# SEVEN SILENT MEN

Also by Noel Behn

*The Kremlin Letter*
*The Shadowboxer*
*Big Stick-up at Brink's!*

# SEVEN SILENT MEN

A NOVEL BY

## Noel Behn

ARBOR HOUSE · NEW YORK

*For Dot*

# Author's Note

*Prairie Port, Missouri, lies some one hundred and thirty miles downstream from St. Louis at a point in the Mississippi River known as the Treachery. Settled in 1737 as a barge-caulking outpost, it is the second oldest city in the region. Prairie Port proper covers seventy-two square miles, as compared to St. Louis's sixty-one square miles, and is topographically diverse. Sheer riverfront rock palisades rise from the Mississippi along its northeastern border. The inland northern and western perimeters are engirded by a curving ridge of lush wooded highlands. The western end of town opens onto the flat and arid prairie.*

*Censuswise, Prairie Port is the third fastest-growing metropolis in the nation. Whereas the population of St. Louis decreased from 857,000 to 622,000 between 1950 and 1970, the habitancy of Prairie Port during this period rose from 78,000 to 507,000. Much of the escalation was directly attributable to the electronics, ultrasonics and missile industries which moved to the area in the early 1950s. Part has to do with the opening of a state university annex and two major medical centers. Some has to do with the simple fact that Prairie Port is a lovely place to live. Despite its astounding growth, a riverfront quaintness, not unlike that immortalized by Mark Twain, lingers. A movement has been afoot to rename the city New Hannibal.*

*Prairie Port has one of the highest literacy and lowest crime rates in the nation. Though there are several "poor" or "trash" sections of town, the inhabitants there are mainly Caucasian and the neighborhoods far from being ghettos or slums. The Prairie Port Police Department is ranked among the finest in the nation. The area's county and state judges are harsh. A majority of arrests and convictions deal with petty offenses perpetrated by the young. But a tradition of smuggling persists, both along the river and inland over the legendary outlaw trails. The practitioners of this ancient art are an elderly and vanishing breed, a colorful group Prairie Port residents often treat as an endangered species rather than a threat.*

*The area's federal law-enforcement agency, at the time of this story, ran into unexpected complications.*

# Prologue

Friday, August 20, 1971

Head bowed and black skin aglisten under the evening glare of outdoor arc lights, John Leslie Krueger toed the pitching rubber with cleated foot and regripped the softball in his hand and bent forward his upper torso and raised his right arm as high behind him as it would go. Held the arm there immobile. Gazed up at Rodney Willis standing at home plate with an unsteady bat poised and rivulets of perspiration running down his face and neck and hairy bare arms. Glanced overhead at the cloudless night, stared down into the dirt again. Breathed deeply. Shook his head sharply to shed accumulating sweat from his eyes. Looked up at Rodney once more. Strained to lift his right arm ever higher. Suddenly whipped the arm down and around in a complete windmill circle and whipped it even faster on the second full windmill . . . at the bottom of the third windmill let loose the softball with such speed and force that Rodney Willis never saw it coming . . . had no idea where it was . . . shut his eyes and swung. The bat shattered clean in half making contact. The softball blooped out over first base, cleared by half a foot the upstretched glove of back-peddling first baseman Sam Wilson . . . fell fair onto the grassy playing field of Delta Island Recreational Park.

It was the first hit the Golden Bricks, a team composed of local FBI agents, had gotten off Juggernaut pitcher John Leslie Krueger in six and a half innings of play. The only time, in fact, any Brick had managed to move the softball, foul or fair, beyond home plate. Even so, the score was close. Thanks to their own batting ineptitude, rather than Golden Brick pitching, the Southern Missouri Bar Association's blue-jerseyed Juggernauts led the game two to nothing.

Sue Willis was the first Brickette on her feet in the rickety, four-tiered wooden grandstand. She jumped up and down and clapped her hands and exhorted her husband to run, run, run . . . not stand around in stunned disbelief. And Rodney, in his golden trousers and gold T-shirt inscribed with the maroon initials "GB," took off and ran like there was no tomorrow . . . amid the shouts and cheers and applause of Golden Bricks and the wives of Golden Bricks . . . pantingly reached first base. Ponytailed Sissy Hennessy bounded off the grandstand and onto the field and, in her short, flared gold skirt, cartwheeled up the third-base sideline and then back down again before leaping high in the air, and with the best form of a Crimson Tide cheerleader, which she had been nine years before, let loose with a kick and thrust and a bellicose "Go, Bricks, go!"

"Go, Bricks, go!" chanted the Brickette rooting section of Helen Perch and Nell Travis and Bonnie Lou Womper and Flo de Camp and Elsie Brewmeister: wives of Bureaumen on the softball roster.

"Lucky swing, J. L.," Juggernaut Jules Shapiro yelled to the pitcher from his position in center field. "He was swinging with his eyes closed!"

"Just like you do at home, Julie," Flo de Camp catcalled back.

"Touché, Florence, touché," Jules conceded with a wave.

John Leslie Krueger looked admiringly away from shapely Sissy Hennessy and tipped his blue cap at Rodney Willis, who was standing on first base breathing heavily and brushing himself off even though he hadn't slid in. Rodney nodded back his appreciation of the Krueger compliment much as Babe Ruth might have nodded to Big Train Johnson.

The Brickettes cheered in renewed enthusiasm, and for good reason. Balding, bull-necked, barrel-chested Cub Hennessy, captain of the Golden Bricks and cleanup batter, stepped to the plate wearing gold satin shorts and the sleeveless training sweatshirt he had been issued a dozen years earlier when he was a reserve linebacker for the St. Louis football Cardinals.

Brickette hurrahs were answered by a chorus of boos and assorted raspberries from an abutting assemblage of Juggernaut

10

wives, the most audible of whom were pert, kinetic Pam Shapiro and overabundant, perpetually tipsy Dori Wilson, who possessed a two-finger whistle of terrifying penetration. Dori's husband, Sam, besides playing first base, was public defender for the City of Prairie Port.

"Cubby, give you six to one you don't lay a bat on the ball," challenged Pam, wife of Juggernaut team captain and assistant U.S. attorney for the Southern District of Missouri, Jules Shapiro.

"You're on, Pam." Cub, who had struck out his two previous times at the plate, ground his heel cleats into the batter's box dirt, assumed his stance . . . called out to the waiting pitcher, "What about you, J. L.? Wanna bet another court order I don't lay my bat on it?"

John Leslie Krueger smiled a polite smile and without benefit of his windmill windup stepped forward on the mound and unleashed a blazing side-arm pitch that not only whizzed by Cub Hennessy undetected but knocked the mitt clean off the catcher's hand and went careening into the wire backstop.

Rodney Willis, alerted by grandstand whoops and hollers, belatedly dashed to steal second base, dove for the bag head first as the throw from the catcher hit the infielder's glove. The baseline umpire signaled that Rodney was out. The home-plate umpire called him safe. Benches emptied.

Sam Wilson rushed toward Krueger saying, "Calm down, big boy, stay calm."

"Forget it's Cub at bat." The catcher hurried to the mound alluding to a recent altercation between Krueger and Hennessy. "Forget it's the feds we're playing, altogether."

"Don't get riled, Johnny," Jules Shapiro urged J. L. from the periphery of the second-base brouhaha over whether Rodney Willis was out or safe.

"Fellas, I'm not riled or angered or otherwise out of control," assured Krueger, who was the assistant U.S. magistrate for the Southern District of Missouri. "I know as well as anyone we only have this half inning to go. That's why I changed windups and bore down more. That last pitch was the best one I've thrown all evening."

11

Jules and Sam and the catcher exchanged unsure looks.

Krueger raised the first three fingers of his right hand. "Scout's honor, fellas, I'm fine."

". . . J. L., go back to the windmill, will you?" the catcher suggested as he started for the ongoing screaming match around second base. "I can't see the friggin' ball when you whip it side-arm like that."

The decision of the home-plate umpire prevailed. Rodney Willis was deemed safe at second base. Only one man was out in the bottom of the seventh and final inning of the game. Cub Hennessy took to the batter's box once more . . . heeled his cleated shoes in place, assumed his batting stance, glowered vengefully at the pitcher, whose head was bowed.

John Leslie Krueger gripped the softball along the seams and bent forward and raised his pitching arm high and held it on high, immobile, and gazed up at Cub at the plate and higher up at the sky above, and stared down at the ground and raised his arm even more and took a second, colder look at Cub . . . and noticed something in the distance . . . peered into the night beyond Hennessy . . . squinted across the thin expanse of Mississippi River separating the delta island ball field from the sprawling bankside city of Prairie Port . . . homed in on the huge illuminated time-temperature sign atop the tallest structure of the downtown business district, the Prairie Farmer Building. "8:12 PM" was dimming and rising on the thousand-bulb display screen. "89°" replaced "8:12 PM," immediately dimmed to near blackness, then rose in power until the numbers were blazing white.

Cub Hennessy, along with most everyone else at the game, turned in the direction Krueger was staring, couldn't help seeing that "89°" had begun to flash on and off . . . saw a dimming and rising "8:12 PM" superimpose itself over the flashing "89°." "You gonna blame that on the FBI too?" Cub called out to J. L.

"If I find out you're responsible again, you're goddam right," Krueger answered.

"You really think we're screwing up Jarrel's sign?" Rodney Willis said in disbelief.

12

"That last time you tried to tap his phones, you blew fuses in a four-block area," Krueger reminded.

It was curious, on many counts, that John Leslie Krueger noticed the trouble before anyone else on the field. First off, not only was Krueger the only black player on either softball team, he was but one of twenty-two hundred black people in a city of five hundred thousand whites . . . Prairie Port, Missouri. And the Prairie Farmer Association, on whose office building the giant sign stood, was as vehemently pro-segregationist an organization as existed in the Midwest. Secondly, the local FBI, whose office team Krueger was pitching against, had conducted a long and much disputed investigation of the Prairie Farmer Association and its board chairman, Wilkie Jarrel, but for financial rather than racial malfeasance. Thirdly, Jarrel's battery of expensive lawyers had petitioned Krueger complaining of unauthorized activities by the FBI against their client. Lastly, it had been Krueger who had ordered the FBI to discontinue its investigation of Jarrel and who, on two occasions, had hauled Cub Hennessy, among other Bureau agents, into his courtroom and reprimanded them for violating that order.

"89°'" stopped flashing on and off, grew constantly brighter. "8:12 PM" remained superimposed over the "89°'" but suddenly began blinking. Just as suddenly the entire electric display screen went to black. A moment later it was on again with "8:12 PM" blinking at half strength. The huge sign went black. Stayed black many seconds. Came on again with all one thousand bulbs burning hotter than ever. Blue-white hot. So hot several bulbs popped into smoke. The board faded to black. Came on with every bulb a faint and shimmering red. Went to black. Stayed black.

"Yes, sir, J. L., I sure t'hell wish that was us short-circuiting Jarrel." Cub shook his head in envy, turned and waited for the other players to reassume their positions . . . stepped up to home plate and raised his bat and adjusted his stance and watched Krueger's windmill windup begin . . . anticipated the release and swung away before actually seeing the ball leave Krueger's hand. The bat missed the hurtling white target by a full foot.

Cub Hennessy walked toward the bench, knelt to rub dirt on

13

the grip of the bat, glanced at the grandstand long enough to notice Sissy grimacing at him with that you-can-do-it grimace he had come to know all too well.

He returned to home plate thinking that maybe he should bunt. Problem was, he was a rotten bunter. And even if he got lucky and the bunted ball allowed Rodney Willis to score from second, the Golden Bricks would still be one run behind. No, if you're going to count on luck, he told himself, then go for broke. Try to hit the little bugger right out of the park like you've been trying to do all night.

Cub took a stance slightly higher than before, choking up on the bat. He saw the windmill windup finish its first and second cycle, then as the arm rocketed down for a third time, clenched his teeth and swung the bat forward with all the strength in him. Swung as before, without really having seen the ball released. The sound and feel of his impacting bat told him he had made perfect and mighty contact.

All eyes turned skyward as the soaring softball disappeared into the blackness above the towering poles of arc lights, remained lost for moments, came back into view far, far out and high in center field.

Jules Shapiro gave chase, running with amazing fleetness for an awkward man, overtook the lazily arching ball . . . positioned himself at a spot he presumed would be in the drop path . . . held up his glove . . . as the white ball seemed to hover in space, restationed himself once, then twice, then a third time.

The ball began to plummet. When it was roughly fifteen feet above Shapiro's waiting glove, the lights went off. The ball park was plunged into darkness.

Then, along the nearby riverfront of Prairie Port, from the looming rock-faced palisades in the north to the flatlands downstream, lights began to lower and dim, and many, many of them, whole stretches of them, blacked out.

The time was 8:16 P.M.

14

# Book One

# One

Little Haifa adjusted the battery-powered light attached to his blue metal miner's hat, hiked up his hip-high yellow vinyl fisherman's boots and splashed forward through the tunnel north of the main cavern; entered and crossed a small grotto; ducked along a low passageway; came out in the improvised command bunker fashioned from a decaying underground control booth of a long-abandoned irrigation and flood-control system. Little Haifa removed his hardhat and checked the first of four television monitoring screens. The bank premises some forty feet above, as expected, were empty . . . were, as expected, illuminated by soft, low-wattage night lights. The second TV monitor screen offered another view of the ground-level office, a moving view which revealed the two glowing red dots of an operative burglary alarm system. He glanced over at the third screen, saw that the street outside the bank was dark and empty. The fourth screen displayed the front of a massive, burnished-metal, walk-in vault.

Little Haifa clamped on a radio headset . . . asked into the tiny microphone if the wires in the main cavern were ready to be connected.

Wiggles's voice told him everything was ready for connection.

Little Haifa asked if the scaffold had been rolled away.

The voice of Windy Walt said the scaffold was away.

Little Haifa called for Worm, inquired of Worm if the supply cave had been sealed off with sandbags.

Worm, via walkie-talkie, confirmed that the cave had just been sealed off . . . that all the supplies were secure within.

Little Haifa asked Rat the condition of the passage leading from the south wall of the main cavern.

17

Rat said the sandbags were in place just inside the passage mouth, that he was already behind them waiting to be joined by Windy Walt and Worm.

Little Haifa raised Cowboy, wanted to know from Cowboy the state of the tunnel leading into the northern side of the cavern, the tunnel through which Little Haifa had traveled to reach the command bunker.

Cowboy said the tunnel was sandbagged shut except for a narrow opening by which Wiggles could enter.

Little Haifa asked Meadow Muffin to return to the command bunker.

Thirty seconds later, Meadow Muffin, his walkie-talkie in hand, emerged through a steel hatch in the floor of the bunker . . . announced that the water level of the irrigation tunnel beneath them was three and a half feet lower than it should be, that the water current must be speeded up.

Little Haifa called into the microphone for Mule. When there was no reply, he called louder.

Mule's voice responded from far off, asked what was so important.

Little Haifa half shouted that the water level and water flow in the irrigation tunnel should be increased substantially.

Mule answered, Gotcha.

The naked light bulb dangling beside Little Haifa's head dimmed. A faint echo of creaking wood and metal rose as the distant water–control machinery activated.

Little Haifa again spoke loudly, ordered everyone but Mule to leave the main cavern and take refuge in their designated shelters with their hardhats on and the hat's miner's light on and hat's plastic visor down.

Cowboy, then Rat, soon were heard saying the order had been obeyed.

Little Haifa told Wiggles to make the final connection and go to his assigned shelter and report in.

Seconds later Wiggles said he was secure behind sandbags and that the connection had been made.

Little Haifa checked the television monitor screens, saw that

18

everything within the bank premises and on the street beyond was normal, announced into the microphone that the countdown was beginning . . . put his hand on the control switch of the console detonator . . . began to count backward from 20 to 19 to 18 to 17 . . . kept his eyes on the monitoring screen showing the front of the walk-in vault . . . at the count of 6 slowed the cadence slightly . . . 5 . . . . 4 . . . . . 3 . . . . . . 2 . . . . . . .

The detonation switch twisted to "activate."

A thud shook the concrete bunker but did not move the vault door he was watching on the TV screen. Little Haifa glanced at another monitor. The two red lights of the alarm system continued to glow. He looked at a third screen. No one was on the street outside the bank.

Little Haifa announced into the microphone that the bank's alarm system had not gone off as a result of the explosion . . . that he would now inspect the results . . . that everyone should remain in place except Wiggles and Cowboy.

He handed the headset to Meadow Muffin, donned his hardhat realizing he had forgotten to turn off the miner's lamp on its front, grabbed an Army-issue walkie-talkie, ducked out the command bunker and through the short low passageway . . . recrossed the small grotto . . . splashed forward through a half inch of water in a long tunnel . . . passed around a barrier of sandbags piled just within the tunnel's mouth . . . emerged from the tunnel into a huge underground cavern . . . a twenty-five-foot-high subterranean chamber of rock and clay illuminated by string after string of suspended, unfrosted electric light bulbs.

Wiggles and Cowboy, both in hardhats, stood beside a portable scaffold pointing up. A large segment of rock ceiling had been blasted away. Lying exposed above was mangled and shattered concrete . . . the concrete floor of the building overhead.

Wiggles limped rapidly forward on a gimp leg, pulled the portable scaffold out and around. Held it firm. Little Haifa shed his fisherman's boots and climbed the scaffold to the ceiling, began pulling at the shattered concrete. It fell away more easily than expected. If his calculations were correct, the bottom of the vault would be four to five feet up. What bothered him as he continued

19

tearing down debris was that the vault hadn't budged one mite during the explosion. This could mean the concrete floor was thicker than the estimated four to five feet. It could mean there wasn't any vault or vault room directly above. Or bank.

Little Haifa signaled for assistance. Cowboy, in black-and-white snakeskin riding boots, ascended the scaffold and with pick and electric drill attacked the more resistant portions of concrete. Little Haifa soon learned his error. Two and a half feet up, not four or five, a metal surface was struck. A hard metal surface.

Little Haifa raised his walkie-talkie and proclaimed he was right on target, that he had reached the bottom of the vault. He checked his wristwatch and saw that it was 9:17 P.M., then repeated the time into the radio and added they were slightly ahead of schedule and should be done with the job and out on the river well before 12:30. He told Meadow Muffin to use the command bunker's powerful radio transmitter to let Mule know everything would now proceed as planned. He ordered Windy Walt and Worm and Rat, who were waiting in the sandbag-shut passage on the southern side of the cavern, to exit out of the opposite end of the passageway and prepare the platform in the irrigation tunnel for their impending getaway . . . turn on the lights and stake out the four areas of embarkation and open the equipment cartons.

More concrete was chopped and drilled away. The exposed bottom surface of the metal vault expanded to a roughly three-foot-by-three-foot square. Little Haifa took up the electric drill, inserted a diamond bit and began boring up into the hard alloy overhead.

Eleven holes were drilled before Little Haifa and Cowboy descended the scaffold. Cowboy and Wiggles went and waited in the southern passageway. Little Haifa entered the partially sandbagged storage cave, emerged carrying a small wooden rack containing eleven vials of nitroglycerin with attached fusing . . . holding the rack of volatile explosives as steadily as possible, he reclimbed the scaffold ever so carefully.

Ever so slowly, so cautiously, the first vial of nitroglycerin was removed from the rack and raised and slid into an angular hole drilled in the metal overhead . . . sealed in by plastic and with its connecting fuse exposed and dangling. The second vial was inserted in the next slot and sealed with its fuse dangling. Another hole was filled and sealed. Then another.

When the final vial was in place, Little Haifa gathered the eleven dangling fuses, twisted them into one central cord and attached the cord to a master fuse already suspended from the ceiling which trailed down the twenty-five feet to the cavern floor below.

Perspiring, Little Haifa descended the scaffold, plunked onto the ground, raised his walkie-talkie, ordered Meadow Muffin to take a final check, listened as Meadow Muffin said all four television screens showed conditions at the bank premises to be normal.

Little Haifa asked for a progress report from the loading platform in the irrigation tunnel.

Windy Walt said all the physical chores had been seen to but that there was trouble with the water level in the tunnel . . . that the water was three and a half feet lower than it should be . . . a good three and a half feet below the platform . . . that the water flow seemed far weaker than was advisable . . . dangerously slow.

Little Haifa ordered Windy Walt and Rat and Worm into the main cavern, then walkie-talkied Meadow Muffin and told him to tell Mule to totally cut off the supply of water to the Sewerage Department's secondary mains and anywhere else . . . to concentrate only on the main irrigation tunnel . . . to divert all the water he could into the main irrigation tunnel.

A minute of silence elapsed before Meadow Muffin's voice emitted from Little Haifa's walkie-talkie saying Mule said it was dangerous to cut off the water to the Sewerage Department's secondary mains . . . that if he did, Sewerage Department officials would see that something was wrong . . . would see that someone was tampering with the water controls of the city.

Little Haifa told Meadow Muffin to tell Mule they would have to take the risk . . . reordered Meadow to order Mule to cut off the water to everywhere except the main irrigation tunnel.

21

Meadow was on the air some twenty seconds later saying Mule was doing as ordered, but not happily.

Windy Walt and Rat and Worm removed the sandbags from the mouth of the southern passageway and entered the cavern. Walt helped Little Haifa and Wiggles and Cowboy remove four large rubber boats from the supply cave and inflate them. Worm and Rat broke open the wooden crates of waterproof and lightweight plastic buoys and land mines and sacks and life jackets, booby traps and plastic explosives and dynamite and timing devices.

Their chores done, the six men stripped naked and put on wet suits . . . went to the storage cave and retrieved the clothes they would be wearing following the getaway, placed the clothes in waterproof bags . . . attached an elastic wrist band to each bag. Windy Walt and Rat and Worm sorted through the pile of discarded work clothes and shoes and rubber boots, rechecking to make certain no identifying marks had been left. After that the discards were stuffed into larger, nonwaterproof sacks. Cowboy's snakeskin boots, however, went into his waterproof getaway bag.

Little Haifa, Cowboy and Wiggles hoisted a rubber boat, tilted it on its side and hurried into a narrow passageway on the southern side of the cavern. They came out on the cement platform of an enormous underground irrigation tunnel lit up, at this juncture, by a line of bare light bulbs set atop stanchions . . . an echoing subterranean concrete aqueduct whose spuming water level was a good four feet below the platform on which the rubber boat was being set . . . a half foot lower than it had been when Windy Walt reported it to the command bunker earlier.

Little Haifa raised his walkie-talkie, tried to contact Meadow Muffin. He couldn't hear over the resounding water rush, not even his own voice.

There were two routes by which Little Haifa could get to the command bunker due north from the platform on which he stood. The easterly path was encumbered, entailed backtracking up the narrow passageway he had just traveled, reentering and crossing the main cavern, going into the tunnel in the opposite, northern wall of the cavern and following it westerly into the grotto and short passage leading to the bunker.

The other way was uncluttered but circuitous, required using the metal catwalk running along the twenty-foot-high irrigation tunnel . . . a curving tunnel which arched northwest, then northeast around the west periphery of the main cavern.

Little Haifa chose the second route . . . stepped from the concrete platform onto the iron catwalk . . . ran along it in his tight-fitting rubber wet suit with the bobbing beam of his metal miner's hat piercing the bending blackness ahead . . . ran for one hundred and fifty yards over the rough grating before reaching the metal ladder rungs set into the tunnel's cement wall . . . climbed the rungs to the steel hatch in the floor of the abandoned irrigation system control booth above. Pushed the hatch open. Boosted himself up and into the improvised command bunker. Without a word to Meadow Muffin, grabbed the radio headset and yelled into it. Yelled for Mule.

Mule's voice could be heard in the earphone, just barely.

Little Haifa screamed for Mule to speak up.

Mule answered, somewhat louder, to stop shouting at him, that he could hear perfectly well when Little Haifa used an ordinary tone of voice, that even if he could speak louder he wouldn't because he had a worsening sore throat from standing around in the friggin' dampness trying to operate the friggin' controls. Then he asked what Little Haifa wanted anyway.

Little Haifa yelled that the water level in the main irrigation tunnel was falling instead of rising.

Mule asked how the hell Little Haifa thought he got his sore throat in the first place . . . by running around trying to get the water level up.

Trying wasn't good enough, Little Haifa countered. The water level was four feet too low. Four feet was a DISASTER.

Mule warned against shouting.

Little Haifa excitedly explained that everything was ready to go . . . that everybody was in place . . . that the soup was even sealed into the box . . . that THE WHOLE OPERATION COULD

GO INTO THE TOILET BECAUSE THE WATER LEVEL IS TOO GODDAM LOW!

Mule cautioned that one shouts at dumb animals and speaks civilly to human beings and told Little Haifa DON'T SHOUT AT ME ABOUT IT! GO SHOUT AT THAT FRIGGIN' PUSS-HEADED NEPHEW OF YOURS ABOUT IT! YOUR PUSS-HEADED NEPHEW DREAMT UP THIS SYSTEM! HE KNOWS HOW IT WORKS, NOT ME! GO GET HIM TO SHOW YOU!

Little Haifa let it be known YOU KNOW GODDAM WELL HE WENT AND VANISHED ON US! YOU GOTTA DO IT! YOU'RE THE ONLY ONE WHO KNOWS ANYTHING ABOUT THEM CONTROLS! YOU GOTTA HOLD UP YOUR END!

HOW? demanded Mule. YOU WANNA KNOW WHAT PUSS HEAD WENT AND DONE? YOUR GENIUS NEPHEW? HE WENT AND TOOK THE IRRIGATION CONTROLS AND THE FLOOD-CONTROL CONTROLS FOR A CITY OF MILLIONS OF PEOPLE AND SPLICED THEM ALL TOGETHER UP HERE IN ONE BIG BOWL OF FRIGGIN' SPAGHETTI! IF YOU FLUSH A TOILET IN UNIVERSITY HEIGHTS YOU'RE LIABLE TO BLOW FUSES AT THE RIVERFRONT MOTEL. I DON'T KNOW WHAT OPERATES WHAT UP HERE! ALL I KNOW IS EVERYTHING IS HOOKED INTO SOME SORT OF FRIGGIN' AUTOMATIC TIMER THAT'S SET FOR GOD ONLY KNOWS WHEN!

WHY YOU KEEPING SECRETS? Little Haifa asked. WHY DIDN'T YOU SPEAK UP LIKE A MAN? WHY D'YOU GO ON SAYING 'GOTCHA, GOTCHA' ANY TIME I ASKED FOR SOMETHING TO GET DONE?

'CAUSE WAY BACK THEN I WAS IGNORANT! WAY BACK THEN I THOUGHT I COULD GET THESE CRAZY CONTROLS UNJAMMED AND WORKING. NOW I SEE WHAT THE PROBLEM IS.

Mule, what we gonna do? asked Little Haifa.

Put the score off, was the reply. Hit it tomorrow like we planned to do. Maybe by tomorrow I'll have these controls figured out.

Can't go tomorrow, Mule. Gotta go right now. Mule, I already

24

put the nitroglycerin in. A bank employee comes in and as much as sneezes in that vault room, it's boom and good-by.

Maybe you can go with the water like is? Mule suggested.

With the water that low, most of the irrigation tunnels downstream will be bone dry. We'll have to walk through them tunnels maybe ten miles carrying the score and our gear. By the time we get to the river, it could be dawn. We'll miss the Treachery. Uh-uh, we're stuck, Mule. We gotta go right now. You gotta come up with something to get us away from here.

Keep getting ready . . . I'll call you back, Mule said.

Returning to the underground excavation site, Little Haifa, with Wiggles and Cowboy, began stringing fuse into the northern tunnel leading to the command bunker. While they did, Windy Walt began piling sandbags at the tunnel's mouth. Sandbags already closed the narrow passage mouth across the cavern leading to the irrigation tunnel.

Little Haifa's walkie-talkie crackled. He raised it up to hear Meadow Muffin tell him the 11 P.M. monitor check had been taken and all was well in the bank premises above and in the street fronting the premises.

Little Haifa ordered Rat to prepare the booby traps and demolition charges for the equipment being left behind in the cavern and storage cave, then went on fusing in the tunnel. News from Meadow Muffin that Mule was on the radio sent him on ahead to the command post.

He had figured out something he could do, Mule explained to Little Haifa, a dangerous thing on all counts. The floodgates leading down from the Tomahawk Hill reservoir could be opened. Emergency gates which would spill out one helluva lotta water. Hundreds of thousands of gallons. That much water would ride them away from the scene like lightning. Or faster. That much water would probably wipe out parts of the city's sewerage system as well.

Mule said that if Little Haifa was worried about the dimouts they'd been causing in the city by draining off electricity in the past, he'd have a nervous breakdown when the floodgates got opened. That to open those gates would require activating not

25

only the huge generator which had created the dimouts but a twin generator as well. That they would be sucking far more electricity out of the city's power supply than they'd ever used before. That whole parts of the city could be blacked out.

Little Haifa wanted to know that if the gates were opened, how fast it would take for the water to rise to the required level at their escape point.

About five minutes, was the answer.

Then do it.

I gotta warn you again, it's gonna be the deluge.

Do it. Open the gates.

Mule said he would need another five minutes of lead time in which to warm up the generators.

Little Haifa told him to start warming them up as of that moment.

Mule said there was one more thing, that Meadow Muffin had best leave the scene with the rest of the gang . . . that Mule might not be able to slow down enough to pick up Meadow Muffin as previously planned.

Little Haifa agreed, instructed Meadow Muffin to put on his wet suit and remain in the bunker until he radioed Mule the order to open the flood gates, then to set the time-delay mechanism which would blow up the command bunker minutes later and run like hell . . . use the escape hatch and get onto the catwalk in the irrigation tunnel and run the one hundred and fifty yards to where the gang would be waiting on the concrete platform like he had never run for anything in his life.

A final instruction Little Haifa intended to give Meadow Muffin was interrupted by Wiggles, who entered the bunker holding up an empty fusing drum and yelling they'd been gypped, that he'd run out of fusing seventy-five feet away, that the second spool contained seventy-five feet less than it should have . . . that it was Little Haifa's fault for dealing with the scumbag nephew of his.

Little Haifa said he'd checked both drums himself, that there was no shortage of fusing.

Wiggles waved the empty spool menacingly, asked if he was being called a liar.

26

Meadow Muffin blanched at the sight of the upraised spool, meekly confessed he thought it had contained rope rather than detonation fuse . . . revealed that he had taken the seventy-five missing feet and given them to Mule when Mule asked for rope.

THE ROPE! THE ROPE! Little Haifa repeated into the microphone. WHERE IS THE ROPE MEADOW MUFFIN GIVE YA!

Mule wanted to know what kind of moron would be worrying about rope at a moment like this . . . at the instant he was about to activate the generators. He again let it be known he didn't enjoy being yelled at.

WE NEED THE ROPE! THE ROPE IS FUSE!

THE ROPE IS ROPE! rebutted Mule. THE ROPE IS CUT UP INTO LITTLE TINY PIECES AND IS GODDAM UNDERWATER AND YOU WANNA KNOW WHY? 'CAUSE THIS CHINTZY OUTFIT'S TOO CHEAP OR TOO IGNORANT TO BUY OR STEAL ANOTHER RUBBER BOAT! SO I BUILT ME A WOOD RAFT AND LASHED IT ALL TOGETHER WITH THAT THERE ROPE! YOU CAN HAVE IT BACK WHEN I FLOAT DOWNSTREAM TO SEE YA! AND TALKING ABOUT DUMB, WHAT KIND OF MORON PUTS IN THE NITROGLYCERIN WHEN HE STILL HAS LOTS OF THINGS LEFT TO DO? THE SOUP GOES IN LAST, ALWAYS! NOW, YOU GONNA GO ON BEING DUMB AND IGNORANT OR SHOULD I TURN ON THESE GENERATORS SO YOU CAN GET WATER DOWN THERE?

Little Haifa told Mule to turn on the generators.

Almost instantly the bunker's electric light bulb dimmed and a far-off echo of humming arose, the whir of an ancient and mammoth generator starting up. A second whirring resounded. The light went completely out, after a moment glowed back to half strength, then to full power.

The detonator was taken from the command bunker and the fusing removed from the northern tunnel and restrung across the main cavern and on into the narrow southern passageway which ran down to the concrete platform in the irrigation tunnel . . . a platform on which the inflated rubber boats rested in rows and tied together by long strands of nautical nylon rope . . . four

27

rubber boats, each being hurriedly outfitted with a plastic tiller and plastic emergency oars and a waterproof rifle and life jackets and two powerful battery-driven, front-gunnel searchlights and cross-gunnel static lines on which waterproof bags of stolen money and getaway clothing would be snapped.

The tunnel mouth on the northern wall of the main cavern was sandbagged shut. So was the entrance to the small storage cave in which the booby traps and demolition charges and other explosives were stowed. Except for a narrow opening through which a man could barely squeeze, a double tier of sandbags closed off the passageway on the southern side of the cavern.

At 11:20 P.M. Little Haifa began his final inspection of the main cavern . . . climbed to the top of the scaffold and examined, without touching, each of the eleven sealed-up holes in the exposed square of metal above . . . studied the fuses leading down from each hole . . . felt the junction at which these lead fuses had been twisted together and spliced into the master fuse suspended from a hook in the top of the cavern.

Once down on the floor of the cavern Little Haifa scrutinized the end of the dangling master fuse while Wiggles rolled away the portable scaffold. Little Haifa dropped to one knee, waved Wiggles off, snapped on his walkie-talkie and asked Meadow Muffin for a report. Hearing that everything was normal on the monitor screens, that no one was inside or outside of the bank premises above, Little Haifa hooked the radio to his shoulder strap and lifted the slack end of the master fuse leading up to the nitroglycerin . . . gingerly connected it to the fuse on the ground and running back the entire length of the cavern and on under the sandbagged opening of the narrow passageway in the south wall.

Little Haifa crawled along inspecting the fuse, traced it back into the passageway and past an interior barrier of sandbags behind which Wiggles, Cowboy, Rat, Windy Walt and Worm were lying. He moved on to to where the detonator rested. He ordered everyone to turn on the miner's lamps on their hardhats. Those whose lamps were not already on complied. He ordered the passageway to be closed off from the cavern. Wiggles and

Cowboy scurried forward, sealed shut the narrow opening with a double layer of sandbags. Little Haifa said he needed only one of the men to stay with him, that the other four should continue down the passageway and go out and wait on the cement platform of the irrigation tunnel. Windy Walt began to get up, but was restrained by Rat, who told Little Haifa they were all staying with him here in the passageway. Little Haifa protested that such an action was stupid . . . that if anything happened and the passageway collapsed they would all be trapped or killed . . . that there would be no one to come and dig them out. He repeated his order for four of the men to leave. No one budged.

Muttering to himself how dumb they all were, Little Haifa raised his walkie-talkie and alerted Meadow Muffin that the connection was to follow and to relay the information on to Mule. He ordered Windy Walt to join him and train his miner's lamp on the detonator. The beam shone down. Little Haifa twisted the detonator's dial switch to "inactive" . . . took a penknife and sliced away the protective coating on both strands of fuse end until the copper wire below lay exposed . . . connected the first strand of naked copper to the detonator . . . connected the second piece . . . announced loudly enough into the walkie-talkie for all in the passageway to hear that the countdown was about to begin. He specifically told Meadow to tell Mule that he would be going on 10 rather than 20 this time.

The detonator crank was turned twice and stopped at "pre-activate." The counting down began aloud at 10 and went to 9 and 8. 7 . . . 6 . . . 5 . . . Fingers seized the "activate" switch, ready to turn it to "activate." 4 . . . 3 . . .

Meadow Muffin's voice cried out from the walkie-talkie to stop everything . . . shouted that a car had pulled up on the street outside the bank . . . a police car with multicolored warning lights spinning on its roof . . . that a second police car with spinning lights was pulling in behind.

The countdown was aborted.

Rat, Worm and Cowboy moved back around Little Haifa and Windy Walt . . . listened to the crackling radio as Meadow Muffin said that the spinning roof lights on the police cars had gone off

. . . that a policeman was getting out of the first car . . . that two more policemen were getting out of the second car . . . that one of the policemen was at the glass doors of the bank, had cupped his hands to the pane and was looking in . . . that one of the policemen standing near the curb had lit a cigarette . . . that the TV picture was clear. Meadow Muffin could read the number on one of the cars: 115.

Meadow Muffin's audible gasp of surprise was followed by word that the cop lighting the cigarette wasn't a cop at all, but a girl . . . a rather young girl, wearing a cop's cap and with a cigarette hanging from the side of her mouth, who was beginning to undress . . . undress on the street . . . that she had dropped to her knees . . . that . . .

Worm, from over Little Haifa's shoulder, implored Meadow Muffin to continue talking.

Meadow Muffin said he couldn't see . . . said the television monitoring screens in the command bunker had begun to dim out, had turned to snow . . . that the electric light bulb in the bunker was also dimming.

Wiggles, lying prone behind the interior barrier of sandbags, told the men crowded around the walkie-talkie he didn't give a hoot in hell who was copping what cop's joint . . . announced he couldn't take the oppressive heat in the passageway one instant longer . . . jumped up and stripped off his wet suit. Cowboy did the same. Windy Walt prayed aloud that the young girl was professional at what she was doing, and rapid.

Meadow Muffin's voice came through with word that the monitor screens had lit up again along with the bunker's light bulb . . . that the cops and girl were rushing back to the two patrol cars . . . that the girl was dressing on the run . . . that they had gotten into the cars . . . that they were driving away . . . that the street was once more empty, and as always, dark . . . that inside the bank premises above, all seemed normal . . .

The countdown resumed at 10. Went to 9 and 8 and 7. To 6 and 5. 4 . . . 3 . . . 2 . . .

The detonator was activated.

Nothing happened.

Little Haifa twisted the switch back to "inactivate," then forward once more to "activate."

No thud resulted. No trembling of earth.

Again the lever was switched off and on.

There was no response.

Little Haifa reached to the side of the detonator, cranked and recranked the primer arm . . . seized the "activate" lever on the face of the detonator and turned it off and on again. And again.

All remained still.

A naked Wiggles and Cowboy attacked the double barrier of sandbags sealing the entrance of the passageway . . . pulled and pushed and tore and lifted and tossed in a frenzy . . . scrambled through the opening they created followed by Little Haifa . . . ran deep into the cavern and stared up.

The three-by-three-foot square of metal in the rock ceiling twenty-five feet overhead was unchanged, still had eleven strands of fusing trailing down from the eleven vials of nitroglycerin embedded in it.

Rat and Worm and Windy Walt stepped up beside Wiggles and Cowboy and Little Haifa and also stared above. One of them wondered aloud, What the hell now?

Little Haifa shrugged and lifted his walkie-talkie and told Meadow Muffin to radio Mule and tell him something had gone wrong and that Mule should be prepared to shut down the generators and forget opening the flood gates at the reservoir.

How can he forget what's already been done? Meadow Muffin asked. Mule's already opened them gates.

WHATYA MEAN, ALREADY OPENED? Little Haifa said.

Mule opened them gates when you counted down and said number 'one' just like you told me to tell him to do.

I NEVER TOLD YOU NO SUCH THING!

Sure did. Said for me to tell Mule he would be going on 10 rather than on 20. And I told him.

ME, YOU TWOT! ME! ME! ME! THAT WAS FOR ME, NOT HIM! THAT'S WHEN I WAS GOING TO ACTIVATE THE DETONATOR! NOT WHEN HE WAS TO OPEN THE GATES! NOW WE GOT HALF A GODDAM RESERVOIR OF WATER

31

HEADING OUR WAY AND THE DETONATOR DON'T
WORK!

No shit?

IS THAT ALL YOU CAN SAY, YOU PEA-BRAINED SCUM-
BAG? I'LL SHIT YOU OKAY! I'LL SHIT YOU TILL YOU
WISHED YOU WAS A PIECE OF RAW MEAT BEING
GROUND UP LIVE, YOU . . . YOU . . . YOU!

Little Haifa, in a rare fit of animated rage, hurled the walkie-
talkie into the dirt with all his might.

The flash was blinding . . . the concussion from the exploding
nitroglycerin so powerful that all six men were knocked flat on
their backsides. And as they lay there stunned and staring up,
dollar bills floated down from on high.

Windy Walt rolled onto his stomach and beat the ground with
his fists shouting, We did it, we did it, while Rat ran around and
around in circles yelling pretty much the same thing.

Stark naked, Wiggles was also running, running the portable
scaffold forward under the perfect three-foot-by-three-foot-
square hole blown in the hard metal surface above. He clambered to the top, hoisted himself up into the opening. An equally
nude Cowboy clambered up the scaffold after him, also disappeared into the hole overhead. Indian whoops were heard.
Money sacks began plummeting down. Handful after handful of
loose bills fluttered after them. Bigger sacks dropped. The men
on the floor scrambled to stuff the loot into the oversized waterproof bags. Filled and bulging bags were run, in relays, out
through the passageway and onto the concrete pier in the irrigation tunnel.

The rumbling rose like evil thunder. Thunder trapped deep
underground and not far off. The cavern's walls and ceiling,
which had hardly quivered when the nitroglycerin exploded,
began to shake violently. Wiggles poked his head down through
the hole in the vault, saw that rock chips and rock segments were
shaking loose all around him and showering down on the four
men in wet suits who were dashing for cover twenty-five feet
below.

Quaking intensified. Thunderclaps became louder and more

32

frequent. The rumbling grew deafeningly near. Little Haifa shouted the men out of the cavern, held the scaffold as steady as he could while Wiggles and Cowboy dropped onto it from the hole above and bounded down . . . grabbed up Rat's abandoned walkie-talkie and, running to avoid the hail of rocks and falling dirt, screamed for Meadow Muffin to drop everything and make tracks for the rendezvous point.

Meadow Muffin, in wet suit and miner's hat, disappeared through the hatch in the command bunker's floor, came out into the tumultuously echoing irrigation tunnel, all but slid down the metal ladder onto the iron catwalk, which was only inches above a swirling river of fast–flowing water. He turned to run along the iron walkway . . . run the hundred and fifty yards in the curving subterranean conduit to where the gang members were assembling for the getaway. Before Meadow Muffin could take a single running step he heard, behind him, a sound like he had never heard. A roaring of unimaginable magnitude. He turned back and saw a sight like he had never seen before . . . a solid wall of water reaching from the top of the twenty–foot–high tunnel to the bottom . . . a wall of water bearing down on him at breakneck speed. A wall from which Mule's head and upper torso protruded as he lay riding the front half of a rickety wood raft as one might ride a surfboard. As he rode, Mule shouted in great glee, only his words were lost in the din.

The rubber boats pushed off one after the other with Little Haifa and Windy Walt in the lead craft and Wiggles alone in the second and Worm riding the third. The fourth rubber boat had been cut loose from the other three, was manned by Cowboy and Rat, who were doing the best they could to hold it close to the concrete platform . . . Rat was shouting into his walkie-talkie for Meadow Muffin.

Seconds later, at approximately 11:58 P.M., Friday, August 20, 1971, the vanguard of 18,000,000 gallons of rampaging water hit the four rubber boats, sucked them in, devoured them like some unspeakable monster . . . shot them through seven and a half miles of irrigation tunnels as a bullet might be shot through a rifle barrel . . . jettisoned them at incredible speed toward a tortuous tangle of sewers and mains and stand ponds and diversion terminals and hairpin turns beneath the sprawling city of Prairie Port.

At 7:36 A.M., Sunday, August 22, 1971, the alarm system at Mormon State National Bank, which had been inoperative since before Little Haifa and his gang blew a hole in the vault more than thirty-one hours earlier, activated and began emitting ultrasonic alert messages to the communications center at the Prairie Port Police Department. The messages, for whatever the reason, were inaccurate. They indicated the long-since-perpetrated robbery was still in progress. The police, while immediately responding to the scene, withheld the information from the Federal Bureau of Investigation. This was not unusual. There was bad blood between the Prairie Port PD and the local resident office of the FBI.

. . . Five minutes after that, a clandestine informant within police headquarters notified his Bureau contact in Prairie Port that the robbery was in progress and where.

# TWO

Screeching reverberated. Green-eyed, sandy-haired, youthful special agent of the FBI William B. Yates looked up and off and saw a four-door black and dented Chevrolet slide to a sideways stop several feet beyond the red light at the bottom of a super-highway exit ramp, watched the driver's arm thrust out the window and flash a finger at a motorist yelling at the Chevy for partially running the light. The light greened. The car lurched forward, screechingly veered into the elm-shaded parking lot of Prairie Port's Marriott Motel and continued on to where Yates, in a freshly pressed, neatly tailored summer suit, stood waiting beside the entrance.

"Yates?" The face of the driver calling through the Chevrolet's half-open passenger window was flat-nosed, square-jawed and fortyish. A Stetson rode low on a wide, wrinkled forehead. Dangling from the collar of his western-style shirt was a string tie. "Billy Yates?"

"Hennessy?" Yates asked back.

"Nope, Jessup." And Jessup, with a fetching smile, pushed open the passenger door. "Resident agent H. L. Jessup. Hennessy will meet us on ahead."

Yates slid in, shook Jessup's outheld hand, pulled the door shut . . . was told, "That's Brew in the back. Marty Brewmeister."

Turning, Yates peered in the direction of Jessup's hitching thumb. FBI resident agent Martin L. Brewmeister lay on the rear seat with his legs pulled up and a narrow-brimmed straw hat covering most of his face. The jacket of his Ivy Leagueish seer-sucker suit lay open on a white-on-white Hathaway shirt, a Dacron tie with blue-and-brown stripes too wide to be Ivy League and a black leather shoulder holster.

"Brew, you awake?" Jessup called.

"No," the voice beneath the hat responded.

"Say 'hi' to Billy Yates."

The hat lifted, revealing a gentle-featured and unhurried countenance with deepset brown eyes. "Welcome to Prairie Port, Billy Yates." Brew replaced the hat on his face, crossed his arms over his chest.

Jessup burned rubber, sent Yates tumbling back against the seat . . . sent the car zooming across the parking lot and out into the street and up a long and winding concrete access ramp. Glancing into the back, Yates saw Brewmeister lying exactly where he was before with his hands still peaceably folded on his chest and the hat over his face.

"We're two-thirds of the robbery squad, Brew and me," Jessup said. "Cub Hennessy, he's the other one-third. You're to tag along with us till you get acclimatized."

The car made a squealing turn onto the elevated superhighway. "We're chasing an eight-oh-five alert that's likely an eight-oh-three," Jessup explained as he swerved the car out into a middle lane and tried to squeeze in between a lumbering oil truck and a Greyhound bus . . . couldn't. He let the Chevy drop back a foot or so. "Eight-oh-three is the Prairie Port Police Department's code number for bank-robbery-in-progress, only this particular call we're chasing went out as an ordinary eight-oh-five robbery-in-progress with no mention made of banks. That's so the police can overlook telling the FBI about it. They overlook telling us lots of things. You could say it's a professional discourtesy." Jessup's laugh was not unpleasant. "Can't really blame them. We have trouble with just about everybody. Local police, state police, county sheriff's office, National Guard, ACLU, U.S. attorney, Boy Scouts, PTA. Biggest trouble of all is with FBI headquarters back at Washington. We piss them off like you cannot believe."

"Amen," Brew added from under the hat.

Jessup cut into the outer lane, tailgated the Dr. Pepper truck ahead. "So when did you get to town?" he asked Yates. "Friday, wasn't it?"

36

"Friday afternoon."

"And the office here didn't get a chance to brief you, that right?"

"Only on routine procedures."

"There's scant little of that to worry about . . . scant little of anything else." Jessup's laugh was more mirthful than before. "Prime malady 'round here, in case you haven't heard, is boredom. Could be we're the boredom capital of America. Not lifestyle boredom, 'cause Prairie Port is the best place you ever could choose to raise a family and improve your tennis game. I'm talking occupationally. Occupational boredom. Diddly-dick doesn't go down around here crimewise. That probably accounts for folks disliking us as much as they do. We get cranky waiting for something to happen. When it does finally happen, we get overzealous.

"You take Ed Grafton. Ed's off on vacation now, but he's our senior resident agent in charge of Prairie Port. He's something of a local legend . . . a cross between Jesus Christ Almighty and Billy the Kid. Ed's been busting the chops of an individual named Wilkie Jarrel. Wilkie Jarrel's as potent a powerhouse as a man can get to be in this part of the country. Not to mention Jarrel being a friend of J. Edgar Hoover. Ed Grafton doesn't give a hoot in hell who or what Jarrel is. Grafton's a friend of J. Edgar's too, so he goes right on busting Wilkie Jarrel's chops. Not as bad as a couple of years back, but still bad. Ed just won't let Jarrel off the hook. He's like a man possessed about nailing Jarrel. Jarrel's no choir boy, but he's surely not worth the time and trouble Grafton's been putting in . . . unless there's nothing else to do. Unless you're killing a little boredom."

Jessup pulled up to an inside lane and finally passed the Dr. Pepper truck . . . to Yates's relief. "Lord-dee-lord, does ever it get boring hereabouts. And I gotta tell you, the prospects for the future look none too rosy. Everything in this city keeps growing except crime. Right this instant in Prairie Port we've got a population nearly as big as Saint Looie. And guess how many FBI agents Saint Looie has?"

"Seventy-five?" Yates guessed.

"Eighty-seven and a potload of support personnel! Guess how many agents our office here in Prairie Port's got?"

"Thirty?"

"Including you, eighteen, and no support people except for a part-time typist who comes in on Friday evening . . . only Friday evening is softball night. Softball accounts for an awful lot 'round here. Grafton organized the team. Even if he hadn't, softball would account for lots. Bridge and backyard barbecues account for lots too. Anything to fill the time. If Prairie Port rolled over and died tomorrow, you could put on its tombstone: The Honesty Was Terrible. Where did they transfer you from? Ohio, wasn't it?"

"Cincinnati," Yates told him. "I was assigned to Cincinnati and then loaned out to Columbus for a while."

"The missus come with you?"

"Yes."

"The kids too?"

"We don't have kids."

"Couldn't find a better place to start than Prairie Port. Good neighborhoods, good schools, lotsa churches . . . almost no crime, like I mentioned. For boys it's 'specially good. Boys get all the regular sports plus riding and hunting and exploring. Even surfing. Surfing right here on the river. The Mississippi River has a freak midstream current running the length of Prairie Port and beyond called the Treachery. It's like shooting the rapids getting on it. Yes, sir, if you're a lad, Prairie Port is indeed a wondrous place. Tom Sawyer grew up just north of here. Hannibal, Missouri, is just upriver past Saint Looie. What kind of trouble did you get into back at Cincinnati?"

". . . Why would you think I had trouble?" asked Yates.

"You're here, aren't you?"

"So?"

Jessup glanced at the placid agent, who in three-quarter profile reminded him of Paul Newman. "Don't you know about Prairie Port?"

"Know what?"

"It's Siberia."

38

"Siberia?"

"Billy Yates, you've been exiled."

Yates seemed not to comprehend.

"Prairie Port may be heaven on earth to little kids and aging FBI men waiting to retire," Jessup said, "but for most of the other agents it's Siberia without snow. The Gulag. Elba. Banishment." He reconsidered. "Well, maybe it's not the ultimate exile that can be imposed. Not Butte or Detroit. When they're not quite sure you qualify for Butte or Detroit, you come here. It's kinda Purgatory's waiting room. For years now, Bureau headquarters hasn't sent Prairie Port anything but misfits, rebels and crazy people. It's their way of getting back at Grafton for doing what he damn well pleases about Wilkie Jarrel and everything else. Headquarters brass won't risk challenging Grafton directly. Not with him being as tight with J. Edgar Hoover as he is. So they punish Ed with transfer agents. You have no idea what they've dumped on this office in only the time I've been here. We had one agent transferred down from North Dakota who swore he understood animals. Actually could talk to animals and have them talk back to him, like in that song Rex Harrison sang. Know what, we darned near solved a case on what he told us a billy goat told him.

". . . We have another agent who's always dying and getting himself reborn. A regular Lazarus. Ain't that right, Brew?" Jessup happily called back over his shoulder. "A real live Lazarus, that guy?"

"Real dead," Brew yelled out from under his hat. "Tell him about Mata Hari."

Jessup grinned, said to Yates, "We got this other agent they call Mata Hari. He sees spies everywhere. Under the bed, in your soup. Thinks Washington is always sending in secret operatives to snoop on Grafton. Probably thinks you could be the latest spy working for Washington."

"Looney-toon thing about Mata Hari is," Brew's hat-muted voice interjected, "Mata's the only agent in Prairie Port who doesn't look on Ed Grafton like the second coming. Mata thinks Grafton's nothing but gloss, but he goes right on protecting Grafton against spies."

"Yessiree, it's crazy time 'round here okay," Jessup assured Yates. "So crazy even sane agents start going wacko. Grafton was born a little prairie-mad to start, so he don't really count, but not so Cub . . . Cub Hennessy, who was supposed to pick you up instead of us this morning. Cub's a real good guy and honorable mention All-American at football. He even played a couple of seasons of pro as second-string middle linebacker for the Saint Looie Cardinals. Cub's thirty-eight now and know what? He wants to make a comeback at football. Cub's out there every free moment hitting the heavy bag and pushing a sled like he was twenty years old and expecting a coach to call. That's real looney-toon, like Brew would say. Some folks think it's Cub's wife, Sissy, who's driving him to it. Only Sissy's one of the best wives and mothers ever, ain't that right, Brew?"

No answer came from the rear seat.

"Strom's even worse off than Cub," Jessup went on. "Strom Sunstrom. Strom's the assistant senior resident agent here and solid as a totem pole. Strom's second-in-command to Grafton and the man behind the legend . . . the one who makes Grafton's image look so good, if you ask me. Without Strom, Grafton's shoeshine. Strom's about the nicest guy ever born and the most efficient. He keeps the office running smooth as oil. Now even Strom's gone wacko on us. Strom's seeing ghosts! Real friggin' ghosts!"

"And holding exorcisms," the voice beneath the straw hat addended.

Jessup thought about Strom Sunstrom for a moment, noticed Yates watching him think, asked Yates, confidentially, "So who did ya hit?"

"Hit?"

"Slug. Belt? Punch out, to get sent to us?"

"You have to punch out somebody to be transferred here?"

"It surely does help," Jessup said. "This is a very picky asylum. Very snooty. No matter who headquarters sends, damn few damned souls get let in. Technically, Grafton does the accepting or rejecting of transferees. When it's left to Graf, he usually goes for some hotheaded, looney-toon bronco buster. Nine times out

40

of ten, thanks be to God, Strom Sunstrom makes the actual selections, whispers in Grafton's ear who to take and who to slam the door on. Strom favors the hotheaded and noble, but not looney-toons. Noble or chivalrous. I don't figure you for looney-toon. Give you odds it was your SAC back in Cincinnati you laid out. Strom cottons strong to SAC beaters."

Billy Yates, for the first time during the trip, if only in bemusement, smiled. "You're the one who sounds looney-toon."

"Oh, I am," Jessup gladly admitted. "I'm the fella who thinks you're the spy Washington sent in."

"You're Mata Hari?"

"In the flesh."

"I'm no spy," Yates assured him.

"It would be a helluva lot easier to swallow that if I knew who you slugged."

"Isn't it conceivable I didn't slug anybody?"

"Young turkey, you're speaking to a member of the FBI. Granted not the youngest member, but even these weary old eyes of mine don't need specs to notice you're covering up the knuckles on your right hand . . . skinned and bruised knuckles." Jessup winked a self-satisfied wink at Yates. "Could be, of course, that you're a slicky, that you're covering up them knuckles kinda awkwardlike with malice aforethought . . . so I'll think you're too inept, so to speak, to be the spy?"

"Mr. Yates?" Brewmeister, to be heard more distinctly, was holding the hat away from his face. "Might as well 'fess up to the fighting or he'll go on and on. Like Jez told you, his eyesight's not for dick. He wouldn't have noticed your knuckles in a hundred years if the assistant SAC from Cincinnati hadn't called up yesterday and told our office your personnel file hadn't been sent on yet . . . and to watch out because you pack one helluva wallop. Only problem was, he hung up before saying who it was got walloped. Jez has been skulking around like something wild and unwashed wondering who it could have been."

Yates studied Brewmeister. "Did you hit someone to get here?"

"No, sir," Brew replied. "I'm an exception to the rule. I re-

41

quested to be transferred in. I come from Prairie Port. That's not to say I'm any less looney-toon than the rest of the agents."

"So who got slugged?" Jessup asked eagerly. "I say it has to be the SAC or assistant SAC."

"Neither," Yates answered. "Cops."

"You hit police*men*? In the plural?"

"Afraid so. Around Columbus, Ohio. Maybe that's why the Cincinnati office didn't have the details."

"Details such as?" pressed Jessup.

"I broke one cop's jaw." Yates was none too happy. "Did some pretty ugly damage to four more."

"*Five* cops in all?" Jessup said in awe.

Yates nodded.

Jessup thought it over, frowned. "You bulling me?"

Yates shook his head. "Nope."

"Let's have a closer look at them knuckles!"

Yates slid his right hand from under his left, held up the severely bruised knuckles for closer inspection.

"It's raw okay," Jessup conceded. "When you say this happened?"

"Four nights ago."

"Brew, you see that hand?" Jessup called back.

"I'm seeing."

"So whatcha think?"

"I think if he hits a softball as good as he hits cops, we can take the county championship."

Jessup glanced expectantly at Yates. "You heard the man, young turkey. How d'you rate yourself at softball?"

"Better than with cops," Yates told him.

Jessup, unsure exactly what the answer meant, took a second, harder look at Yates.

"I'm good at softball," Yates said. "Very good."

Jessup laughed. Yates grinned. Brew smiled, then almost rolled off the rear seat as Jessup made a two-wheel cut back across three lanes of the superhighway, held on for dear life as the careening car, at seventy miles an hour, rocketed down and around a circu-

42

lar exit ramp. Reaching the newly constructed service road at the base of the ramp, Jessup accelerated.

Yates stared ahead through the windshield at the looming sky-scrapers of the River Rise apartment project, some of which were completed, many of which were still under construction. An electrified billboard announced that River Rise was the "recreation of yesterday today."

"So what caused the fight between you and the five Columbus cops?" Jessup asked Yates.

"Leave the guy alone for chrissakes," Brewmeister said.

"I was only being neighborly."

"Neighborly like a boa constrictor," Brew commented.

"I wanna know," Jessup insisted. "A man's got a right to know who he's serving beside in the trenches." He glanced over at Yates. "So why didya bash them, young turkey?"

". . . Ass." Yates spoke softly.

"Ass?"

"As in behind," Billy qualified. "I'm addicted to it. But only my wife's behind. My wife's name is Tina Beth and she's as blonde and tall and blue-eyed and beautiful as any woman ever born. No bosoms to mention. But my God . . . my sweet Jehovah . . . what an ass! I am slave to a high-slung Nordic ass. Any little wiggle, any minimal flex of her derrière and I fall to my knees panting like a puppy dog. I once followed her down the street like that in daylight. She loves showing me her ass as much as I love looking at it. Generally she loves showing it without clothes on, which is why we both got picked up back in Cincinnati . . . got nabbed bare–ass as Venus right on the front lawn of the Taft Museum. Then came Columbus, the Ohio State football stadium at two in the morning. We only got a warning on the front lawn of the Taft Museum. At Ohio State it was the real thing. I understand all my file record says about the incident is 'mistaken arrest for justifiable exhibitionism.' Don't you love that phrase? Don't it just knock your socks right off?"

Jessup remained silent, kept his eyes hard on the road ahead.

"Anyway, there I was, chasing Tina Beth in Ohio State football

43

stadium at two in the morning. I tried telling the cops I was an FBI agent and not to worry. I kept yelling at them to go away and leave us be. But what would you believe if you were a bunch of Ohio cops who found this stark-naked character scrambling, on his hands and knees, across the fifty-yard line after a naked lady's tail?"

Again there was no reply from Jessup.

"Still feeling unchatty, are we?" There was a ring of amusement in Billy's tone. "Can't say that I blame you. Right now, if I was listening to all of this, I'd probably be wondering how a punk brick agent could get caught jaybird nude by seven cops and not be booted out of the Bureau in two seconds flat. Part of the answer is I was a flasher for the FBI. I was covert. Underground. Spying on the great American menace gnawing at the fiber of our university system . . . student radicals. When you look as young and rosy-cheeked and Norman Rockwell dewy-pure as I do, infiltrating campuses is no sweat. I ate and slept and rioted and skinnydipped with them. But I only slept with my wife. I don't know if Mr. Hoover counted on the skinnydipping, but infiltration fattens on the motto, 'Do what you have to do and don't get caught.' By the way, I met my wife skinnydipping. Not long after, we were married. With our clothes on. She was a coed at Ohio State University. My wife, Tina Beth, wasn't a student radical. She was just in love. So was I. Ever been in love?"

Jessup kept his eyes on the highway. "What about the cops you hit?"

"I was chasing Tina Beth's glorious bottom. The cops caught us and put blankets around us and took us down to the station house. One of the cops at the station house pulled the blanket off Tina Beth to have himself a look. I broke his jaw. I beat up four of the other cops who came at me." Yates grinned sheepishly. "Now you know who's serving in the trench beside you."

". . . You bulling me, turkey?"

"No, sir."

Brewmeister was sitting up. "Jez here grows on you, if you have undue patience. Every now and again, a real live beam of human sunshine breaks through that B.S. of his." He gave Yates a reassuring pat on the back. "Any questions I can help you with?"

Yates thought for a minute. "How much B.S. was his saying this is the boredom capital of America?"

"He exaggerated some," Brew said. "There was real big excitement around here in 1935. Ma Barker drove right through Prairie Port in 1935 and almost got killed. Not that the FBI knew she was in town or had anything to do with her nearly getting crushed to death. It was those looney-toon mud volcanoes that erupt west of town every ten or fifteen years that knocked Ma's car off the road and turned it upside down. Ed Grafton was the only FBI man in the territory in those days and he heard about Ma's accident pretty fast. Ed could have arrested Ma if he wanted, but he was more interested in who she might be going to meet. So he let her steal another car and keep on traveling. He notified the boys down the line Ma was heading south. And they got her down the line. Had a gun battle at a place in Florida called Lake Wier and shot Ma and her boy Freddie to death. That's when Edgar Hoover took a shine to Grafton, or so the story goes. According to one story, Edgar even thought of adopting Grafton as his own son."

Jessup slowed the car and prepared to display his FBI credentials at the police roadblock ahead as Brewmeister told Yates, "Maybe you're the lucky charm. Maybe you brought us luck like Ma and mud volcanoes brought Grafton luck way back when. Maybe this bank robbery alert is the real thing. I sure do hope so . . . most fervently."

The clifftop mall ran the length of a massive high-rise apartment building at River Rise and had been built to resemble a turn-of-the-century Missouri street. A Sam Clemens street with each storefront a replica of what Huck Finn might have encountered. Fronting the shops were a wooden sidewalk with gas-lamp posts and a brick street. Beyond that ran a wide expanse of thick grass lined with stone benches and shaded by large, graceful trees. Beyond that was a forty-foot drop to the Mississippi River.

Behind each tree and bench, toward the upstream end of the

45

mall, was a helmeted and visored policeman in flak jacket with either a rifle or shotgun aimed. More combat-ready police lay prone behind the benches and trees, their weapons trained on the last storefront of the mall, the one at the corner of the building, directly over the water . . . the Mormon State National Bank, whose facade was an exact copy of the 1815, long-defunct Mormon State Bank in Chillicothe, Missouri . . . the bank Jesse James always meant to rob but was afraid to, according to legend.

A solitary policeman in a flak jacket and holding a machine gun squatted on the narrow ledge of bank roof which protruded from the riverside face of the forty-story-high building. In the windows above him, several more armed policemen waited.

"The police say they have seven to eight men trapped inside," Cub Hennessy explained as Jessup and Yates and Brewmeister moved forward and lay beside him on the lawn. All four FBI agents were observers at the scene, voluntary observers who had encountered resistance trying to cross the police line blocking off the mall. "Six men are downstairs. One or two on the staircase leading up the bank proper."

"According to who?" asked Brewmeister.

"According to the scanner," Hennessy answered. "They've got that new Thermex ultrasonic scanning system on the premises. That heat and space variation gadget. It's usually accurate when it's been thoroughly checked out. Only this one hasn't been totally checked. The bank doesn't officially open until the day after tomorrow. The scanner was due for one last inspection and adjustment."

A SWAT team, with rifles upraised, dashed past and deployed.

"We are asking you for the last time to come out and surrender," a helmeted officer said through his electric-powered, handheld amplifier. "For the last time, come out and surrender."

Jessup recognized the two men behind the officer. The shorter of the pair was Ned Van Ornum, head of detectives for the Prairie Port PD. The taller man was Chief of Police Frank Santi.

The officer with the bullhorn and Van Ornum turned to Santi. Santi, tugging at an earlobe, regarded the ground. He said something to Van Ornum. Van Ornum cocked a finger and pointed.

46

A flak-jacketed policeman in tennis shoes rushed from cover and zigzagged across the brick street and dove forward on the wooden sidewalk below the bank's front window, rolled on his back, training his weapon on the glass above. Moments passed. He reached up and tried the handle of the front door. It was locked. He signaled as much to Van Ornum. Van Ornum motioned the cop on the rooftop away, waved to the police in the windows above to get back . . . cocked his finger at the bank facade. The man on his back removed a glob of plastic from his flak jacket, slapped it to the bank's door, stuck in a detonating pin, rolled over and ran for cover.

The explosion was muted. The front door disintegrated. A wave of police stormed through. Then a second and third wave. The ground-level floor on the bank premises was secured within moments. Not a crook was to be found.

Ned Van Ornum, over the objections of Frank Santi, decided to lead the assault on the basement vault room. Rigged out with a flak jacket and combat helmet and bulletproof visor, he took a shotgun and started down the steps alone, his back sliding against the wall. Sharpshooters at the head of the stairwell aimed their weapons beyond and below him. Once near the open door at the bottom of the steps, Van Ornum stopped, cocked his finger up at the battery of guns.

The officer with the electric bullhorn moved in behind the poised sharpshooters, implored the criminals in the vault room to give up.

No response came from the open door.

Van Ornum crouched as low as a ski jumper at trestle top, keeping low, bounced up and down on his haunches. Once more he cocked a finger at the head of the stairs. Before the bullhorn officer could get out more than an amplified word or two, Van Ornum dove through the open door with shotgun raised. Landed on the cement floor on his elbows, ready to fire.

The large room was empty. The burnished metal walk-in vault stood in the middle of the chamber with its huge hydraulic door securely locked.

Chief Frank Santi and Ned Van Ornum and a robbery squad

47

detective by the name of Hogan conferred near the vault with the bank's manager, who said there could be no doubt someone unauthorized had violated the premises, since all the doors leading down to the vault room were opened instead of being closed as they should have been. The official pointed out that not only had all those doors been electronically locked, they were electronically programmed to remain locked until nine o'clock the next morning. Hurrying down into the sublevel chamber was the assistant bank manager, the ranking expert on ultrasonic alarm systems, who imparted, urgently, that while the vault door looked unopened, even untouched, one of the many control panel dials upstairs indicated that someone had definitely been inside the vault . . . could, conceivably, still be inside.

Flak-jacketed police were rushed in to keep their machine weapons trained on the vault door. When the area engineer for the Northern California-based ultrasonic alarm company could not be found, H. L. Jessup, the seniormost FBI agent at the scene, was asked to join the vault room confab. Jessup, after hearing the specifics of the situation, confessed to having little knowledge of ultrasonic alarm systems and volunteered to phone Bureau headquarters in Washington for expert advice. Detective Hogan said if someone was trapped inside, they'd best try to contact whoever it was before the person suffocated. Hogan had seen too many vaults to suspect this one of being booby-trapped. His offer personally to check for explosives and try to contact anyone inside was accepted.

Hogan moved toward the vault. The others in the room moved back, far back. The detective, without touching, studied the hydraulic door. Finding no indication of booby-trapping, he began feeling it with his hands . . . tapped on it with a finger . . . made a fist and knocked on it . . . knocked again hard.

A rumbling occurred. The room quivered. Hogan jumped back. Others bolted up the stairway. A mighty and echoing crack resounded. The vault tilted to one side. A second, louder cracking reverberated. Atilt, the vault sank straight down into the cement floor. Stopped after a foot's descent. The cement cracked further. The vault sank deeper. Tilted more. Stopped.

48

# Three

Martin Leo Brewmeister was a native-born Prairie Portian. Like many other boys of the area, he had spent a goodly part of his childhood at the Mississippi River. He swam there and boated there and, on two occasions, took courage by the flying mane and rode the Treachery. Much more time had been given to the river's western bank. Specifically, the sheer rock-faced palisades running from Warbonnet Ridge down past Lookout Bluff. Martin, from the earliest of years, had been an inveterate spelunker. Hardly a cave existed on the cove side of Lookout Bluff he hadn't explored. His prepubescent thirst for suspense and discovery was slaked by these often perilous forays into uncharted darkness. The passion later mingled with a more sophisticated interest, geology. He had briefly entertained hopes of going to the Colorado School of Mines, where, among other electives, two lecture courses in speleology were offered. Martin's parents, a proud and proper Hessian married to a proud and practical Junker, which was which didn't matter all that much, counseled their seventeen-year-old son that whereas geologists and speleologists were each a stalwart and noble breed, examining rocks and exploring caves was hardly an endeavor to provide bread for the table of the children they expected him to have after wedding Elsie Heeren that coming June. If he wished to be a criminal lawyer, as he always professed he wanted to be, or attend a proper agricultural college, the family would see to many of his and his wife-to-be's needs during the ensuing years of higher education. But he might as well stay home on the family farm for all the good a university degree in anything else, speleology included, would do him, for all the help he would get from his parents. Or his betrothed's parents, who were lifelong

49

friends of his parents. Though he was reverential toward his family, threats of such disenfranchisement hadn't mattered to Martin. What had were his future wife's desires. He explained to Elsie that he might like becoming a geologist. That geology, even more than criminal law, had been a devotion. He told Elsie he had no idea where a geologist could work or live in this day and age or how much money the two of them would have in the beginning. But he thought it best she should know how he felt. He asked her opinion on their future. What she wanted, expected. Elsie told him she possessed but one desire after their marriage . . . to have children as soon as they could afford to.

Martin Brewmeister married his childhood sweetheart, Elsie Louise Heeren, and sired their first son his freshman year at Illinois Central College and their second his first year of law school. He passed his bar exams and spent twenty-one months working for a Springfield, Illinois, attorney in an office across the street from a parking lot reputed to be the location of a building in which young Abe Lincoln had once practiced law. Just before a scheduled move to Chicago to take a position with a distinguished criminal law firm on Michigan Avenue, he accidentally got Elsie pregnant. There was no consideration of abortion. Both parents loved and wanted their unborn child. But Elsie was frugal and Martin was practical. They had barely managed to get by on what Martin earned from the Springfield law job. The Chicago position, being more prestigious, paid less than Springfield, was, more than anything, a career move. Sustaining themselves in Chicago would be costlier than in Springfield. Nor would Martin entertain going ahead alone, separating the family for even a short period. Martin and Elsie were fiercely self-reliant. Borrowing money from their parents, even though they could, was out of the question. Every month since taking his Springfield job, Martin had paid back a small amount of what he owed his father for financing his education. Another mouth to feed simply meant that Martin must forgo both Springfield and Chicago and find a better-paying law job. Elsie grew larger. Martin shopped vigorously for a position in criminal law. Elsie gave birth to twin girls. Martin joined the FBI, had another son and served with the

Bureau in three other cities before being assigned to the resident office in Prairie Port. In the six months since arriving home, Brewmeister had had little interest in, and less time for, spelunking.

. . . Now, listening as construction engineers for the River Rise project tried to assure skeptical police welders that the concrete floor in the vault room was absolutely safe, that there was sheer rock underneath the crack, Martin Brewmeister was reminded of boyhood legends of certain palisades in this area being beehived by passageways and caves. Caves used by the underground railroaders of Civil War repute and favored by the bootleggers of Prohibition days.

When a compromise was reached whereby an acetylene torch and its police operator would be suspended over the vault in a harness attached to the walls and ceilings, Brewmeister got Jessup's permission to scout about a bit. He went to the clifftop cul-de-sac in front of the bank, looked over the edge, saw that the rock below slanted outward, that certain ledges existed far below . . . that segments of an age-old, rusted metal ladder hung to the cliff. Despite the sharp angle below, Brewmeister was tempted to rig a climbing line and descend to the ladder segment and ledges. He thought better of the idea and gazed off along the sharp wall of cliffs running upstream. He spotted what he thought to be a crease in the rock front. The crease seemed to have a gentler slope and be filled with slag and overgrowth. Staring at it, he noticed something else. Segments of another decaying metal ladder trailed down the rock front some thirty yards beyond the crease. The lowest segment of ladder ended beside a dark spot in the cliff. A spot whose general shape could be that of a small, roughly hewn opening. A door or tunnel mouth cut into the rock face five feet above water level.

Brewmeister had to drive through the construction site of Prairie Farmer Industrial Park to reach the stretch of clifftop above the dark spot. Peering over the edge, he could not find the metal ladder. But he did see rusted iron rungs, climbing rungs, like those used by the utility company, protruding from the rock face right on down to what appeared to be river level. Brewmeister tested the uppermost rung with his hand, then his foot. It held. He pressed on the rung below with a length of plaster-splattered two-by-four. It too seemed firm. He backed down over the edge of the cliff, with one foot felt for the first rung. Found it. Applied weight. Brought the other foot down and located the second rung. Stood on it. Rung after rung he descended the rock face. Halfway down he saw a segment of corroded metal ladder several inches to his right. More ladder could be seen below that. The next rung he stepped on gave, pried itself out of the rock and fell into the water below. Brewmeister clung to the rungs above, hoped they would hold as he dropped his body, eased a foot down past the missing rung to the one beneath that. It was firm.

Fifteen more minutes of cautious descent brought him beside the dark spot. It was indeed an opening in the rock. A dark tunnel mouth five feet above river level. An entrance apparently intended to be reached by the line of rungs, since the last rung ended here beside it. The step from the rung into the opening was easily negotiated.

Bending somewhat, Brewmeister started up the dark tunnel, almost immediately ran into a barricade of wooden boards and screening. He pushed against it. The barricade was loose. He kicked at it. It gave somewhat. Reaching out and pressing his hand firm against the tunnel walls for leverage, he kicked harder. The barricade crashed over backward. Brewmeister studied the darkness beyond, thought he saw a glimmer of light in the far distance, heard a murmur. He proceeded forward. Feeling the rock walls as he moved, he knew this was a man-made pasageway cut in the cliff. Why it had been excavated, what its purpose was, eluded Brewmeister. The passage grew lower, forcing him to bend more. It grew even smaller.

Brewmeister got on all fours and crawled toward the fragile light source. The tunnel began to slope downward. His hands touched on something smooth and powdery. Dried mud. He felt the walls, the ceiling. All was coated by dry mud. The tunnel turned. The mud carpet grew thicker, firmer. He crawled around the turn into a cavern. A cavern illuminated by cross shafts of overhead, filtering light. A cavern totally and completely encrusted by dried mud. Stalactites of dried rich brown mud hung down from the ceiling like chocolate icicles. Stalagmites of mud rose up from the floor as round and dark as scoops of ice cream. Further back in the cavern, the stalactites met with the rising stalagmites to form twisting columns.

Brewmeister damned himself for not bringing a flashlight along from Jez's car. He had heard of underground mud eruptions, but never of a cavern being crusted in the stuff. He went to the wall on which a sliver of light played, felt it . . . dug into it with his fingernails. The mud had an almost moist texture to it.

A sound was heard nearby. A sound louder and clinkier than the continual murmur. Brewmeister followed the lowest light shaft back around through the cave to a half wall of rolling, smooth brown balcony stalactites. Beyond the wall he could see an opening in the cave. One sure kick crumbled a section of balcony stalactites. He walked through and into the opening and along a natural tunnel beyond. A turning tunnel which ended at a mud-crusted spiral staircase encased in a circular mud-coated shaft. Gazing up, Brewmeister saw that the shaft ascended thirty feet into a bright light source which was definitely electric in origin. He also noticed the mud covering went up only ten feet. Beyond that the red brick of the shaft wall and the dark iron of the circular steps were in plain view.

Brewmeister climbed to the top and came out on a cement platform in a large underground construction he assumed erroneously was part of the Prairie Port sewer system. Far below the platform murmured a fast-moving stream of water which disappeared into a nearby tunnel mouth. The glowing light bulbs on the cement-beamed ceiling were unglazed. Brewmeister tried the metal door at the far end of the platform. It was locked. He looked for another way off the platform, noticed a metal catwalk leading into the huge tunnel. He took it.

Brewmeister followed above the gurgling stream for fifty yards before entering a small natural cave where the catwalk ran onto a platform. The catwalk continued beyond the platform and into a larger tunnel. For whatever his instinct Brewmeister chose to climb the short metal ladder leading up from the platform. He ascended into another small cave. Here there were no stalactites or stalagmites. Only walls and ceilings and floors covered in smooth dry mud. Illumination was ample but not electrical. It emanated from a far opening. As he had done earlier, Brewmeister followed the light source, entered a second cave which had a natural stream trickling through and which was also coated by dried mud. Beyond the stream was another natural tunnel. It too was mud-coated. Then he came out into someplace he couldn't believe.

The underground chamber he stood in was as wide as any cavern he had ever seen in the area, ever heard of. Went up twenty-five feet. Was electrified by string after string of glaring light bulbs suspended from on high. In the middle of the floor an enormous metal scaffold rose to the ceiling. To a spot from which the rock had been chipped away. To where something black and square was exposed.

Brewmeister walked around for a better view. One couldn't be had from this distance. He climbed the scaffold. Red and white microflashes sparked above. He stopped below the huge metal square block protruding down through the rocks. A hole had been torn out of its bottom. Up inside the hole he could see a white-hot flame cutting through the darkness. The flame withdrew. A loud metal bang echoed. Something fell and clanged, leaving behind a circle of light above. A circle into which the plastic-masked face of a police welder appeared.

The mask popped up. The police technician stared down in disbelief at the face of Brewmeister looking up at him from the hole in the bottom of the vault.

A terrible rumbling occurred. Brewmeister's face undulated back and forth, in and out of view. Disappeared. The police technician stared harder down through the hole in the bottom of the vault . . . saw surging, foaming water . . . torrents and eruptions of water as if a dam had burst. Before the lights below went off he caught a glimpse of Brewmeister's face gasping for air, of his hand clutching for help. Both face and hand disappeared in a swirl of froth.

"Have you reached Grafton?" It was 1 P.M. and the long-distance voice of A. R. Roland spoke from SOG. SOG was the acronym for Seat of Government. Seat of Government was J. Edgar Hoover's own personal and preferred title for the Washington, D.C., headquarters of the FBI, where Roland served as assistant to the Director, the fifth–highest–ranking man in the Bureau.

"No, sir, not yet." This voice was from Prairie Port and belonged to forty-six-year-old, silver-haired John Lars Sunstrom III. "We did get through to Silver Lake and they're sending someone after him."

"Silver Lake?"

"The fishing camp in Montana he's vacationing at."

"Damnable time for a vacation."

Sunstrom thought of saying it was a damnable time for a robbery as well. "Yes, sir."

"But they have found our man Brewmeister?"

"Twenty minutes ago," Sunstrom said. "They're bringing him to the University Hospital now."

"How badly hurt is he?"

"It's hard to say. He's unconscious and pretty well banged up, from what I'm told."

"He's not about to die, is he?"

". . . I don't know."

"He was found in the river? The Mississippi River?"

"Yes, sir. The River Patrol spotted him lying on a delta island three miles below Prairie Port."

"So he was spit out into the river somewhere along the way, is that right?" Roland asked. "He was swept out from under the bank and spit into the river?"

"Yes, sir, that's right," Strom, as Sunstrom was known, said.

"Amazing."

"What might prove more amazing, sir, is how far he was swept in those tunnels. We've been told there's no outlet to the river

55

between the Mormon State National Bank and on down into Prairie Port proper. This could mean Brewmeister traveled a minimum of seventeen miles underground, assuming he came out through the Sewerage Department's tunnel in the middle of town. If he came out of the tunnel on the far end of town, which empties out into the river close to where he was found, you can add five miles to the seventeen."

"Twenty-two miles underground? Underground in water?"

"If he came out the far tunnel, yes, sir."

". . . You said in your earlier report that the robbery was receiving an inordinate amount of publicity. Is that still the case?"

"I was referring to local media coverage, and that is still true. Now national television news people have arrived in Prairie Port. People from ABC and NBC—"

"And only the local police are conducting an investigation?"

"We're investigating, sir, but not for the record."

"You personally, Mr. Sunstrom, are uncertain if the FBI should enter the investigation officially, am I correct?"

"At this time, sir, yes."

"Would Mr. Grafton share this opinion?"

"I doubt so, sir. I'm the conservative in the family."

"What is the status of the police investigation?"

"Pretty much what the media is saying, sir. It's large scale, but not much headway is being made. There is no evidence as to when exactly, over the weekend, the perpetration occurred. The amount of money stolen hasn't been established as yet. There is no indication at all as to who the perpetrators are or how many of them there were. The police are certain they came in under the vault through a series of caves and tunnels north of the bank and then made their getaway along the route Brewmeister was taken . . . through the tunnels south of the bank . . . but they don't have details. Some of the tunnels are still flooded. Others drain out and then suddenly reflood. The police suspect the robbers may have booby-trapped the tunnels . . . somehow arranged for this spot-flooding so as to keep from being followed."

". . . That smart, are they?" Roland's voice was barely audible.

56

"Sir?"

"I was telling myself, Mr. Sunstrom," he said in normal tones, "this appears to be an imaginative perpetration. Well thought out."

"Seems so."

"Is there a rough estimate on how much may have been stolen?"

"Only rumors, sir."

"Rumors where?"

"Both in the media and around police headquarters."

"Of what amounts?"

"The police think between four to six hundred thousand may have gone. The media's been claiming a million and up."

". . . Did I hear you say," Roland asked, "all three networks were at the bank? National news teams from ABC, CBS and NBC?"

. . . There is a structure to FBI field offices and resident agencies which the operations at Prairie Port managed to defy. And an obsequiousness. A common denominator for FOs and residencies, Prairie Port included, is population. High-density urban areas usually host a field office. Legalistically and geographically, the field offices, fifty-nine in all, correspond to the boundaries set for federal court districts. Certain field offices cover more than one court district and therefore develop cases for more than one United States attorney. However, each of the nation's ninety-four U.S. attorneys, who are the court system's federal prosecutors, is served by only one FBI field office. Whether housed in a government building or leased commercial space, each field office appears to be a replica of the next in general layout and operations. FOs are run by the special agent in charge and an assistant special agent in charge, the SAC and ASAC respectively, who have private offices on the premises. Supervisors and chief clerks function from their own cubicles. The workaday "bricks," or special agents, operate from large squad rooms, are usually assigned to "squads" which specialize in specific categories of crime.

57

Strewn between the galaxy of field offices, and subservient to them, are five hundred and sixteen satellite operations known as resident agencies. RAs, or residencies, are predicated totally on population and range in size from one agent covering a territory to as many as thirty. Each resident agent, according to protocol, reports officially to the squad in the parent field office . . . from this squad receives his formal assignments. Most residencies have some sort of office space. Many do not, with the resident agents of the area mailing or phoning in their reports to the field office. Few RAs boast the luxury of secretaries or stenographers. Certain of the larger RAs designate a senior resident agent, SRA, and an assistant senior resident agent, ASRA, who have no formal authority over the other resident agents at the office and who are responsible only for matters of administration and coordination. Not so at Prairie Port.

Prairie Port, technically, was in the dominion, and therefore under the jurisdiction, of the St. Louis, Missouri, field office. But Ed Grafton would have no truck with St. Louis. He had, as long as anyone could recall, dealt directly with Washington headquarters . . . very often took his orders from no mortal less than J. Edgar Hoover himself . . . operated Prairie Port as its own entity . . . seemed to be the only SRA or SAC in the Bureau who had the power to reject agents sent to his residency by Washington headquarters. A decade of enormous population growth in the Prairie Port area and the assignment of an assistant U.S. attorney to cover the newly built federal courthouse in the city added credence to those headquarters men pushing for the residency to become a full-fledged and proper field office. The pervasive enemy to such a plan was Grafton. He wished Prairie Port to remain as it was . . . a curious creature vacillating somewhere between residency and field office. Ed Grafton didn't have to bother about the chaos such vacillation created. John Sunstrom did. Sunstrom served as assistant senior resident agent, the second-in-command to Grafton, and was in sole and total charge of the administrative end of things at Prairie Port.

\* \* \*

The telephone conference call with A. R. Roland at Washington headquarters which Strom had hurriedly arranged began at 1 P.M. sharp in the eleventh-floor residency offices in downtown Prairie Port. Since the temperature outside was ninety-two degrees and the building's central air-conditioning system was nonoperative on Sundays and the office's three auxiliary window air-conditioning units had long since broken down, the seven attending Bureau agents were in their perspired-through shirtsleeves. Twenty-eight-year-old Rodney Willis recorded the Prairie Port end of the conversation on the office reel-to-reel Magnavox tape machine. Billy Yates was relegated to operating the speaker box so all in the room could hear, be heard by, or converse with, the man to whom Sunstrom was talking on the tie-line phone to Washington, assistant to the Director of the FBI A. R. Roland.

Jessup was the first of the group Strom summoned to the speaker box. Reading from his notes for Roland, Jessup recapitulated learning that the Prairie Port police had not told the FBI a robbery was in progress at Mormon State National Bank . . . how the police rushed the bank thinking the robbers were still inside . . . how nobody was found inside . . . how the vault sank into the concrete floor . . . how the top of the vault was blow-torched open . . . how nothing was seen inside the vault except Brewmeister's face staring up through a hole in the bottom . . . how Brewmeister was swept from sight.

Attention shifted to the true reason for the conference call: determining the FBI's legal right to enter the investigation. The robbery of any bank that was federally chartered, as most were, afforded the Bureau automatic jurisdiction to investigate the felony. So did the theft of any bank funds guaranteed under FDIC, the Federal Deposit Insurance Corporation. So did, when all else failed, suspicion that the perpetrators had fled across state lines to avoid arrest. Ed Grafton's liberal use of this last federal statute, both for bank theft and other violations, had prompted vehement media and civic condemnation from Prairie Port and other large Midwestern cities in which Wilkie Jarrel held sway. Jarrel was Grafton's white whale. Grafton was Jarrel's *bête noire.*

Wilkie Jarrel headed the all–powerful Grange Association, a multibillion-dollar agricultural combine, as well as its subsidiary, the Prairie Farmer Association, both of which Grafton never stopped investigating. Grafton was forever amassing evidence to prove Jarrel had misappropriated funds for the singular purpose of corrupting elected officials. A. R. Roland had to deal with many of these officials on Capitol Hill in Washington and, more often than not, had to soothe their Jarrel-ordered wrath against Grafton and his ongoing investigation of the Grange Association's top man.

Roland had been the Bureau higher-up who instructed Grafton never to invoke catchall statutes, such as crossing-state-lines, without receiving his prior approval. Now, learning via the conference call the difficulties resident agents were having in determining whether federal laws governing bank theft and FDIC guarantees had been violated, the Grafton-Jarrel feud loomed ever larger in the consciousness of the assistant to the Director of the FBI.

Thirty-one-year-old Donald Bracken explained to Roland, over the speaker box, that Mormon State National Bank did not officially open "until the day after tomorrow," Tuesday, August 24. This in itself, Bracken estimated, created somewhat shaky grounds for citing violation of FDIC statutes in claiming jurisdiction to investigate the robbery of Mormon State. A strong case might be made proving an investor's deposit could not be insured until such a deposit had been made and that it was physically impossible to deposit funds before a bank was open . . . that, therefore, FDIC statutes were both invalid and nonapplicable in the Mormon State situation. As if this were not enough, Bracken went on to say his talks with bank officials revealed the FDIC papers had not been signed or made out by the bank's president.

Portly, forty-seven-year-old Madden "Happy" de Camp provided Roland, and most other men in the room, with the dourest information of all . . . that a strong argument could be, and might be, made against the federal bank statute itself having been violated. Happy related that his cursory institutional check showed

60

that Mormon State National Bank had obtained a state charter under which to operate rather than a federal charter. And federal bank robbery laws applied only to federally chartered enterprises. What was more, the bank premises, as well as the entire River Rise project, stood on a strip of unincorporated state park land that was exempt from federal taxation . . . and possibly federal bank statutes legislation.

Happy de Camp saved the worst news for last. He had found, he told his listeners, that Mormon State National Bank was owned by Old City State Bank of Prairie Port and that Old City was owned by the Platte River Bank of North Platte, Nebraska, which in turn was a subsidiary of Rapaho Investments Incorporated. Rapaho Investments, Happy pointed out for those who didn't know, had been purchased three months before by the Grange Association, of which sixty-eight-year-old Wilkie Jarrel was controlling stockholder, board chairman and chief operating officer.

Resident agent Rodney Willis, in his turn at the speaker box, told of checking at Brink's Incorporated several hours earlier and obtaining verification that the money-moving company delivered twenty-one sacks of currency to the Mormon State National Bank at 4 P.M., Friday, August 20, in armored truck number 12-311. If the delivered funds had come directly from the Federal Reserve Bank in Prairie Port, the currency would have constituted federal monies, the direct theft of which gave the FBI automatic jurisdiction to investigate. Willis's preliminary findings showed, however, that the twenty-one sacks had been picked up at, and transferred from, Old City State Bank in Prairie Port, the parent company of the violated Mormon State National Bank. The twenty-one sacks, Willis had been told, represented the first of five consigned transfer shipments from Old City. The five shipments contained an aggregate of $1,100,000 in currency which had been packaged in sixty-eight sacks, locked trays and metal money crates. No specific record had been kept as to what each individual package was worth. How much money was in the twenty-one sacks missing from the Mormon State vault could not be determined until a recount was made of the four undelivered

61

money shipments still at Old City State Bank. Since it was Sunday and Old City was having trouble getting cashiers in to count, Rodney Willis had been warned by Brink's officials not to expect a final figure until midmorning of the next day, Monday, August 23.

Cub Hennessy was the final resident agent Strom had speak with Roland. Cub explained that over the last eight days Prairie Port had suffered a mysterious series of electrical dips and dim-outs, the cause of which Missouri Power and Electric Company, better known as Little Mo, had not been able to trace. Cub, just prior to the conference call, had chatted with a senior vice-president and a supervising engineer for Little Mo, both of whom were now absolutely certain the bank robbers had somehow tapped into the utility's main power lines, thereby creating the electrical failure. The two officials were also certain that these power dips would continue until Little Mo troubleshooters could get down under the bank and correct the chaos wrought by the missing thieves. The presumption of deliberate interference in electrical power, Hennessy guardedly proffered, might open up new avenues for claiming jurisdiction, such as those covering the sabotage of public services. Roland said he doubted that it would.

The room was cleared and the speaker box shut down so Roland and Sunstrom could continue their conversation in private. Asked for his assessment of events, Strom confessed never having experienced a situation in which just about every avenue for gaining legal jurisdiction appeared, for the moment anyway, to be blocked. He quietly joked that perhaps God was trying to tell the FBI something, then went on to say he was certain these impasses were temporary, that, as more information became available, a way would be found for entering the case through either the bank theft or FDIC statutes, should the Bureau deem it worthwhile to do so. Strom was fairly certain the Prairie Port Police Department would soon have to put out an official all-states fugitive alarm, which would make "escaping across state lines" more defensible if the FBI chose this path to follow. Sunstrom counseled that when the statutes in question were finally violated, every propriety should be observed in the hope of minimizing the inevitable anti-Bureau criticism to come . . . that it was wise not to automatically enter the investigation, even when they could, but first to petition for such jurisdiction from the assistant United States attorney of the district, Jules Shapiro.

A. R. Roland thanked Sunstrom for his candor but made no comment, signed off telling Strom he wanted to be kept apprised of all events under discussion or relative to the discussion. He emphasized that a careful eye should be kept on the amount of television and press coverage of the crime and manhunt, as well as any perceptible public reaction to this information. The assistant to the Director made no mention of Grafton. Sunstrom thought this odd.

. . . By 1:30 P.M. Sunday a small crowd of curiosity seekers had joined the media people gathered in front of the Mormon State National Bank, and the Prairie Port Police Department, which had already picked up some fifty known criminals for questioning, launched a city-wide dragnet but still avoided issuing any out-of-state alarms for the fugitives even though state troopers from Missouri and Illinois had voluntarily erected roadblocks on both sides of the Mississippi River, and the county River Patrol, by itself, was making sweeps of the Prairie Port waterfront and examining midstream islands on which the robbers could have taken refuge. Between 3 and 4 P.M. the Grange Association offered a $10,000 reward for information leading to the apprehension of the robbers, and police teams searched every departing carrier at the bus terminal, the air terminal, the rail terminal, and Army Corps of Engineers divers descended into the flooded tunnels of the rock palisade below the looted bank, and the Prairie Farmer Association added $5,000 to the reward already posted by the Grange Association, and the switchboards at the police station and state police barracks were barraged with tip calls. Even the FBI, which hardly anybody in the area much cared for, got rung up a few times with offers of information.

From 4 to 5 P.M. the vacationing Ed Grafton was finally contacted in northern Montana, and Martin Brewmeister gained consciousness in University Hospital long enough to give Sunstrom a brief accounting of his adventures in the flooded tunnels, and WJKB, Prairie Port's leading country-and-western radio station, not only set up a robbery "hot line" telephone number for those wishing to provide information on the crime but added $5,000 of its own to the already $15,000 reward money jackpot. Also, River Patrol frogmen jumped from a hovering helicopter into the Mississippi River to retrieve a floating corpse that had been spotted by waterside picnickers some twenty minutes before, and the local rock-and-roll radio station, WQXY, WJKB's main competitor, thrice interrupted programming with bulletins of the robbers having fled in two airplanes, one of which had crash-landed in a cornfield west of town . . . claimed that a gun battle was under way between the survivors of the crash and encircling state troopers.

At 5 P.M. Prairie Port's three television channels expanded their half-hour local newscasts to sixty minutes so all aspects of the robbery and manhunt could be gone into depthfully . . . reported that the latest estimate of missing money was put at four to five million dollars . . . that the plane which state troopers had surrounded in the cornfield had actually crashed five weeks earlier . . . that the fishing of the corpse out of the river by frogmen had drawn a shoreline crowd of nearly fifteen hundred spectators and that the body had tentatively been identified as that of sixty-year-old mental retardee Mary Hill, who had disappeared from a county medical institution and who wasn't thought of as having any connection with the robbery . . . that Mormon State National Bank was also becoming a sightseeing mecca that currently boasted, as live TV coverage showed, a crowd of four hundred neck-craners plus hot dog, soda and ice cream vendors . . . that no fewer than one hundred and fifty known criminals had been interrogated by the police . . . that the FBI was not involved in the investigation and would make no comment other than that divers had been frustrated in their efforts to descend into the flooded tunnels but that these tunnels were draining fast and were expected to be unflooded in the coming hours . . . that the police switchboard was receiving almost two hundred phone calls an hour offering information on the crime . . . that the city and state police had already checked

64

out some forty-five false leads but were still soliciting the public for more information . . . that empty money sacks, possibly stolen from Mormon State National Bank, had been found in a midstream tower of the recently begun suspension bridge over the Mississippi River, which when completed in three years would link Prairie Port, Missouri, with Illinois. The scoop of the day came on ABC's local affiliate with the live interview of Franklin Ulick, assistant manager of Mormon State National Bank. Ulick, who was hurrying from his car into police headquarters when he was spotted by an alert news team, stopped long enough to display a typewritten page and explain that these were the names and addresses of the one hundred and eighteen people who had visited the bank premises over the last two or three weeks. He gazed hard into the camera and let it be known that one or more of these one hundred and eighteen people was the key to solving the crime, had to be the robbery gang's inside contact, since this crime was unequivocally an inside job. All of what Ulick said, as well as everything else on the local television, was relayed to an assistant in A. R. Roland's Washington headquarters office by Sunstrom.

There was as yet no mention of the robbery on the national newscasts of CBS or NBC or ABC. Matters were too inconclusive. Nor by 7:30 did the Prairie Port Police Department know anything more about the crime than it did six hours earlier. Brink's Incorporated and bank personnel were counting the balance of the money shipment intended for Mormon State but couldn't yet say how much was stolen. The resident agents of the FBI's Prairie Port office were still unable to develop a clear-cut method by which legally to enter the case . . . but this didn't seem to matter when at 11 P.M. Sunstrom received a phone call at home from an aide to A. R. Roland by the name of Denis Corticun.

"Get to the assistant U.S. attorney and claim jurisdiction any way you can," he was ordered.

# Four

"Tell me, if you would, where it was you went?"

A right pinstriped trouser leg crossed over on top of a left pinstriped trouser leg. Manicured fingers lowered and rubbed against one another as the fingers of a pickpocket might rub together prior to dipping into a passing purse. A strand of lint was lifted from the right knee and disposed of. The fingers returned to the pinstriped lap, came to rest on fingers already lying there. A throat cleared. "I am sorry to have awakened you, but it is important I know where it was you went. What happened?"

Brewmeister, in traction on a hospital bed and bandaged at the neck and shoulders, tried to move, get a better view of the man in the pinstriped suit sitting bolt upright in the chair beyond the bedstead.

"You left the scene of the robbery and went where?"

Brewmeister strained more.

"Is something amiss, Mister Brewmeister? Discomfort? Shall I summon a nurse?"

"I can't see you," Brewmeister said.

"See me? I'm in plain sight."

"Not your face."

Pinstripe got up.

"Should I record that too?" asked the crisp young man with a stenographic pad. He wore a gray chalk-stripe suit and sat just within the door of the private hospital room.

"No, Mister Quinton, not that." Pinstripe reset his chair, resat himself, bolt upright and downbed, in plain view. His right knee crossed over on top of the left knee. His manicured hands settled in his lap.

"Where did you say you're from?" Brewmeister studied what

he would later describe as Pinstripe's "nondescript eastern seaboard face."

"SOG," Pinstripe told him. "I'm Special Deputy Inspector Corticun. Denis Corticun."

"I got that part. What department did you say?"

"Strategic Review," answered Corticun. "It's a monitoring program, recently innovated."

"To do what?"

"Among other things, record outstanding achievements by individual agents such as yourself."

Brewmeister, frowning, glanced at the closed slats of a venetian blind behind Corticun. Light filtered through. "What time is it?"

"Four in the afternoon."

"Four Sunday or Monday?"

"Monday."

"I slept for twenty-four hours?"

"Yes."

"What was the loot?"

"Loot?"

"The take from the bank robbery."

"They're still attempting to establish that."

"I'll bet it's big." Brewmeister spoke more to himself than anyone. "A real big loot."

Corticun snuck a fast look at Quinton, who was biting the tip of his pencil. "May we proceed with the interview?"

"Why not interview Sunstrom? I gave Strom the whole story yesterday."

"We've talked to Mister Sunstrom. Now it's time to talk with you."

"I'm tired. Come back later, okay?"

"Is there some reason, Mister Brewmeister, you do not wish to speak to me?"

"You go riding a goddam underground rapids and fracture a goddam leg and sprain a shoulder and tell me if you don't feel like sleeping too!"

"You rode twenty-two miles underground from what we can

67

assess, Mister Brewmeister. A heroic and harrowing feat by anyone's measure. And I understand your displeasure at my appearing here to question you at such a moment. You are, however, a member of the Federal Bureau of Investigation. I am here on matters of importance to that selfsame organization. Our organization. Yours and mine."

Brewmeister stared at the ceiling.

Pinstriped legs recrossed themselves. "I am told that on your own initiative you left the scene of the robbery and went exploring the caves, is that so?"

Brewmeister nodded.

"You've had experience with caves, have you not, Mister Brewmeister?"

"Spelunking."

"Pardon me?"

"Spelunking," Bremeister repeated. "That's the colloquial for exploring caves. Speleology is the science of studying caves."

"Is that 'ie' or 'ee'?" asked Quinton.

"One 'e.' S-P-E-L. It comes from the Greek *spelaion. Spelaion* is cave in Greek."

"According to agent Jessup the bank vault had cracked through the cement floor and discussion arose as to what was under the floor," Corticun stated. "Engineers for the building said there was no danger, that there was solid rock under the cement, but you knew that might not be so. You knew there were caves down there?"

Brewmeister shook his head. "The caves I'd explored were miles downstream and around behind a cove. I explored them a long time ago. The only thing I knew about the cliffs where the bank was, was hearsay."

"What sort of hearsay?"

"Childhood rumors about caves existing and rumrunners using them during prohibition. Things like that. Fairy tales."

"And that's what you went looking for, childhood fairy tales?"

Brewmeister thought it over. "I'm still sort of a child, I guess. About caves."

68

"From the point of the discussion as to what was under the bank vault floor, what did you do?"

"I walked out of the bank and looked upstream and thought I saw an opening in the cliff . . ."

"An opening how far upstream?" Corticun interjected.

"Four or five hundred yards from where I was standing. I drove over and climbed down the cliff face and had a look. It was the mouth of a passageway. I went in. The passage led me into a series of caves and tunnels and large water tubes. I followed one to the other, meandered all over hell for a while and got lucky. Or unlucky. I ended up directly under the vault."

"How long did all of this take?"

"From the time I entered the tunnel, maybe half an hour or forty minutes."

"Tell me about the area directly beneath the vault."

"It was a natural cave, say twenty-five-feet high. I didn't explore all of it, but from what I could see, it ran quite a ways. My guess is it was the dome of a network of linked, smaller caves. Part of the ceiling had been cut away, excavated by the men who were trying to get to the vault."

This time it was Corticun's arms which crossed. "Once you arrived in this dome cave under the vault, what did you do?"

"I climbed the scaffold."

"What scaffold?"

"A steel scaffold. A portable scaffold that reached up past the lights."

The arms uncrossed. "There were lights in the cave when you were there? Electric lights?"

"How do you think I could see the scaffold? There were about ten strings of electric lights. Hundred-watt unglazed Mazdas. Hasn't anyone been down there since? Is it still flooded?"

"It took half a day for the cave area to drain out enough," Corticun said. "The men who went down into it after that didn't find a scaffold or lights. Or you."

"What did you say," Brewmeister began. "How many miles was it I traveled?"

"From the spot you were found on the island to where the cave is measures just under twenty-two miles."

Brewmeister whistled.

"I realized this might prove difficult, if not impossible to talk about," Corticun said, "but what can you tell me about the flooding and after?"

"It's the only part I do like talking about." Brewmeister shifted as best he could in traction. "Like I told Strom, I was standing on the scaffold looking up into the hole in the bottom of the vault, watching the torch burn through the top of the vault. Then came a looney-toon moment when the torch man and myself were staring at one another. The next I knew I was being swept up in a tidal wave. A raging tidal wave trapped in a cave. Swirling water started spinning me around and sucking me down. By the time I realized the water was spinning out like water going down a drain I was already far below the surface and sinking deeper. I was spinning and being sucked legs first. Being sucked into something horizontal. Probably a large main. I was holding my breath and praying for I don't know what. My eyes were closed. When they weren't closed, the darkness didn't allow much to be seen. Then I got stuck. Wherever I was, whatever I was in, I was stuck. My lungs hurt to the point of bursting but some . . . some primal instinct told me to keep holding my breath . . ."

Brewmeister stared contemplatively at the ceiling as if watching the events play out on an overhead screen. "Then there was . . . well, I guess a water cannon describes it best. I had the sensation of being shot out of a water cannon or maybe a torpedo tube. I was being propelled forward, under water, at an incredible speed. I tried opening my eyes but couldn't from the sheer pressure of the thrust. I may have passed out at this point. Passed out or . . .

"What I remember next was riding an avalanche of water. My body was sticking out of what was a solid wall of water surging through the tunnels. I was traveling at the same incredible speed as before and knew I was dangerously close to the top of the tunnel. I knew that the top of the tunnel was only inches above me and that if I looked up my face would scrape off. I kept my head down. The ride, as fast as it was, was smooth for a while. Then it became rougher. I was being buffeted along now, taking sharp turns and rises and falls. Coming around one exceptionally fast turn I crashed into something and fractured my leg. Then I was carried over a series of cascades into steadily declining levels of tunnel. I was tumbling head over heels down these. I came around another turn and here the water course ran straighter and faster than in quite a while. I was almost body-surfing along. Up ahead I saw a solid wall of brick. A tunnel's end of brick. I was being driven at it like a pig on a spit . . ."

Brewmeister stopped speaking, watched the crisis continue on the memory screen.

After waiting several seconds, Corticun asked, "Then what?"

Brewmeister went on staring at the ceiling. His eyes half-closed. His face twisted into an anticipatory expression somewhere between pain and elation.

"Mister Brewmeister, you were being carried toward the wall and then what?"

"Ask Strom. Anyway, I got past the wall and was swept on through another couple of tunnels, got dumped out into the river and crawled onto an island and came to in this room."

Corticun and Quinton exchanged a long look. The pinstriped knees recrossed before Corticun asked, "Mister Brewmeister, what is your assessment of the men who robbed the vault?"

"They're rich."

"Bear with me while I propose a scenario," said Corticun. "A group of criminals penetrates a system of tunnels and caves, a complex system, and comes up directly under the spot where a bank is being built. They bring in electricity and a large portable scaffold and God only knows what other paraphernalia. They excavate away the top of the cave until they have reached the bank floor. They cut through the floor and reach the vault itself and then cut right through that. Somehow they have arranged to neutralize the electronic alarm system on the vault and throughout the bank. What's more, somehow they have manipulated their escape by flooding the tunnels and caves they had

71

used for the perpetration. Not only that, by flooding those areas they also erased the physical evidence of having been there in the first place."

"Is that what they did?" Brewmeister said. "Flooded the tunnel intentionally?"

"It appears so. The perpetrators may have tested their escape and flooding plans quite a few times prior to the actual perpetration. This could explain the electrical shortages and brown-outs in the Prairie Port area over the last week and a half."

Brewmeister's nod was appreciative. "Pretty slick."

"Very slick," Corticun suggested.

"The crime of the century," added Quinton.

"It may well be." Corticun was on his feet. "Mister Brewmeister, I would like to have your opinion on what sort of person, other than yourself, could find his way through those caves?"

"Anyone who works down there, I'd guess. Sewer or water company personnel. Maybe people from the electric company?"

"I'm referring to the caves. Who could have seen a bank being constructed and known that underneath there was a natural cave? Any local criminals?"

"It's possible some of the old rumrunners knew."

"I thought that was a childhood rumor."

"An oft-repeated rumor. I give it credence."

"Are any of those old rumrunners still around?"

"One or two."

Corticun's thumb hitched into the fob of his vest. "You've been extremely helpful, Mister Brewmeister, extremely. I hope your recovery is rapid." He took several steps toward Quinton, who had stood up, then turned. "For the record, Mister Brewmeister, what happened at the brick wall in the tunnel?"

"Never for the record." Brewmeister, for the first time during the interview, spoke lightly.

"Off the record then? For my own curiosity."

"I don't think you'll want to know."

"Why not allow me to be judge of that?"

". . . I had a religious experience."

72

"Religious experience?"

". . . I saw the kingdom of heaven. It was on the other side of that wall."

Had Corticun been seated, he would have crossed his legs or folded his hands or removed lint from a knee. Standing, all he could do was clear his throat.

"Mister Corticun, I'm Lutheran to my eyeballs," Brewmeister told him. "German Lutheran. Hardly a promising recruit for divine revelation . . . being reborn. We had an agent here for a time who claimed always to be dying and reborn, it wasn't me. I don't believe in such things. But in those tunnels something miraculous happened. I crashed through the brick wall headfirst and lived. A brick wall lay in the path of the avalanche of water I was riding. I was ramrodded through and sprained a shoulder . . . and I wasn't unconscious. What I saw on the other side of that wall, it was like I was in God's temple, water was swirling around me, spinning me in a circle and when I looked up I saw the domed roof of a great cathedral . . . and all the walls around me, while I spun, they were tall and arched—"

Corticun broke in. "And how long did you dwell in God's temple?"

Brewmeister looked at him, looked hard. "Only a millisecond, then I shot out through one of the arched doorways. Was shot into another tunnel and carried along on another crest of rampaging water. You know what I did then, Mister Corticun?"

". . . What did you do, Mister Brewmeister?"

"I sang. I went whizzing along on my back through the darkness with a shoulder badly sprained and leg fractured and I sang my damned fool head off—"

The knocks on the door were sharp and impatient. Corticun squared his shoulders and motioned. Quinton slipped the note pad inside his jacket, barely managed to unlock the door when it burst back into his face, shoving him to the wall.

Big and burly and unkempt Ed Grafton strode through, followed by Happy de Camp and Cub Hennessy.

"What the royal hell is that enema doing here!" Grafton's voice

73

was as stentorian as his full, large-featured face was ruddy. "I told that enema not to come here." Grafton looked at de Camp but was pointing at Corticun. "What's he doing here?"

"Why are you here?" asked Happy de Camp.

". . . I had a few follow-up questions," Corticun said.

"I told the enema it wasn't to bother my people!" Grafton walked to the bed, looked down at Brewmeister. "How you feeling, lad?"

"Good, Graf, thanks."

"How's the brick wall?"

"Strom told you?"

"Yep. One helluva trick. Might come in handy sometime." Grafton patted Brewmeister's cheek. "What's that D.C. bunghole bothering you with?"

"Interviewing me about the cave."

"You need anything? Food, booze . . . a broad?"

"A cigarette."

"Smoking's bad for ya."

"I know, but that's what I'd like."

"Who's got a cigarette?" Grafton faced the others.

Corticun held out a pack.

"Not you, someone human."

Cub Hennessy tossed over a pack of Kool Milds. Grafton gave one to Brewmeister, lit it. Brewmeister took a long, satisfying puff.

Grafton moved into the center of the room, stood with his back to Corticun. "I need a chair."

Corticun pushed his empty chair forward.

Grafton sat. "Ask the enema what it was he wanted to know about caves in particular."

"What did you want to know about caves?" Cub asked.

Corticun stepped beside Quinton. "I wished to know how agent Brewmeister found the cave and survived the flooding."

"Tell the enema that's what he asked permission to do earlier. And I said no."

"You heard the man," Happy told Corticun.

". . . I have to get back to Washington and wanted—"

74

"Brew," Grafton called out to Brewmeister, "this bunghole give you his crime-of-the-century routine? Rave on about it being the slickest loot ever?"

"That he did, Graf."

"There were electric lights in the cave, hundred-watt bulbs," Corticun said. "A line of them. And a portable scaffold."

Grafton turned in his chair, studied Corticun, who backed closer to Quinton. "Look at those two fuckers, would you? Pinstripes. Who would have ever fucking believed pinstripes in the FBI?" He shifted around so he could half-face Brewmeister and partially see Corticun and Quinton. "Okay, you two walking dildos think you got the crime of the century on your hands, I won't discourage you. Only take notes." He pointed at Quinton without looking at him. "I want you to report every last word of this back to Washington."

Quinton had the stenographic pad out and ready.

"Everything I told you back at the office checks so far," Grafton began. "We've put together a couple of more things since then, including a little present or two we brought over for Brew. But now we'll share." Grafton beckoned. Cub handed him a large, damp brown paper bag.

"The robbers probably escaped from under the bank on rubber boats." Graf's hand went into the bag. "Big black rubber boats made of this." Graf tossed a piece of shredded, black heavy-duty rubber at Corticun. "They found this not far from where they found Brew on that delta island. They've got the rest of it over at the River Patrol boat house. It's a six-man boat or what's left of it."

A strand of waterlogged, gray window sashing was tossed at Corticun as Graf explained, "Several of these were connected to inner rungs on the gunnels of the boat. And one of these was connected to the rope."

Corticun caught a soggy gray canvas bag in both hands, held it away. A small, open padlock dangled from the zipper opening at the bag's top. Stenciled on the bag's side was the name "Brink's."

75

"Reach inside," Graf ordered.

Corticun obeyed, removed a thick packet of one-dollar bills. A water-drenched packet.

"Guess the crooks were in too much of a hurry to take it along, but it's Mormon State money okay," Graf brought the packet of bills to Brewmeister. "Fifty dollars in all, and believe you me, they're going to miss it dearly."

Grafton returned to the chair. "So now we know the crooks not only took in safe-cracking equipment, a scaffold, electricity . . . oh, by the way . . ." He tossed a mud-caked orb to Corticun. "There's a light bulb under that goo. A hundred-watt light bulb. A string of them were tangled in the boat's rudder, or what remains of the rudder."

The paper bag dropped on the floor beside the chair. Grafton bit into a plug of tobacco. "Like I was saying, now we know for pretty damn sure those crooks beat it the hell out of there in rubber boats. That's why they flooded the tunnels. And if you think they were a slick crowd in cracking the vault, wait till you hear the razzle-dazzle they pulled with the flooding.

"According to the Sewerage Department, the crooks did a bigger and better job with the flooding than anyone thought. The sewage people think as much as an extra four to eight million gallons came through their pipes over the weekend, only they can't be sure. The extra water knocked hell out of their monitoring equipment. Ripped lots of it clean away. The water knocked hell out of the sewage system itself too. It wasn't till Sunday afternoon, with the beginning of those mud explosions over west, that engineers started going down into the tunnels and saw that all hell had broken loose.

"Another thing about that extra water is they don't know where it came from exactly. Up north of the city, around the bank, a couple of old irrigation and water systems hook up together or at least intertwine. They link into the city's water and sewage systems at different places. If you think the riddle can be solved by asking who the hell is missing four to eight million gallons of water, don't. No place seems to be. What they do know is the area under the bank was probably flooded three times.

76

"As for the matter of intelligence, we have two choices. Did the crooks have an inside source of information, a human source, say at Brink's, to tell them when the money was going to be shipped to the Mormon State National Bank? Did they have someone inside Mormon State itself giving them tips? Or did they rely on the bank's own monitoring system? Did they tap into the bank's main monitoring cable and see for themselves when an armored truck pulled up on the street outside and began unloading money . . . see the money sacks being brought downstairs and put into the vault? There were splice marks found on the main monitoring cable of the bank's security system."

Grafton nodded to himself, took long and studious notice of Corticun . . . pointed to an empty chair. "Sit!"

Corticun came forward and seated himself. Crossed his legs.

"This sound like the crime of the century so far?" Grafton was less abrasive.

". . . I would say," Corticun cleared his throat, "it sounds extremely well planned and well executed."

Grafton spit tobacco into the potty. "One way or another the crooks knew when that first shipment of money arrived. It was delivered by Brink's armored truck number 12-311 at four P.M. on Friday, August twentieth, and put in the vault. By Sunday morning, August twenty-second, the shipment was missing from the vault. So was everything the crooks had used to pull the job except for a demolished boat and piece of rope and string of mud-caked, hundred-watt light bulbs."

Grafton leaned forward and smiled at Corticun. "Assuming you were me, what would you do now?"

The legs recrossed. "You mean after going to the assistant United States attorney?"

"Go to the assistant U.S. attorney? Why?"

"To receive jurisdiction," said Corticun.

"Jurisdiction for what?"

"To investigate the robbery you just described."

"That's what you would have done, barreled ass right over to the assistant U.S. attorney and got yourself some jurisdiction?"

77

"Mr. Grafton, that is what Director Hoover expects to be done. *Must* be done."

"Make this here robbery an official FBI investigation, no matter what, huh?"

"Absolutely."

Grafton looked over at Quinton writing. "You getting all this down, son?"

"Yes, sir."

"Tell you what, Mr. Headquarters Pinstripe Junior G-Man," Grafton said to Corticun, "you go see the assistant U.S. attorney on your own and claim jurisdiction. Claim it for Edgar Hoover or whoever else sent you sniffing around down here. Claim it and bring in all the photographers and reporters and TV cameras and hire a fine brass band to march up Main Street investigating your crime of the century. My men, they're keeping as far away as possible from that robbery." He got up and stretched. "Me personally, I'm keeping a thousand miles far away and pronto. I'm catching the first airplane back to Montana and finishing out a duly earned vacation just like planned. Anything pops up, wire me at Silver Lake."

Grafton walked to Brewmeister. "Know what these fancy pinstripe desk jocks forgot to ask? They forgot to ask how much money was in those sacks Brink's delivered to the bank. How much money was stolen. How much money them dumb bastards who call themselves bank crooks made off with."

"How much?" Brewmeister asked.

"Guess, Brew."

"It's too good to tell you outright," Cub added.

Happy was smiling. Cub fought not to smile.

Brewmeister made a deflated estimate. "Half a million dollars?"

"Sixty-five hundred dollars!" Grafton broke up. ". . . Sixty-five lousy hundred dollars . . ."

"In singles," Cub spit out between belly laughs. ". . . There were only one-dollar bills in those money sacks . . . only singles."

"Those poor dumb crooks did all their labor and digging and

78

planning for probably under a thousand bucks a man." Happy nearly choked laughing.

". . . Under a thousand *in singles.*" It was the funniest thing Cub had ever heard.

"Those dumb clucks would have been better off on unemployment." Happy doubled over in pain laughing.

"Sixty-five hundred, oh my God!" Brewmeister nearly ripped down the traction rig laughing.

"It's the crime of the century okay . . ." Grafton pounded his fist against his leg and roared louder than ever, ". . . the poorest crime of the century."

"The Polish crime of the century," Cub howled.

Grafton dropped to his knees in laughter, with tears streaking down his face, gasped, "There ought to be a law against doing that to crooks."

Happy fell into the wall laughing, laughing even harder he shouted, "Good Lord, I'm peeing in my pants!

The twin-engine blue and white Cessna 210 airplane dropped through a rip in the early evening cloud cover, banked steeply, leveled off and, maintaining an altitude of five hundred feet, droned downstream above the Mississippi River; passed over a turn in the river known as Cyclone Bend and an enormous gray rock cliff rising from the turgid water of the western bank called Warbonnet Ridge and a patchwork of forest preserve and lagoons and reservoirs and recreational areas; on down above the outer limits of the city of Prairie Port and a midriver current known as the Treachery and riverfront rock palisades on which loomed the construction sites for the Grange Association's nearly completed high-rise complex and the just-begun Prairie Farmer Industrial Park and the River Rise project, which housed Mormon State National Bank; further downstream over Lookout Bluff and the recently constructed 60,000-seat sports stadium; over the twinkling evening lights of Hennings Wharf and Steamboat Cove and Nigerton and ten blocks of downtown "Old City" and twenty-five modern acres of New City, which was ringed to the north and west by wooded and lush hills of riding trails and

79

hunt clubs and golf courses and fashionable homes and large estates and low, modern industrial buildings housing much of the area's burgeoning aerospace and electronics industries; on above the river's delta islands, one of which contained a softball field, and a grand turn-of-the-century waterfront luxury hotel and gabled houses and the university and the last ridge of high ground and horse farms and pastures; on out over the prairie whence the city received its name.

As the plane banked to start an upstream sweep, the lights of Prairie Port began to dim and raise . . . dim and raise in geometric clusters of approximately four square blocks each . . . dim and raise with no cluster in synchronization with the next.

"Jesus, look at that," the pilot said, staring down through his side window.

The two men behind him said nothing, continued unscrewing the side bolts of a metal refrigerator locker.

"The city looks like a huge blinking checkerboard," the pilot continued. "A checkerboard run amok." He glanced back at the pair of men kneeling over the locker. "You oughta see."

"You see for us, friend," the shorter man said. "You keep your eyes straight ahead or down on the city . . . but *not* back here."

"Sure thing." The pilot turned back to the controls. He hadn't liked his two passengers from the moment he picked them up, and their big metal locker, in East St. Louis an hour and a half before. They sure as hell weren't from East St. Louis or anywhere in the Midwest. They were too close-mouthed, too well dressed, too hard to pin down to suit him. He couldn't be sure if they were mob guys or big business guys or CIA. He'd flown all of them in his day and could usually sense who was who, sooner or later. But these two on board now eluded him. Ah, what the hell, he told himself, Lieutenant Jake Oferly of the Chicago PD had asked him to take the job, so how bad could the pair be? . . . anyway, when you fly charter in and around Chicago it's smart to stay on good terms with Jake. And they did pay in advance, $1,400 on the spot. Why worry?

"Lose altitude," the short man ordered.

The plane dove and leveled off. The two men slid the heavy

lead lid from the locker . . . lifted and lay on the cabin floor a hermetically sealed plastic body bag . . . unzipped the bag. The corpse of Teddy Anglaterra lay exposed. A naked cadaver that the two men began dressing in a light green initialed work shirt, a dark green tie, dark gray slacks and a dark gray suit jacket. Once the body was dressed, the shorter man moved forward to make sure the pilot continued looking ahead. The taller man strapped a broken watch to the corpse's wrist, draped a silver crucifix around the discolored neck. A battered wallet without identification went into the rear pocket of the trousers. Keys and change and sixteen dollars in waterlogged bills slid into a side pocket.

"You're still too high." The short man was standing directly behind the pilot.

"If I go any lower we can't glide." The pilot indicated below. "Is that the spot you want?"

The short man looked down through the window and told him it was.

The Cessna 210 flew due north and made a wide, one-hundred-and-eighty-degree turn and started back down over the river, flew at wingtip past Warbonnet Ridge and on down over the Treachery and palisade-top construction sites for the Grange Association and Prairie Farmer Association and River Rise Realty Corporation, on beyond Mormon State National Bank and Lookout Bluff and Hennings Wharf.

"We're here," the pilot said.

The tall man jerked up and opened the trapdoor in the cabin floor, pushed the corpse through, hung his own head down and out and watched Teddy Anglaterra splash into the Mississippi River at a spot not far from where the body of a lunatic lady had been retrieved by helicopter two days earlier.

"So there the danged boys are, Ed Grafton and Cub Hennessy, hunkering over the office desk and sniffing away like they can't tell something dead from something hissing." Billy Yates, his face lathered with aerosol soap, spoke into the motel suite's bathroom mirror as he stood in neatly ironed pajama bottoms shaving with

81

a straight blade. "They were telling the rest of us what happened at the hospital with Brewmeister. Telling, hell, they were putting on a full production. Partying too. They brought a half case of white lightning in with them. I mean, real mountain moonshine. The kind that peels paint off fenders. And they'd been drinking pretty fierce before they came barging into the office. I didn't know what to expect. It was old hat to the other agents. Most of 'em ate it up. A few didn't. There're some real tight butts up there.

"So anyway, Ed Grafton and Cub Hennessy are telling us about talking to Martin Brewmeister and the Brass Balls. Brass Balls is what they call anything from Washington, D.C., around here. They don't say SOG or Seat of Government or Headquarters or even Washington if they can help it. Everything's Brass Balls or Brass-Balled Monkeys to them."

A long and languid "Ohhh" emanated from the dark bedroom beyond the open door.

"Actually, it's Ed Grafton who's telling what went on," Yates amended. "Cub Hennessy's passing around white lightning. Right in the middle of a sentence, Ed Grafton stops talking and gets this expression on his face and hunkers over and starts sniffing. Sniffing and sniffing all around. Cub Hennessy hunkers and starts sniffing too. They sniff and sniff, the two of them. Ed Grafton makes like a hunting hound, leaps up on top of a desk and gets on all fours, points his nose at the conference room door and lifts his hind leg and freezes. Cub Hennessy, he starts in howling at the moon. Then they both take out these toy pistols, these cap guns, and they sneak up on the door. Whammo, they pull open the door and guess what bursts out, Tina Beth!"

". . . What bursts out?" Yates's wife, Tina Beth, asked from the unlighted bedroom.

"Happy de Camp does."

"Who?"

"Happy de Camp. He's the agent whose son burned his draft card."

"Ohhh."

"And guess what Happy's wearing, Tina Beth? Nothing! He's

82

bare-bottom naked 'cepting for a pinstripe jacket and a one-dollar bill tied around his you-know-what. Happy bursts out and goes racing round the office letting out these war whoops with Ed Grafton and Cub Hennessy snapping caps at his naked behind."

Yates grinned off into the darkness of the bedroom. "Remind you of anything, Tina Beth?"

"Shush up, naughty boy."

Shaving resumed. "Then Ed Grafton stands on another desk and proposes a toast to Denis Corticun and Harlon Quinton. They're the two Brass Balls up in Martin Brewmeister's hospital room who thought the bank robbery was the crime of the century. Pretty soon everybody starts in toasting everything and even the tight-butt agents are a little loaded and having a good time. It was crazy up there, Tina Beth, and getting crazier. Only around here they like to say looney-toon for crazy.

"They're drinking white lightning and warning Ed Grafton he better shag out if he's going to catch the evening plane back to Montana. Ed Grafton's enjoying the toasting too much to leave. They're toasting some things two or three times. Toasting Denis Corticun and Harlon Quinton and all the Brass Balls at headquarters. Toasting Frank Santi, the chief of police, and all the Prairie Port cops who went chasing the bank robbers. Toasting the bank's alarm system which said the crooks were trapped in the vault. Most of all, they're toasting the crooks themselves, who went to all that trouble to make so little money.

"The scuffle kinda started when they toasted going over to the assistant U.S. attorney's office and getting jurisdiction to investigate the robbery. Somebody or other said the assistant U.S. attorney never did catch the softball when the lights went out the other night. I don't know what the hell they were talking about, Tina Beth, but Cub Hennessy got good and mad about it. Someone was accusing the assistant U.S. attorney of dropping a softball in the dark and finding it on the ground and holding it up when the lights came on, saying he caught it all the time. Cub Hennessy said the assistant U.S. attorney was the only public official he knew who never lied and that if he said he caught it in the dark, he sure t'hell caught it in the dark. Arguing turned to shoving,

83

and that's when Ed Grafton announced he's got to go catch the plane for Montana. He put an arm around the agent who was arguing against the ball getting caught in the dark, Lester Kebbon, and says, 'Come on, you're driving me to the airport.'

"They leave and somebody or other grabs for the one-dollar bill on Happy. Happy de Camp's still only wearing a pinstripe jacket and the one-dollar bill around his you-know-what. Remember where I told you the dollar was wrapped around, Tina Beth?"

"Billy Bee, does this story have an end?" asked the voice in the dark.

"Sure does, hon. What happens when one agent grabs is that other agents start grabbing too. They're chasing Happy de Camp around the office giddy as schoolboys. Happy starts grabbing back on the run. Pretty soon everybody's grabbing at everybody and laughing and scrambling and, whammo, they end up in one big pile on top of Happy de Camp. And whammo again, guess who walks in, Tina Beth?"

"You're treating me like a little kid again," Tina Beth said in the darkness.

" 'Course I'm not."

"Y'are so. You go on stopping and asking me questions like I was a little kid taking a test."

"Tina Beth, that's my way of telling things. Always has been, you know that."

Hearing no further objection, Yates turned back to the mirror, tilted up his head, began to slice away foam from beneath his chin. "Right in the middle of everything, Denis Corticun walks into the office."

"Who?"

Billy Yates glanced off through the door. A giggle rose in the darkness.

More under-chin foam was cut away. ". . . Denis Corticun was the Brass-Balled Monkey talking to Brewmeister. The one they were toasting. The pinstripe guy I told you about earlier. Don't you see, it's his pinstripe jacket Happy de Camp has on. Happy de Camp and Jez Jessup snuck into Denis Corticun's hotel room and lifted his pinstripe jacket.

"Tina Beth, you cannot believe the expression on Denis Corticun's face when he walked into that office. I mean, he was ash-white horrified. And he hadn't even spotted Happy de Camp yet. Happy was buried under a pile of agents. All Denis Corticun saw was a white-lightning free-for-all. Corticun's got this habit of clearing his throat, and he did so loudly to get attention, only it didn't get anybody's attention. He had to call for attention like a drill sergeant. Had to call a couple of times. When everyone quieted down, he said someone had broken into his hotel room and stolen his jacket and he wanted to know what the best procedure was for reporting the loss to the police . . . whether he should do it through our office or call the police directly.

". . . Which is when he saw Happy de Camp. The pile got off Happy, and Happy stood up wearing Denis Corticun's pinstripe jacket and nothing else but the one-dollar bill. Corticun was speechless. He pointed a finger and damn near choked before he could finally shout, 'That man doesn't have his pants on!' Faster than you can blink an eye, every agent in the place dropped his pants and was asking, 'Which man?' Poor old Preston Lyle forgot he had on these panties. Little teeny underpants that look like girls' panties, only they're not. They're manufactured for men. You could have fooled me they're manufactured for men. Once the other agents see them, they start chasing Pres like they were chasing Happy earlier. Chasing and shouting, 'Panty raid, panty raid.' It was a sight, Tina Beth, a sight indeed."

"Preston Lyle? He the one married to the redhead?"

"Uh-uh. That's Butch Cody. Butch is thirtyish. Pres is more our age . . . twenty-six or twenty-seven."

"Twenty-six or twenty-seven! Billy Butler Yates, you maybe can flimflam the riffraff with talk like that, but *I'm* nineteen. Twenty come December. I'll have it no other way. You go and be whatever you want. Only jest leave me home, hear?"

Yates grinned a feeble grin reserved for those ever-increasing moments when he wasn't sure if Tina Beth was truly offended or faking. As usual, he traveled the road of least peril. 'You're nineteen, and what say I promise to stop kidding about age?"

No response came from the blackness beyond the door. "All kidding stops," Yates declared, "and I'll settle in at a firm twenty-eight?"

"You won't be twenty-eight come November," stated Tina Beth. "Why do you make everything older?" She began to cry, loudly.

Yates put down the straight razor and hurried across the bedroom.

"Tina Beth," he said, dropping to a knee beside the bed on which the cross-shadowed silhouette of a shorty-clad young woman lay facedown atop the sheets. "The last thing I want to do in this life of ours is make anything older, specially you and me."

She buried her head deeper under her arms.

"Hear what I'm telling, Tina Beth?"

"Stop lookin' at my bottom," came her tearful demand.

"Honey, I'm not looking at your bottom," he lied.

"Yer always lookin' at my bottom," she said. "Every time you squinch down like that, it's to see my bottom close. That's all I am to you, a bottom—"

"That's a pernicious lie." He rose and sat on the bed, bent over her. "It's the top I love, not the bottom."

"Stop drippin' shavin' soap on my back." She threw a hand blindly up behind her to fend him off. "You're always *drippin'* on me."

"Shows to go how all wet I am."

". . . Stop tryin' to make me laugh."

"Shows to go what a big drip I am."

Tina Beth rolled over, sat up abruptly and crossed her arms. "I'm no dopey-dope. I read three books a week and coulda even finished college if I had a mind to. 'Stead I married you, unfortunate to say. You never talk to me like I coulda finished anything, college included."

"Sure I do."

"Show me one ferinstance. Tell me in plain old unsyrupy words when you ever once treated me like I coulda finished college."

Yates gambled on repentance. "I see your point, Tina Beth. I'm ashamed and I apologize. If fences could be mended, how would you like me to talk to you?"

"Shorter. You go on and on like some whiskery old guide in museums. You tell me all them tiny details like who's wearing one-dollar bills and who isn't—"

"A man in my job's no better than what he sees and remembers, Tina Beth."

"Then remember it for yerself and don't repeat it a hundred times. You know how many times you told me Mr. Grafton sniffed and sniffed? You told me and *told* me. Once woulda done."

"I . . . I see what you mean. How else you'd like me to talk to you?"

"I want you to *listen* to me. I know things too, lots of things. Things jest as exciting as one-dollar bills. Only you never do ask. You don't rightly care what I do. All that counts round here is what you do. That's why you're always in one mess of trouble after the next mess with folks. You never once asked how my luncheon with the wives went today. That's 'cause you don't listen!"

Experience had taught Billy Butler Yates that his wife was a one-two puncher in situations such as this, that her second complaint was usually the critical complaint. Answer too quickly and Tina Beth would accuse him of blind placation rather than considered understanding of her viewpoint and feelings. Tarry too long before responding and she would strafe him for indecisiveness, evasion, vaguery and disconcern.

"Hey, yeah, how was that old luncheon anyway?" He asked enthusiastically . . . after counting off eight seconds under his breath. "You were going out to that country club, weren't you? They a nice bunch of wives? You have a good time?"

"A fine old time . . . considering I coulda been killed for all you cared. Coulda been buried alive under the landslide!"

"Landslide?"

"Someone hide your ears?"

"A landslide in Prairie Port?"

"What else would you call a whole side of hill, trees and all, sliding down under your very nose? On our way home it happened. Whole slices of hill slid onto the road. Mud gurgled up where the trees and earth had been, and it came oozing down too. State troopers had to block off miles and miles of road because of that mud. And it isn't a country club at all. It's a hunting and riding club, the Laggerette Hunt and Ride Club. We've been asked to become members. Sissy Hennessy wants to put us up."

"Whatever you like," Yates told her.

"Sissy Hennessy's a very fine woman and so are the other wives, but my Lord, do ever they chitchat." She reached out in the darkness for the bed lamp. "Land o'loving, Billy Bee, do ever they talk around here. Gossip like there's no tomorrow. That's probably what God was saying with that mud slide of His . . . hush your mouths, catty ladies."

Tina Beth Yates, the night light revealed, was as blondly beautiful and provocatively formed as any young woman who ever graced an outdoor billboard advertisement for swimsuits . . . which she had done quite often for a short period of time prior to marrying Billy. Billboards primarily in the South and Southwest. Her daddy had been outraged at such wanton exposure, but only with Billy's help was he able to terminate his daughter's brief career.

From the moment Tina Beth Lodes set eyes on Billy Yates, she was his. Not unconditionally, but his if he acted wisely and rapidly. Cut bait and shaped up to her expectations. Tina Beth was surprised by this reaction. Never had she thought she would give herself to so handsome a man. Handsome men were too self-centered for her. Too ungiving. The world came to handsome men the way the world comes to beautiful women. Demanding little. Offering all. The handsome men she had known had demanded all, offered little. Never, never had she met anyone she thought was quite as handsome as Billy Yates. His blue eyes and

88

square chin reminded her of a younger, better-looking Paul New-man. The quizzical expression he made when he wasn't certain of something had, for her, all the fetching vulnerability of an unsure Jimmy Dean. His resolve, on those occasions when he finally made up his mind to do something, was not unlike that of Tina Beth's most revered film idol, Gary Cooper.

Images of movie heroes to the side, Billy Yates, from the first night she had allowed him, was the greatest lovemaker she had ever conceived of knowing. Never since they had been together had she thought of infidelity. There was no need. No interest in anyone but Billy.

Billy Yates, as Tina Beth got to know him, was able to do another thing she hadn't suspected, talk to her as she had never been talked to before. This above all became the linchpin of their love. His talking wasn't anything specific, no particular vocal technique or imparted wisdom. Merely a manner. A shy warmth. An awkward passion. If anything, Billy sensed what subjects to avoid, such as having children. Tina Beth has no intention of bearing children until she was middle-aged, at least twenty-five.

She was seventeen at the time they met. They had to wait until she was eighteen before they could marry. Now another year and a half had passed, and things were as good as ever . . . or almost. During their final months in Ohio he had become preoccupied and taciturn. It had occurred to her the reason for this was un-happiness about his work, with his assignments, but it didn't matter. He had spoiled her with his attention and understanding, and she knew this and knew she had become too reliant on him, too selfish, to settle for anything less than she had before. When all he could provide was less, her resentment deepened. She grew to hate Ohio and the FBI, but never Billy. Never her Billy Bee. He was still whom she loved and dreamed of. Still as boy-ishly sensitive as Jimmy D., if not as handsome as Pauly N. At least not lying on the motel room double bed with his face partially covered with shaving soap.

"Night of horrors, what a sight!" Tina Beth had eeked as the bed lights came on. "March right into that bathroom and unmess yourself, hear?"

89

Billy Yates trooped obediently off to the bathroom, straight-razored away the last of the shaving soap in record time, vigorously washed and rinsed and dried his face, then standing in the doorway, profiled the finished product. "That unmessy enough?"

Tina Beth patted the bed. "Come sit here, good boy, and I'll tell you all the gossip. Well, maybe not all. There's certain things we girls best keep between ourself."

Once Yates lay down beside her, Tina Beth raised up and sat cross-legged facing him. "Remember how you're always telling me FBI agents never discuss any 'ficial business with their wives, Billy Bee? Well, maybe that's true some places, but not here in Prairie Port. Those girls cluck on like the wildest hens I ever did hear. 'Bout everything and anything. FBI work included. And lovin', my gracious, they do love talkin' lovin'! They're downright scandalous."

Tina Beth, to her husband's disappointment, popped a pillow down into her lap, leaned confidentially forward over it and, raising a single finger as might a child about to reveal the most precious of secrets, said, "The happiest of all the couples at Prairie Port is Elsie and Martin Brewmeister, Doris and Lester Kebbon, Sue Ann and Rodney Willis and Tricia and Ralph Dafney. Cub and Sissy Hennessy used to be one of the happiest but what with all the babies they keep having and Sissy wanting Cub to become a SAC, they may not be as happy as they used to. It's not Cub's idea having all the babies, it's Sissy's, and how she manages to maintain her figure is a marvel. Billy Bee, you will not believe that woman's shape. She has the body of an eighteen-year-old. Bearing children seems to have no direct relationship with unhappiness. Sue Ann and Rodney Willis don't have any children and Tricia and Ralph Dafney have one girl, but they're every bit as happy as Doris and Lester Kebbon and Elsie and Martin Brewmeister, who have a small football team between them."

"Tina Beth, what's your sudden interest in kids?" Billy asked.

"Hush, I'm telling about lunch," she told him. "The younger couples, like the ones I just mentioned, tend to keep more to their own group except for Sissy. Sissy is everybody's den mom. Pauline Lyle, she's the biggest snob of all the wives and most everybody's least favorite. Flo de Camp, I guess that must be Happy de Camp's wife, is the best cook. Helen Perch is the cheapest. Sally Jessup is the sweetest . . . and worst at keeping a secret, poor thing. Sally Jessup's been going across the river to the University of Illinois and telling everybody it's to see a gynecologist because of female trouble. It's not female trouble at all. It's male trouble. Sally's been accompanying her husband, Jez Jessup, who has testalgia but doesn't want anybody to know.

"The most beautiful wife of all is Alice Sunstrom. She's much younger than her husband, Strom Sunstrom, and maybe that's causing problems. No one can be sure. The Sunstroms aren't very social. They stay up in a great big house on the hill they bought a while back. Tramont Hill, that's one of the fanciest sections of Prairie Port. It's out in the western hills. Mister Sunstrom comes from money. Old southern money. Mister Sunstrom really runs the office here, and everybody, men and women, trust and respect him the most of anybody 'cepting Mister Grafton. They like Miz Sunstrom too, but she's very hard to talk to even when you do get to see her. Sue Ann thinks Mister Sunstrom is going through mid-life male withdrawal. Sue Ann says it's conceivable Miz Sunstrom is having an extramarital romance because she's much calmer recently."

"This is what the wives talked about at lunch?" Yates was mildly benumbed.

"Billy Bee, this was hors d'oeuvres! Meat on the hoof comes later. 'Course I was with the younger wives, and they do admit to being somewhat more gossipy than the older wives. Like Sue Ann says, the older wives still believe in Christmas and the Monroe Doctrine. Sue Ann told me the biggest secret around here is that Mister Grafton never did get shot by the man Mister Jarrel hired. Sue Ann says Mister Grafton shot himself on purpose to make people think it was Mister Jarrel who ordered it."

"Are you speaking of Wilkie Jarrel?" he asked.

Tina Beth nodded. "Only one of the richest and most powerful people in Prairie Port, and the man Mister Grafton has sworn to arrest. Mister Grafton thinks Mister Jarrel is the corruptest man in Missouri and has been investigating him for years and years.

91

Mister Jarrel exerted Senate pressure to have Mister Grafton stopped. Shooting himself was one way Mister Grafton could fool Edgar into letting him go on investigating."

"Edgar?"

"Edgar Hoover."

"The wives call Director Hoover, Edgar?"

"Just like all their husbands have a name for Washington, D.C., they have one for him . . . Edgar plain. Sue Ann says Mister Grafton can play Edgar easy as an accordion."

"Sue Ann seems to be quite an expert."

"I should hope so. Sue Ann's been fucking Mister Grafton for six months almost."

"What kind of garbage-mouth talk is that! You're not some low-species sidewalk floozy!"

"Dear child, that's how every last wife round here talks, leastways the ones at lunch, 'cepting for maybe Sissy Hennessy. I told you, it's their favorite subject . . . along with Edgar. When they cease talking 'bout Edgar, they're talking 'bout who's doing that word to who. 'Course Edgar gets included in that word too."

"If Sue Ann's so happily married," Yates thought aloud, "what's she doing with Grafton?"

"Making sure she stays happily married!" With a hand on a hip and a finger wagging in Yates's face, Tina Beth gave every appearance of being angry. "Billy Bee, interrupt me one more time and I swear something violent and ungainly will occur. Jest moments ago you apologized for being inconsiderate and ungiving, now you're back at your old selfish ways. May I finish what I was relatin'?"

Billy nodded gloomily.

"Cross your heart?"

He crossed his heart.

"As I was telling, Edgar gets included with that word you're so offended by. Only not with women. Sue Ann says Edgar almost married Carmella Hebbelman of Chicago, only the female body displeased him. Tricia Dafney says he prefers young boys of the Mediterranean persuasion . . . ones with curly hair and big—"

"For God's sake, Tina Beth, you're talking about the Director of the FBI!"

"You said lots worse after him."

"I was referring to headquarters policy, not sexual proclivity."

"Edgar seems a mite more partial to proclivity than policy . . . on all counts." Tina Beth rolled onto her stomach and reached out beyond the opposite side of the bed for the record player, by reaching out hiked what there was of the shorty nightgown high onto her back, thus rendering thoroughly naked her magnificently formed upper legs and buttocks. " 'Cording to Tricia Dafney, the solitary one thing which genuinely does interest Edgar is who's doin' that naughty word to who."

Tina Beth snapped on the record player, then still lying fully extended turned her head, gazed intently back at her naked bottom, studied it for a bit, shifted her stare to her legs, smiled to herself, finally looked up into the flushed face of her husband. "We can't much fault a person for that, can we, Billy Bee?" She spoke in her little girl's voice. The opening strains of "Yesterday" softly drifted from the portable's speakers. "For being lustfully inclined like Tricia says Edgar is?"

Billy Yates, his stare frozen on a barely visible tiara of golden pubic hair, managed to shake his head.

Tina Beth tittered her childlike titter. "Billy Bee, you got an inclination in doin' that naughty word to me?"

Eyes transfixed, Yates nodded.

"An itsy-bitsy inclination or a great big powerful inclination?"

"Powerful."

"I don't believe you one bit." Tina Beth swiveled around on her stomach, propped her chin on an open hand only inches from her husband's lap. "Show me how powerful?"

Billy Yates tentatively felt for the drawstrings of his pajama pants.

"Standin' up," she chirped. "Show me standin' up."

He rose, stood at bed's edge facing her, uneasily searched for the drawstrings, found them, gave a weak tug, followed by a stronger tug. The pajama pants dropped away.

93

Tina Beth studied his erection with all the intensity of a child viewing a new sight. Then she let out a low and appreciative whistle.

The instrument went limp.

"I told you never to whistle at me," Yates nearly yelled, clutching up the pants as much to hide his shame as in anger. "Neither men nor women are animals to be whistled at!"

". . . Yer right, Billy Bee, and I apologize." Tina Beth flopped over on her back, wriggled toward the head of the bed, wriggled up into a sitting position with her knees drawn up to her chest and pressed tightly together. "I've been nothin' short of wanton." Her lips formed into a pout. "I don't know what overtakes me at times. Whatever it is, I'm goin' to fight it fierce."

Tina Beth slowly parted her raised knees. "I won't ever go showin' off this ol' tantalizer no more neither," she pledged, lowering both hands over her private parts. But not completely over. A slight space was left between the forefingers and thumbs of the two clutching hands. A space where the color pink was vividly discernible. A moist and luminescent pink. Pink ridged by occasional strands of blonde hair.

Despite her pout and downcast eyes, Billy Yates knew that Tina Beth knew exactly where he was looking, where he was incapable of not looking. He knew that she knew he knew this. That she wanted him to know. That this convoluted and infantile rut of "I'll-show-you-mine-but-don't-look" had invariably heightened his passion and hers. He knew that she knew these machinations weren't necessary. Not to arouse him at least. She knew all that she had to do, one way or the other, was display a little bottom . . . clothed or unclothed. Shashay in full regalia. Flash a flank. Whatever, he was lost.

Tina Beth glanced at Yates, feigned a gasp, again lowered her eyes, this time demurely. "Billy Bee?" she asked, managing to produce a 100 percent bona fide blush, "Is that there adorable creature trying to tell me something?"

Yates peered down upon his revitalized lust, attempted to cover it up.

"Billy Bee, why you trying to hide all that glory from me?"

He didn't know, couldn't answer, looked helplessly to the bed.

Tina Beth turned over, lay on her stomach staring back at him. Lay with a pillow under her. With her sublimely naked bottom propped high and thoroughly on display. "You sure what yer hiding ain't fer me?" she asked quietly.

"Be right back."

Once in the bathroom applying Pepsodent to his toothbrush and temporarily free of his wife's influence, Yates called out, "I never want to hear you whistling at anyone, home or out! Persons who come from prime background like yours don't go around whistling! And I don't want you swearing! Swearing's for floozies and tenant farmers!" After a rapid brush, rinse and gargle, he added, "And you oughta find a better crowd of women to have lunch with!" He stepped out of the pajama bottoms which had fallen to his feet, snapped off the bathroom light and headed into the dimly lit bedroom. Dimly and blue lit.

Somewhat to Billy Yates's surprise, Tina Beth had changed the bulb in the nightstand lamp during his brief absence. A blue light now burned. The record on the softly playing phonograph had been switched to the Beatles' "Let It Be."

"I don't want you repeating dumb gossip, either." He moved past a portable floor speaker. "I don't care who's sleeping with who, dumb gossip is not to be believed."

"Hush," Tina Beth ordered as he fell into her outstretched arms. "I like this town," she said, squeezing him tight. "I feel good here. Lucky." She squeezed harder. "Oh, Billy Bee, we're going to have the biggest and best life anybody ever had. We're going to have kids, if you want, and a proper house and all the things a proper young couple should have. Cats and dogs and goats even, and everything, I know it. We'll never be away from one another. You won't be preoccupied and distant. And you won't get into trouble, ever again, will you, Billy? Promise me you—"

Billy Yates silenced his wife with a kiss, trapped her wagging tongue under his own, sucked it back into his mouth pressing it tightly between his lips, bit her tongue. Bit gently. Slowly. Began biting more rapidly. Harder. Began squeezing her bottom.

95

The telephone rang and was ignored.

Billy bit her lips. Bit quickly. Began biting and kissing her chin and neck.

The telephone gave up, lapsed to silence.

Tina Beth seized his head in both hands, kneaded her fingers in the thick curly hair, pushed slowly and persistently . . . as she did, steered the biting, licking, kissing face down her neck and over a breast and onto her stomach, maneuvered his lips down to her ridge.

Billy bit along the edge of the hairline. Intensified his grip on her bottom. Raised his head. Simultaneously raised her as well. By the bottom. Held her several inches above the sheets. Pressed his thumbs into her skin. Gently twisted his hold, forced the dangling legs wide apart.

Gasping his name, she threw her arms flat and outstretched onto the bed. Gasping, she told him how much she loved him.

Someone knocked at the door. Continued knocking.

Billy Butler Yates paid no heed. He had Tina Beth where he wanted her. By the bottom.

She thrust her pelvis higher, grabbed his hair and tugged him toward her, shouting out his name and her love for him.

Someone else started shouting from beyond the door. "Yates, this is Jez. Sorry to bother you, but we gotta get a move on."

"Go 'way!" Billy yelled.

"I can't. God beckons."

". . . What!"

"God wants to see us! Or vice versa . . . on TV! We have to go rent a TV set."

# Five

Never, in response to an FBI invitation, had so many journalists and photographers and television news cameras crowded into the Justice Department's ground–floor Great Hall at Washington, D.C. Far more media people than the allocated one hundred and fifty seats could accommodate. Excited people. J. Edgar Hoover, in an unprecedented move, had called a mass press conference. Only once before, that anyone could remember, had Director Hoover faced reporters . . . in 1968, when he responded to Martin Luther King's allegation that the Bureau was being "laggardly" in its enforcement of Civil Rights legislation. Hoover, at the time, termed the black leader "the most notorious liar in the world." The King rebuttal had occurred in the Director's private fifth-floor offices, where a relatively small press corps had been brought together. Here, in the Great Hall, over two hundred members of the national and international media were jockeying for elbow room and noisily speculating on what the Director's forthcoming message might concern. Overwhelming consensus held he would be announcing his long-anticipated retirement as head of the FBI.

At 9 A.M. sharp, Tuesday, August 24, some forty-eight hours after the alarm had sounded at Mormon State National Bank, he entered. J. Edgar Hoover. Promptly. Looking tired and drawn and older than his seventy-six years. But striding strong and flanked by the associate director of the Bureau, Clyde Tolson, and followed by the assistant to the Director, A. R. Roland. Jowls a–jiggle and bulldog lips pursed, Director Hoover mounted the dais. Halted before a cluster of microphones. Squinted out beyond a bobbing thicket of camera lights and lenses. Blinked into the flood of upturned faces. Loosened his jaw and pointed a

97

friendly finger and offered a "Hi there, Pileggi, haven't seen you in a dog's age." Pointed farther back with a "Good to see you, Jane." Peered down at the cameramen and photographers directly in front of him and suggested, "What say you keep low, fellows, and give the cheap seats behind you a break." When people laughed at this, Director Hoover laughed too, which was something almost no one ever recalled him doing in public. When he threw a half salute and winked at his audience, which absolutely *nobody* ever recalled him doing before, many were prompted to clap. More clapped. And damn near everyone clapped.

J. Edgar Hoover let them clap on for many moments before raising both hands for silence, which he got. He pinched the tip of his nose. Wet his lips. Looked off at nothing. Grew pensive. Shot his cuffs. Squared his shoulders. Leaned into the microphones.

"Evil sleeps with one eye open," Edgar told them. "It distinguishes neither between adult or child or God or democracy. It cojoins with atheism and alienism and amorality and opportunism both here and abroad. Commingles, piratically, with the pious and political. This very morning, fishing trawlers belonging to Communist Russia were spotted near Little America examining the glaciers. Examining, or trying to melt them, I ask you? We know one thing, they won't be building churches out there. We know . . ."

Clyde Tolson, unseen by all except A. R. Roland, touched Edgar gently on the elbow.

Edgar resquared his shoulders and intoned that he had called this meeting to make an announcement of great importance to himself and the FBI and the nation, but before he did so, he wished to share a few thoughts.

"There are those in high and respected places who would have you believe that in a society such as ours there is no longer need for federal operations such as the FBI. That the FBI's fiscal funding should be drastically reduced, if not abolished. I tell you those funds must be increased. I tell you that experience persuasively shows us that effective law enforcement must stand as a para-

98

mount cornerstone of a just and progressive society. I tell you that the forces of evil are on the march. I tell you that our nation suffered grave and unparalleled threats to its freedom and internal security this last year. From without, forces antagonistic to a free government sought through espionage and other clandestine-type activities to weaken the United States and its contribution to the defense of the Free World. From within, shocking excesses of criminal activity, organized and otherwise, and violent attempts to subvert democratic processes and promote racial discord lacerated our society. Destructive acts of senseless rebellion by increasing numbers of our youth and widespread contempt for properly constituted authority greatly supported the causes of lawlessness and subversion throughout the country."

Edgar stopped and looked away.

A smattering of applause broke out.

"There are those who say that crime is on the decline and what crime there is is a matter for local, not federal, law enforcement. I tell you criminal activity is on the rise. Not the simple crime of our parents' and grandparents' day but sophisticated and ever-changing crime. The contemporary federal lawbreaker has the intellect and skill to prevail over nearly every modern technological and strategic deterrent . . . except one. The FBI. Today more than ever before we are the last and first defense against sophisticated law-breaking. This was demonstrated only hours ago, vividly."

Hoover folded his hands in front of him. "Over the last weekend the Mormon State National Bank in Prairie Port, Missouri, was burglarized by a gang of brilliant and dangerous criminals who effected a spectacular and successful getaway. The felons' identities and whereabouts remain unknown. Local law-enforcement and banking officials cursorily estimated the money stolen to amount to under ten thousand dollars. Thorough follow-up work by the men and women of the FBI has just revealed this figure to be far, far too low. The FBI has established that prior to the robbery, under the strictest of security and therefore unknown to local authorities, a shipment of used currency belong-

99

ing to the United States Treasury Department, and earmarked for destruction at a federal incinerator at St. Louis, was shunted to the Mormon State National Bank for overnight safekeeping the evening of the robbery. This money is also missing and assumed to have been stolen by the perpetrators of the Mormon State Bank theft. No serial numbers are recorded. The shipment was carried in an armored semi-trailer truck leased from the Gulf Coast Armored Security Corporation and, due to its unusual size, took over an hour to unload and store at the Mormon State National Bank. The minimum estimated value of this missing money is thirty-one million dollars . . . I vow to you the FBI will not rest until we bring the felons to justice and recover the thirty-one million dollars . . ."

Watching the press conference over a rented television set in their downtown office, the thunderstruck FBI resident agents of Prairie Port could not believe what they were hearing. No one had informed them of the Federal Reserve currency shipment or that the Bureau would be entering the investigation . . . just as no one had yet informed them that Ed Grafton was en route from Montana to Washington, D.C., and would soon be relieved as head of their resident office. What most every Prairie Port Bureauman did realize, painfully, was the importance of the reestimated bank-theft loss. Thirty-one million dollars was more money than had ever been stolen anywhere in the world.

# Six

Pert and comely Nancy Applebridge, a recently hired stringer reporter for United Press, was the first person to reach the eleventh-floor FBI offices in downtown Prairie Port following J. Edgar Hoover's nationally televised press conference. The one previous Bureau office Applebridge had visited, in her native Chicago, was motion-picture spick-and-span. Rushing into the FBI anteroom in Prairie Port, she found a threadbare rug, two unmatched wooden chairs, a small wood coffee table with a split and reglued surface, and, resting on the table, an uncleaned souvenir ashtray from the St. Louis World's Fair. The walls were in critical need of new paint. Bending over and peering up through the tiny receptionist window, when the buzzer didn't work and knocks on the locked interior door brought no response, she saw that the plaster was chipped and cracked along the ceilings beyond . . . and°that seven FBI men, in shirt-sleeves, were dashing about the inner offices picking up and slamming down ringing telephones. What Nancy Applebridge was witnessing, and would later write about, was the end result of a long-standing policy of punitive penury sanctioned against Ed Grafton by his detractors at FBI headquarters.

No sooner had J. Edgar Hoover announced to the country that $31,000,000 had been stolen from the Mormon State National Bank than the telephones erupted in the Bureau's Prairie Port offices. Unfortunately, a malfunctioning switchboard for the dozen and a half phones strung across the eight-room suite had not been repaired because, over the last three weeks, Washington headquarters had failed to appropriate often–requested funds for such fixing. An incoming call could ring on any or all of the eighteen instruments . . . or not one. "Hold" and "Intercom" buttons did not necessarily hold calls or intercommunicate. Nor had Prairie Port been allocated monies to mend its teletype machine to headquarters. The teletype, like the office's window air-conditioning units, had been on the fritz for two months. A short-wave radio transmitter was operative, but recurring and inexplicable power failures throughout the metropolitan area rendered it ineffective in reaching all but the nearest radio cars. Not that there was much time for radioing.

Whatever the dismay Strom Sunstrom, Cub Hennessy, Jez Jessup, Butch Cody, Happy de Camp, Ted Keon and Yates may have registered at learning they had underestimated the largest cash theft in history by approximately thirty million, nine hundred and ninety-three thousand, five hundred dollars was instantly eradicated by a deluge of telephone calls. Phone calls from Prairie Port FBI agents away from the office trying to find out what was coming down. Calls from local media people and national media people and city officials and county officials and state officials and federal officials and law-enforcement agencies across the Midwest, except for the Prairie Port Police Department, which eschewed the Bureau in general and the local office in particular. From professional tipsters and cranks and well-meaning citizens who thought they possessed relevant information regarding the crime. From seers and mystics who had no doubt they possessed relevant information. From amateur sleuths and waiting posses such as the Agatha Christie Garden and Deduction Society of Armbruster, Illinois, and the Covington Vigilant Riding Association of Covington, Kansas. From family and friends. From the masses of unknown curious. Twenty-eight hundred calls in all, before the day would be out, at an office which had never recorded more than one hundred and ten calls in any twenty-four–hour period.

Assistant senior resident agent John Sunstrom and his six shirt-sleeved subordinate agents, with their switchboard gone haywire, rushed from room to room and ringing phone to ringing phone trying to keep up with the incoming traffic blitz . . . not noticing in their scramble that a prophetic pattern of mud and the river and exploitation had begun to emerge. The fifth call

102

into the office, logged by Cub Hennessy, was from an over-wrought local druggist who requested the FBI come quickly because two mud geysers had just erupted through the sidewalk and street in front of his shop and he had no doubt the robbers were trapped below and up to no good. Ted Keon took and recorded the eleventh call, a tip from a Wayne County farmer with a "talking" mule, a beast which reputedly could tap out messages with its front left hoof and had just let it be known, tappingly, that the missing robbers were hiding on a Mississippi River delta island sixty-one and three-quarter miles downstream from Prairie Port. Butch Cody was recipient of the first "breather" call, number twenty-three, from a whispering voice which identified itself as "TA" and offered, for one million dollars in unmarked paper currency, to name every one of the actual robbers. TA allowed twenty-four hours for his offer to be considered and then hung up. Callers six, nine and fifteen each complained of home electrical power failures and were referred to the Missouri Power and Electric Company by exasperated agents who coded the messages "irrelevant" to Bureau business until Jez Jessup received the second mud alert, call number twenty-eight from the assistant deputy commissioner of the Prairie Port Fire Department, warning that the massive underground flooding not only had caused severe electrical short-circuiting and power failures but had activated a long-dormant mud river under the western section of the city . . . that three square miles of land in the western section was besieged by mud eruptions and the area was being cordoned off and evacuation procedures were under way . . . that at least two city councilmen thought the flooding and mud eruptions might be the result of international sabotage and terrorism and that these two council members would like the FBI to drop everything and immediately look into the matter. Cub Hennessy handled call number thirty, a reputed Mississippi River tour-boat captain who wanted to know if any of the missing millions had spilled into the river . . . and where. Strom took the thirty-third call, spoke to a St. Louis manufacturer of novelties who inquired as to a franchise for official robbery T-shirts. Butch Cody picked up on caller thirty-six, a hydrologist named St. Ives

103

from the Missouri Valley Geological Survey who said the assistant deputy commissioner of the Prairie Port Fire Department had gotten his facts about the mud jumbled, then went on to explain that the geysering of mud in the three-square-mile area in the western section of the city was certainly caused by a subterranean mud river, but that the real danger was that this river was trapped and building up pressure at an enormous rate . . . that if this pressure wasn't substantially eased, by yet undetermined means, a mud volcano could rapidly form and erupt with enormous force as had been the case in that area in 1926 . . . that in 1926 thirty-one people had died in the earthquake effect accompanying the volcano explosions. It was call number forty-one, however, taken by Ted Keon, which was to prove pivotal to the career of John Sunstrom . . . and to the fate of his resident agents.

Following his conversation with the St. Louis T-shirt maker, John Sunstrom went out into the tiny anteroom and confronted a crunch of thirty-odd reporters, press photographers and TV cameramen. The soft-spoken and forthright Sunstrom stated that he had no official comment other than "no comment" and that, in fact, he hadn't yet been able to get through to Washington headquarters. It was at this juncture Ted Keon emerged from the inner offices and, leaving the door behind him open, forced his way forward through the crowd. Keon whispered something into Sunstrom's ear. Sunstrom politely excused himself from the gathering, kept apace as the fast–stepping Keon led the way back into the inner offices and onto a receiver lying off the hook and picked up and handed him the receiver.

". . . Agent Sunstrom," Sunstrom said into the phone.

"Sir," an eminently familiar voice began, "this is J. Edgar Hoover speaking to you from Washington, District of Columbia. Why have you kept me waiting?"

"I'm sorry, Mister Director—"

"Look at your watch, sir. What time do you show?"

Studying his wristwatch, Sunstrom said, "Nine-fifty-one A.M., Mister Director."

"Sir, are you aware we began to teletype orders through to you twenty-six minutes ago and received no response?"

"Our teletype machine is broken, Mister Director."

"Then fix it."

"Yes, Mister Director."

"Are you, sir, further aware that I have been personally attempting to reach you by telephone for exactly seventeen minutes now and that your lines have been busy?"

"Mister Director, I was aware our telephones were busy but not that you were trying to reach us."

"Repeat after me: Romor 91-22535!"

"Romor 91-22535?"

"Effective this moment," Edgar Hoover proclaimed, "the code name for the investigation of the Mormon State National Bank theft is Romor . . . Robbery-Mormon State. The case number is 91-22535. You know what 91 stands for, do you, sir?"

"Yes, Mister Director."

"What?"

"It's the prefix designation for bank robbery."

"*Federal* bank robbery, sir."

". . . Federal bank robbery, Mister Director."

"91-22535 . . . the twenty-two thousandth, five hundredth and thirty-fifth case to be investigated by the FBI since the enactment of the Federal Bank Act of 1934. And it is your case, sir. Yours and the men of your command. Romor 91-22535! It has a good ring to it. Make us proud of it, sir. Please stand." After a moment Edgar asked, "Are you standing?"

Sunstrom, who had never sat down in taking the call, told him, "I am standing, Mister Director."

"All that I am about to say is binding and irrefutable," J. Edgar Hoover told him. "Effective this moment, Edward A. Grafton is relieved as senior resident agent for the Prairie Port office of the Federal Bureau of Investigation. You, Mister John L. C. Sunstrom III, effective this moment, will replace Mister Grafton in his role as senior resident agent and assume all responsibilities inherent in that position. This promotion is temporary. Nonetheless, your expense remunerations will be adjusted upward upon receipt of proper vouchers. Your previous position as assistant senior resident agent will forthwith be filled, also on a temporary basis, by

105

Mister Harold H. Hennessy. You will please inform Mister Hennessy of his good fortune and instruct as to his new duties. You are free to assign to Romor 91-22535 whomever you wish as supervisor and case agent. You and your men will, as of this moment, desist in referring to the investigation of the theft at Mormon State as anything but Romor 91-22535. Effective this moment, you and you alone, Mister Sunstrom, are in charge of Romor 91-22535. How does that strike you?"

". . . It strikes me very positively, Mister Director."

"Assistance is en route for deployment at your discretion. Thirty agents and support personnel. Prepare for them and disregard expense. Denis Corticun will arrive to assist you in any manner you so deem. He will tend to the additional personnel for you. I have suggested to Denis Corticun that he create a flying squad to answer directly and only to you. How does a flying squad strike you?"

"Very positively, Mister Director." Strom had no idea what was meant by a flying squad.

"That broken teletype machine of yours, how old is it?"

"I'll find out, Mister Director."

"Bother not, bother not. You shall have new machines. New whatever you need. You will turn the full skills and attention of your personnel to recouping the stolen monies and bringing to justice the insidious perpetrators of this momentous incursion. God be with you. God be with your men—what's all that clatter in the background?"

"The telephones, Mister Director. They haven't stopped ringing since your speech."

"It was quite a speech, wasn't it?"

"Indeed, Mister Director."

". . . I don't know you, sir, but I like you."

J. Edgar Hoover hung up.

. . . John Sunstrom, in the fall of 1960, was accepted by the FBI and sent to the Bureau's training academy on the grounds of the United States Marine Corps base at Quantico, Virginia. The recently widowed southern aristocrat had just turned thirty-five.

Although the maximum age for acceptance into the FBI was forty-one, Sunstrom was considerably older than his academy classmates and was called Pappy by them. The moniker was short-lived. John's skill in investigatory and administrative matters, as well as his relaxed and gentlemanly and winning manner with co-workers and the public, first at the Minneapolis, Minnesota, field office and later at New Orleans, earned him the affectionate nickname of Strom. It also won him a transfer to Washington headquarters, where he began training for a supervisory position. Except for being slightly too old, Strom Sunstrom was all the FBI could hope for in a prospective special agent in charge at some field office. The FBI, in turn, had proved to be all Strom had hoped for and more . . . an endless string of challenges he could rise to . . . an enveloping, all-inclusive way of life . . . an escape from his long-grieved-over ghosts, memories of his first wife. He was happier than he had been in a long time.

On December 17, 1965, Strom Sunstrom married his dead wife's younger sister. She was twenty-three years old to the day, a graduate student of design, ravishingly beautiful and a virgin. He was forty, prematurely silver gray, in his second year of duty at FBI headquarters and anticipatory about sleeping with his bride. Their wedding night he was overwhelmed. She was, in bed, an extraordinary lover. He had never been so gratified, so free.

The marriage proved an instant asset. This sleek, dark-haired beauty and her tall, elegant, Lincolnesque husband made a charming and striking couple in a place where charm and appearance counted mightily. On July 1, 1967, a year earlier than most agents of equal experience would have been given such an assignment, Strom Sunstrom was made assistant special agent in charge of the Denver, Colorado, field office of the FBI. He and his wife, in their low-keyed, mellow manner, won the hearts of all whom they encountered. He became the official area spokesman for the Bureau. She was asked to speak on the women's club circuit. They entertained often and well. They were, briefly, a golden couple. FBI golden.

But John, secretly, longed for action . . . the challenge of field investigation. His wife sensed something was wrong, coaxed him

107

into admitting he may have made a mistake becoming an administrator. Given his druthers, he confessed to her, he would revert to being a brick agent who could get out into the field and work cases instead of sitting in an office pushing pencils and practicing speeches. She urged him to resign as assistant special agent in charge. He cautioned it wasn't all that simple. Told her such a resignation could be taken as a betrayal by Bureau superiors who had championed his promotion. He warned he might be banished to some hellhole like Detroit or Butte, Montana. She chided him for believing such goosey–gander rumors as FBI retaliation, insisted the Bureau and Director Hoover were too noble for such pettiness . . . said if he would be happier in Detroit or Butte, she would be. So he requested of headquarters they reduce him in grade back to brick agent.

Punishment was swift.

Had Strom been alone, the retribution might not have been so vexing, but his wife insisted on accompanying him on each leg of the journey. Aside from Detroit and Butte, three other FBI offices, according to general agent consensus, qualified as bona fide "Siberias," places of exile and often oafish and unpredictable SACs. He was first sent to Maine, arrived during a midwinter blizzard to find no one was expecting him. When written orders did catch up, his demotion wasn't mentioned and he stayed on as assistant SAC during the balance of the winter, living with his wife in a rented suite of rooms. Costly rooms due to the number of expensive ski resorts in the area. The couple leased a house and, with the first break of spring, sent for their furniture. No sooner had the furniture arrived and the house been redecorated than Strom was sent to the FBI office at Brownsville, Texas. The transfer order reduced him in rank back down to a brick agent. The Sunstroms again trucked their furniture to storage, this time at their own expense, and abandoned the Maine house with nine months left on the lease.

Brownsville, Texas, was as hot and humid as Maine had been cold and snowswept, but at least the local FBI office was awaiting John's arrival. So were the old nickname "Pappy" and whispers he had been shunted off into exile because he was too old to cut the mustard as ASAC in Colorado. Whispers also had it that Strom and his wife were blood relations. Other whispers emphasized the age difference between them. The most audible promoter of the rumor campaign was the SAC, a loutish alcoholic who, drunk or sober, was also contemptuous of nearly everything non-Northern and nonwhite. Strom, the composed southerner, took the slurs in stride. Not so the whispers that his wife had suffered a series of nervous breakdowns. Hearing the SAC loudly repeat this to a fellow special agent, Sunstrom lost control of himself for one of the few times in his life. Grabbed the SAC by the neck and in a display of rage and strength that would surprise even him on reflection, with one hand lifted the man from his feet by the neck and held him dangling on high. Hurled him into the wall. Had he not been restrained by the special agent, a fellow named Jez Jessup, Strom might have gone after the crumpled rumor–monger and struck him and gotten into irreparable trouble. As it was, Jessup kept Strom back and warned the SAC that if he reported the incident to Washington, let alone pressed charges against Sunstrom, Jez would tell Washington he had seen the SAC hit Strom, deny Strom had retaliated. The SAC elected to overlook the matter.

Strom didn't find it so easy to forget . . . might have quit the Bureau then and there if it weren't for his wife. Knowing how much investigatory work meant to him, she begged him to put the incident behind him, ignore everything. She argued that his exile was nothing more than official hazing at the most, bureaucratic bungling at the least. She went out and rented a house and redecorated it. Shortly after, as in Maine, Strom was ordered to yet another FBI office. This one reputedly the newest and worst Siberia on the banishment circuit. Worst not because of the physical environment, which was supposedly quite pleasant, but because of the quirky and eccentric special agent in charge . . . a man named Ed Grafton, who held sway in a place called Prairie Port, Missouri.

. . . They faced one another over black coffee and whiskey at four-thirty in the morning at a Prairie Port railyard diner frequented by trainmen and bloody-smocked packing house workers and weary vagrants allowed in from the chill, this tall quiet southern gentleman known as Strom and the unkempt, fierce-eyed renegade Grafton, who had defied nearly everyone he could find to defy at FBI headquarters. Each man, from the beginning, recognized something in the other that engendered esteem and trust. Grafton did most of the talking, sat staring down at his coffee cup and in hushed and hoarse words explained how this eatery was his favorite spot for business meets and the time his favorite time. How offices were anathema to him, including his own Bureau offices in Prairie Port, which he seldom visited unless forced. How the running of these offices was left to whatever woebegotten subordinates he could saddle with the assignment. Grafton granted he should not be calling other resident agents "subordinates," since technically they were independent residency operatives with great autonomy, only here at Prairie Port every one of them damn well did what he wanted them to do, when he wanted it and how he wanted. Grafton added that the agents liked, rather than resented, him for this. Grafton said that this was his "gift": making subordinates like him. Grafton said he had gone through Strom Sunstrom's file and had heard scuttlebutt on Strom's exiles to Maine and Texas. He said that Strom's banishment to Prairie Port might turn out to be more propitious than punitive if he and Strom were of the same mind. Grafton said there was a good chance he could take Strom's latest exile and jam it right down the throats of the Bureau Brass Balls at headquarters who ordered it . . . force the Brass Balls to choke on the order . . . make them rue the day they had issued it, and soon. He said to do this would require not only Strom's cooperation but a considerable emotional sacrifice on Strom's part. Then, as if to play for suspense by delaying his proposition, Grafton downed a large tumbler filled with whiskey and washed out his mouth with coffee and poured more whiskey into the glass and a goodly portion into the coffee cup. Stirring the rye into the coffee with a fork, Grafton said that perhaps Strom was the very man he had so urgently been in need of . . . the man he had been so patiently waiting for.

Grafton told Strom that of all the battles he had fought with

Bureau Brass Balls in Washington, the bloodiest was under way. That he had begun to investigate a local Missouri man named Wilkie Jarrel and that the cries of anguish and outrage rising in the hallowed hallways of FBI headquarters were not unsimilar to those of a pack of pained hyenas giving communal breechbirths at midnight. That Wilkie Jarrel was wealthy and powerful and politically well-connected on Capitol Hill in D.C. That many of these Capitol Hill connections, fearing Grafton would expose the corrupt control Jarrel wielded over them, which was precisely Grafton's intention, were exerting enormous pressure on FBI headquarters to drop the investigation. That the Brass Balls were responding to the pressure and doing everything possible to deter Grafton from continuing with the Jarrel matter, short of ordering him to stop. The reason the Brass Balls didn't issue such an order, Grafton explained to Strom, was because they knew Grafton would not obey it even if it came from J. Edgar Hoover himself and that the Brass Balls didn't dare go to Hoover with the problem out of fear that Hoover might side with Grafton, even though Hoover knew Jarrel and rather liked the louse.

Grafton sat back and rested his hands in his lap. "J. Edgar Hoover is the greatest man who ever lived," he told Strom in sermon-certain tones. "The FBI is the greatest crime-fighting organization ever conceived. But time has betrayed both of them. Edgar seems to have lost control of himself and the FBI. He should have quit when he was invincible. Before he was gotten to. The Brass Ball Monkeys have gotten to Edgar. The Brass Ball Monkeys have taken over at Washington headquarters. They are petty and venal and incompetent men. Not all of them. But most. Edgar is falling slave to them. A prisoner locked in the tower of his own past . . . his own bygone glory. Edgar has never countermanded an investigation I've chosen to begin. I doubt if he would do so with the Wilkie Jarrel matter. But if Edgar did, I would still go after Jarrel and hang him from the highest tree. That is what the Brass Ball Monkeys have come to realize. They see *me* as someone out of control. They figure if they can stop me with the Wilkie Jarrel case, they can stop me for good. Topple me from command in Prairie Port, maybe from the FBI itself, without ever having to go to Edgar. They are second-rate, these Brass Balls, but they have a chance to win out this time. Not because of themselves. Because of Wilkie Jarrel. I underestimated Jarrel."

Grafton returned to stirring the coffee and rye. "I am not a bending man, Mister Sunstrom. I've rarely acknowledged needing help or assistance. Now I do. I need your assistance if I am to win out over Wilkie Jarrel. I know these headquarters monkeys, Mister Sunstrom. Their grand strategy is to bring the Jarrel matter . . . and myself . . . to a close, to include assaults on the administration end of our operations here in Prairie Port. Cutting back on expenditures, such as those for maintenance and repair. Delaying remittance of what has already been paid out by myself and the other agents. Along with this, they will up their demands for paper work and protocol, require three times the number of reports and requisition forms and gripe to high heaven if a word is misspelled or a comma missing. Minor things, I grant you. Pesky things. But on the aggregate, debilitating. This I need from you, Mister Sunstrom . . . to fight the battle of the filing cabinet so I and my men are free to fight the battle of Wilkie Jarrel."

Grafton slowed the stirring. "You're displeased with my proposal, aren't you?"

"I was hoping for an investigatory rather than administrative assignment," Strom had admitted.

"What's your passion?"

"Passion?"

"Each of us has an overriding passion," Grafton had expounded. "Mine is the misuse of privilege. Not privilege in and of itself. Not power and wealth because they are power and wealth, but the misapplication of that power and wealth, the distortion of it at any level. I suppose you could just as easily replace the word privilege with the word advantage. The police officer who extorts from a shopkeeper, the jail matron who abuses an inmate, these rankle me. A scoutmaster embezzling funds from his troop's treasury, and we had a case like that, is as offensive to me as Wilkie Jarrel. The Brass Balls' defense of Jarrel is loathsome. All of them are misusing their privilege, and advan-

112

tage. That's my passion, such misuses. It allows me to crusade. Without a crusade, an old fart like myself is best committed to dust. And you, Mister Sunstrom, what is your passion? What makes you pick up lance and sword and ride the great white horse into battle?"

"All crime . . ."

"Nothing more specific than that?"

"No . . ."

"And each and every one of these crimes thrill you beyond redemption?"

"I'm not exactly the thrill-seeking type."

"That's a pity. I heard of you early on, Mister Sunstrom . . . when the Brass Balls tried to turn you into one of their own and you refused them. Odd as it may seem, I have a friend or two left in Washington. They told me about you in passing, and I said to myself, There's a brash fellow who deserves watching. I have watched you from a distance. Learned about you. Southern gentry, Confederate cavalrymen and preachers, isn't that your stock?"

"Volunteer, not professional, cavalrymen . . . and one Anglican minister, my paternal grandfather."

"Could be your bent is with the cloth?" Grafton had spoken evenly. "Do you wish to be a competent investigator, or the best investigator?"

"The best."

"I doubt that you will make it. To be the best, in my mind, requires two God-given talents: instinct and passion. The instincts of a criminal and the passion, if you like, of the charging cavalryman. You seem to possess neither. You will be a *competent* investigator, Mister Sunstrom. In this day and age, with the Bureau, competence suffices. Do I depress you?"

"It's hardly the most optimistic assessment of my capabilities I've heard," Strom replied.

"But you will pursue the investigatorial end nonetheless, won't you?"

"Yes."

". . . Let me propose an arrangement, Mister Sunstrom. A

113

covenant whereby you do what I ask and in return I will make you into a better than competent investigator. Not a great one, but a damn sight abler than competent. And who knows, perhaps I can goad you even further than that. Perhaps I can ignite a spark, get some passion flowing. Have you lusting for the thrill of the charge. For riding the great white horse into battle."

Strom Sunstrom took over the administrative operations of the FBI's Prairie Port office January 20, 1969. Within weeks the paper-work end of things was running with computerlike efficiency. Ingenious rebudgeting and tight fiscal management deftly handled the predicted financial squeeze begun in March by antagonistic personnel at headquarters. It was in the selection and processing of transfer agents that Strom's talents exceeded Grafton's maximal expectations, and his own. His gentlemanly manner caught the Brass Balls off guard, allowed Strom to turn away transferee after transferee until he found what he wanted, without any undue ruffling of feathers or fur . . . without really being noticed all that much at headquarters. As hotheaded and recalcitrant as many of these newly selected deportees were on arrival, Sunstrom could somehow win them over. Prepare them. Indoctrinate them with the legend of Grafton. The very first transferee Strom had arranged to be sent to Prairie Port was the special agent who had acted on his behalf during the fracas with the SAC of the Texas office, Jez Jessup. Jez resisted the adoration of Grafton, directed his loyalty and respect to Strom.

Over the years that followed, Grafton more than fulfilled his pledge to Strom. Brought Strom in on virtually every ongoing case. Worked with him shoulder to shoulder. Taught him by example, as was his method with most of the men. Imbued him with a sense of pride and a new respect for the role of leadership. Strom began to hear the far-off clap of hoofbeats . . . saw the great white horse rear up riderless on a nearby hill . . . wanted very much to join the charge.

. . . Now, standing with the receiver to his ear amid six scurrying agents trying to keep up with the seventeen telephones in other parts of the office, Strom Sunstrom listened to J. Edgar Hoover hand him the reins to the Mormon State robbery and

114

temporary control of the Prairie Port residency and then hang up. Strom cautiously returned the receiver to its cradle. Stood motionless with at his hand still on the phone. A trembling hand. Such trembling was unusual, but he didn't have time to dwell on this.

"Graf got the boot," Strom told Ted Keon, who had fetched him back from the anteroom of reporters minutes before . . . who knew it was J. Edgar Hoover on the phone. His fingers left the receiver and clenched into a fist. *"Grafton got sacked . . ."*

Cub Hennessy glanced over. So did Jez Jessup and Butch Cody and Happy de Camp and Billy Yates. Telephones continued to ring.

Strom had never been known to shout or swear or bark out commands before, but now he did all three. "KILL THOSE FUCKING PHONES! PUT THEM IN A DESK DRAWER OR RIP THEIR CORDS OUT OR DO WHATEVER YOU HAVE TO DO TO KILL THEM! DON'T STAND THERE GAWKING, DO AS I SAY! CAN'T YOU UNDERSTAND, GRAF GOT THE SHABBY BOOT . . ."

Strom Sunstrom, who in memory had not displayed anger in front of his fellow resident agents, stormed off quivering with rage. "THE SHABBY BOOT HE GETS, AND THEY EXPECT ME TO REPLACE HIM. I'LL NOT HAVE IT! NOT FOR A MOMENT!"

The door to his office slammed resoundingly.

Siren wailing, wheels spinning and skidding, a River Patrol ambulance plowed through the deep sand leading from the access road down to the riverfront swimming area at Prairie Port's South Beach. A burly lifeguard was applying artificial respiration to the corpse of Teddy Anglaterra. Ambulance paramedics took over, gave oxygen to the motionless body. Eight minutes later, at 10:21 A.M., a first-year intern at Missouri Presbyterian Hospital's emergency room cut away Teddy's shirt and discovered that the dead man's upper torso bore fourteen deep stab wounds. The administrating doctor was summoned. After examining the wounds, as well as the ugly bruises on Teddy's head and chest,

115

the doctor berated the intern for admitting an obvious homicide victim to the overcrowded emergency room of a private hospital. The doctor ordered that the corpse be put back in the ambulance and sent directly to the city morgue. The intern wondered aloud if the police and next of kin shouldn't be contacted. The doctor railed that this was exactly what he was trying to avoid . . . that there were far more important duties for the hospital's hard-pressed staff than getting embroiled in the paper work of processing a murder victim. *Forget the body was ever here,* the doctor raged as he left the room. The intern called the garage and ordered an ambulance to the emergency room. He searched Teddy's pockets. No identification was found in the water-soaked wallet. The ambulance driver appeared and was told to deliver the unidentified corpse to the city morgue as a John Doe and to merely state it was found at South Beach. Later, conscience-stricken by his actions, the young intern called Channel 10, the city's leading television station, and told a desk assistant in the news department that a corpse had been found at South Beach. A murder victim. The desk assistant, inundated by phone calls resulting from J. Edgar Hoover's televised address, couldn't have cared less about the tip, made no notation of having received it. Even if there had been interest, little could have been done. Every news person at the station, and anywhere else in the city, was assigned to the story of the decade . . . the Mormon State bank robbery.

Rubber-booted scientists from the Missouri Valley Geological Survey dropped through the hole in the bank vault . . . descended a rope ladder into the mud-crusted cavern . . . planted tall metal measuring rods firmly into the huge chamber's wet floor, secured other hydrological measuring instruments in the opening in the north side of the cavern as well as in the tunnel mouth on the south wall before returning up the rope ladder. Five minutes later, at approximately 10:41 A.M., water gushed forth from both openings . . . and in the incredibly short period of nine seconds reached a level of nine feet.

And stopped.

116

# Seven

116s led the master case assignment list. Classification 116, the FBI's numerical prefix for Energy and Research Development Applicants . . . background checks on persons seeking employment at the newly built Atomic Energy Commission research laboratories west of the city. 116s accounted for sixty-three of the five hundred and seventy-one cases being investigated by the eighteen agents of the Prairie Port residency at the time J. Edgar Hoover ordered Sunstrom to become temporary senior resident agent in charge as well as to assume personal responsibility for the Mormon State robbery manhunt, a case titled and prefixed: Romor 91.

Gracing the cellar of the numerical count were such esoteric single inquiries as Classification 74, Applications for Executive Clemency; 142, Illegal Use of a Railway Pass; 103, Interstate Transport of Stolen Cattle; 66, Bureau Automobile Accidents. Due to an oceangoing yacht running aground a delta island on the Prairie Port side of the Mississippi River and the suspicious disappearance of the ship's captain, the office was investigating a rare Classification 45 . . . Crime on the High Seas.

The remaining five hundred and three cases, between the top and bottom of the list, covered another forty-odd classifications equally distributed, more or less, among the major subsections of Civil Rights, Accounting and Fraud, Fugitives, and Employee Security/Special Inquiries other than for the A.E.C. Woefully lacking, in the minds of most Prairie Port agents, were cases involving "pure" or "hard" criminal violations such as bank robbery.

The sixty-three Classification 116 Energy and Research Development Applicant investigations, like Romor 91, had originated in Prairie Port and were, therefore, Office of Origin, or OO, cases whose prime jurisdiction lay with the originating office. Fifty percent of the other inquiries being worked on by Grafton, Strom and their men had originated elsewhere, leaving Prairie Port merely the IO, or Investigating Office, with no control over the case other than to provide requested information and send it on to the OO. Agents of the Prairie Port residency, already invested with more autonomy than most field office operatives, favored OO cases, preferred the control of origin, the insulation from outside meddling.

Personal preferences regarding specific classifications contributed to what Assistant to the Director of the FBI A. R. Roland cited as the "contentious group temperament" of the Prairie Port resident agency. Ed Grafton's abhorrence of Classification 26, Interstate Transportation of Stolen Motor Vehicles or Aircraft, resulted in those investigations receiving the lowest priority possible. Grafton so despised I.T.S.V.s for being "unpure" and "soft" and "demeaning to the integrity of honorable field operatives" that he twice said so on local television interview shows . . . further denounced I.T.S.V. on one of the two shows as "paltry statistical nonsense created by important headquarters brass monkeys who wouldn't know a field investigation from a dry martini without olives."

Classification 100, Internal Security, involved the investigation of seditious and hate organizations. Ironically it was Connecticut's Ralph Dafney who felt it questionable that except for some follow-up IO inquiries related to the May 5, 1970, burning of the Air Force Reserve Officers Training Corps building at Washington University in St. Louis, the full effort of the Prairie Port agency's Classification 100 cases were directed at the local KKK. Strom explained that the matter had more to do with Ed Grafton's vendetta against Wilkie Jarrel than the Klan per se . . . that Grafton wanted to link Jarrel to anything deemed derogatory such as the Klan. And Grafton did eventually establish this linkage. Bigotry, in the circa 1971 FBI of J. Edgar Hoover, was not a stranger. At least not the bigotry of omission. No women and

118

precious few blacks, Hispanics and Jews could be found among the Bureau's 8,548 nationwide agent population.

It was Classification 25, Violation of the Selective Service Act, which rendered the Prairie Port office a divisive cut. Ten of the eighteen agents assigned to the residency had served in the armed forces prior to entering the FBI. The eldest of these men, Madden "Happy" de Camp, had taken part in World War II. The youngest, Rodney Willis, had fought in Vietnam. The remaining eight were veterans of the Korean conflict. All had been officers. All were not of one mind as to the Vietnam War itself, the peace movement, draft dodgers, conscientious objectors and deserters. Nor was there unanimity on these issues among the eight resident agents who had not been in the military. Differences of opinion, in the past, seldom had affected the men's discharge of official duties.

With Vietnam, though, work had been affected. As attitudes polarized, antagonisms grew. Conflicting viewpoints erupted in divisive verbal exchanges. Twice, heated discussions of the war provoked a near fistfight.

Grafton, not unpredictably when matters of this nature boiled over, had walked away . . . left the tempest to the one person who could calm the waters, Strom Sunstrom. Strom, friend of all . . . diplomat and father-confessor and house hand-holder who read the men of the office and their wives much as a concert pianist read music . . . and who at times played them with comparable skill. Strom Sunstrom, the master of everybody's life but his own . . .

Following J. Edgar Hoover's call to the Prairie Port resident office, a reversal of roles occurred. It was Cub Hennessy and Jez Jessup who attempted to do the calming. It was eternally even-tempered Strom Sunstrom who had exploded and marched, cursing ringing phones and the expulsion of Grafton, across the floor and slammed the door and locked himself in the combination office-conference room he had shared with Grafton.

Jez and Cub allowed thirty minutes to elapse before going to the door and lightly rapping and reminding Sunstrom that much had to be done. No answer came. They persisted. The lock un-locked. The door remained shut. A voice on the other side said to come in.

Strom sat at the head of the conference table with his hands folded together on top of a yellow pad. In front of the pad lay his pipe and tobacco pouch. Resting on a cart to his immediate right was the Magnavox tape recorder. "Didn't mean to be self-indul-gent out there, lads." He sounded like the old familiar low-keyed Strom Sunstrom. "Haggish and rude as well. Forgive me. Hag-gishness will bring us short shrift now. You're correct. There's much to do. Fetch the others, would you?"

"What about the phones?" Cub asked.

"Take them off the hook, as I said."

Hennessy, Jessup, Cody, de Camp, Keon and Yates seated themselves around the table. Strom explained how J. Edgar Hoover had ordered him to replace Grafton on a temporary basis as SRA and that Cub Hennessy was to move up and become assistant senior resident agent, and more immediate than this was Romor 91, the investigation of the Mormon State National Bank robbery . . . Romor 91 was now officially their case . . . Prairie Port was the Office of Origin . . . so additional agents would be transferred in for back-up assignment and haughty Denis Corticun would show up and probably try to hog the show but this wouldn't be easily accomplished because of what J. Edgar Hoover had proclaimed to Strom. Beyond Prairie Port being the OO for Romor 91, J. Edgar had designated Strom Sunstrom his own personal proctor in the investigation. His chieftain. His sur-rogate.

"Let's have at Mormon State, shall we?" Strom paused to watch Rodney Willis and Donnie Bracken hurry into the room and seat themselves at the table. "There's something I'd best get out of the way first, if you'll bear with me."

Strom rose, began to pace slowly around the table, thrust his hands into his trouser pockets. "I'm not all that adept at speech-making any more. I'm uneasy talking to you right now. I know if all the men were here, I could not say what I wanted to. Could not get it out.

120

"What I want to say, to tell you, is that I believe Washington wouldn't be too unhappy if we failed with Romor 91. They could be, conceivably, counting on our failing. Maybe not Director Hoover or A. R. Roland, but the rest of the Brass Balls who've been flogging this office for so many years. And why shouldn't they expect this? I would, wouldn't you? We're an odd lot at best. The Brass Balls probably think anything we've achieved is because of Graf . . . that without Graf to lead us we're nothing. They might even feel with Graf gone there's no reason to continue penalizing him with the likes of us . . . that they should send all of us packing and repopulate the office with safe and sane agents.

". . . Ed Grafton, of all the men I've known, was a remarkable leader. He elicited from us a supreme effort and led as a true leader should lead, by example. He could, quite honestly, do anything we could do better. And he cared about us. That, to say the least, is unusual at the FBI.

"Graf has been banished, and I have been ordered to serve in his stead. I am no leader by experience or design. My skills, whatever they be, lie elsewhere. I know you are my friends and wish me well. I beg you, in the name of that friendship, to face the reality that I am not Ed Grafton. What I can do for you in the four to six weeks allotted to us . . . and that is how much time I estimate we have to strut our stuff or be deported, or worse . . . is to estimate the most efficient use of our personnel, of each of your skills. We are, in spite of our troubled histories, a talented bunch. If you bear with me, abide my often rather pedantic approach to matters, maybe I won't let you down as I worry I will at this moment. Maybe, with the help of God or beyond, we might even surprise a Brass Ball or two."

Preston Lyle, striding in on the conference with a big "Thirty-one mil, can you fucking believe it?" would later confess having felt as if he had violated a prayer meeting at which the pastor was stepping down from a pulpit and the parishioners, heads bowed, were mumbling quiet amens.

"Who died?" Pres wanted to know.

"Sit down and shut up," somebody or other told him.

Pres complied.

121

"Now for Romor 91," Strom announced with noticeable relish. He reseated himself at the head of the table and began passing out yellow pads and pencils. "Romor 91, past and present. What we know, don't know, ought to know and had better damn well find out. Let's recapitulate . . . and stop me if I'm wrong.

"We know that Mormon State National Bank was not due to officially open until Tuesday, the twenty-fourth of August . . . which, come to think of it, is today. By the way, is it opening today?"

"No," Jez answered, "they put it off a week."

Strom continued. "We know that at approximately four P.M. Friday, the twentieth of August, a Brink's truck delivered twenty-one packages to Mormon State which were placed in the vault. We know that two days later, at seven thirty-six A.M., Sunday, the twenty-second of August, the alarm went off at Mormon State. We know the alarm system, a Thermex scanning mechanism, indicated that seven or eight perpetrators were in the bank, six downstairs, one or two on the staircase leading up from the vault. We know that splice marks were later found on the main cable of the Thermex system. We know that the vault sank into the concrete floor and that when it was cut open on the top there was already a hole cut in the bottom . . . a hole through which Brewmeister was seen looking up. We know Brewmeister was washed from sight and found twenty-two miles away on a delta island in the river.

"We know that the perpetrators somehow gained access to the cave beneath the bank. We know firsthand, from Brewmeister, the perpetrators brought in a metal scaffold reaching up to the roof of the cave and that one-hundred-watt electric bulbs were burning. We know from the cuts in the rock ceiling and in the bottom of the vault that the workmanship was very professional and that specialized high-powered electric drills had to have been used. This would presume the perpetrators had a source of electricity . . . perhaps a generator, perhaps a tap into a commercial supply of electricity . . . by the way, was there a report on the explosives in the cave?"

"The police lab says nitroglycerin was used both in the vault and the rock below," Cub Hennessy answered. "Used quite expertly."

"Make sure you personality-profile aficionados don't overlook another already–mentioned professionalism," Strom told the writing agents, ". . . electricity. Someone was playing with large amounts of electrical power down there. Perhaps lethal amounts.

"We can presume additional supplies were brought into the cave. Fusing, detonators, food, clothing, communications devices. We can presume at least one large rubber boat was brought to the cave, the one whose remains were found near where Brewmeister was discovered in the river. We can presume from the static line in that boat and the Brink's money sack snapped to the static line that the perpetrators anticipated a somewhat rocky getaway in that boat. We can presume that the perpetrators were able to somehow flood the tunnels to effect their getaway subsequent to the robbery. Flood the tunnel with millions of gallons of untraceable water, if we are to believe the Sewerage Department people. We can presume that in their getaway the perpetrators followed a route similar to the one traveled by Brewmeister . . . twenty-two miles through underground tunnels before being dumped out into the Mississippi River at the southern end of Prairie Port. We can possibly presume the perpetrators further contrived to flood and reflood the tunnels and cave beneath the bank for two more purposes, the removal of all physical evidence and, secondly, to act as a booby trap, or time deterrent, for anyone investigating the scene.

"Adding this to our profile would presume the perpetrators were also knowledgeable in both tunnels and underground water control, or at least more knowledgeable than the people we've talked with so far. I don't believe half those tunnels have been inspected yet, have they?"

"Not the ones going west, that's for sure," Jez Jessup said. "The deputy fire commissioner called again saying the tunnel flooding has turned into a river of mud under the western part of town. That's what's been causing mud geysers on the surface. He thinks it could be pretty serious, that mud."

"So does a guy named St. Ives," Butch Cody added. "He called in too. He's with the Missouri Valley Geological Survey. He says if the mud stays trapped and builds up pressure, we could damn near have an earthquake."

"Strom," Happy de Camp called out, "think our perpetrators could have ended up inland by mistake?"

"No way, José," Lester Kebbon interjected as he entered the room with E. G. Womper. "I talked with the water commissioner myself when Brew got washed out to sea. He says the Sewerage Department is covering up on what really happened. He says there were all kinds of floodings over the weekend the sewerage people didn't tell anybody about. The biggest floodings came first and they were doozies. They went right under town and spilled into the Mississippi. Brew was on one of those. Right after that the sewerage people tried to contain the flooding and opened the wrong gates in one of their transfer terminals . . . started sending all the water into the western tunnels. Sending it inland to the mud."

"What would the water commissioner know about what goes on in the Sewerage Department?" Happy asked.

"What would he know about anything?" Jez Jessup said.

"He's not as dumb as you guys think," said Kebbon.

"Come on, Les, the guy's an asshole," Jessup maintained, "a certifiable asshole."

"He's not as bad as the sewerage commissioner."

"The sewerage commissioner is in the right job," Hap said.

"E. G.," Strom turned to Womper, who was co-founder and lead actor of a local amateur theater group, "go out front and man one of the phones. Tell the urgent calls we'll get back to them. Slough the rest. Charm them all."

E. G. Womper, nodding, started for the outer offices. Never before could he remember Strom giving a direct order to himself or anyone. What Les Kebbon noticed as he took his place at the conference table was that Strom, a chronic pipe–smoker, had left his pipe and tobacco pouch untouched.

"Is there anything else we should know in recapitulation?" Strom asked the group. "Anything I overlooked or one of you hasn't mentioned? Cub, didn't you and Jez sneak a couple of interviews at the bank yesterday morning?"

"Sure did, with risk to life and limb," Cub admitted. "Don't forget, it was still the police department's investigation as of yesterday, and they were leering at us every step we took. According to the bank's assistant manager, a nervous wreck named Franklin Ulick, nobody was in the bank from the time it closed Friday afternoon until the police crashed in Sunday morning. No one authorized. Like you said earlier, Mormon State's official opening date wasn't until today. According to Ulick, most of the regular staff had been hired and wasn't due to show up until Monday morning . . . but people were in and out of the bank on Friday. In and out between ten A.M. and four–thirty P.M. About twelve people in all, but none of them regular staff. The first in were painters and maintenance people, and they stayed a good part of the day. We have their names and addresses. From twelve–thirty to two–thirty P.M. the bank manager and assistant manager interviewed job applicants for the positions still unfilled, including those for night watchman. Ulick gave the police the names and addresses of these people. He took them over to police headquarters Sunday night along with names and addresses of everyone who had come in or out of the premises for the last three weeks. A list of one hundred and eighteen names. Our guy inside the PD got us a copy the next morning . . . The last job applicants were out of the bank by two–thirty P.M. on Friday, August twentieth. The rest left at four–thirty. Brink's made its delivery of money around four P.M. . . . between the time the interviews ended and the workmen left."

"Cub, let's get this straight." Strom lifted his pencil, reread his last notation. "There were workmen present at the time Brink's made the delivery, is that right?"

"According to Ulick, the assistant manager."

"Painters only, or painters and some of the maintenance people?"

"Painters only. The maintenance people were all out at three sharp because the bank didn't want to pay them union overtime.

The maintenance workers were union. The painters were non-union. The painters started working about ten A.M. They were still there when the Brink's truck arrived."

"Then what?" Strom asked as he made his notations.

"The Brink's driver and a Brink's guard brought the load into the bank," Cub said. "Another Brink's guard waited in the armored truck outside. The Brink's driver and guard brought the load down into the vault in the basement. Twenty-one small canvas sacks is what the load was. Giles Julien, the bank manager, was with them. Ulick, the assistant manager, and the painters were upstairs on the main floor of the bank. Ulick doubts if the painters noticed the shipment come in, since they were painting the back offices. After the sacks were put in the vault, the manager closed the vault door and activated the television scanning equipment connected to the alarm system. Once the vault door was closed, the manager activated the system for just downstairs, for just the vault in the basement. The manager went upstairs and left the bank. That was at four-fifteen P.M. The painters were let out by Ulick, the assistant manager, at four-thirty. Then Ulick checked the offices and shut off the lights. The last thing he did was activate the alarm system for the entire premises. That was at ten to five, which is also when he went home . . .

"We know the Friday afternoon shipment to the bank by Brink's was only the first delivery in an overall shipment of some sixty-plus packages worth over a million dollars in cash. This was the working money to get the bank operation started on its opening day, Tuesday. No individual value records had been made on the cash contents of the Friday delivery. As it turned out, that first delivery was only meant to provide the bank with supplies from Brink's, extra sacks and locks, lading forms, tabulation forms, et cetera. Some of the sacks contained paper currency . . . sixty-five hundred dollars in one-dollar bills. That's when some of us had a good laugh and Graf pulled out of the investigation. Before pulling out," Cub added, "we picked up other information through secondary sources and the media, but on a direct knowledge basis that's what we had."

126

All eyes were on Strom, who was reading his notes and dropping his pencil, eraser end first, on the tabletop, catching it as it bounced back up, reversing ends, dropping it lead first . . . on the bounce, catching it . . . reversing . . . dropping . . . catching.

"You said there was no watchman at the premises over the weekend?" Strom asked.

"Or anyone else," Cub replied. "According to Ulick, the assistant manager, no watchmen had even been hired. Three applicants were accepted and waiting approval from the bonding company."

"But the alarm system had been activated before the bank was locked up for the weekend on Friday?" Strom asked.

"Right."

"And you said the television–scanning portion of that system had been activated as well, which would mean that the premises were being scanned by closed-circuit television cameras whose pictures were relayed to a monitor screen somewhere?"

"Four monitor screens. All in a control room beside the assistant manager's office at the bank," Cub said.

"All four screens were active over the weekend?"

"So I was told."

"Who was there to watch?" Strom asked. "Why bother to turn on television cameras and monitor screens if there's no one there to watch the monitor screens?"

". . . I should have explained," Cub said, "it wasn't activated as much for security reasons as for testing. It's a sensitive and complex system. Installation is a bitch. It takes adjustment after adjustment to fine-tune it. Technicians from Thermex had been at Mormon State Thursday afternoon making final adjustments. The system was left on over the weekend to see if it was functioning properly."

"You talked with the Thermex people?"

"Not yet," Cub said. "The assistant manager told me about it."

E. G. Womper stood in the doorway. "Strom, Denis Corticun's on the line."

"Tell him I'll get back to him."

"I did, but he said to go get you."

127

"Say I'm in conference and can't be disturbed."

E. G. shrugged and disappeared.

Strom returned to dropping his pencil, finally asked Cub, "Was any mention made by either the bank people or Brink's regarding the shipment of another thirty-one million dollars to Mormon State? Thirty-one million from Federal Reserve?"

"Absolutely not. I'll tell you something else. Julien, the bank manager, sure as hell didn't expect the shipment before it arrived. Or know about it after it got here. He was the one who set the alarm system on the vault. Then he locked the system into a master timing mechanism which would keep the vault door locked until nine-thirty A.M., Monday morning. If he was expecting something to arrive before Monday morning, why go to all that trouble, no matter what the Thermex technicians needed? Uh-uh, he wasn't expecting zilch. From his tone of voice today I'd say he was as surprised about the shipment as we were."

"You talked to the bank manager today?" Strom asked.

"He called while you were talking to Director Hoover," Cub said. "He wanted to know what we knew about the thirty-one million."

The pencil bounced and was caught. "Did the manager say if the vault could be opened once the alarm and timing mechanisms were set?"

"He did," Cub said. "He claims two people had the double keys and knowledge needed to do it, the manager himself and the bank's president, Emile Chandler. The manager said he didn't open the vault and doubts if Chandler could have. He says Chandler was out of town over the weekend, and is still out of town."

"Tell me about the bank manager."

"Giles Julien . . . if you can believe a bank would have a manager named Giles and a president named Emile . . . he's a real oddball type. Creepy. The kind who brings his lunch to work in a brown paper bag and buys used shoes. He looks like yesterday's throwouts. But I don't think he's up to lying."

E. G. Womper was back in the doorway. "Corticun says he's about to catch a plane from Washington to here and wants to know if there's anything special you need besides a teletype machine and switchboard."

"Tell him a little information on that thirty-one-million-dollar shipment would be appreciated."

E. G. threw a salute and was gone.

"What about the police investigation?" Strom asked Cub. "How had that progressed until Mr. Hoover's press conference?"

Cub shook his head. "They were running around in circles, if you ask me. Rounding up every punk they could find. The commissioner of police supposedly told the state's attorney general the robbery had probably been perpetrated by a group of out-of-town criminals. That's usually a giveaway they don't know what the hell's going on."

"No suspect then, even out of town?"

A thumbs-down, a headshake. "The only thing they're sure of is that the bank got robbed and the crooks flooded the tunnels for their getaway."

"Do they have any idea when over the weekend the bank was scored?"

"Nope."

"I suppose it would be asking too much for them to know where the water for flooding came from."

Cub nodded.

"Is that what you guys are after, where the water came from?" Les Kebbon said. "Hell, I know where it comes from. It comes from Tomahawk Hill reservoir."

"Who told you that, the water commissioner?" asked Jez.

"No, Chet Chomsky. The reporter on KTY who's thick with the mayor and city hall crowd. He's usually accurate. E. G. and me just heard him on the car radio driving over here. Chet Chomsky said the Tomahawk reservoir reported losing millions of gallons of water over the weekend and that the city engineers are sure this is the water that flooded the tunnels . . . only they don't know where it went to get there."

"How the hell can you lose millions of gallons of water and not know where it went?" Jez protested.

"I'm only reporting what Chet Chomsky reported," Kebbon said. "He said the main water ducts leading from the reservoir didn't show any unusual amounts of water coming through over the weekend, leastways not forty to fifty million gallons. That's what they estimate was lost, forty to fifty million. Chomsky said all kinds of old tunnels and water systems everyone's forgotten about are all over the place. He said the tunnels right under the bank, the ones that flooded, have been identified as being part of an old system called CCC or something. But none of the engineers can figure out how the hell the millions of gallons from the reservoir got way the hell over to the CCC tunnel at the bank. There's nothing connecting them that anyone knows of. He said a state geologist thinks the tunnel flooding is directly related to the mud slides and explosions west of town. According to WQG, which we were listening to earlier, the mud is so serious the governor's thinking of declaring west Prairie Port a disaster area. Getting back to Chet Chomsky, he said the flooding has to do with the electrical dimouts too."

"Sounds like we should hire Chet Chomsky," Happy de Camp said.

"Promise him a uniform and six-shooter and a-running he'll come," Les Kebbon said. "Chomsky is a trooper freak. He's a member of every auxiliary state police organization that lets him buy a fancy uniform and carry pearl-handled pistols. He loves riding in prowl cars. Maybe that's why his county crime information is usually accurate. He's buddy-buddy with one helluva lot of state troopers and sheriff's deputies. But the city cops hate him."

Strom surveyed the conferees. "Is there anything else we know about the perpetration? Any first-, second- or third-hand data?"

No one at the table said anything.

Strom laid aside his pencil. "Like it or not, lads, I'd say we are smack-dab back at the basics. Back to the WhoWhatWhyWhere-WhenHows, and in no particular order." He was on his feet pacing and thinking aloud. "Why did the perpetrators select Mormon State in the first place? And When? When exactly, and How did they enter the caves to perpetrate the actual theft?

130

What, precisely, was the *modus operandi?* What specific equipment did the MO dictate be brought along? Who are they? How many are they? Where have they gone? And When? When! We'll look a fine lot of fools if we can't even establish When the haul came down."

John Lars Sunstrom's abilities as an organizer and administrator were generally unrecognized beyond the confines of the residency. Now freshly invested with what he considered to be temporary but near irrevocable authority by J. Edgar Hoover, he found himself in top form.

Prairie Port's complement of seventeen resident agents, Strom told the men seated at the table, would be split into two groups, a three-man Caretaker Force and a Strike Force of the remaining operatives. The Caretakers would immediately evaluate the status of all five hundred and seventy-one investigations currently being conducted by the resident office. High-priority cases would stay within the residency's purview and be worked on by the Caretakers. Everything else, the bulk of the investigations, would be shunted on to Denis Corticun and the thirty backup agents expected at Prairie Port in the coming hours. The Caretakers would assist the backups with these cases as best they could. Strom suggested the building's landlord be called at once by Happy de Camp and space on the empty floor above the residency be rented short term to provide offices for the new arrivals. Hap was further instructed to arrange billeting and whatever else might be needed to accommodate Corticun and the thirty other out-of-towners.

The three-man Caretaker team would, in short, relieve the fourteen-man Strike Force of all responsibilities other than pursuing Romor 91. This pursuit would follow soon-to-be-detailed Channels of Investigation, and whatever assistance might be required could be provided by the support personnel headed by Denis Corticun. Should the Caretakers have any availability, they too would assist on Romor 91.

Pacing and pointing, Strom then began to list what the individual Channels of Investigation would be and exactly which ones each of the fourteen resident agents would be assigned to.

131

Heck Bevins, hurrying into the conference room with Ralph Dafney, sensed a difference in Strom. A confidence he had not seen before. Ralph Dafney felt it was more a sort of puckishness. What Billy Yates and most agents already at the table took note of was Strom's insistence, while rattling off the channels and channel assignments, on answers to three questions: When did thirty-one million dollars arrive at Mormon State National Bank? How, precisely, did it get there? When exactly, between the time the assistant manager locked up on Friday afternoon and the police arrived early Sunday morning, was Mormon State National Bank robbed?

Early afternoon papers in Prairie Port and across the country headlined what radio newscasters had been bulletining since J. Edgar Hoover made his speech hours before, the largest cash robbery in history. The most immediate response from the local populace was to rubberneck in front of the Mormon State bank, thereby creating a minor traffic jam in the area. The national response was reflected in a run on Prairie Port hotel and motel rooms by out-of-town media people.

At 11:45 A.M. Strom noticed a headline in one of the papers an agent had brought him. "My God," he said to Jez, "I forgot the reporters outside."

"Don't worry, Washington will make up for it," Jez assured him. Strom did not listen, hurried out into the anteroom . . . was swallowed up by the crunch of press people.

The first interview to be conducted by any member of the Prairie Port residency since the creation of Romor 91 was unofficial and occurred at 12:05 P.M., when a curious Billy Yates, waiting for assignment, decided to call the Prairie Port Sewerage Department. Since repairmen had temporarily shut down the FBI office switchboard, Yates took the back elevator down to a lobby paybooth. The only person not out to lunch was a cheery secretary. Yates identified himself, explained this was an unofficial call and asked if the electrical power shortages over the last week or so had in any way affected the electrical equipment used by the department. Had it ever, he was told. It had knocked all the central control room's measuring gauges for a loop. No one had the vaguest idea what had gone through the sewerage system since Friday afternoon. Whole sections of tunnel had been nearly demolished, but there was no way of knowing when or by how much water. What was true for the sewerage monitoring system was true for the Water Department. If he didn't believe her, Yates was told, call the Water Department. He did call. The secretary there refused to give out any information.

The first official communication Washington headquarters received from the originating office of Romor 91 occurred at 2:07 P.M., when acting ASRA Cub Hennessy placed a call over the newly repaired switchboard and requested detailed information on the shipment of $31,000,000 to Mormon State National Bank.

The first official communication the Romor 91 office received from headquarters was logged into the Prairie Port communications book at 2:55 P.M.

"What's the idea of calling headquarters and not calling us?" Harlon Quinton, Corticun's aide-de-camp, demanded.

"I didn't know we were supposed to," Cub replied.

"Like hell you didn't. We've been calling you all day."

"Then you'll know our phones went out."

"That's no excuse. When we call we expect an immediate answer. That's how it's going to be."

"How what's going to be?"

"Chain of command. You answer to us, mister. When we call we expect an immediate response."

"Then I'll give you one." Cub, without further ado, hung up.

The first official report from Prairie Port to Washington began at 3:10 P.M., after Denis Corticun called Strom Sunstrom and politely apologized for the behavior of Harlon Quinton. Corticun said there was no doubt Strom was in total charge of Romor 91. Again Corticun apologized for Harlon Quinton . . . casually asked what progress was being made. Strom, without hesitation and calmly, began rattling off the Channels of Investigation to be followed by the Prairie Port residency: Mormon State National

133

Bank Premises and Personnel; Shipment of $31,000,000 to Mormon State Bank; U.S. Treasury Department Procedures for Transport and Destruction of Currency; Inspection of Tunnels, Caves and Underground Systems Running Under or Near Bank; Inspection of Tunnels, Caves and Underground Systems Running North and South of Bank Including Sewerage and Water Department Systems of City of Prairie Port; Background of All Persons Having Access Physically and/or Informationally to Such Tunnels, Caves and Systems; Inspection of Dams, Locks and Flood-Control Systems Twenty Miles North of Bank; Inspection of Mud Explosions West of City to Determine Relationship with Crime, If Any; Reconstruction of Crime; Projection of Potential Equipment Utilized in Crime; Check of All Retail and Wholesale Stores Stocking Such Equipment; Projected Profile on Perpetrators; Local and State Check on All Known Criminals with "Capacity to Perpetrate" Mormon State-Type Crime; Nationwide and Interpol Check for Known Criminals with "Capacity to Perpetrate"; Local Check on Airports, Bus and Rail Terminals and Hotels, Motels and Rooming Houses for Strangers in Prairie Port at Time of Perpetration; Neighborhood Checks to Find Eyewitnesses at or Near Bank Premises; Area Checks for Eyewitnesses at Location Downstream from Bank Where Agent Brewmeister Was Found; Nationwide Alert for "Big Spenders" of Unmarked Money; Interpol Alert for Large Shipments or Deposits of U.S. Currency; Crime Lab Examination of Robbery Premises, Rubber Raft, Rope, Money Bag; List of the Unknown Perpetrators on Ten Most Wanted List; Alerts to City, State and Out-of-State Law-Enforcement Agencies on Rented or Stolen Vehicles Possibly Used by Perpetrators; Media Monitoring for Additional Leads; Establishment of Emergency Lines of Communication with Public Regarding Additional Leads; Assignment of Special Liaisons to City, County, State Law-Enforcement Agencies; Contacting of Informants; Development of Additional Informants.

Corticun was also told by Sunstrom that assignments of specific agents to these channels were currently being made.

Corticun told Sunstrom that the special "flying squad" would expedite the needed data for him. He informed Strom he would be arriving in Prairie Port early that evening . . .

Wet-suited divers, one by one in the stillness of the late-afternoon heat, rolled off the pontoon raft and into the dark waters of Tomahawk Hill reservoir west of Prairie Port, sank forty-seven feet, touched bottom, deployed and scanned the basin floor with powerful portable searchlights. The team was from the United States Army Corps of Engineers, and had been trying, for many hours, to locate leaks or cracks or other unsuspected openings which might account for millions of gallons of missing Tomahawk water. And the shortaging hadn't ended. Startling amounts of water, intermittently, continued to disappear.

Diving team leader Sergeant Mel Wallinor spotted dense undergrowth looming up ahead. Suspecting they had reached the original bed from which the reservoir had been expanded three decades before, he signaled the other swimmers into the area. Muck mushroomed as they flippered through the vegetation. Wallinor heard metal creaking, turned in time to see a flailing diver to his right shoot backward out of sight. Wallinor made for his comrade, was spun around and sucked through the undergrowth with amazing force. He banged into the moss-crusted latticework of a huge iron gate against which the diver was pinioned . . . through which reservoir water was escaping.

Watching the evening television news on the rented set as well as on one brought in by Heck Bevins's wife, the agents of Prairie Port took a dinner break and saw the anchormen of local NBC and CBS channels simultaneously announce the largest cash robbery in modern history, then cut to J. Edgar Hoover making his press conference statement earlier in Washington, D.C. After commercials reporters for both networks recapitulated the crime from in front of the Mormon State National Bank. CBS went to another reporter standing before the residency's office building. Pointing up to the lighted line of windows, the reporter stated these were the Bureau's current offices and that the enormity of

135

the manhunt to come could best be judged by the additional space just taken by the FBI: the entire floor above. NBC went directly into the jam-packed anteroom of the Prairie Port residency office, where senior crime reporter Theodore Howel revealed the media expected an announcement of major significance at any moment.

CBS cut to Prairie Port's Municipal Airport, where a cargo plane was being unloaded. An off-camera reporter announced this was the FBI office equipment flown in from Washington for what was expected to be the greatest manhunt in U.S. history.

The reporter appeared on screen with Denis Corticun, who was introduced as "J. Edgar Hoover's man-at-the spot." Corticun graciously explained he was here merely to assist the senior resident agent in charge, John L. Sunstrom, and the men of the Prairie Port office, who had already made significant progress in their investigation of the crime, details of which would be described more fully at a ten-o'clock press conference in Prairie Port the next morning.

The progress was news to Strom and his viewing agents.

NBC went remote to "special guest crime–analyst Chet Chomsky," a pudgy fellow in an Anzac hat who was standing in the control center of Prairie Port's Sewerage Department holding a metal gauge. Chomsky, after declaring history was in the making and Mormon State would go down as the greatest criminal masterwork of all time, announced the FBI had just discovered another ploy invoked by the brilliant perpetrators. Wandering along a wall of glass-enclosed dials and gauges, Chomsky revealed the FBI had determined that by dimming and raising electrical power levels in the Prairie Port area, the criminals had caused most electrical-sensitive mechanisms, such as the Sewerage Department gauge he was holding, or those on the wall behind him, to be knocked out of commission much as an electric clock is knocked out of whack when power is shut off and later restored. Chomsky said the gauges at the Sewerage Department as well as the Water Department had definitely been put out of commission by the power fluctuations and as a result it could not

136

yet be determined when the actual flooding of the tunnels took place. Chomsky then added that the mere discovery of the technique used to neutralize the gauges was the major break in the case FBI men had been hoping for . . . that it boiled the list of suspects down to a very specialized few. Chomsky leaned into the camera and confidentially advised his viewers to expect a big announcement soon.

Seated in the family station wagon parked in the open-air lot across the street from the office, Cub Hennessy and his wife, Sissy, ate a home-cooked picnic supper while listening to radio station KTY, over which Chet Chomsky's prerecorded voice relayed substantially the same electrical gauge information he was currently presenting live on NBC.

"Sounds like you're making progress," Sissy said.

"The gauge thing was Yates, the new boy," Cub told her.

"He has a lovely wife. Young and smart."

Cub switched off the radio, popped an olive into his mouth.

"What's wrong?" asked Sissy.

"Nothing."

"When you eat an olive after your custard, something's wrong."

". . . What Strom said up there could be true."

"Which was what?"

"He warned that Washington might be setting him up, might want us to fail with this case."

"That's foolishness. It sounds like everything is going fine."

"We've got to get out into the field. Strom is up there organizing for D-Day. There's nothing he hasn't thought of . . . on paper. But so far we're still upstairs planning."

Sissy kissed him on the cheek. "You'll be out on the bricks soon enough."

". . . Grafton? Why remove Graf at this particular moment?"

Sissy peered at her husband. "You don't think Strom can handle the case?"

"Maybe the case by itself," Cub told her. "Any investigation is luck, you know that. Ten percent hard work, ninety percent luck.

137

If we get the breaks fast, fine and good. But I . . ." Cub turned and faced Sissy. "I have a feeling something else is going on. Something I just don't understand . . ."

Alice Maywell moved naked through the darkness to the open window. She folded her arms, stared absently out across the narrow street at the lighted but empty third-floor office. The large clock on the office's far wall showed the time to be 10:18 P.M.

"Don't stand there with nothing on," Elaine Picket said from the bed.

"Don't tell me what to do. No more!" Alice warned.

"People can see in."

"Let them!" Alice tore aside the sheer curtains, raised her beautiful face, threw back her arms. "Look at me," she shouted into the night. "All of you out there, look at me . . ." She clasped her high and firm breasts and dug her fingernails into the smooth flesh.

"Idiot." Elaine felt about in the bedclothes.

"You're damn right I'm an idiot." Alice spun around. "That and a lot more for ever loving you!"

"Love? You're a grown woman. You wanted a fling, I gave you a fling. Flings end."

"I believed in you, I needed you—"

"And I need a smoke. Get away from the window so I can turn on the light and find my cigarettes."

Alice remained motionless.

The nightstand lamp illuminated. Auburn-haired, freckle-faced, bone-naked Elaine Picket was on all fours on top of the mussed satin sheet searching. "Go home," she said, belly-flopping on the mattress and reaching down for a pack of Virginia Slims on the shag rug. "You belong at home. Work it out with that husband of yours. You don't cut it as a dyke."

Alice glowered at the long, lithe woman draped over bed's end lighting a cigarette. She turned abruptly away, again gazed outside.

A man who looked like Groucho Marx was standing at the closed third-floor office window across the street staring at her

138

...a tall man in red fright wig and long black frock coat and white gloves. On seeing Alice had noticed him, he doffed the wig politely, revealing a totally bald head. Then he danced several high-stepping steps of a jig and leapt into the air clicking his heels. He was wearing cowboy boots.

Alice retreated several paces. As she did, the bedside lamp behind her snapped off.

A second, far shorter man moved quickly up beside the first at the closed window. He too looked like Groucho Marx. The shorter man wore gray gloves and an unzipped black windbreaker over a dark green T-shirt and was huskier than the taller man. He also had on a fright wig, only his was blue. Powder blue. The short Groucho was visibly agitated. He carried an open cash box, held it upside down in front of his partner to show it was empty, shook it a time or two, tossed it aside, stalked off out of view. Tall Groucho went on staring in Alice's direction.

Alice backed farther into the dark bedroom, but couldn't stop watching. She had already discerned what their disguises were ...snap-on, half-face Groucho masks. Short Groucho rushed back to his partner holding a newspaper . . . a newspaper he had obviously just come across . . . a paper whose front-page headline he kept slapping with the back of his free hand while he talked animatedly at the taller man. Tall Groucho paid scant attention ... went on looking for Alice. Short Groucho grabbed Tall Groucho by the arm, jerked him around, held the newspaper up in front of the masked face, pointed at the headline, screamed something. The tall, red-wigged Groucho stared hard at the headline, slowly shook his head, shrugged, glanced back toward the window and Alice. The shorter, blue-wigged Marx Brother again grabbed the other man's arm, tried pulling him farther back into the office. Tall Groucho broke the grip with ease. Short Groucho pointed a finger at Tall Groucho and stamped a foot. Tall Groucho put a disbelieving finger to his chest. Short Groucho nodded, stamped again, pointed his finger off in the distance, stamped twice more. Tall Groucho shook his head, waved his hand as if to tell Short Groucho to get lost. Short Groucho threw a fit, went into a veritable tarantella . . . jumped up and down and

139

kicked the floor with his heel and shook an accusatory fist first at Tall Groucho and then off at some distant entity, and ripped the headline in half and ran to one side of the office and then the other, kicking desks, as if trapped or going crazy or both, and then came back and jumped up and down in front of Tall Groucho. Suddenly stopped jumping and just stood there looking up into the taller man's masked face. Tall Groucho again shrugged and motioned the smaller man away. Short Groucho tapped a gloved finger against his own windbreaker pocket, raised the finger at Tall Groucho and wagged it . . . held up his second gloved hand . . . made both hands into fists . . . lifted three fingers of the right hand and one finger of the left hand.

Alice could hear Short Groucho's muted shouts of "Thirty-one, thirty-one" . . . saw Tall Groucho shake his head vehemently and yell back, "Don't blame the world on me, you lousy mule-fucker, you."

"Did you say something?" Elaine Picket called from the darkness.

"No." Alice watched Short Groucho wildly brandish a fist. Tall Groucho appeared to be angry, started toward Short Groucho. The office lights began to dim and raise. Both Grouchos looked around. The lights dimmed and raised again . . . dimmed and went completely out.

Alice moved up to the bedroom's open window, peered through and around. Every electric light along the block and beyond was off. In the blackness of the office across the street muffled shouting was audible. She strained to see what was happening. The office lights glowed on. Tall Groucho was standing near the window looking in her direction. Then he turned . . . directly into a gun Short Groucho had raised to eye level. A long-barrel handgun with a silencer encasing the tip.

Alice did not hear the double thuds all that distinctly, but she clearly saw Short Groucho's gloved hand kick to the right twice and two puffs of faint white smoke ring the muzzle of the gun and expand . . . watched the red fright wig pop high into the air . . . witnessed the side of Tall Groucho's bald head explode as she had once seen a Halloween pumpkin explode when a lit fire-cracker was dropped inside.

Exploding, Tall Groucho crumpled from sight beneath the sill of the office window. Short Groucho stood staring down, the smoking gun in hand. He ripped off his wig and mask and went on staring down contemplatively, angrily. He dropped the gun inside his windbreaker. He turned and looked up and blinked in surprise. Only then did she realize she was directly in front of the open window and could be seen. She backed away too late. Alice Maywell Sunstrom, wife of FBI man John Sunstrom, and Marion "Mule Fucker" Corkel had gotten a good look at one another.

# Eight

Six new teletype machines were among the FBI equipment on the chartered cargo plane that had landed in Prairie Port earlier in the evening. Shortly before 10 P.M. two of these machines arrived at the eleventh-floor resident office of the FBI. The remaining four instruments had gone up one flight to the hastily rented twelfth floor, where support operations for the residency were to be housed. Installation of all incoming machines had begun immediately. Some four hours later, at 2 A.M. Wednesday, August 25, the first teletype, one of the four instruments on the twelfth floor, was activated. The message which began clicking out shortly after was from special agent Alexander Troxel, a member of the newly formed flying squad organized by Corticun at J. Edgar Hoover's bidding. The communication was a summary report made in conjunction with U.S. Treasury Department operative H. C. Kundra and dealt with nineteen interviews conducted days earlier, between Sunday, August 22, and early Tuesday morning, August 24, regarding the shipment of money to the Mormon State National Bank. The text read:

J. F. Dunlop, Senior Vice President, Federal Reserve Bank Branch Office, 5252 St. Charles Avenue, New Orleans, Louisiana, states his bank regularly reprocesses paper currency from depository banks and replaces bills no longer fit for circulation. Unfit bills usually old or damaged or otherwise disfunctional. Unfit bills burned on premises in Fed Bank's basement incinerator. On 11 August 1971 Dunlop says incinerator broke down. Six days subsequent, Tuesday,

142

17 August 1971, Dunlop telephoned Arthur G. Klines, Assistant Director, Projects, United States Treasury Department, Washington, D.C., to express concern at delays in repairing incinerator and amounts of unfit currency amassing at branch bank: nearly twenty million dollars ($20,000,000).

Arthur G. Klines confirms Dunlop story. Klines says such emergencies are not unusual and that twenty million dollars is a "relatively small sum" considering Fed moves hundreds of millions in currency weekly. Klines states, agreeing with Dunlop, that a transfer of amassing unfit currency should be made to an operative incinerator elsewhere. Klines states telephoning Allen J. Noble, Security Director for Gulf Coast Armored Security Corporation, Corpus Christi, Texas, the afternoon of 17 August 1971. Noble confirms Klines's story, further says Gulf Coast Armored Security is "small, flexible" money-moving company which often assists in emergency or "spot" governmental projects of this kind. Subsequent to Klines's phone call on 17 August 1971, Noble diverted armored semi-trailer truck from Tampa, Florida, to New Orleans. Truck bore no name other than "Gulf Coast Transit" and did not appear to be armored. Truck driven by Gulf Coast Armored Security Vice President, David C. Swoggins. Security guard Jack W. Manly accompanied Swoggins. Swoggins and Manly former Green Berets. Swoggins and Manly, due to company security policies, claim no prior knowledge of mission other than to meet Noble in New Orleans. Noble, Klines, Dunlop say communications between them conducted

143

in strictest secrecy. Klines states being only person to know destination of shipment prior to truck arriving at New Orleans.

Swoggins and Manly arrived New Orleans early evening, Thursday, 19 August 1971, and rendezvoused with Noble. Subsequent to refueling truck and dining, Swoggins, Manly, Noble drove to Federal Reserve Bank branch office on St. Charles Avenue, arriving 8:00 P.M. Bank Vice President Dunlop was waiting for them alone. Between 8:00 P.M. and 9:30 P.M. Swoggins, Manly, Noble state loading some five hundred and fifty (550) canvas sacks of unfit currency into truck trailer.

Money sacks described as heavy-duty canvas of two sizes. Smaller sacks in majority, measure two feet (2 ft.) width, three feet (3 ft.) height, weight estimated at thirty (30) to forty (40) pounds when filled with paper currency. Larger sacks described as three feet (3 ft.) width, four and half feet ($4\frac{1}{2}$ ft.) height, weight estimated eighty (80) to one hundred thirty (130) pounds filled. Sacks, large or small, white or gray in color. Sacks, large or small, stenciled either FRB or Federal Reserve Bank. Some sacks, large and small, without stenciling. Some sacks have zipper tops with padlock attachments but no padlocks inserted. Some larger sacks have draw-rope tops.

Paper currency described as old, used, faded, torn or otherwise damaged bills. Bills banded together in stacks according to denominations . . . one-dollar notes, ten-dollar notes, fifty-dollar notes, one-hundred-dollar notes. Bands are of varying colored paper . . . white, gray, manila, yellow. Most bands have no markings. Some white and gray bands might be printed with: U.S. Federal Reserve Bank.

Dunlop states total amount of unfit bills loaded onto Gulf Coast Armored Security truck was thirty-one million dollars ($31,000,000) and that this figure appeared on lading voucher given Swoggins. Dunlop further says duplicate inventory list of serial numbers for every one-hundred-dollar ($100) bill in shipment provided Swoggins.

Swoggins confirms receiving lading voucher for thirty-one million dollars ($31,000,000) as well as copy of inventory list of hundred-dollar bills. Swoggins, Noble, Manly, Dunlop say only after truck was loaded and ready for departure did Dunlop reveal shipment's destination was Federal Reserve Bank at St. Louis, Missouri. Dunlop told them if trouble was encountered en route, Arthur Klines should be telephoned.

Swoggins, Manly, Noble state leaving New Orleans 10:00 P.M. Thursday, 19 August 1971, in armored truck with Noble driving, Swoggins in cab as armed guard, Manly in trailer as armed guard. Anticipated travel time: sixteen (16) hours. Estimated arrival St. Louis: 2:00 P.M. Friday, 20 August 1971. Truck departed New Orleans westward on U.S. Highway 10 to U.S. Highway 55, followed 55 northward for balance of journey. Truck overheated at McComb and Canton, Mississippi, causing delays of two and four hours respectively. Each delay was telephoned to Arthur Klines by Noble. Overheating problem was partially corrected by reducing driving speed from sixty-five (65) miles per hour to forty (40) miles per hour. Once inside Missouri border, Noble reached Klines by telephone advising engine trouble was worse. Noble doubted truck could hold up till St. Louis. Noble suggested replacement vehicle come for load. Klines told Noble to wait by telephone. Klines called back many hours later saying no replacement truck was available. Klines instructed Nobel to deliver load to Mormon State National Bank in nearby Prairie Port, Missouri, for weekend safekeeping, then take truck for repair.

Truck reached Mormon State National Bank at 6:45 P.M., Friday, 20 August 1971. Emile Chandler, President, Mormon State Bank, was waiting at premises. Noble, Swoggins and Manly transferred the entire load of unfit money from truck to bank vault. Transfer completed 8:00 P.M.

Noble, Swoggins, Manly moved truck to Majestic Garage, 45 Clayton Street, Carbondale, Illinois, where they remained for weekend while radiator was replaced. Early Sunday morning, 22 August 1971, Noble, Swoggins, Manly departed for Prairie Port in repaired truck to pick up money at Mormon State and complete delivery to St. Louis. En route heard news of robbery on cab radio and stopped to call Klines in Washington, D.C., for instructions. Klines unavailable. Noble called Dunlop in New Orleans. Dunlop ordered them back to Carbondale to await instructions.

At 7:45 A.M. Sunday, 22 August 1971, Emile Chandler, President, Mormon State National Bank, telephoned at home by Chief of Prairie Port Police Department, F. R. Santi, who reported robbery-in-progress at bank premises. Chandler reached premises 8:15 A.M. Chandler unable to contact Klines. 8:30 A.M. Chandler notified Dunlop of robbery-in-progress.

Dunlop states being unable to find his copy of inventory list of serial numbers for unfit hundred-dollar bills. Dunlop further reveals only two such copies of list existed. Dunlop called Chandler, who had no memory of seeing any such list. Dunlop called Swoggins and Noble in Carbondale, Illinois. Swoggins remembered only his own copy of inventory. Noble remembered placing two copies of inventory list into envelope containing lading voucher. Noble stated envelope then put on top money sack nearest hydraulic door inside vault of Mormon State National Bank.

At approximately 9:45 A.M. Sunday, 22 August 1971, Chandler and Dunlop informed vault is empty. Subsequent search revealed no inventory lists or voucher forms in vault or premises. Chandler, Dunlop agree to say nothing of missing thirty-one million dollars ($31,000,000) until speaking with Klines, who was still unavailable. Klines first contacted by Dunlop and Chandler 8:00 P.M. Sunday, 22 August 1971. Subsequent to being told of robbery and continuing count to establish amount of missing money, Klines expressed fears over potential criticism of Treasury Department for mishandling transfer of thirty-one

147

million ($31,000,000) as well as for losing inventory lists. Klines ordered Chandler and Dunlop to continue not to reveal that thirty-one million dollars ($31,000,000) was missing from the vault.

At 7:00 A.M. Monday, 23 August 1971, Klines met with A. R. Roland, assistant to the Director, FBI, and explained matter. Subsequent to hearing missing thirty-one million dollars ($31,000,000) had not yet been declared to the auditors from Brink's Incorporated and Mormon State who were tabulating the loss, Roland suggested information continue to be withheld until facts could be confirmed. Roland dispatched special headquarters team to investigate Klines's statements. At 3:00 P.M. Monday, 23 August 1971, money counters for Brink's Incorporated, without authorization, announced publicly total amount stolen from vault was sixty-five hundred dollars ($6,500). Klines upset by revelation but deferred to Roland's wish that nothing yet be said about shipment of unfit currency. Confirmation of Klines's statements established. Late evening Monday, 23 August 1971, Roland referred matter directly to Director Hoover. Subsequent to reviewing Roland information, Director Hoover ordered press conference for following morning.

9:00 A.M. Tuesday, 24 August 1971, Director Hoover met with press and revealed an additional thirty-one million dollars ($31,000,000) stolen in robbery of Mormon State National Bank.

148

"Swiss cheese!" Billy Yates muttered as he stood beside the twelfth-floor teletype machine reading the message.

Denis Corticun, prim and immaculate, who was entering the communications cubicle, looked over at him. "What's that?"

"This report has more holes in it than Swiss cheese," Billy told him.

"What's your name?"

"Yates, W. B."

"From what field office?"

"He's from down on the eleventh floor," the communications agent said from a far desk. "They sent him up to get that teletype."

Corticun took out a pad and pen. "Your full name."

"William Butler Yates."

"Any relation to that poet?"

"Not unless he's Jewish."

". . . Jewish?"

"Jewish like in Hebrew. Gog like in synagogue. The other William Butler is Irish. I'm of the Hebraic persuasion. He spells his name Y-E-A-T-S. I spell mine Y-A-T-E-S."

Corticun scrutinized the flaxen-haired young man who looked every bit as Aryan as a recruitment poster for Hitler Youth, then jotted down the name. "I suggest, Mister Yates, you behave like a courier rather than an analyst and bring that report to Mister Sunstrom without delay or comment. Only Mister Sunstrom."

The second assistant medical examiner, as he routinely did on his midnight-to-eight A.M. shift, reviewed the day's autopsy reports to make certain everything was in order. The folder on Teddy Anglaterra, listed as a John Doe, stated the unknown cadaver had sustained severe beating on its head, shoulders and chest, possibly inflicted by a lead pipe, and then had been stabbed in the upper torso fourteen times. The cause of death was attributed to a stab wound in the right ventricle of the heart. Shortly after expiration the corpse was submerged in water, most likely river water from the look of secondary bruise marks and traces of sludge and water both on the skin and in the internal

149

organs. The time of death was placed between Thursday, August 19, and noon on Friday, August 20.

Noticing that no fingerprints had been taken, the conscientious second assistant M.E. went upstairs to the forensic department's cadaver room, brought out Teddy's body and printed all ten fingers and the heel of each hand twice, once on the autopsy form itself and then on a state police identification card. When the ink had dried he put the card into the morgue's latest toy . . . a facsimile machine for relaying fingerprints and photographs directly to the crime information center at state police headquarters. Transmission began at 2:45 A.M.

Sister Huxtable, her long-sleeved nightgown properly covered by a linen robe, hurried down the steps of the convent kitchen and out into the blackness of the night holding on high a butane lantern. Seventy-eight-year-old Sister Eleanora, attired in a scapulary chemise, hurried behind carrying a crowbar . . . followed the older Huxtable down the hillside and through the peach orchard and beyond the vegetable garden and pig sty and ancient stone dairy barn . . . on into a small, unelectrified brick building that once, long ago, had been used for sheep-dipping. A half-dozen more nuns, most of them hurriedly dressed in their Benedictine habits, stood near the far wall. The knocking had been going on for many minutes, Sister Eleanora was told. "It's like someone's trapped down there." Sister Eleanora took the butane lantern from Sister Huxtable, lowered it over a heavy iron cistern cover in the floor and with the crowbar clanked on the metal twice.

Three distinct answering thuds sounded from under the cover.

Sister Eleanora clanked four times more.

Six thuds echoed back.

Sister Eleanora turned and looked up at Sister Huxtable. Huxtable pondered, then nodded. Aged Eleanora gave the lantern to the nearest nun, with the crowbar tried to pry under the lid. The lid resisted. She began hitting it around the edges. The lid still wouldn't give. Sister Eleanora called for a chisel and hammer and when the tools arrived, chipped away at the heavy rim, managed to get the chisel down under the edge of the cover, slid the crowbar in beside the chisel, stood and leaned on and pushed the long end of the lever. Fell onto the bar with all her weight. Had other nuns fall onto it with her.

A hiss, like air escaping from a punctured tire, was heard. Grew louder. With a pop, a geyser of mud blew the heavy iron cover high into the air and away, splattered the cowering nuns.

Wiggles, jaybird-naked and covered from head to toe in mud, clambered out of the opening . . . free at last from the underground maze of tunnels and caves where he had been trapped since after robbing Mormon State. On his hands and knees he kissed the stone floor beside the cistern hole. Continued kissing.

He looked up. Saw the semicircle of thoroughly startled and mud-flecked nuns staring down at him. Crossed himself. Grabbed the nearest hand and kissed it. Thanked it for releasing him from purgatory. Began moving on his knees and kissing every hand, muttering snippeted Hail Mary's and Glory Be's and Confiteors. Then he leapt to his bare feet, thrust a mud-crusted wad of something into the hand of an astonished Sister Eleanora and limped rapidly off through the open rear door into the night.

At 3:30 A.M. the state police communications center, which since a call from Cub Hennessy some three hours earlier had been putting out alerts for all known criminals in Missouri with a capacity to perpetrate a Mormon State-like crime, transferred the just-received photocopies of Teddy Anglaterra's fingerprints into a transmission machine that tied into the identification division in Jefferson City as well as trooper headquarters in adjoining states.

Music woke Alice Maywell Sunstrom at 4:55 A.M. Downstairs she saw her husband standing over his desk in his bathrobe and slippers . . . obviously pleased. Spread on the blotter before him were photographs and open files.

"John, are you all right?" she asked.

"Best day of my life." He turned and looked at her. "Best except for the day I married you. I was just about to go up and wake you. You are beautiful."

She was also dumbstruck. It had been quite a while since Strom had said anything of this sort to her. "Can I fix you something to eat?"

"Drink would be more fitting." He indicated the silver wine bucket off to the side, a bucket containing an opened and chilling bottle of Dom Perignon. "Fetch it, will you, darling? Two glasses."

Alice, unsteady and unsure, did as she was asked and brought two filled glasses back, handed one to him.

He clinked his glass against hers, raised it in a toast. "Here's to all the misery I've caused you of late. I apologize and pledge it shall never happen again."

They went upstairs, and he made love to her for the first time in years. Her silent prayers had been answered. She wept in both joy and passion.

# Nine

Warbonnet Ridge is a three-quarter-mile-long, slate gray granite cliff rising out of the fast swirl of Mississippi River at a place called Cyclone Bend. The Bonnet runs in a due north-south direction, on the Missouri side of the river. Its upstream or northern or "tall" tip reaches an altitude of three hundred and fifty-one feet. The southern or downstream or "low" tip is an even hundred yards above river level. For most of the ascent from Low Tip toward Tall Tip, Warbonnet Ridge is seldom wider than fifty yards. Over the final fourth of the journey, to the northern crest, the width almost doubles. The drop to the forest floor, beside the Bonnet, is sixty-eight feet at Tall Tip and seventeen feet at Low Tip. No one quite recalls when the roadway leading up to Low Tip was built.

In 1958 Warbonnet Ridge was officially incorporated as part of the United States National Parks system. This had created problems, since in 1945 the same cliff had been incorporated as the northeasternmost corner of the city of Prairie Port. Older residents were vaguely aware that the State of Missouri had spent years working out a compromise whereby the park site remained within the city limits, but as a federal enclave. In exchange for their mediation, Missouri officials had managed to have the United States fund construction of a scenic, double-lane road running along atop 12.6 miles of rock palisades fronting the river between Warbonnet Ridge and Lookout Bluff downstream. Under whose orders the Army Corps of Engineers shored up sections of palisades over this same stretch was never made known. But they did shore up and shape. The initial deal between Missouri and the federal government seems to have also included the U.S. going fifty-fifty with the state in restoring a

153

historic corner of the city, the old pre-Civil War riverfront village of Steamboat Cove, which lay right behind Lookout Bluff.

Lookout Bluff is a far smaller and less imposing cliff than Warbonnet Ridge. Quite a few oldtimers recall when the city limits ended at Lookout Bluff. One or two even remember back to the days when Lookout Bluff was named Sentinel Bluff and Warbonnet Ridge was known as Lookout Ridge.

What no one, except a geologist, could be expected to know was that the Bonnet, as Warbonnet Ridge is generally called, was actually a coxcomb, a fifty- to ninety-six-yard-wide crown on a rock formation meandering northeast from the Salem Plateau and ending here on the Missouri side of the Mississippi River. The specific "rock" which the Bonnet fronts runs inland nearly three-quarters of a mile. In 1935 it was hollowed out.

Only a fraction of Prairie Port's population was old enough to have lived through the Rooseveltan era of WPA and CCC. In those Depression years and in this particular area, the singular job-creating project was MVA, the Mississippi Valley Authority . . . an ill-conceived predecessor to the Tennessee Valley Authority. Beyond building pyramids for the pure and Keynesian sake of putting people to work, MVA hoped to convert the untamed Mississippi River into a source of inexpensive hydroelectric power for lower Missouri and Illinois, northern Arkansas and Mississippi and western Kentucky and Tennessee. The project was also intended to provide lower Missouri with flood-control systems and mammoth-scale irrigation. Another objective was to somehow drain off underground leakage responsible for intermittent explosions of the salses, or mud volcanoes, at the township of Prairie Port, which in 1935 had a population of forty-six thousand inhabitants.

It was the core of the master plan that was faulty. Rather than build a dam in Tomahawk Hills just west of the Bonnet, behind which raw water power to turn turbines could be stored, the forgotten architects of MVA concocted what can only be ponderously described as an anti-gravitation bypass-infusion scheme. For whatever the explanation, the Mississippi flowed with extreme rapidity around one midstream island and two river bends. The

Bonnet stood on the outer arc of the second, and southerly, of these curves, Cyclone Bend. The intention of the engineers was to divert portions of the river, at the point of highest water velocity, directly into the waiting path of reaction turbines.

One area of high water speed was along the semi-arid riverbank of the valley lying at Warbonnet Ridge's immediate north. Here construction began on a series of canals which were to shunt river torrents into the turbines without losing a milliwatt of potential power. Basic, straight-edge geography and a New Dealish desire to, wherever possible, maximize work gangs, dictated the best place to station the first set of turbines . . . inside Warbonnet Ridge.

Huge chambers and channels and shafts were hollowed out of the massive granite formation on which the ridge rested. Pipes and valves and generators and pumps and Francis Reaction Turbines and ventilators and lighting and elevators were installed in the underground, six-level-deep hydroelectric plant. Boring and installation went on even farther down in the rock . . . all the space and equipment needed to operate the main terminus for both the flood-control and irrigation systems.

A second engineering feat, equally as remarkable as what had been achieved within Warbonnet Ridge, was the most extraneous of the project. The southward underground tunnels, needed to control lowland flooding as well as to provide irrigation, could very well have been dug out of the soft earth west of the riverfront palisades. Instead, the engineers chose to bore the wide subterranean channel within the rock palisades themselves. The rationale for this at the time was that the rocks were veined by caves and caverns, which if incorporated as part of the drainage-irrigation system could save appreciable construction costs and time. Chopping and blasting through the palisades proved infinitely more expensive and time-consuming as tunneling to the west would have, caused numbers of cave-ins and accidents, accidentally killed three workers and injured many more and missed connecting with Prairie Port's sewerage and water systems, which had been the original target, by a full one-eighth of a mile. Nor did the engineers bother connecting into the drainage and

155

water systems at the time. Their energies veered due west, burrowed through the earth and caves and caverns under the western section of Prairie Port searching for the elusive underground rivers of mud responsible for the intermittent eruptions.

A monumental and scandalously expensive undertaking occurred when the State of Missouri came to the rescue and built an eighth-of-a-mile-long tunnel under Lookout Bluff linking the MVA system to underground water and sewerage passageways of Prairie Port.

Two years and two months after it began, the MVA project was abandoned. Not one drop of river water had flowed into the turbines or through huge underground channels built for irrigation. Sections of the flood-drainage system were being tested, but like everything else, that too was shut down. Closed off with temporary wood barriers, but not permanently sealed, were the 12.6 miles of arterial tunnels linking the ridge with the water and sewerage systems of Prairie Port.

At the time the hydroelectric project was aborted, reforestation began. Thousands of federally paid unemployed descended on the recently constructed diversionary canals north of the Ridge, filled in some, remodeled others, planted trees and shrubs and created, in a formerly semi-arid valley, fifty square miles of forest and lagoons and streams. These legions then moved into the partially wooded Tomahawk Hills west of the Ridge and worked their wonders again.

Soon all that was left was the ridge itself: Lookout Ridge, according to the map titling of that day. As barren a slanting slab of granite clifftop and shrub as existed in the territory. Labor gangs shoveled into place a solid earth bridge connecting Low Tip with the hills below. Built a single-lane roadway up the bridge and on across the entire length of the ridge to Tall Tip. Reforesters swarmed forward with their picks and spades and seedlings and earth-laden dump trucks and flatbeds lugging full-grown or near to full-grown trees. And whatever was set into the thick blanket of clifftop soil seemed to batten, grew wildly, provided as unindigenous a display of species as ever had collected anywhere along the entire Mississippi. Dense stands of red oak and blue ash and white

156

ash and elder. Paper birch and black walnut. Hawthorn and horse chestnut and linden and sycamore and cherry. Maple and hazel and dogwood. Willow and hickory. Even a redwood. Lush along the man-laid ground were briers and hedges and vines and flowers, both wild and domestic . . . berry and juniper and honey-suckle and grape and rose and bluebell and sweet William. At any daylight moment from spring to October the ridge was a profusion of shapes and hues. In the fall the colors exploded. No explosion was more magnificent than that at Tall Tip. For some reason the trees at the northern and widest part of the ridge had grown taller than the rest, were, as winter neared, more multitudinous in colors, more tumultuously bright. Looking up from the far bank of the river to the north ridge, one fall day long past, a local newspaper writer was reminded, by the form and coloration of the forest at Tall Tip, of an Indian headdress. Of a warbonnet. He said so in print. Other locals began calling the place by that name. The 1947 city plat of Prairie Port cites the cliff as Warbonnet Ridge rather than Lookout Ridge, as had been the case on the previously printed official city map in 1937. On the 1947 plat the former Sentinel Bluff is titled Lookout Bluff . . .

Jez Jessup had little curiosity and less knowledge about how the names evolved as he drove toward the single-lane highway leading up to Low Tip. His attention, after fifteen miles of circuitous small talk, had come to focus on the latest snippet of resident office scuttlebutt: Billy Yates's run-in with Denis Corticun.

"Swiss cheese?" Jessup repeated. "All you said was Swiss cheese and Corticun filed a complaint about you with Strom?"

"Swiss cheese got his attention. The Jewish bit knocked his wind out."

"What Jewish bit?"

"My Jewish bit."

"Make sense."

"I'm Jewish."

"Since when?"

"Birth and possibly before."

"T'hell you say?" Jez just couldn't believe it. "You sure don't look like any Jewish person I ever saw."

"I'll get a nose job."

Jessup flashed his puckish grin. "I think you're kinda cute as is. So you say the teletype report is as full of holes as Swiss cheese and that you're a Jewish person and then what?"

"I go downstairs with the report and give it to Strom, and he tells me Corticun has filed a complaint about my being insubordinate and not wearing an identification card. It's the first I ever heard about needing an identification badge on the twelfth floor and I think it's the first Strom ever heard too, because he tells me to forget it. That's all there was to it."

"You should have bashed Corticun, like you bashed the cops in Columbus." The grin widened.

"Should have kept my mouth shut," Yates sighed.

"You did just fine. He apologized, didn't he?"

"I still should have kept my mouth shut."

"If you shoulda done anything, it's not malign Swiss cheese. Swiss is my favorite."

"Then you ought to read that report."

"I did. Didn't seem all that cheesy to me. Or holey."

"Jez, nothing makes sense in it. First off, we are expected to believe two bank presidents and a high Treasury Department official conspired to keep secret the theft of money for over forty-eight hours."

"Bank presidents are the first to fib about anything to do with money." Jez spoke matter-of-factly. "Particularly their own money. And how many government officials, Treasury Department or Bureau of Cuckoo Clocks, won't commit grand perjury rather than admit they made a mistake? Wake up, turkey. Live in the world around you."

"I'll give you bank presidents," Yates conceded. "What about coincidence? Suddenly thirty-one million dollars in untraceable bills finds its way into the bank vault at Prairie Port because of not one coincidence, but two. Two acts of God. Two breakdowns. First off, the incinerator used to burn unfit currency at the Fed Bank branch in New Orleans breaks down. Not only breaks down but seems unrepairable. Thirty-one million dollars in old bills piles up and nobody yet knows when the incinerators will be working.

158

"Act of God number two: the truck hired to take the money to an incinerator in St. Louis also breaks down. Presto, the truck limps into the nearest port-of-call, Mormon State National Bank. If you want a third coincidence, count in the missing list of serial numbers. The chief honcho of the Fed Bank in New Orleans, for some mysterious reason, makes up only two inventory lists of serial numbers for the hundred-dollar bills in the shipment. He keeps one copy and gives the other copy to one of the truck drivers. Or so he thinks. The banker finds the truck has driven off with both copies of the inventory list. Whammo, the envelope with both inventory lists, the only two lists that exist, is left inside the vault and is stolen along with everything else. Jez, how the hell far do you want to be carrying acts of God? And there's one other point of, if not coincidence, then contradiction. The armored truck leaves New Orleans for St. Louis with explicit instructions that if trouble occurs only one person is to be contacted —Arthur G. Klines, the assistant Treasury Department director, who not only engaged the truck in the first place, but solely arranged for the transfer of money from New Orleans to St. Louis. The truck does run into trouble, and Klines is there to take the phone calls and direct them to make an emergency stop at Prairie Port . . . drop the thirty-one million off at Mormon State until repairs can be made. But what happens the second time the truck calls him? When on Sunday the truck, after repairs, is en route back to the bank to pick up the money and continue its trip to St. Louis? Klines isn't there to get the truck's phone calls saying they've learned the bank has been robbed. All day Sunday, August twenty-second, Klines is unavailable to the truck crew as well as the bank president of Mormon State and the vice-president who heads the New Orleans Fed Bank. Klines, the maker of the plan, the core of the operation, can't be reached for twelve hours. So what say, old turkey? You still think that report isn't Swiss cheese?"

Jessup scratched at his neck. "You have a favorite sports team, Yates?"

"A few."

"Any of 'em ever great teams?"

"What's this got to do with the report?"

"Ever remember a great team that could do no wrong? Was perfect in all respects? Then one game everything goes haywire. The team suddenly can't do nothing right. It makes error after error. Mistakes a ten-year-old kid is smart enough not to make? For no rhyme or reason it all falls apart? Seems to me what's true for the team could be true for the transfer of that money, and more so. When mere mortal men start screwing up, sometimes there's no end in sight. Dumb error begets dumber error."

The car sped up the approach bridge and onto the one-lane asphalt roadway atop Warbonnet Ridge. Trees pressed in from both sides, blocked out the sun, made the narrow pavement seem a dark stream meandering through lush shrubbery on a great cavern's floor.

"Could be that you're right and I'm wrong," Jessup said. "That Corticun's flying squad of headquarters agents got everything fouled up. But we'll know better when the individual reports that summary was written from come in. Anything else on your mind I can help with?"

There was, but Yates shook his head.

Jez pulled the car to a stop on a concrete observation platform jutting out beyond cliff's edge three hundred feet above the river. Ahead, through the lazy morning mist, the mighty Mississippi wound northward across an infinite panorama of flatland and forest and farm. Directly below the platform, along the Missouri bank, were the clearly defined outlines of the long-abandoned canals and water basins built by the MVA thirty-four years before. Inland and stretching across tens of miles of hilly, tree-choked terrain, lay a huge reservoir lake.

Once out of the car and walking along a dirt path running back through the trees, Yates asked Jez, "Who planted this place?"

"Planted?"

Yates continued to survey the forest about him. Above him. Beneath him. "Who put in the vegetation? Trees, flowers, grass?"

"God."

"God never allows yellow poplar and blue juniper into the same space at the same time. Look over there. Three different

160

species of cottonwood. Plains, Narrowlead and Black cottonwood trees . . . none of them indigenous to this part of the country. That one there's a cedar elm . . . and there are no cedar elms in Missouri. No tawnyberry holly or dahoon or yaupon trees either. Only you've got one of each right behind us. This is some crazy forest. I see all kinds of species that don't belong here. If God grew it, he must have been on pot."

"You grow up around trees?" asked Jez.

"Nope."

"How come you know so much about them?"

"Because I used to know everything."

"Everything?"

"Everything. Absolutely everything there was to know, I knew."

Jez slowed his pace, cautiously estimated the taller, younger, poker-faced man walking behind him.

"Aren't you going to ask why I knew everything?" Yates said.

". . . Why did you know everything?"

"Because I studied everything. Granted, I was slightly weak on minor Peloponnesian deities, but besides that, I knew absolutely everything there was to know."

Several more steps were taken in silence before Jez asked, "You still know everything?"

Yates shook his head. "Nope."

"How come?"

"When I knew everything, no one asked me questions."

Waiting in a clearing directly ahead of them stood several wide-brim hatted, green-uniformed rangers from the Forestry Service. Beyond the rangers was a scattering of picnic tables and beyond that a phone booth. A ranger lieutenant, when introductions had been exchanged, thanked Jez and Yates for responding so promptly to his call to the Bureau office. "The Geo guys discovered something you might want to see."

"Geo guys?" Jez questioned as he and Yates accompanied the lieutenant toward a red marking flag rising up from the tall grass at the other end of the clearing.

"Geological Survey," the ranger said. "The group trying to find

161

out what's causing the mud trouble west of Prairie Port. Earlier this morning they ended up here."

Jez glanced around. "Where?"

"Right under you."

Despite being marked by a red flag, the moss-covered hatch in the high grass had gone unnoticed by Yates and Jez until they were nearly at it.

The lieutenant said, "I thought there was nothing underneath here except solid rock. The Geo guys say someone else knew better. Knew about this hatch and used it. They say it could have been the bank robbers you're looking for. Check the hinges on the hatch. They've been oiled."

Jez knelt down, bent back the tall grass. The ground around the hatch was well trodden. The moss had been neatly cut away from the two hinges. Touching the hinges, he felt oil and grease.

The lieutenant pulled the heavy metal hatch open, lowered himself onto the ladder in the circular hole beneath, said this was an auxiliary, or emergency, means of egress and disappeared into the darkness beneath. Yates followed. Then Jez.

A lightless descent ended on a narrow, dimly lit catwalk which wound several hundred feet through a curving crevice in the rock to an iron door. Passing beyond the door, Yates and Jez found themselves on yet another catwalk . . . this one looking down into an immense six-story-deep chamber cut in the rock heart of Warbonnet Ridge. Crisscrossing the vast space, at various altitudes, were pipes and support struts and other metal walkways and lines of glowing unglazed light bulbs. More lines of glowing lights rose perpendicularly up the rock. On the floor, eighty feet below, lay bare concrete foundations on which electrical turbines once reposed. Moving among the foundations were tiny metal hats of the inspecting engineers and scientists.

The ranger lieutenant reached the end of the catwalk and pulled open the railing gate on a cageless elevator of two seats fastened to a solitary rail which ran eighty feet to the floor below.

"You want us to ride this?" Jez said.

"Or use the ladder over there." The lieutenant pointed back

162

across the short walkway to metal rungs trailing down the rock face.

Yates, gingerly, moved out onto the far seat of the open elevator. Jez, very slowly, got into the near seat. The ranger lieutenant shouted down. Metal hats far beneath tipped upward. Hands waved. A yellow metal hat crossed the floor to the wall, extended an arm, pulled something. Whirring sounded from an unseen generator. The elevator started down, jerkily.

"What the hell is this place?" Jez asked.

"Beats me," Yates said.

"I thought you knew everything."

"Only above ground."

A willowy yellow-helmeted man in chinos and lightweight safari shirt introduced himself as Henry St. Ives, divisional director for the Missouri Valley Geological Survey and nominal chief of the team of experts trying to neutralize the mud eruptions. Also in the party welcoming Jez and Yates were Chester Safra, a short, doll-faced hydrologist from the Mississippi River Control Authority, and Jamie E. K. Thurston, senior engineer for the Missouri Power and Electric Company.

"Never dreamed this operation existed," St. Ives said. "Should have, I suppose. Heard rumors of it long enough. Some of the others had too. Only no one we know ever set foot inside. Imagine our feeling when we stumbled in here last night."

"What is it?" asked Jessup.

Chester Safra held out rolls of dusty, discolored blueprints. "Pump-priming idiocy."

"That is very clever, Chester. Very double-entendre." St. Ives applauded once and turned back to Yates and Jessup. "Chester's terminally Republican, which is to say, the initials FDR are poison to his tongue. What we are standing in is New Dealism at its fiercest."

"It didn't work," Safra insisted. "*None* of it worked."

"Not thirty-four years ago, Chester," St. Ives agreed. "But someone has certainly put part of it back into operational shape and recently. Mister Jessup, Mister Yates, we are gathered at the

163

common crux of everyone's individual problems. Mister Thurston's power shortages, Mister Safra's and my mud . . . and most definitely, your robbery . . . stem from in here. Come."

The party descended a concrete staircase past two more levels of empty chambers, with St. Ives giving a history of MVA. They continued down through fifteen feet of solid rock into a low-ceilinged, rectangular room, two of whose adjacent walls were constructed of glass. Glass looking out on utter blackness.

St. Ives slapped a hand against the plaster wall bearing an eight-foot-long, five-foot-high, faded overlay drawing of the Missouri Valley Authority of the early 1930s. "There it is, the entire system. MVA, in all its glory."

"Pork-barreling!" Safra called it. "Trotting, not creeping, socialism."

St. Ives turned to Jessup and Yates. "Thirty-four years ago, in 1937, the electricity-producing aspect of the project was closed down without ever having been used. The machinery was mothballed, and all the chambers above us were sealed shut.

"The irrigation-flood facilities were kept operative and made self-sufficient. Its terminal, where we now are, was equipped with its own power plant and master-control apparatus regulating the water flow throughout the system as well as up here. Should the power plant, or any part of it, fail, plans were formulated for connecting into whatever source of commercial electricity was near." His finger moved back onto the wall overlay, stopped at a point west of Warbonnet Ridge. "This was another phase of the MVA, construction of a reservoir network in the hills behind the Bonnet to supplement both the city's water supply and the irrigation system. With the hydroelectric capabilities aborted, it was hoped expansion of the reservoirs could make them the primary source for irrigation water. Plans were revised. An underground tunnel was built linking this irrigation terminal in the Bonnet to the reservoirs under construction in the hills. It was the discovery of these tunnels yesterday afternoon that led us here."

St. Ives checked his notes. "The entire MVA was disbanded in 1938. Work stopped on the incompleted reservoirs. The irrigation-flood control center here in the rock, like the hydroelectric facilities before, was sealed closed. The irrigation tunnels themselves were not sealed, simply left to lie fallow. The water gates in the tunnels were also left to rot. Before long they were pretty much forgotten. All of MVA was." He went on to say how early in World War II a need for heavy electricity-producing equipment made the government open up the hydroelectric plant above them, and they found the machinery was missing. No one knew where it had gone or who had taken it. "Those chambers were resealed more permanently than before. Nobody seems to have remembered the irrigation-flood control area down here, including the looters.

"In 1954 the State of Missouri, with federal funding, resumed construction of one of the reservoirs abandoned in 1938, an immense basin more than a mile deep in places that today is called Tomahawk Hill reservoir or lake. The state engineers had no information or interest about where the old water gates in the original basin led, even though there were two sets of these gates —some ten small ones built directly into the reservoir's eastern wall and two enormous slab gates built directly into the basin's floor near the eastern end. The state engineers even ignored the fact that every gate, floor or wall, was counterweighted and hydraulicized. They let all this be and installed a new system of gates miles away at the other end of the reservoir, on the western side . . .

"And those old gates are what was opened over the weekend, Mister Jessup and Mister Yates, three of those original gates. The two enormous slab gates in the basin floor and one of the small wall gates. That is what caused the flooding and the mud. The fact that three thirty-four-year-old gates were opened is startling enough. How it was accomplished is even more amazing.

"This, where we're standing, was the nerve center of the irrigation-flood system abandoned in the 1930s." He played his penlight on a wooden counter running the length of the dark glass. "The electrical equipment controlling water flow throughout the tunnels rested here."

The light beam shifted onto a faded line-rendering thumb-

165

tacked to the counter surface. "It's a 1937 electrical wiring chart for the whole system. For everything from the tunnel's diversionary locks twelve-point-six miles south of here to the forgotten gates in the reservoir a mile and a half to the west . . . and someone has rewired part of this system . . . rewired it in the last few weeks."

The beam moved back and in tighter on the electrical wiring chart. "If you look closely at the plan you'll see pen markings for what areas the connected wires are controlling . . . it's everything in the main tunnels between here to right there." St. Ives's finger tapped at a distinct check mark on the faded paper. "The tunnel directly under Mormon State National Bank.

"The crucial element, at the risk of sounding melodramatic, is behind us." St. Ives's penlight swept along to the wall at their backs, stopped on a large, rusty iron box imbedded in the plaster, with two forked switches, one on either side, in the down or "off" position.

"That is your culprit," St. Ives told Jessup and Yates. "The aider and abettor in the robbery at Mormon State National Bank . . . Mister Thurston is better qualified to provide specifications."

Jamie E. K. Thurston, senior engineer for Missouri Power and Electric, went to the wall with his own, more powerful flashlight on. "This is the original fuse box/circuit-breaker. It wasn't a standard make even in the 1930s. I would say it was manufactured specifically for this operation, as was most of the other equipment down here."

Thurston opened the door of the box. The fuses within were thick and glistening and a half foot high. "These are not the original fuses," he said. "They are far more resistant than the specifications on the old chart, and as you can see, they are brand new. They were handmade. Expertly made."

The light beam played on a thick cable descending from the bottom of the box, new cable. "This lead line was recently installed as well. Tracking it down through the floor, you'll find it stretches a mile and a quarter through a side tunnel and ties into the main power line near the highway. Only a suicidal son-of-a-gun would try splicing into that much voltage midline. The splice

166

was made hot and midline. That's one reason we hadn't found it till now. He did it midline and hot."

"Is that what caused the power failures?" Jessup asked. "His splicing into the main power supply?"

"Not by itself. This had more to do with it." Thurston seized the forked switch on the right side of the fuse box. Pushed it up and on.

Moaning resonated. The control booth shook. Whirring replaced moans. Shaking ceased. Dim-burning electric light bulbs grew visible in the blackness beyond the glass walls of the room, became brighter . . . jumped in intensity. Illuminated below the shorter of the adjacent glass walls was a vast room in which stood two massive generators and six large engines. The view through the longer glass wall was of brightly burning light bulbs in an enormous square concrete chamber. Twenty yards in was a large wood-and-metal water gate. A closed gate, five feet high.

"Only one of the two generators has been activated," Thurston said as he moved up to the shorter glass window overlooking the machinery. "Everything you see down there is original equipment, the same ones installed back in 1936. Whoever put them into working shape was something of a wizard. Those are old-fashioned contraptions, old-time power-guzzling machines. They're guzzling three times what they did back in the 1930s because the two generators were not only reactivated, they were converted into motors as well . . . and connected to the high-voltage line out west. Instead of creating electricity, they were using it. Everything you see down there was sucking power out of the city's electrical supply. The generator running now and the two engines nearest it are the power sources for the tunnel between here and Mormon State National Bank. Most of the water-control gates in the tunnel are operated by it. If the criminals used any sort of electrical devices . . . air hammers, drills, lights . . . this system would more than provide the power. The two engines and generator by themselves probably are responsible for the power losses and dimouts in the earlier part of last week. But not for what happened on Friday or over the weekend. Help was required for that."

167

Thurston reached for the fuse box, let his fingers rest on the handle of the second switch of the fuse box. "This activates the other generator and the last four engines. The major blackouts on Friday took place not long after this switch was thrown." His hand moved away from the box. "The second generator and four engines are what was required to open the sluice gates in the reservoir. Those gates were so old and resistant that the machines literally blew a fuse getting them to move. Or I should say, blew Prairie Port's fuse. There are indications that no more than one of those reservoir gates was ever meant to be opened, that opening the others may have been an afterthought, as will become evident when we go downstairs."

The party descended into the immense concrete chamber beneath the glass-fronted control booth. Along the base of two of the area's three walls were large round openings which had been bricked closed. The fourth, or southern, wall was missing, had only the wood–and–metal water gate.

"This structure is a rudimentary shunting terminal not untypical of engineering beliefs in the 1920s and 1930s," Chester Safra, the expert on hydrology, explained. "As you can see, those pipe openings in the north wall beneath the booth have been sealed shut, but they were the original source of intake from which this entire system evolved. Through those unsealed mouths, thirty-five years ago, was supposed to have gushed the discarded river water which had been used to turn the turbines of the hydroelectric plant overhead."

Safra pointed to the bricked-over holes in the east wall. "Those were one of two routes of water outtake. The pipes behind them go right through the rock base of Warbonnet Ridge and pour into the Mississippi River." He pointed to the water gate at the southern end of the chamber, started walking to it. "That was the second route of outtake. By closing the valves in the eastern wall, the water would head for there."

Jessup and Yates moved up beside Safra, looked beyond the gate into a high, wide concrete tunnel running from their right to their left, from northwest to southeast. The drop beyond the gate to slowly flowing water was twelve feet. A narrow metal stairway zigzagged down the wall beneath to a rusty metal dock and several bobbing motor boats. Farther to the left, water rippled over a series of closed gates.

On Safra's instructions, Jez and Yates peered past those gates to where the tunnel began to curve due south. Lines of round openings were visible on the far, or western, wall.

"That is your second source of intake water," he told them. "Those are sewerage and drainage tubes leading down from the western hills, bringing in the natural rainshed and spillage. On the other side of the tunnel are the outtake pipes." Safra pointed in the opposite direction . . . pointed uptunnel to the northwest. "That's where the reservoir is . . . where the third source of intake water can be found."

Thurston took over. "All of this, all the intake and outtake systems, whatever the initial water sources, was controlled from the booth we were just in . . . until a recent innovation was made."

They went down the metal steps on the tunnel wall and onto the dock, with Thurston saying, "Going right in this tunnel for a mile and a half brings you to the water gates in Tomahawk Hill reservoir. Follow the tunnel five miles to the left and you're at Mormon State National Bank. Keep following beyond the bank seven and a half miles and you're at downtown Prairie Port."

Thurston reached into the water, searched below the surface, brought up a long, rectangular metal instrument panel. Attached to its underside, and trailing back down into the water, were several thick cables and twenty-one wires. "I believe this is how your criminals originally meant to regulate the water flow in this tunnel. Automatically. It's a timing device. A homemade device, but ingenious." He held the instrument out for all to see, tilted up the bottom. "Those cables tie directly into the generators . . . can activate or shut off the generators one at a time or together. The smaller wires lead to the intake-outtake gates down the tunnel to the left . . . the section of tunnel between here and the Mormon State bank.

"To make the system operative you set the timing mechanism on the inside. At the specified time the device turns on the generators, then it opens the outtake gates and closes the intake

169

gates. This fills the tunnel with water. At a later moment the device shuts the intake gates and opens the outtake gates. This drains the tunnel of water. The device then shuts down the generator.

"That's how it's now programmed. The original intention of the device's design was to use the natural watershed from the hills for flooding the tunnel . . . with an exception. A wire may have been connected to one of the small water gates in the side of the reservoir. But I believe some last-minute adjustments were attempted."

Thurston turned the instrument and tapped its end. "If you look inside you'll see the timing mechanism is scratched and dented, as if someone clumsy, or in a very big hurry, was trying to turn it off or alter it." He displayed the other end of the device, indicated a large connecting screw. "This was probably the pole for the sluice gates at the reservoir. One of the small gates in the reservoir's eastern wall. A decision to open other reservoir gates seems to have been made on the spur of the moment. The line attached to this pole was most likely disconnected and brought over here." Thurston walked to the other edge of the dock, indicated a group of cables running along the tunnel wall. "These lead to every reservoir sluice gate, those in the wall as well as the two in the basin floor. The other ends of the cable have been attached directly to the second generator and its four support engines. The splicing and taping here is sloppier than with any of the other connections. It's likely a second person did this work. Someone who was racing the clock. One way or another, the hookup was completed by eight Friday night and tested out right away. We estimate it took another four hours of adjustment before they got the gates to open. Three gates in all . . . one in the reservoir wall, two on the basin floor."

"Got the bottom gates to open," Safra emphasized. "Dismiss the side gate and it's a trickle. Bottom gates opened! Discharged twice as much water as the system was capable of containing. Demolished whole sections of the tunnel network. Sent tens of millions of gallons of water west for the mud instead of going into Prairie Port's sewers and then out into the Mississippi River."

170

Safra reached over and patted the time device Thurston was holding. "All because of this little hell box. Our good Mister Thurston omitted mentioning that no one shut this hell box off until we came along late last night."

"The box went on operating?" Jessup asked.

Thurston nodded. "It didn't start the initial flooding on Friday night, but it activated shortly after and shut down the generators. It didn't matter that the device wasn't directly connected to the reservoir gates. Those gates were tied in to the second generator, and the device controlled that generator along with the other. The reservoir gates were hydraulicized. Once the power to them was cut off, they automatically closed. It was holding them open which caused the power drains and blackouts. Opening them under that much water was like tilting up one end of a New York City skyscraper."

". . . You said the initial flooding took place on Friday night," Jez said. "Which Friday night?"

"Last Friday, August twentieth . . . the night of your robbery."

"We haven't established when, precisely, over the weekend, the perpetration occurred," revealed Jez.

Safra put in, "No robbery, I can assure you, could have happened in the cave under the bank after the first flooding occurred on Friday. The area was totally inundated."

Jez asked, "Do you have some idea when on Friday night the robbers would have had to leave the cave or be inundated?"

"Eleven-forty-five," Thurston answered.

"Not eleven sharp or one A.M. Saturday?" pressed Jez. "Not maybe ten–fifty or midnight?"

"No, sir," Thurston said. "Our monitoring equipment recorded three specific incidents of power dips other than the ones that began in the middle of last week. Those earlier dips bear the characteristics set when the first generator is operative. The three dips I'm referring to, the later dips, are identical to the characteristics made when the second generator is operative.

"The first of those three dips came at eight P.M. Friday and was brief. This, we now know, indicates the second generator was activated and immediately turned off. Activated and turned off,

171

I assume, as a test to see if the equipment would function. Twelve minutes later, at eight–twelve P.M., the first blackout occurred in the Prairie Port area . . . a result of the second generator being activated again and given a trial run of perhaps fifteen minutes.

"The dips disappeared until eleven forty-five P.M. Then the largest dip of all was registered. I have little doubt that's when the gates opened in the reservoir. When both generators and all six engines were operative. When eighteen million gallons of water came through."

Yates looked to Safra. "Why would Prairie Port's Department of Sewerage show no record of excessive water in its system until late Saturday afternoon and early Sunday morning?"

Thurston answered for Safra. "The second electric dip at eight–twelve Friday was sharp enough to put their monitoring equipment out of commission. Theirs and the Water Department's. We have special instruments for just such an incident. Their measuring equipment was affected the way a digital clock is affected when power is shut off and then restored. It blinks on and off repeating the time of the disruption. This happened to the display sign on the Prairie Farmer Building. The Prairie Farmer outdoor timeboard kept repeating eight–twelve P.M. that night until it shorted out. It seems," Thurston said not unkindly to Yates and Jessup, "that your robbers presented a calling card of their intentions for all of Prairie Port to see . . . the flashing eight–twelve on top of the Prairie Farmer Building on Friday night."

Safra spoke up. "If what the newspapers say is so, and the thieves escaped by boating through the tunnels, which is the only practical way they could leave, it might be that they wanted to catch the Treachery. The Treachery is the curious midstream current flowing in the river along Prairie Port and below. It's a fascination for us hydrologists. The Treachery comes and goes for no apparent scientific reason, but on a very projectable schedule. We thought it might have something to do with the inland flooding and mud so we got that schedule. The Treachery would have been strong until one A.M. Saturday, August twenty-first, until an hour and a quarter after the first and major flooding by eighteen

172

million gallons of water. If the thieves had gone through the tunnels under Prairie Port and gotten out into the river and onto the Treachery by one A.M. they would have been carried forty miles downstream faster than by car. If they reached the river after one, motors or paddles would have been needed. The Treachery disappears promptly at one A.M. Saturday, August twenty-first . . . does not start up again for another seventy-six days."

Jessup stood mute.

"Those later floodings," Yates asked, "the ones after Friday night, August twentieth, did they occur at regular intervals?"

"Precisely at ten twenty-two, as the timing device prescribed," Thurston answered. "As I mentioned, the device's inner mechanism seems to have been tampered with, but it was set for ten twenty-two. Neither A.M. nor P.M. was stipulated. There was a second tunnel flood at ten twenty-two Saturday night, August twenty-first. Twelve hours later, at ten twenty-two Sunday morning, there was a third. They were even larger and longer than the first flood. Between them, they spilled another forty million gallons of water into the tunnels. The electricity the generators required for the Saturday and Sunday flooding caused the severest power dips and blackouts . . . each at ten twenty-two, A.M. or P.M., as the case might be. After the Sunday morning flood the timing device shifted to a twenty-four-hour cycle and far shorter operative periods. Floods were recorded at ten twenty-two A.M. Monday and ten twenty-two A.M. Tuesday. The accompanying power dips were less extreme. We estimate seven million gallons were discharged from the reservoir at each instant. Overall, in the five-day period from Friday until we disconnected the device late last night, Tuesday, a total of sixty-two million gallons of water was released into the tunnels . . . the first half of which flowed right through the Prairie Port sewer system and on out into the Mississippi River . . . the second half of which was diverted inland, west to the mud."

Jez took the timing device from Thurston, turned it over, studied the maze of wires and cables. "What sort of person would have the skills to build this . . . to manage the other electrical and mechanical work? To make fuses and read old charts and rewire

173

and splice into high-voltage lines and get antique generators going?"

Thurston shook his head. "No one I've come across in thirty years with Missouri Power and Electric. Maybe one of those Ph.D.s at the university or up at the aerospace labs could have. They're pretty strong in the wizard department. As I said before, there was wizardry at work down here."

St. Ives's motorboat led the way through the opening water gates of the partially flooded tunnel. Beyond the gates St. Ives throttled up, trained his twin flood beams on the bending blackness ahead. Thurston rode with St. Ives. Yates and Jessup followed in the boat operated by Safra.

"How did you know about the Sewerage Department report?" Jez yelled to Yates over the motor roar.

"Remember I used to know everything?" Yates called back.

"Cut the crap."

"I'm inquisitive. I read every report coming into the office that I can . . . including the one from the Sewerage Department."

St. Ives shouted, trained his search beams on the line of large round holes in the wall to their right. Safra explained these were the mouths of the drainage pipes leading down from the hills above, intake pipes the timing device had opened and closed.

St. Ives, with another holler, turned his search beams straight up in the tunnel. On the ceiling far above was silt and mud . . . residue, Safra explained, from the highwater mark of the rampaging floodings.

The first stop, five miles from where they began under Warbonnet Ridge, was at the platform leading into the passageway that brought them out into the cave beneath the Mormon State National Bank, where a special team of FBI lab technicians was at work chipping away the caked mud that encrusted every surface.

Seven and a half miles farther downtunnel, St. Ives and Safra cut the motors, let their boats drift into an array of flares and electric lights. Yates and Jez saw scores of frogmen working in

174

the shallow water, piling up sandbags and reenforcing walls of what seemed a wide, high cathedral-like structure.

This, St. Ives told them, was the bypass terminal beneath Lookout Bluff, a subterranean diversion point leading into Prairie Port's sewerage system immediately south and connecting to the spur tunnel running due west . . . the very spur tunnel built thirty-four years ago to drain out the caves and crevices beneath the western sectors of Prairie Port and which had remained sealed until the recent flood smashed it open.

"It will stay open a good while now," Safra predicted. "Draining it out will take years."

Yates asked, "What are the divers doing?"

"Buttressing for the backlash," Safra told him. "We'll be trying to tap the underground mud crown west of the city within the hour. Drilling down into the mud dome and easing the pressure before it erupts. If it erupts before we drill, or if we misdrill and cause it to erupt, a river of mud could be coming in this direction. They're preparing for the river."

The boats putted across the bypass terminal, entered the city's sewerage tubes.

"This is where your robbers went." Safra was emphatic as he pointed ahead. "They rode the crest of the water through here and then on to the sewers ahead."

"Why couldn't they have gone west, into the spur tunnel?" Yates asked.

"There wasn't enough room to get through on Friday night," Safra said. "It wasn't until later, until the water began backing up in the spur tunnel and collapsing the walls, that there was enough room. Even so, area and velocity was with the sewage tubes. They acted like vacuums by then, sucked everything through with tremendous force . . . sucked tile right off the ceiling."

Safra's flash beam swung up to the ceiling. Tile chip after tile chip was missing.

The motorboats came out onto the Mississippi River at the far southern end of Prairie Port . . . came out 21.6 miles downstream from Mormon State National Bank. A helicopter was waiting . . .

175

# Ten

Teddy Anglaterra, ever since washing up dead on South Beach on Monday night, had been bureaucracy's child. South Beach was a county beach even though it fell within the city limits of Prairie Port. When Teddy's body, mistakenly thought to be alive, was picked up by the River Patrol ambulance, it should have been taken, dead or alive, to University Hospital, a county facility. Instead Teddy had arrived at Missouri Presbyterian Hospital, which was private. Had Presbyterian admitted Teddy and made out his death certificate, copies would have been sent to the appropriate city, county and state authorities. Since he had obviously been murdered, a state inquest would have been mandatory. Had the inquest decided further investigation was required, the matter would have fallen to the state police. Presbyterian Hospital, however, had refused to accept Teddy and ordered he be shipped to city morgue. And he was, in one of Presbyterian's own ambulances rather than in the River Patrol vehicle which had brought the body over originally.

City morgue was situated in the basement of University Hospital. The two facilities, while having direct access to one another, had separate entrances and receiving docks. Had Presbyterian's ambulance brought the body directly into city morgue, Teddy would have become exclusively a city case and the Prairie Port PD would have been notified. The ambulance, as was not unusual, delivered him into the main emergency room of University Hospital, which once again made Teddy a county ward. Seeing that the ambulance belonged to Presbyterian, the administrative nurse classified Teddy as "a Missouri Presbyterian Hospital patient-on-exchange, deceased" and made out the ap-

176

propriate admittance papers but nothing else . . . no mandatory "suspected murder notification," no "unidentified person report." The nurse assumed, erroneously, that Presbyterian Hospital had followed correct procedure and notified all city, county and state agencies of the unknown murder victim.

Rather than perform an autopsy on an unidentified body, as it had the authority to do, University farmed the task out to city morgue, which more and more had begun to handle county cases such as this. The city medical examiner, rather than bring Teddy down into the basement morgue, took him up to the second-floor operating area in the hospital wing housing the state university medical school, where he performed the autopsy in front of a group of forensic students. Because it did not occur on its own premises, the morgue did not list the event on its daily log of autopsies . . . a log made available to law-enforcement agencies on request. The med school kept no records whatsoever on such educational procedures.

The medical examiner put a copy of Teddy's autopsy report in his own file in the basement and sent the original upstairs to the County Medical and Health Administration on the third floor of the building. Adhering to correct procedure, the M.E. notified no one else of the incident. A clerk in County Med and Health, assuming Presbyterian Hospital would make the necessary follow-up contacts on what was listed as Presbyterian's patient, did absolutely nothing except file the report in its own record room and send Presbyterian a brief teletype resume of the M.E.'s findings. Presbyterian had no record of the unidentified person referred to in the teletype and disposed of the communication.

Teddy, through it all, remained in a refrigerated locker on the second-floor hospital wing occupied by the state med school. Statistically he was a nonentity, had not been included on any city or county or state official tabulation of unidentified persons or murder victims—or even as a death, for that matter. The state police had put out a five-state make for Teddy's fingerprints with instructions to contact city morgue if information was available, but that was the extent of it. This sort of macabre snafu in ac-

177

counting for dead bodies had occurred before in Prairie Port. Occasionally an incident was publicized, but with little outcry ensuing.

At 11:50 A.M. Wednesday, as Jessup, St. Ives and Safra helicoptered west toward the mud fields and Thurston drove Billy Yates into downtown Prairie Port, Teddy's body was identified in the med school's cadaver room by a short, muscular young man in a tight black T-shirt and sharply creased chinos who produced verification he was the decedent's nephew, Fred C. Anglaterra, of Sparta, Illinois. Fred, whose well-coifed hair was parted in the middle, volunteered no information as to how Teddy might have ended up in Prairie Port, nor was he asked. He merely filled out a med school release form stating he intended to take Teddy back home to Sparta for burial and that he had a hearse waiting outside. The med school had to summon its dean, who in turn signed a form releasing Teddy to the authority that in this instance held jurisdiction over the state and med school. Then the medical examiner made out his own forms that released Teddy to the agency that held sway over the morgue under these circumstances: the County Medical and Health department three floors above in University Hospital.

. . . Jessup, Safra and St. Ives watched the spinning bits lower, one by one, from a line of derricks set along a field not far from Laggerette Hunt and Ride Club, saw them chew into the ground and spin straight down, spin deeper, spin from earshot. For a long time silence held. Then a tremor was felt. Hissing echoed. Hissing from all sides of the field. The land quaked and rumbled. Mud geysered up from under the second derrick, spouted twenty feet into the air. The third and first and fourth derricks followed suit, erupted into towers of gushing mud. The pressure deep beneath the surface had been tapped, the incipient mud volcano neutralized.

. . . The clerk in the County Med and Health office stapled the release forms from the state med school and city M.E. to the county release forms, stamped and signed the form on behalf of the county, recorded the $50 in cash and $150 in traveler's checks that had been handed him and made out a receipt, gave the receipt and release forms and an out-of-state hearse permit to the short, muscular young man in the black T-shirt and chino pants.

. . . Happy de Camp and Ted Keon went over the latest data obtained at state police headquarters. Neither Teddy Anglaterra nor his vital statistics appeared on the long list of names or descriptions of persons reported dead or missing in the immediate five-state area since the robbery. Nor would they appear in the future. Except for two secondary sources of information which law-enforcement agencies seldom bothered searching, the files of Prairie Port's medical examiner and the County Medical and Health records, Teddy Anglaterra, dead or alive, did not exist.

Ailing, sixty-eight-year-old Wilkie Jarrel, bolstered by an unseen arm at his back, stood against a tree on his vast estate and for the first time in his life gave a press interview, telling a battery of television cameras that he would personally match all reward monies posted for information leading to the apprehension of the Mormon State robbery perpetrators. It was a matter any public-spirited citizen was obliged to become involved in if possible.

Teddy Anglaterra rode in the back of the rented hearse being driven by the young man in the tight black T-shirt, the corpse's self-described nephew. Beside the driver sat a much taller man. The two of them had dropped Teddy from the airplane into the Mississippi River on the previous Monday evening. Both were delighted with how things had gone.

Strom, pacing and poker-faced and puffing his pipe as he listened to Yates's detailed report on what had gone on at Warbonnet Ridge and in the tunnels earlier that day, was pleased. Pleased that so much relevant information had been garnered this early in the investigation. The time of the robbery was now established. The entire getaway route had been laid out. The source of the flooding was known and the means. Critical physical evidence had been obtained, a timing-control device and

179

handcrafted fuses and wires and wire splices and blueprints and charts and everything else required to convert two old-fangled generators into motors and make them, with the other machinery in the Bonnet, operative. This new physical evidence might provide what the previous already in tow, the money sack and dollar bills and light bulbs and wire and segments of rubber boat, had not: a latent fingerprint. The new evidence might prove traceable to places or persons who could lead them a step closer to the unknown perpetrators, if not directly to the perpetrators.

Equally important for Strom, a profile on one of the actual robbery gang members was becoming clear, the so-called wizard of electricity. The wizard more than anyone or anything else kindled Strom's guarded optimism for a fast break in the case being within their grasp. He counseled Yates and Cub that the strictest confidentiality must be imposed on what they had just learned.

But Denis Corticun told the world.

# Eleven

Haughty Denis Corticun, as Strom liked to call him, showed another face. After blowing up at Billy Yates and hurling harsh words at other personnel the Tuesday night of his return from Washington, he had become progressively more unhaughty. Granted, he was still wearing his pinstriped suit when, early the next morning, he went down to the eleventh-floor office and sought out Yates and openly apologized for being so nasty . . . the sight of the pinstripes did elicit a chuckle or two from several of the resident agents. But when he came down an hour later and reaffirmed that Strom had the final say with Romor 91 and vowed that he and his twelfth-floor personnel would assist the investigation in any way Strom wished, Corticun was in shirt–sleeves with his tie loose. Returning to the residency office several hours after that . . . accompanied by a brand-new switchboard and another teletype machine as well as seventeen autographed copies of J. Edgar Hoover's *Masters of Deceit* for the resident agents and seventeen tortoise-shell lockets with a picture of Edgar himself for their wives . . . Corticun was wearing a sweat shirt, jeans and tennis shoes. When he passed out the books and lockets, he was downright friendly with the men. Even joked and laughed. And his throat-clearing had disappeared.

Corticun became as convivial on the twelfth floor as he had been on the eleventh. He created in a short time both a physical and emotional environment of efficiency and care. The thirty incoming FBI agents meant to support the eleventh-floor residency were processed and billeted and given assignments and twelfth-floor desks and were eagerly at work within hours of their arrival. Twenty-five secretaries and stenographers from other offices were flown to Prairie Port until clearance could be gotten on local office personnel. Corticun gave the eleventh floor first priority on the steno pool. Gave the eleventh floor priority on almost everything. Went along with most suggestions from the eleventh-floor Caretakers while tending to the Prairie Port case load. Everyone from the twelfth floor liked Denis Corticun. Quite a few converts were being made on the floor below as well.

Decor and layout lent a surprisingly un-FBI atmosphere to the vast twelfth-floor office. Absent were the traditional bare-wood austerity and small rooms. The space was open and multileveled. Design and colors varied for different areas of operation. The ten agents assigned to handling the five-hundred-odd routine cases of the Prairie Port residency were in a main-level section of office which had a deep orange and white motif . . . deep orange rugs, white vinyl desks, orange vinyl desk lamps, white plastic room-dividers for privacy. The pool of twenty agents on hold for eleventh-floor Romor 91 chores and assisting the ten other agents with the Prairie Port case load, should no Romor 91 assignments be forthcoming, had a turquoise and eggshell-white color scheme. A glass-enclosed communications section, containing three teletype machines, four radio transmitter-receivers and an auxiliary switchboard, was on an elevated platform covered by dark gold carpeting. Gold trim adorned its black vinyl desks and filing cabinets. The glass-enclosed media section, with white copying machines and small printing presses and a television monitor screen connected to the press conference room, was also elevated and carpeted in green, with green trim on the white vinyl desks and cabinets. Silver and eggshell-white was the choice for the small office Corticun shared with Harlon Quinton.

The most expensive chambers to decorate were down the hall and around a corner from the main space on the twelfth floor. One was a long cafeteria-lounge done in yellows and grays and hung with silver-framed newspaper front pages whose headlines extolled the FBI's most notable achievements over the decades. The abutting area was also dual-purposed, a combination press conference auditorium/television studio containing two hundred and ten seats and two stage sets. One set was the speaker's podium facing the seats. The other, hidden from view, was an

182

exact replica of J. Edgar Hoover's office in Washington, D.C. Here, in the press conference room, was where Denis Corticun reverted to his pinstripes and, occasionally, his former haughtiness.

Corticun, from his arrival in Prairie Port following J. Edgar Hoover's announcement of $31,000,000 having been stolen, was relentless in pursuing the media. He had talked to reporters as he deplaned from the aircraft that carried equipment for the twelfth-floor offices. He had ridden in from the airfield with reporters, chatting with them nonstop. Two hours after reaching the office, he met with them again, in a hallway. Ten hours later the cafeteria-lounge had been completed . . . a place in which the press could hang out and receive an endless stream of news releases created and printed by a three-man team of headquarters public relations specialists operating within the enclosed green-and-white media section.

The cafeteria-lounge, from inception, was a hit. A visiting reporter, if he waited around long enough, could usually extract a fresh bit of data from Denis Corticun or one of the three FBI PR specialists, who all made a point of dropping around between officially scheduled press briefings. Also available to the reporter were reproductions or typed recaps of what the print media, nationally and worldwide, had to say about the robbery at Mormon State. Taped shows and the transcribed texts of local, national and international television and radio coverage could also be had.

Even without Denis Corticun and the PR section's efforts, the media focused on the Mormon State robbery as it had rarely focused on any other event of this kind. Every major American newspaper, in the wake of J. Edgar Hoover's announcement of August 24, carried the story on the front page, with a majority headlining the revelation. All national newscasts led off their programs with it.

The visiting press created within Prairie Port, and for a twenty-five-mile radius around, a hotel-room and rental-auto shortage of paramount proportions. Private detective Jeb Stuart Wile, the man who solved the sensational Black Mass murders of the previous year, arrived and held his own press conference and announced he knew for a fact the robbery gang included five members, all local men, three white, two black, and that he aimed to prove it and claim for himself the rewards.

Rewards were a factor in creating what one national magazine writer stated "can only be described as a jamboree spirit around Prairie Port." The Grange Association upped its previous cash offer for information leading to the arrest of the unknown thieves to $100,000. The Prairie Farmer Association added another $50,000; the Chamber of Commerce of Prairie Port, $15,000; the Rotarians, $8,000. Country-and-western radio station WJKB reestablished its hot line for crime information and sweetened the reward kitty by another $15,000. WJKB's competitor, rock 'n' roll station WQXY, put up its own hot line and offered $17,500 for information. The local FBI office opened its own well-publicized hot line number and soon was getting so many calls that it diverted much of the traffic up to the auxiliary switchboard on the twelfth floor, where each hour new records were set for incoming "tip calls" regarding a federal crime.

Receiving somewhat less publicity than Jeb Stuart Wile was the appearance of Newark, New Jersey's, famed bounty hunters, M. L. Konvits and Pretty Boy Schline. The North Dakota Mounted Posse let it be known they too were here to seek the rewards. The Agatha Christie Garden and Deduction Society of Armbruster, Illinois, claimed to have driven over just for an outing and that any money they received in rewards would go to provide the poor and infirm with food, shelter and flowers. Thousands came just to sightsee. Robbery shirts and pillows, along with postcards and toy guns, were selling as briskly as hot dogs and soda, not only at the shrine site but throughout the city.

On the Mississippi River, tourist boats had been prospering since the early media speculation that the robbers may have fled via the river . . . that millions of dollars of stolen money may have fallen into the river. Craft from as far away as Louisiana and Minnesota started up or down the Mississippi for Prairie Port as the greatest treasure hunt in modern times got under way. Everything that was navigable seemed to travel the river to Prairie

Port, including a two-man submarine. Maps of the Mississippi sold at a premium, as did alleged "original pilot's charts" from the glorious steamboat days of yore. Scuba gear and scuba instruction became a hot new industry in town. Treasure-hunt boats left Prairie Port hourly. Spano's, the largest department store in town, filled its fifteen display windows with masked and scuba-equipped mannequins reenacting various stages of the theft and getaway. The River Patrol and the U.S. Coast Guard implemented emergency right-of-way rules so the flotilla of fortune-seeking craft would not interfere with normal water traffic, so searchers would stay off private property along the river's banks or on its midstream islands.

The expanding treasure hunt at Prairie Port escalated the jamboree aspects into an out-and-out holiday festival. A joviality and abandonment, not seen since the last state fair or when the local high school basketball team went to the state finals, permeated, transformed the missing robbers and the efforts to catch them into a civic celebration at which a vocal majority hoped the thieves would not get captured. A joint Elmo Roper-NBC national poll reflected the same sentiment.

The more attention and publicity, the more difficult became the maneuverability of Strom and his agents in pursuing the Channels of Investigation laid out for Romor 91. Reporters hung around the parking lots used for Bureau cars, gave chase to agents driving out on assignment.

Despite this the residency was able to accomplish a great deal of work in the early days of Romor 91, interviewed four hundred known criminals and underworld contacts without the media finding out, followed up another hundred leads unnoticed.

Then came the wizard.

Strom Sunstrom had briefed Denis Corticun on what Jessup and Yates had learned inside Warbonnet Ridge and traveling through the tunnels. Suspecting Corticun had made leaks to the press as to missing millions being dumped into the Mississippi River, Strom curtly warned that none of the recent Warbonnet Ridge information must reach the press.

"How can it not reach the press?" Corticun had asked Strom.

"It *is* news. Spectacular news. The scientific team and their assistants inside the Bonnet know of it, and do you suppose they'll not pass on it? Tell a wife or son or associate in the strictest of confidence? People connected with the Water and Sewerage Departments and the mud eruptions have learned the old reservoir gates were opened, learned how they were opened and by whom and for what purpose. Can we expect them *all* to remain silent? No, Strom, everyone will know, with or without me or you. If you wish, when it begins getting out to the media and the media come to me for confirmation, I will either deny any of it is so or have no comment. This has always been policy . . . the reason, more often than not, that the FBI has lost credibility."

Strom countered, "Critical and corroborating information was discovered at the Bonnet. Information only the actual perpetrators could know—"

"I'm not arguing, dear fellow. I'm simply saying it is not within our control to keep it from the media. Strom, the media of the world have come to Prairie Port. Not a few local newsmen but a national and international corps. Four hundred and eleven persons in search of a story. Our story."

"So we hold a press conference and tell all, is that what you suggest? You've been doing that since you got here."

"Has it hurt us so badly?"

"If you ask me, yes."

"How?"

"For one thing, the criminals seem to be coming off better than the FBI. Are you sure you're not their press agent?"

"What else is bothering you, Strom . . . about me?"

"Now that you bring it up, I have this curious suspicion that in addition to plain old conferences, you do a bit of unofficial leaking to reporters on the side."

"You mean as in the instance of several million dollars spilling into the Mississippi River?"

"Yes."

"I did leak that. Your local newsfellow, Chet Chomsky, somehow got wind of it and was going to say so on the air. I found out he found out and what he intended to do, so I beat him to it. I leaked it to Nancy Applebridge and the Associated Press. I made two new friends for us, Applebridge and AP, and one enemy, Chomsky. The next time out I'll leak something to Chomsky and he'll become a friend as well . . . and *we'll be in control.*"

At the special 3 P.M. press conference on the twelfth floor Denis Corticun wore his pinstriped suit, stood at the podium in front of a large FBI seal and said that, no doubt, all the reporters present had learned of the mud volcano being neutralized and water having escaped from Tomahawk Hill reservoir . . . stated that these two events tied directly into the robbery of Mormon State National Bank . . . revealed that long-forgotten sluice gates in the reservoir were opened and the tunnels flooded by the very same man who caused the power dips—a scientific wizard.

Details on how the gates were opened and what exactly caused the power shortages weren't answered. Nor did Corticun disclose other aspects of the operation. It made no difference. Wizardry prevailed. A Wizard of Darkness, as the ABC commentator said after ABC's nightly national newscast led off with Corticun's revelations and on-the-scene reports from Tomahawk Hill reservoir and the Prairie Port headquarters of the Missouri Power and Electric Company. CBS's man invoked the images of Professor Moriarty, Dr. Fu Manchu, Raffles, and Jekyll and Hyde. A well-known TV host made his entrance dressed as the Wizard of Mormon State, accompanied by six frogmen whom he introduced as the rest of the Mormon State robbery gang, with a half-minute ovation of clapping and whistles and foot stomps. The wizard, like the Mormon State robbery itself, seemed to be just what a diversion-starved media and public were in need of.

A period of dullness and uneventful waiting pervaded as the summer of 1971 came to an end. Children were going back to school and Mark Spitz captured the AAU final in 220-yard free-style swimming and World Series fever was nearing and professional football had begun its exhibition season and Chase Manhattan, the country's sixth-largest bank, had lowered its lending rate one full percentage point and the pullout of United States troops in Vietnam had left only 22,000 GIs there and had deescalated combat to a near standstill. Little else was new or good. The economy was in such ragged shape President Nixon had imposed a 90-day wage freeze, which the AFL-CIO agreed not to challenge in court. Crime was up. George Jackson, convict and author of *Soledad Brother,* was killed in a San Quentin shoot-out.

Had not the wizard materialized, there wasn't all that much to make headlines with over the final days of August and the opening week of September except for death and politics. The wizard and Mormon State dominated all other news. Corticun leaked to Chet Chomsky a startling item: the wizard had spliced into the city's main power line while that power line was "live" or "hot," a feat few mortal men could do. A second leak, which Corticun provided the UPI via Nancy Applebridge, dealt with the wizard having rewired critical generators inside Warbonnet Ridge.

The faceless wizard made the cover of national magazines. A London newspaper decried the wizard as being nothing but a second-rate, made-in-America plagiarizer of England's spectacular Great Train Robbery. Until Mormon State, the train heist was title-holder for the largest cash theft in recorded history, over $7,000,000. Nonetheless it concurred with the quoted evaluations of experts who assessed the wizard, and at least some of his accomplices, as possessing skills equal to those of electrical engineering Ph.D.s or above. A review of international psychology profiled the wizard as having one or possibly two Ph.D.s, possessing, at minimum, a 175 IQ and having genius skills in mathematical probability and theoretic electronics. Television was the prime commercial beneficiary of the manhunt, generating estimated profits of three to five times its investment. Prairie Port's economy had also gained. One commentator likened the windfall from the robbery investigation to that of the Super Bowl moving to the city and staying two whole weeks.

On Monday night, September 6, Alice Sunstrom and Sue Ann Willis and Tina Beth Yates and Sally Jessup and Helen Perch and Heathia Keon and Jolene Bracken went to Sissy Hennessy's home for a Mormon State Desertion Party. Many brought their young children with them. None had seen their husbands for more than a few hours a day since the Romor 91 investigation had started. In honor of their missing spouses, they did what their husbands

188

usually did on Monday nights this time of year—drink beer, eat a buffet dinner and watch Monday-night professional football. Much was drunk and eaten and said by the wives. Little football was seen.

Corticun, at the time of the hen party, held a full-house press briefing intended to shift media interest back to the FBI. He dryly cited many of the investigatory activities to date, stated that 2,500 known criminals across the nation had been interviewed, that hundreds of scientists with electrical expertise had been talked to, that twenty-three other Channels of Investigation were under way. Corticun would not divulge what those Channels of Investigation were. The next evening, Tuesday, September 7, while Billy Yates took time off to help Tina Beth move into their rented house, Corticun revealed for the first time at any press briefing what Ed Grafton and Cub Hennessy and Strom Sunstrom had learned shortly after the robbery had been discovered: that segments of a rubber boat belonging to a robber had been found in the river.

The night after that, Wednesday, September 8, as Doris Kebbon and two of her five children watched "The Carol Burnett Show" on television and Pauline Lyle, Tricia Dafney and three of their children viewed "Adam-12" at Pauline's house and Helen Perch studied for her real-estate license examination and Hinky Cody read Erich Segal's still best-selling novel, *Love Story,* Denis Corticun made a startling admission at his evening press briefing . . . that money stolen in the robbery had been recovered from the river. Corticun avoided saying the amount found was fifty one-dollar bills or that the discovery had been made back in August at the same time the boat segment was discovered. He had used the money-in-the-river ploy before, had unofficially leaked it to Chet Chomsky in the early days of the investigation. Now, as then, it worked. Attention shifted to the Mississippi. And tour boats and the scuba industry thrived more than ever.

Martin Brewmeister, with a slight limp and a bandaged shoulder, followed Yates through the door of the twelfth-floor offices

189

supervised by Corticun. He stopped, gazed about the sprawling, multilevel, multicolored premises and asked, "What the *hell* is this?"

"The future," Yates told him. "Like it?"

"It's a Venetian whorehouse."

"Been to Venice, have you?" Yates indicated the section of office to the left. "Those agents handle our old residency case load and are doing a pretty good job. Those guys over there," he said as he pointed to the right, "they're the reserves for Romor 91. They assist our guys down on the eleventh floor."

After touring the public-relations sector, the main communications area and the still unoccupied office of the flying squad, Yates walked to a horseshoe-shaped enclosure lined with shelves and containing several copying machines and a long table laden with reports. Sorting the report pages, making copies and inserting them into red, white or blue binders, were three secretaries.

"The binders, regardless of color, contain Romor 91 reports." Yates held up a white binder. "White is the operative color for out-of-town reports whether they come in from the flying squad, other field offices and agencies or whatever. White reports go into white binders. Duplicate copies go into the master casebook." He pointed to a line of white binders on the wall shelf. "That's the totality of out-of-town reports reaching us to date."

A longer line of red binders on the next shelf was indicated. "Red is for the eleventh floor. Our floor. The residency. Residency information gathered by us directly on the Prairie Port end of Romor 91. On events that happened only in Prairie Port . . . which is almost everything. The thicker blue binders are the master casebooks containing the entire investigation, the material from both the white and red binders. One set is up here, and we have a second set down on the eleventh floor. Each master binder holds between one hundred and one hundred and ten reports. As you can see, we're already up to eighty-one volumes. With nearly nine thousand reports on tap so far, we may become the biggest investigation in Bureau history, if you believe projected statistics. We've become very big with statistics while you were away."

190

"Where does the *case* stand?" Brewmeister asked.

"It doesn't. It's lying flat on its back, stone dead."

"What about those breaks inside Warbonnet Ridge?" said Brew. "The machinery? The timing device? All the other physical evidence?"

"They ran us down half a hundred garden paths . . . and didn't cough up a thing," Yates told him. "Not one lead. Not a thousandth of a thumbprint. We're at a dead end."

Brewmeister lowered into a form-fitting plastic chair. "You can't have that much physical evidence and not break a lead."

"We can. And have."

"It isn't logical."

"Maybe that's the trouble."

"What?"

"Trying to think logically when you don't know all the facts," Yates said. "That's what we've been doing, trying to think in a logical way. But we don't have all the facts, so how can we be logical?"

"I'm not getting you."

"Examining the evidence at hand, logic has told us this was a supercaper and, ergo, that the perpetrators must be supercrooks. Particularly our wizard. We've interviewed and investigated more electronics Ph.D.s than Edison had amps. But if you follow our own logic, just to this point, you realize we are faced with an illogical supposition. Somehow we've deduced that the wizard and his gang are experts in everything. Experts in electricity and tunnels and tunnel-flooding and geology and caves and drilling and explosives and alarm-jamming. My God, do you know how hard it is to ride a rubber boat through a mild rapids in daylight? It's hard, I've done it. But we're presuming this crowd of crooks could do it in total darkness and on the crest of eighteen million gallons of escaping water. We're supposed to believe this is the most exquisitely conceived and executed crime in modern times . . . that power shortages and mud eruptions were charted out to act as decoys. Well, I'll tell you something, God Himself in a month of miracle Sundays couldn't do as many things as expertly as we've convinced ourselves these guys can do."

Brew considered, then shook his head. "Billy, this gang aren't dunderheads."

"I'm not saying they are," Yates replied. "But they could be. If you want, I can make a pretty good case for a bunch of dumb-cluck crooks stumbling onto a mark, in their dumbness concocting an off-the-wall plan for taking a vault and screwing up half the time and still being lucky enough to pull it off."

Brew shook his head again. "That wouldn't explain the wizard. The wizard did one hell of a job with that machinery in Warbonnet Ridge. I read your own reports on it."

"That's so, but there's one thing we were told down in the tunnel that everyone ignores . . . the electric timing device wasn't used for the actual robbery, only after . . . that someone tampered with the device and tried to bypass it . . . that wires were run directly between the reservoir's water gates and the generator, conceivably run by a different person. It's in the report. Thurston, the electric company engineer, told us that the electrical connections to the reservoir were different from any of the other connections attributed to the wizard. That they were sloppier. Maybe, for whatever the reasons, a different man made that electrical connection to the reservoir gates. A second man. Maybe it was the second man who disconnected the electric timing box too. Maybe the second man didn't have all the skill the wizard did. But maybe what the wizard did just didn't work. Maybe he got the old machinery operative but the flooding end of things was beyond him and someone else had to step in. Someone who didn't give a hoot about doing anything but getting some water into the tunnels any way he could."

Brew didn't see it. "You tell this to Strom?"

"To Strom and anyone else who will listen."

"What do they say?"

"They don't. They turn and flee. What the hell, it's only an idea. Imagine the look on Corticun's face if any part of it was true. If his supercrooks turned out to be the Katzenjammer Kids."

# Book Two

# Twelve

Cub Hennessy drove through the "restricted" gate at University Hospital and down the ramp and on between the bearing beams under city morgue. He had expected Ned Van Ornum to be waiting for him, assumed it was Ned sitting on the edge of the loading dock in the distance. Van Ornum was head of detectives for the Prairie Port Police Department. He was also Cub Hennessy's confidential informant on police force operations. Grafton, the only other FBI man to know the Prairie Port PD was being spied on by one of its own, considered Ned Van Ornum to be Cub Hennessy's finest recruitment. Cub wasn't all that certain. Never had been.

Cub Hennessy ran informants for the FBI's resident office in Prairie Port, which is to say he was in charge of selecting candidates for the small and generally clandestine ring of information-gatherers, then, after clearance from Grafton, recruiting the prospects, convincing them by whatever means possible to "run" for him and Grafton. Other agents at the Prairie Port residency developed their own informants, but these were usually less crucial sources. Strategic recruitments were left exclusively to Cub.

Neither Cub nor Grafton had been keen on recruiting an upper-echelon officer of the Prairie Port Police Department, saw no particular need to do so. Relationships with the PD, though not ideal, had been cordial, at least as long as the force had been run by Chief B. C. Hankler. B. C. "Before Christ" Hankler was, as the saying went, viable. When Hankler's impending retirement was learned, FBI headquarters in Washington had grown restive. More precisely, the assistant to the Director, A. R. Roland, became anticipatory. Roland suggested to Grafton, in his polite and persistent manner, that a change of Prairie Port PD leadership

195

could change the climate of the Wilkie Jarrel investigation and that since Jarrel would undoubtedly be doing everything in his power to influence the selection of a new chief of police, it might be prudent to develop a reliable contact within the PD who could apprise them of developments . . . a contact who might also prove useful in the future. Grafton, to keep Roland from "pestering us to death," finally told Cub Hennessy that should the opportunity for a PD recruitment pop up: "Follow through." What popped up was Ned Van Ornum. Unfortunately, he popped up after a new police chief was selected by the Prairie Port city council . . . a career police officer Grafton strongly suspected was partial to Wilkie Jarrel or worse.

Cub Hennessy's strategy for the recruitment of Ned Van Ornum was based on age, ethnics, career frustration and patience. Ned was thirty-one years old, by far the youngest police officer ever to hold the prestigious position of chief of detectives. Ned during his previous seven years on the force had amassed one of the best records in memory. Though somewhat taciturn, he was personable and bright and college-educated and a graduate of the National Police Academy course sponsored by the FBI. His parents were third-generation WASPs, which in predominantly white Anglo-Saxon Protestant Prairie Port was still important. His wife was from Prairie Port and WASP and had been his schooldays sweetheart. Ned Van Ornum, needless to say, was a comer at the police department. But not the only comer.

Frank Santi, at thirty-four years of age, was the youngest man ever to be made chief of the Prairie Port Police Department. Like Van Ornum, Santi had been born in Prairie Port and married a local girl and had the reputation of being bright and, when he chose, personable. Unlike Ned, Frank had finished only one year of college, never attended a crime seminar given by the FBI and had grown up in the poorest section of Prairie Port, a crime-afflicted, often volatile riverfront area called Old Port and most recently named "the Battle Zone." Whereas Ned Van Ornum's record on the police force had been one of the best, Santi's record was the best. His rise from the ranks had been faster and more spectacular than Ned's. Frank was something of a local hero. He

196

had played on the Prairie Port High School basketball team that was runner-up in the Missouri State championship finals sixteen years earlier. Between dropping from college and joining the Prairie Port PD, Frank had served with the Marine Corps. One of the two other candidates Santi had beaten out for the top police department post was fifty-one-year-old Tim Shipley, the man former chief B. C. Hankler had handpicked to be his successor. The other was Ned Van Ornum.

Policemen and FBI agents of Prairie Port, except when brought together on official business, politely avoided one another. Didn't even have their respective softball and bowling teams compete. What institutional socializing had to be done was taken care of by Strom Sunstrom. Even chronically gregarious Cub Hennessy didn't fraternize with cops. But he did play golf and was finally accepted at a local country club where Ned Van Ornum had long been a member. This was just at the time Frank Santi was chosen to be new chief of police. Though Cub had never had any direct dealings with Ned, he knew who he was. He also knew that Ned had been a candidate for the police department's number one job . . . had come very close to winning the position. And Ned knew who Cub was. Cub took his time moving. One Sunday morning ended up in a golfing foursome with Ned. Played with him two weeks later. Showered and took steam with him from time to time. Had drinks at the locker room bar with him. The luckiest break of all was that Cub's wife, Sissy, knew Ned's wife, June. Both women had served as chaperones at the 4-H dance. Cub had Sissy invite Ned and June to dinner. It was one of the few times all four of them would be together. Cub didn't like getting Sissy involved with his work. Especially when he couldn't tell her what he was up to. And anyway, that first night when they were all together had provided him with more than enough to go on.

Cub, in his subsequent recruitment of Ned Van Ornum, cautiously followed up on June's dinner-table allusion to "Eye-talians" and the fact that, because of Frank Santi's presence, Ned had gone as far as he could in the police department. Cub, on the golf course or in the locker room or steam bath in the days to

197

come, would good-humoredly exhume for Ned that flaccid rumor of Santi having a relative in the Mafia. A rumor the FBI knew to be true, but which Cub never dealt with as fact, used only as a subliminal barb. One of the many passing irritants to be unleashed. Prods for discontent. Slowly, at Cub's careful instigation, all fell into place. Casual discussion of police and FBI techniques led to more precise subjects . . . allowed Cub to occasionally slip in a direct question of interest to the FBI. Ned always answered. Cub dropped the pretense of discussion, offhandedly made a specific inquiry from time to time. Ned continued to answer. Cub grew bolder but not surer. Against his better judgment he broached the subject of Wilkie Jarrel.

Cub from the outset of the recruitment was acutely aware that certain bonds existed between Ned Ornum and Frank Santi. One of the strongest was that both men were career police officers with a fierce pride in their work and their organization. Under the best of circumstances urban police were leery of the FBI. Most did not like or trust the Bureau. Many considered the feds to be more of a natural enemy than criminals. Throughout their friendship, Ned had never expressed interest in becoming a member of the FBI, even though Cub continually dropped hints that this might be possible.

There was another link between Van Ornum and Santi which troubled Hennessy as much if not more than the police connection. Ned and Frank shared a common heritage. A uniquely regional heritage, Cub had come to realize, which was capable of superseding blood and economic and social ties. Hennessy himself was a native St. Louisian steeped in the lore and pride of Missouri and the Midwest and the Mississippi River. But never had he witnessed the likes of Prairie Port. Prairie Port, despite almost three decades of spectacular growth and modernization, clung so steadfastly to its pioneer traditions that all but the oldest families were looked upon as unwelcome newcomers. Ned Van Ornum was a fourth-generation resident and therefore an automatic member of this fraternity intent on, if not actually reversing progress, certainly holding it in check. Frank Santi's ancestors arrived in Prairie Port long before those of Ned Van Ornum, had

198

settled in the place when it was little more than a barge stop on the Mississippi River. Unlike the immigrant Italian laborers brought to Prairie Port in the 1930s by Franklin D. Roosevelt's NRA and CCC projects, Frank Santi's great-great-great-great–grandfather had come from Italy in 1848 to be a barge caulker.

The more Cub Hennessy reflected on the Prairie Port of Ned Van Ornum and Frank Santi, the more unsure he became of Ned's reliability as an informer. Cub could almost visualize Frank and Ned growing up in Prairie Port, traveling upstream to the rustic riverfront section of the town called Steamboat Cove, where young boys still go, and like Tom Sawyer and Huckleberry Finn building crude rafts and floating on the near bank currents . . . could see them, when they grew to be teenagers, taking to the longboats and trying to ride downstream on the Treachery.

Cub concluded that children growing up in Prairie Port forged too strong, too close-knit a relationship for his professional liking, that even without the police connection he never could be all that certain of where Ned Van Ornum's loyalties lay in regard to Frank Santi. Reviewing the Van Ornum situation, and he constantly reviewed each of his recruited informants, Cub came across another fact to ponder. Ned had never once voluntarily provided information. Everything had come as a direct request from Cub.

Ultimately, the matter of whether Ned Van Ornum could or could not be relied upon was of secondary importance. His recruitment, after all, had been a Washington headquarters idea, a possible ploy for learning if Wilkie Jarrel had influence over Frank Santi. When asked directly by Cub, Ned said Jarrel had absolutely no input with Santi, that no one did, that Santi was his own man and could be influenced by nobody. Whether or not this was so, or if Ned Van Ornum went on providing information, had no effect on strategy at the FBI's resident office in Prairie Port. Ed Grafton would continue investigating Wilkie Jarrel regardless of the situation with Frank Santi or the Prairie Port Police Department or God Almighty.

Still, Cub Hennessy was fond of Ned Van Ornum and saw no pressing reason for breaking off relationships with him . . . particularly on the golf course. Cub merely stopped asking Ned questions. Then, on August 7, Ned called to say there was someone Hennessy might be interested in . . . a man in the employ of Wilkie Jarrel who would possibly consider informing on his boss if the price was right. A man named Willy Carlson.

Ned claimed never to have seen or met Carlson, only to have learned of him through a reliable underworld middleman. Ned, via the middleman, arranged for, but did not attend, a clandestine chat between Hennessy and Willy Carlson. Willy explained he had just done time at Statesville Penitentiary in Illinois on armed robbery, needed money and was currently employed as a fill-in, weekend security guard/chauffeur at Wilkie Jarrel's estate, and that Jarrel was, among other things, a crusty old geezer obsessed with the notion he was being followed by the FBI. Jarrel, according to Carlson, routinely had his home and offices searched for eavesdropping bugs and wasn't above using a public booth for more important calls. He had scrambler telephones in the private study and bedroom of his home and in his limousine. On one occasion, with Carlson driving, Jarrel had tried to reach J. Edgar Hoover from his car but couldn't get through.

Cub Hennessy liked what he saw and heard and recruited Willy Carlson as a paid informant for the FBI. Willy, thirty-six hours later, delivered a list of phone booth locations frequented by Jarrel, was paid in cash by Cub, given a new assignment and handed more money on the spot. This took place Thursday, August 19, three days prior to the alarm going off at Mormon State National Bank . . . one day before the actual theft was perpetrated.

Shortly after discovering the bank's vault had been looted, on Sunday, August 22, Ned and Cub met and concurred that Willy Carlson, recently out of prison and familiar with the crime community of Prairie Port, as well as southern Missouri and southern Illinois, might be a valuable source of information concerning Mormon State. The policeman and the FBI agent agreed to join forces, expand Willy's informant chores and share the information he would, they hoped, provide. Willy couldn't be found. Cub and Ned looked high and low. Willy Carlson had dropped out of

200

sight. Not, of course, uncommon behavior for an ex-convict when a massive manhunt is under way . . . when the con has reason to suspect a law-enforcement agency he's been making money from might want him for riskier assignments.

Earlier this evening, when the emergency phone call from a police dispatcher to FBI night-duty officer Butch Cody had requested that Cub go immediately to the morgue for a meeting, Cub had assumed it was Ned Van Ornum who wanted to see him . . . who had intentionally made contact in this official and clumsy way rather than ring up directly. Ned, on learning that only $6,500 had been stolen from Mormon State and that the FBI was deliriously giddy over the Prairie Port Police Department being stuck with the case, had been none too cordial toward Cub. Later, after it was established $31,000,000 was missing and the FBI stormed ashore with full media pomp to claim the investigation for its own, Ned Van Ornum made his resentment of Bureau behavior known to Cub in a brief, two-word phone call: Hoover sucks.

Driving now through University Hospital's private underground parking lot toward the morgue's loading platform in the distance, Cub Hennessy still thought it was Ned who would be waiting for him. Pulling to a stop, he saw that the man sitting in civilian clothes with legs dangling over the edge of the dock wasn't Ned Van Ornum. It was Frank Santi.

Cub had seen Santi in newspaper photos and on the television newscasts but for some reason never in person, except at the Mormon State bank the Sunday after it was robbed. Cub's impression had been of a very tall man with a small head. Climbing the cement steps up to the loading pier and watching Santi stand, he saw that the recently ensconced chief of Prairie Port police was shorter and stockier than previously supposed. His shoulders were extremely broad and powerful-appearing. Santi's head was indeed small, his features almost delicate.

"Special agent Hennessy?" He ambled toward Cub with an amazingly long arm extended. "Harold Hennessy?"

"I'm Hennessy," Cub said, shaking hands.

"Frank Santi." The chief spoke in an unrushed, somewhat

high-pitched voice. "Thank you for coming out so late. If you'll follow me, there's something you might be able to help us with."

Santi led the way down the morgue's corridor in those long, loping, slightly pigeon-toed strides of a former high school basketball player whose team made it to the state finals.

No one was in the autopsy room. No one alive, that is. Four of the six dissection tables held cadavers. Uncovered cadavers. Naked and waxy-looking corpses lying on their backs with an identification tag tied to a toe. Cub didn't relish seeing dead bodies. He followed Frank Santi across the autopsy room. The chief of police walked directly between the two lines of operating tables, stopped beside three of the corpses.

"This seem familiar?" Santi handed Cub a slip of paper with the numbers 476-3312 on it.

"That's my phone number," Cub told him. "An unlisted number."

"I know, we had it traced. Is that your printing on the paper?"

"No."

Santi walked to one of the mobile tables in the corner, spun it around, ripped off the covering. "Know him?"

Cub glanced down at a bald-headed man, half of whose face had been exploded away . . . a badly decomposed corpse who, nonetheless, was still recognizable to him as being Willy Carlson.

Cub realized Ned Van Ornum might have disclosed their intended sharing of Willy to Frank Santi, that Ned could also have told his boss about Carlson being an FBI informant. It was equally possible Santi knew nothing of either arrangement. Hoping the latter was true, Cub chose to lie. "No, I don't know him," he told the police chief as he turned away from the corpse. "Maybe if there was more of him left . . ."

"Take another look, would you?"

Cub did. ". . . No, I don't know who he is." Sensing Santi was watching him rather than Willy Carlson, he waited several moments before looking up.

Frank Santi shifted his gaze to the dead man. "Not too pretty, huh? The river never helps. They found him in the river. He was probably killed a few days after the Mormon State robbery, on

202

Tuesday or Wednesday, August twenty-fourth or twenty-fifth. Then he was weighted down and dumped into the river. Whatever was holding him under gave way, and he floated to the surface. Mister Hennessy, do you have any idea how he came to have your private phone number?"

"No."

"I don't mean to pry into official FBI operations, but could you tell me whether you use that phone for Bureau business?"

"Sometimes. It's more a private line my wife can reach me on at the office."

". . . Or at home, if she happens to be out?" Santi suggested. "The phone company said you had an extension at home as well as at the office."

"At home it's so my boss can get me," Cub explained good-naturedly. "Chief, am I being interrogated?"

Santi showed a stiff, prudish grin. "I guess so."

"Anything I can help you with I will. Don't be afraid to ask."

"Thank you, Mister Hennessy." Santi's large hand reached up and scratched at a small ear. "Mister Hennessy, is it conceivable that, in some way, you could have had dealings with this man?"

"I come across a lot of people, chief, as you do. He may have been one of them. But it wouldn't have been anything important. Anything I remembered."

"No one you knew well, is that right? No one *bald* you remember?"

"That's right."

"I suppose it's not all that easy to forget a bald man, is it? Sorry to have bothered you, Mister Hennessy."

"Sorry I couldn't help out."

"May I have that phone number back?"

Cub returned the slip of paper to Santi, watched the chief stare down at the number, then up at him, then back to the paper. And Cub realized something he knew he should have seen from the beginning . . . the slip of paper was dry . . . showed no sign of ever having been wet . . . Willy Carlson's corpse, according to Chief Santi, had been in the river for some time.

"Where did you find that paper?" asked Cub.

203

"In his apartment."

"You know who he is?"

The grin flickered. "His fingerprints came down a few hours ago," Santi said. "He's a pal. An old pal of lots of people. Willy Carlson is what he goes by mostly. Ever heard of him?"

"No."

"He was a character, Mister Hennessy. A local character. Great horseman. Loved the beasts and rode them in a fair number of rodeos. His nickname was Cowboy. All in all, Willy was a pretty good egg. Only problem was, he stole. He tried legitimate work from time to time, particularly work around horses, but he was addicted to thieving. Nothing big. Penny-ante B&E's and small-time hustles. He did some light time for a questionable smuggling scam. Then three years back he reached for the stars and got collared on an armed job. He was paroled from Statesville Penitentiary five months ago and went to one of those new rehabilitation programs run by the university. Counseling, confession and lots of pretty young criminology coeds to lay. It looked for a while as if some of it was working, that Willy had settled down, sociopathically speaking. Had rejected thievery. But obviously he was up to something he shouldn't have been . . . or he wouldn't be lying over there with half his head missing, would he? Have any ideas what it could be, Mister Hennessy?"

Cub experienced the same uneasiness he felt when Santi had asked him to take a second look at Willy's corpse. Something about the chief had momentarily changed when he just said: "Have any ideas what it could be?" Not a change of intonation or of voice or of phrasing. Nor was there a difference in Santi's generally placid expression. "No," Hennessy answered, trying to figure out what the difference was. "Why do you think he was killed?"

"Maybe it was sex," the chief said. "Willy was sick that way. An exhibitionist. Maybe he flashed the wrong person and instead of getting blown got blown away."

It was Santi's eyes that changed, Cub told himself. Santi had a way of making his eyes go dead, of looking at you as if he was blind, as if he was saying, "I'm listening, go ahead and lie."

"I suppose you could be killed for flashing," Cub said.

Santi looked down at the corpse.

"Sorry I couldn't be of more help," Cub told him.

"Good night, Mister Hennessy."

"Good night, chief."

Cub knew before he started walking that he would have the feeling Frank Santi was staring at him every step of the way out . . . would have bet that before he reached the door Santi would tell him what he really had on his mind.

"Mister Hennessy," Frank Santi called when Cub was passing the last of the dissection tables. "There is one detail."

Cub stopped, turned around, stood beside the naked corpse of a wizened old woman, only one of whose eyes were open. He waited for the chief of police's next words.

"About Willy Carlson," Santi said. "He had a sideline I forgot to mention. One he picked up in prison and continued on after his parole. Willy had become a rat. A professional informer. An informer-for-hire when he got back here to Prairie Port. And he had several takers. He ratted for the county liquor commission against a go-go bar operation. That was from June seventh to June thirtieth of this year, and he got paid one hundred and seventy-five dollars for his trouble. From June nineteenth through July twenty-sixth he ratted across the river for the Kentucky State Crime Commission against the whorehouses over near Paducah. His fee was four hundred dollars. The Paducah houses paid him three thousand during the same period to rat for them about the state crime commission. Between July and early August he had three more gigs, and then he picked up some very fancy clients indeed. It's all in here." Santi held up a ledger. "We found this in Willy's room. He recorded each job as neat as can be. Date and price all set down like he was planning to have his books audited and pay taxes. Willy 'Cowboy' Carlson, if you hadn't figured it out, was a crackpot. Mad as a hatter. Luckily for the police department, we knew it. What we didn't know was he kept a ledger on the madness."

The eyes with which Santi watched Hennessy were not at all blind or impassive. They stalked Cub. But the voice droned on as matter-of-factly as ever. "Willy managed to show some discretion in his account-keeping. He didn't enter names as such. He put down initials or phone numbers. In some instances, both initials and numbers." Santi peered into the open ledger. "It's the last page that might be of interest to you. Only three entries appear. The second entry from the top has both initials and a phone number and shows that some weeks ago Willy received five hundred dollars for a snitch job. The number is the same one as on the slip of paper we found in Willy's room . . . your unlisted phone number, Mister Harold Hennessy. But the initials before the number aren't HH. They are CH. CH as in Cub Hennessy?"

Cub waited for Santi to look up from the ledger, trying to think of something to say. But the chief of police continued gazing down. "The last entry in the ledger, after you, is Friday, August twentieth. No phone number is given. No amount of payment received. Only the initial: M. If you feel foolish learning you've popped up on a tinhorn hustler's books, Mister Hennessy, you're going to feel even worse. The entry directly under your initials and payment . . . is for the Mormon State bank robbery."

Frank Santi ripped the page from the ledger, came forward and handed it to Cub. Cub studied the three neatly printed listings:

$$8/7 \quad VO \ 476\text{-}1881 \quad 150$$
$$8/19 \quad CH \ 476\text{-}3312 \quad 250 + 250$$
$$8/20 \quad M$$

"Who is M?" Cub asked.

"A man named Marion Corkel. Heard of him?"

Cub shook his head and gave the page back to Santi.

"Aren't you going to comment on the first entry, Mister Hennessy?" the chief asked. "On the one hundred and fifty dollars VO paid Cowboy on August seventh?"

"What about it?"

"VO is Ned Van Ornum."

"Is it?"

"We set you up, Mister Hennessy. Ned and I set you up."

Cub said nothing.

"We meant to embarrass you and Mister Grafton severely, Mister Hennessy. When the time came. Meant to slap the FBI's wrist as hard as we could for reaching in and trying to recruit a police officer. Meant to teach you a lesson you'd never forget. All of you and your kind."

"You've succeeded."

Frank Santi lit a match, held it to the page torn from the ledger . . . let the page go up in flames.

"You're destroying physical evidence." Cub, even before the sentence was complete, felt foolish for saying it.

Santi watched the ashes float to the floor.

"I'm saving your ass is what I'm doing, Mister Hennessy. Your ass and the police department's ass. Or would you prefer the media let the world know how the FBI and the Prairie Port Police Department had a Mormon State bank robber in their employ at the exact time Mormon State was looted? That neither the FBI nor the police had an inkling Willy Carlson had anything to do with Mormon State . . . and probably never would have an inkling?"

Cub, again, had nothing to say.

"I'm afraid, Mister Hennessy, that you and your Mister Hoovers and Mister Graftons have won out again. I have no choice but to hand you the case . . . hand you, most likely, all of the robbers and an outside co-conspirator. I damn your luck. It should have been my luck. Thank the river. Talk about coincidence, the key to it all floated in right after Willy. He's up there waiting for you."

Chief of Police Frank Santi pointed to the staircase.

Two women sat on a wood bench in the small, gray-green room at the top of the stairway leading down to the main room of the morgue. The younger, seventeen at the most, was pregnant and in widow's weeds and weeping. The older woman was as tearless as the prairie itself. Her gingham dress was faded. Her white bonnet, frayed. The casket opposite them lay open. The corpse inside was water-bloated to the point of being unrecognizable. Standing against the far wall with his arms folded as Cub entered was Ned Van Ornum.

"This is Mister Hennessy of the FBI," Ned told the women. "He's the one who will help you now. Cub, this is Natalie Hammond. That's her husband, Samuel J., in the box. And that's Sam's mom, Ida."

Natalie glanced at Cub through crying eyes and said nothing. Ida managed a lost and weary nod.

"Sam was twenty-six and a native-born Prairie Portian," Ned explained to Cub. "He worked for Missouri Power and Electric since dropping out of high school. Worked as an assistant lineman. Missouri Power and Electric says he's a reliable employee and good electrician but lacking in formal education . . . had trouble filling out the written reports they require of the linemen. We show Sam clean as a whistle. Not as much as a parking ticket. They found him in the river at Cape Girardeau three weeks ago but didn't ID him until now. Girardeau's medical examiner attributes death to a concussion and drowning. He says Sam hit the water from a very high altitude, was probably knocked unconscious and drowned. Says there's no indication if he slipped, jumped or was pushed."

"He was pushed," Natalie said. "T'was Bicki what pushed him."

"We don't know that, girl," Sam's mother said.

"I know, ma, I know! Sam wouldn't go along with what Bicki wanted!" She turned to Cub. "Bicki's responsible! Find Bicki!"

"Sam, my son, he got the sulks right often," Ida told Cub. "Since he was a boy, he got them. Bad ones."

"It weren't no sulks, ma. It were your brother Bicki!"

"Meanness don't help no one, girl," Ida answered.

"He killed your son!" Natalie insisted. "Whether Sam was pushed or jumped, your brother Bicki done it!"

Ida turned away.

"Missouri Power and Electric says Sam got moody now and then, went into depression, but it never affected his work," Ned informed Cub. "Sam's superintendent describes him as a shy,

208

nervous guy who's slow to make up his mind, but once it's made up, watch out, he'll plow through walls doing what he's decided. Company records show that on Monday, August ninth, Sam took a four-week leave of absence."

"He was going to Florida for some fishing," Ida explained.

"You didn't say that earlier, Missus Hammond," Ned Van Ornum told her.

". . . I just remember. He was going for fishing."

"Ma, he was going to rob! You said so yourself, right here."

"I got confused. He was going for fishing."

"He was not! He was going with Bicki and them men."

Ned Van Ornum opened the door. "They know who did it and told us," he said to Cub, "but I'll be damned if I'll help you out any more. Not even you and your strutting peacock pals will be able to blow this one. Then again, who knows?" he said, exiting the room. "You've surprised us before."

"There was seven men who came with Bicki," Natalie told Cub as the door banged shut. "I only seen three of 'em myself. That Mister Corkel and the one with the limp and Reverend Walt. Sam told me about the rest. The whole seven of 'em and Bicki. There was seven men and Bicki. Most was from Illinois, where Bicki is from, and I just wouldn't let 'em in the house no more. Specially Mister Corkel. He's from around Prairie Port, Mister Corkel is. I seen him in town lots. The limpy one with the game leg, I think he's from Kentucky. The one they call the cowboy, he's from here too, but I never met him or none of the others. They all come 'cause of Bicki, though. Don't go thinking Bicki don't have nice points," Sam Hammond's pregnant widow allowed. "Bicki never once was unpolite towards me, and he dressed good. When Sam's daddy died, Sam was small when that happened, Bicki was like a second father for him till he got put back in jail. Bicki was always talking big and getting put back in jail. He didn't talk nowhere's big as Reverend Walt did. Reverend Walt, he was promising all kind of things to Sam. I never heard so personally, but Sam told me everything Reverend Walt promised. Reverend Walt and Mister Corkel was the ones I couldn't stand. I put my foot down and said, 'Sam, I don't want them or none of 'em coming back to our house no more.' And they didn't. They stopped coming."

"What was it Bicki and Reverend Walt wanted Sam to do?" Cub asked.

"Take off weeks from the electric company and get some old gen'rators working," Natalie answered. "They had some big, old-fashioned gen'rators in a cave and knew Sam couldn't resist fixing them. That's what Sam liked best, fixing up old machines. That's what Sam wanted most too, us moving to Nags Head and him opening up his own shop for fixing old electric machines and collecting them too. Nags Head is where my people is from. Nags Head, North Carolina. That's the thing they promised Sam the most, his own shop."

"Did Sam tell you where these generators were?" Cub asked.

Natalie exchanged bitter stares with Ida. "Yes, he told."

"Where?"

She was looking at Cub now. "Down inside Warbonnet Ridge."

"Did you know, Missus Hammond," Cub said gently to Natalie, "those generators have been linked to the Mormon State bank robbery?"

"Can't you see, that's why Sam couldn't go along with them," she stated. "They got Sam to take off from work and fix them gen'rators 'cause he likes doing it and because of the shop in Nags Head. Next thing he knows, them gen'rators is fixed and they got him doing other things. Got him putting underground water gates in working order. Sam still don't know what for. Bicki asks him to build a clock machine to open and close them water gates when nobody's around. That got to Sam 'cause he likes inventing machines. When he finished building the clock machine, he finds out what it's for and he got depressed like I never seen."

"What was it for?" Cub asked.

". . . To rob a bank."

"Mormon State bank?"

"Sam didn't know which bank, only that it was a bank. They was going to dig up underneath it and get away by boats, by flooding the water sewers and going through 'em in boats. Sam came home when he found out and lay down on the sofa and

210

started crying like a baby. Crying and shaking. He told me Bicki and the other men meant to rob the bank the next night, only plans had changed and they was gonna do it later that night. And they wanted Sam to come along and be part of it. Sam said they would kill him if he didn't go along, but that he couldn't go along . . . couldn't do it. He cried and shaked, and I held him for hours and hours. When he wasn't crying, we talked about other things maybe we could do. We didn't have no money to run away with, and we didn't have no place to go if we had money. We talked about seeing the police, but Sam was too afraid of Bicki for that.

". . . Then he said he was gonna commit suicide. I said, 'No, don't you do that, Sam.' " Her voice cracked. "I said, 'It's better you go along and do what Bicki wants than kill yourself.' I said, 'What about me and Christopher' . . . that's what we're calling the baby in me, Christopher . . . 'if you go and kill yourself? Do what they want, Sam. Do it!' " Sobbing resumed. "Only he didn't go along with them."

Cub Hennessy waited for her tears to subside before asking, "Missus Hammond, did Sam say what they wanted him to do if he joined them?"

"We talked about that, Sam and me did," Natalie answered. "He had to pack a change of clothes and take them with him. They was gonna give Sam one of them frog suits you see in movies. Rubber suits for swimming in water. Sam was gonna put on the rubber suit and give Bicki his change of clothes for later. Sam was gonna go down into Warbonnet and disconnect the clock machine he built, the machine that was gonna open and close the water gates. They wanted Sam to control them gates himself, let the water in when they told him to. Keep it at the right level while they was robbing the bank. After the bank was robbed, Sam was suppose to let lots more water through the gates and get in a rubber boat and go down through the sewers and join up with Bicki and the other men under the bank. Bicki and the other men was gonna be in boats too, under the bank. All of 'em was gonna ride away in the sewers and come out into the river and get on the Treachery. That's the part that frightened Sam

211

most of all, riding on the Treachery. He almost drowned as a kid doing it. But that ain't why he wanted to say no to Bicki. He wanted to say no 'cause Sam ain't no criminal. Robbing is a crime, and Sam couldn't do it. You gotta believe, Sam didn't do it!"

"What did he do?" asked Cub.

"Sam decided to go talk with Bicki and tell him he couldn't go along. And that's what Sam did, I know it. He didn't take no change of clothes with him. I swear he didn't."

"If Sam had gone along, what would have happened after riding on the Treachery?"

"Sam and the Prairie Port men, I think that was Mister Corkel and the cowboy, they was suppose to turn their boats into Big Muddy and—"

"The Big Muddy River?"

She nodded. "Where Big Muddy goes into the Mississippi River they was suppose to land and a truck would be there. A truck belonging to Mister Corkel. They would get in and drive back to Prairie Port. I was suppose to say, if anybody asked, Sam was home with me all the while."

"The rest of the men who stayed in the boats, where were they going?"

"Sam never said."

"The money? When was the stolen money to be distributed?"

"I can't speak for the rest of the men."

"When was Sam to get his money?"

"Last weekend. Sam said he and me would have to make a trip to Baton Rouge, Louisiana, if he went along with them."

"He was to be given his share of the money at Baton Rouge?"

"From Bicki. If Sam and me wanted, Bicki would arrange us going to South America. Get us the tickets and passports and all that."

"Some of the robbers were going to South America?"

"Bicki told Sam some was."

"If Sam had gone along with the robbery, how much money would his share have come to?"

"Bicki didn't say exactly. Only that it would be high enough for a repair shop and a half."

"Missus Hammond, you're certain Sam didn't go along with them?"

"I told you, Sam didn't take no change of clothes with him. He walked out to go see Bicki and tell him no, that's all!"

". . . When did Sam come back?"

Her hand rose toward the casket. "Now."

"What time did Sam leave the house to see Bicki?"

"About quarter of six, in the afternoon."

"Do you recall the date?"

"Friday . . . August twentieth."

"The night Mormon State was robbed?"

"I suppose, I don't know . . ."

"Your husband never mentioned the name Mormon State?" Cub asked.

"All he said was 'bank.' That he found out they was gonna rob a bank and needed him there to help."

"Is it possible, Missus Hammond, that Sam went to see Bicki and Bicki managed to change Sam's mind for him? Convince Sam, at gunpoint, to do what they wanted?"

Natalie shook her head. "Sam went and seen Bicki. He told Bicki he couldn't go along. Bicki said Sam couldn't walk out on them now and had to go along. Sam walked out anyways. Sam run and hid."

"How do you know that?"

"Sam called me."

"When he was in hiding?"

"When he was coming out from hiding."

"What did Sam say to you?"

"'Pologized."

"Apologized for what?"

"Having to do what he was gonna do."

"What was that?"

". . . Jumping off Warbonnet Ridge."

"Commit suicide?"

She nodded.

"He told you that on the telephone? Said he was going to kill himself?"

213

"Jump off Warbonnet Ridge." Her voice was barely audible. "He told me he was already at Warbonnet Ridge. He said even though he wasn't going along with Bicki and the men, he was as much a criminal as anybody. He said he'd never be able to live with that on his mind. He said he was scared of jumping and scared of Bicki and the other men. He said he knew Bicki and the other men would be back after the robbery to kill him and that scared him most because it wasn't only him they would be killing, they might be killing me and the baby too. He said one of the men with Bicki, Mister Corkel, liked killing women and children. Sam said . . . he told me the only thing to do was what he was gonna do and not to argue with him 'cause he felt bad enough as it was. He said he put his junior class ring in an envelope and mailed it to me for Christopher when he grows up. He said he was sorry for the sorrow he was causing me. Then he hung up."

Cub Hennessy looked over at the open coffin again, again grew nauseated. Time and the river had left Sam hideous. "Did you receive the envelope with the ring?" he managed.

She withdrew a thin silver chain from her bodice. A ring dangled at its end.

"After the phone call from Sam, what did you do?"

"Waited."

"For what?"

"For it not to be so, I guess."

"Did you think of calling the police?"

She nodded.

"Did you call the police?"

She shook her head.

"Why not?"

"I didn't want Sam to get arrested."

"Arrested for attempted suicide?"

"For going along with Bicki. I was hoping Sam would change his mind and do what Bicki asked. If Sam went along, I wouldn't want him arrested even if he broke the law."

"Where did you think Sam might be, if he had gone along?"

"Down south meeting Bicki."

"Getting his share of the money at Baton Rouge?"

She nodded.

"And you never let anyone know he was gone?"

"I told Ma here from the beginning," she said. "Four days ago I let Sam's supervisor at work know he was gone."

"Why the supervisor?"

"Sam's leave of absence with the electric company was over. He had four weeks coming, and he'd used it all. If Sam got paid by Bicki, it woulda happened last weekend. They was suppose to meet and get paid last weekend. Sam woulda called me once that happened. Only he didn't. I knew his electric company supervisor would be wondering where he was. I called the supervisor and said I was worried 'cause Sam was gone. I guess the supervisor told the police. Early this evening Ma and me got called and told Sam was here . . ."

"Do you have any idea where Bicki is?" Cub asked.

"That's what I want you to find out! I want you to get him and all the others!"

"Do you know the names of the others?"

"I told you . . . there's Mister Corkel and Reverend Walt and Bicki. Bicki Hale."

"Do you know Mister Corkel's first name? Reverend Walt's last name?"

She shook her head. "Ma does. Ma knows all of 'em."

"That's a lie," Ida protested.

"They was around your farm," Natalie said. "When I kicked Bicki out, he brought them around to your place. Seven of them, Sam told me, especially that last week."

"If Bicki did, I disremember," insisted Ida.

"Ma, you ain't never forgot nothing in your life! Sam said they was at your place and even got some mail there. Tell the man who they are. Please tell him!"

"I won't hear no more of this!" Ida went to the coffin and stared in. "He didn't do nothing, my boy! My brother, he didn't do nothing neither!" She strode from the room.

"You're sure she isn't right?" Cub asked Natalie.

215

* * *

The house was small and clapboard and in excellent repair. The tiny lawn and sparse shrubbery had been well attended to. Natalie had Cub drive around to the back, pull into a prefabricated, metal garage. The workbench and machines and tools at the rear were the kind of mundane standard equipment to be found in any home workshop. Cub, an amateur carpenter himself, noticed this, wouldn't have expected a wizard to create his wizardry here.

Natalie stepped to several large cardboard cartons piled in the corner, removed them, pulled up a trapdoor in the cement floor. Cub lifted out with difficulty a very large metal workbox.

"Everything doin' with the Bonnet he kept in there," she said, opening the top. "I was suppose to get rid of all of it, but I didn't. Sam told me to get rid of it in that last phone call of his. Get rid of it so no shame would fall to me and our baby."

Cub went through the contents, phoned Yates and Jez back at the office about what to bring along and where to meet him.

Ida sat rocking in a rocking chair on the sloping porch of her dilapidated three-story farmhouse. Beside her rested a suitcase. Beside the suitcase were Jez and Yates.

"She was out near the road when we got here," Jez called as Cub walked from his car with Natalie. "Says she didn't have any particular destination in mind, only that she was leaving so you'd stop pestering her."

"Got the gizmo?" Cub asked.

"Sure do," Jez answered.

"I don't mean to pester you, Missus Hammond." Cub spoke gently, came and sat on the edge of the porch in front of Ida's rocking chair. "Don't mean to malign your son or your brother either. Don't intend to arrest you or search your house or do anything like that. You want to get up and go where you were going, that's fine with me. I won't interfere, I won't follow. What I'm asking you to do is listen . . . and if you've a mind to, help. I need your help, Missus Hammond. We all do. A crime has been committed. And that's against the law. You're not lawless, Missus

216

Hammond, I know that. You don't have to like the FBI. Just do what you can to protect the law . . . if you're inclined."

She said nothing, went on rocking.

"See that object Mister Jessup is holding up, Missus Hammond?"

Ida impassively looked at the handcrafted fuse Jessup was displaying.

"That was found at the place the robbers used to flood the tunnels, Missus Hammond," Cub said. "It's a wonderful job of craftsmanship, that fuse. We've searched all over trying to find the person who made it. But you know that from the media, don't you, Missus Hammond?"

Ida rocked in silence.

"You've been following what television and the papers are saying about the robbery, haven't you, Missus Hammond?"

"She don't have the TV or read papers," Natalie told him. "Neither do I."

"Missus Hammond, let me tell you what the TV is saying about that fuse and the other electric devices found. They say it's the work of a wizard. A genius. Your son, Sam, is that genius. That wizard. Only no one knows it. His genius didn't show up on his employment record or his school tests. Those methods have been unreliable before, they were again with Sam. We've questioned hundreds of electrical engineers and electronics experts trying to find the one who could have built that fuse and the other amazing objects. Men who earn fifty, a hundred, two hundred thousand dollars a year. Who teach at universities, write books about electricity. Sam was better than any of them, Missus Hammond. Sam did what they couldn't have done. Sam was a . . . a wizard. Only good will come of this, I promise. If you want the world to know how talented your son was, we can do it so we show Sam was forced to do what he did. Or, if you want, we won't mention it. We'll do anything you want, Missus Hammond, to get your cooperation . . . to learn what you know. But believe me, your son Sam was involved with the robbery. He was the one who made much of it possible. Look what I found at his workshop."

Cub displayed a second handcrafted fuse. "No one but Sam had

217

the skill to build these." The second fuse was brought next to the first fuse being held up by Jessup. They were identical.

Ida stopped rocking, contemplated the two fuses, turned toward her daughter-in-law. "Why you doin' this to me, girl?"

"Why you denying your own son?" Natalie shot back. "Whether Sam jumped or got pushed off that cliff, Bicki done it! Why you protecting your brother over your son?"

"'Cause he is my brother! Blood kin! The last I got!"

"What about this here!" Natalie was slapping at her huge, pregnant stomach. "What kinda blood's this baby in here got if it ain't your own? Your own and your son's own? Who killed my baby's father? Who killed your grandson's father?"

Ida wilted. Her eyes wettened. Hesitantly she began to identify the eight actual robbers of the vault at Mormon State National Bank . . . Reverend Wallace Tecumseh "Windy Walt" Sash . . . Lamar "Wiggles" Loftus . . . Willy "Cowboy" Carlson . . . Thomas "The Worm" Ferugli . . . Elmo "River Rat" Ragotsy . . . Lionel "Meadow Muffin" Epstein . . . Marion "Mule Fucker" Corkel . . . Bicki "Little Haifa" Hale.

Later, giving her deposition at the FBI offices, Ida revealed that Bicki was to be in Baton Rouge the coming weekend, not the previous one, as Natalie believed. That was where Ida was heading with her suitcase when Jessup and Yates intercepted her, to see if she could reach Bicki before he left Baton Rouge.

# Thirteen

He appeared out of place on the tree-shaded street of Baton Rouge, everything about him did. The short-sleeved shirt was imitation Hawaiian and too large. The pants were wool and old and baggy, and when he hiked them up it could be seen rope was used as a belt. The shoes, at the distance Yates, Brewmeister, Jessup and other FBI men were watching from, seemed not to match. His arms were long and dangling. The torso short. The shoulders round and slumped somewhat forward.

"He looks more like an ape than a mule–fucker," Jessup commented. He lowered his binoculars and stepped back from the window of the darkened stake-out room established the day before by Baton Rouge's FBI. "That's what they call him, you know. Mule Fucker."

"We know," Pete Kirkwood, a local Bureauman, answered.

Brew fixed his binoculars tighter on the man loping along the sidewalk three floors below. Mule appeared to have no neck. His hair was reddish and unkempt, his face narrow and long with a potato nose. When Mule stopped at the entrance of the Altmont Hotel, directly across the street, and glanced ferretlike back and around, Brew was able to focus in on an abrupt scar at the corner of the right eye.

Jessup headed for the refreshment table at the rear of the room. "Can you imagine being called Mule Fucker?"

"Apparently that's what he prefers," Daughter said.

Vance Daughter was from headquarters' flying squad and like Jessup, Brew and Yates had just arrived in Baton Rouge. It was the first time in the investigation that Prairie Port agents had met a member of the squad designed to expedite all out-of-town aspects of the investigation. Daughter's ostensible mission in Baton

219

Rouge, beyond observing, was to provide surveilling agents with background data on suspected gang members residing anywhere other than in Prairie Port . . . particularly to hasten photographs and descriptions by which the Bureaumen in the area could recognize and identify suspected bank robbers. Photos and data, sketchy as they were, had come in from Prairie Port on the men in its area—Marion "Mule Fucker" Corkel, Elmo "River Rat" Ragotsy and the deceased Willy "Cowboy" Carlson.

The out-of-town suspects the flying squad was responsible for were Bicki "Little Haifa" Hale, Reverend Wallace Tecumseh "Windy Walt" Sash, Thomas "The Worm" Ferugli, Lamar "Wiggles" Loftus and Lionel "Meadow Muffin" Epstein. The squad had revealed that none of these alleged bank thieves could be located at their last known addresses. The only dossier and photograph to have reached Baton Rouge were for Lamar "Wiggles" Loftus. The Baton Rouge Police Department had found a sixteen-year-old photograph of Bicki "Little Haifa" Hale in their files, but the picture was in poor condition.

The fear of the Baton Rouge and Prairie Port Bureaumen was that lack of identifying photos or descriptions had already enabled some gang members to enter and leave town under the surveillers' eyes without being recognized. Daughter seemed to have no such worry, seemed politely unrushed by pleas for expedition.

"According to the Kansas state police," Daughter said, stepping up beside Jessup at the refreshment table, "Corkel has a long teen arrest record for sodomizing mules, goats and ponies. I noticed that wasn't in your report on him."

"At least we sent in a report," Jessup said.

"Who complained about the sodomizing," Yates asked from the window, "a mule, goat or pony?"

"I would have expected a question like that from you," Daughter replied.

"I would have expected you to be up on bestiality," Yates countered.

Vance Daughter and Billy Yates sized each other up through the dim light of the long room. The pair of young agents had gone through the FBI training academy at Quantico, Virginia, together. Scholastically they had ranked number one and number two in their graduating class, with Vance finishing second to Billy. Yates, however, had been overlooked for the most exalted academic honor of that period, admittance to the small, private seminars conducted by Orin G. Trask, professor emeritus at Johns Hopkins University and the nation's, if not the world's, foremost authority on theoretic criminology. Vance Daughter was selected by Trask. Daughter also bested Yates in the hundred-yard dash and high jump. Yates beat hell out of Daughter boxing and at judo. They finished dead even on the gun ranges.

"He's going into the hotel," Brew said, watching Marion "Mule Fucker" Corkel disappear across the lobby of the Altmont Hotel.

Kirkwood moved to the window, looked down at the Almont. "If Corkel does what he did yesterday, does what the Altmont desk clerk says he'd done the last four days, he'll sit in the back of the lobby half an hour and leave. Yesterday Corkel went from the Altmont over to the playground beyond the corner. You can see the playground from the room next door. Yesterday Elmo Ragotsy was waiting for him in the park. Corkel and Ragotsy sat talking to one another about five minutes in the playground, then each went back to their own hotels. Ragotsy got into Baton Rouge the day before yesterday from what we can tell. Checked into the Packard Arms Apartment Hotel under the name of Eric Kenekee from Kansas. The Packard says the reservation was made under Kenekee's name four weeks ago; that would be before Mormon State came off. Corkel is staying at the Firestone Motel two blocks away. He showed up at the Firestone without a reservation and registered as Ted Hotchkiss from Cleveland. We've got the Packard and Firestone covered. We're keeping an eye on every hotel as best we can. We're shorthanded. New Orleans and the residencies have sent in men, but we could use more."

"Personnel is en route," Daughter assured him.

A young Baton Rouge agent, wearing a radio headset, stepped in from the command post in the adjoining room, "Sounds like another one is registering at the Clemments House right now, the one with the limp, Loftus."

221

* * *

... Lamar Jonathan Loftus, aka Thomas Wile, John Lamar and Wiggles, according to the flying squad's summary report, was born 11 September 1924 in Dayton, Ohio, and received the equivalent of a ninth-grade education. His juvenile-arrest record began 22 October 1930 for the theft of candy. The case was "set aside." Twenty-seven more juvenile offenses, all petty thefts, occurred before Loftus, at the age of fourteen, was sentenced to a state correctional facility for incorrigible children from which he escaped five times. On his eighteenth birthday he enlisted in the United States Army, where he was court-martialed twice for petty larceny and critically injured in combat at the Battle of the Bulge when a German Tiger tank rolled over his right leg. There were two different accounts of the incident. At first it was believed that Loftus had displayed cowardice and was running from the tank and slipped. It was later confirmed that Loftus had attacked the tank with a Molotov cocktail and was ground under the vehicle's treads. Loftus's right leg was mutilated but saved from amputation by a series of nineteen operations. He was denied the Silver Cross, for which he was recommended, due to his criminal record. In 1946 he was honorably separated from the military and left the Army hospital where he had been since his injury. From 1950 to 1967 he resided in the Paducah, Kentucky, home of his brother, had no known arrests, no known employment and seems to have subsisted solely on his Veterans Administration disability benefits. During April of 1967 he was employed as a deckhand on the *Mary G,* a Mississippi River tug owned and operated by Elmo Ragotsy, age fifty-eight. Ragotsy, known as "River Rat," a convicted smuggler and fence of minor contraband, was reputed to have been a member of the Prohibition era's bootlegging Treachery Gang. While working on the *Mary G,* which was berthed at Cape Girardeau, Missouri, Loftus maintained a rural residence across the river in western Kentucky. Ragotsy during this same period resided in Prairie Port, Missouri, where he shared an apartment with Willy "Cowboy" Carlson, an alleged pickpocket and petty burglar. On 12 March 1968, Loftus, with Carlson, was arrested for the attempted armed robbery of a liquor store outside of Cairo, Illinois. It was the first known felony arrest for either man. Carlson was convicted and incarcerated at Statesville Penitentiary. Loftus, the accused driver of the getaway car, could not be positively identified, and charges against him were dropped. Loftus was believed to have given up his job on the *Mary G* and returned to Kentucky.

"Some desperado," Yates commented as he finished reading the summary report on Wiggles Loftus. "Only one felony arrest out of almost three dozen collars and that one bungled. Hardly the crook of the century, this clown. Hardly 'the cream of the crime world,' as NBC put it."

"Corticun put it that way too. I saw it in three different press releases Corticun sent out this week." Brew, seated at the desk of the hotel room being shared with Yates, was going through the balance of available data on the gang. "Get a load of what's here on Mule Fucker if you want to see how sour that cream is getting."

"Mule's worse than Wiggles?"

"Worse and funnier. I mean this guy's outrageous, he's so penny-ante. He actually stole flowers off a grave. Got caught and fined for stealing flowers off a grave."

Yates was pleased. "Picture the expression on Corticun's face when he finds that out."

"He already found out," Brew said. "Jez talked to Strom at Prairie Port. Strom said Corticun came down off the twelfth floor and looked over the stuff they were sending us and damn near died of heart failure when he read about Mule Fucker and Cowboy Carlson. I mean, they are really looney-toon. Billy, you think maybe Mule and Cowboy weren't involved with Mormon State?"

"It would be a neat bit of magic if they weren't. Nope, everything fits too snug." Yates handed Wiggles Loftus's dossier to Brewmeister. "This ties Cowboy Carlson, Loftus and Ragotsy together tight as can be. Add that to what Sam Hammond's mother and widow said, and it's a lock. Loftus and Cowboy even got arrested together on a screw-up armed job. That's what sent Cowboy over to Statesville Penitentiary, that job."

Brew said, "And that's where Cowboy met Bicki Hale. They were cellmates at Statesville."

"Who told you that?"

"Jez," Brew answered. "Jez said Strom said so. Strom found out yesterday with a lot of other information, but Corticun's holding everything up. Corticun's being a pain in the butt about jurisdiction. Strom thinks Corticun's nose is out of joint, that he's white-hot jealous we're breaking things so fast. Anyway, Corticun's pulling rank and playing by the book, insisting that information coming from beyond the city limits of Prairie Port go directly to the flying squad for dissemination. That's the worst idea yet, that flying squad," Brew said. "Who the hell are they anyway? Who the hell is that guy Daughter you don't like?"

"Exactly what he appears to be," Yates said. "A tight-butt junior Brass Ball who salutes the flag five times a day. He's so far right he thinks the Nazi party is a communist front organization."

The phone rang. Brew picked up.

"It's Wiggles Loftus, all right," Kirkwood's voice said. "He's left his hotel and is heading for the playground. If you want, I'll pick you up in our surveillance truck. A Good Humor truck."

His right leg kicking out to the side and slapping rigidly onto the pavement at every other step, Lamar "Wiggles" Loftus crossed the street under the red light at the corner, crossed as Yates and Brew and Kirkwood watched from inside the Good Humor truck. Wiggles was five foot eight or nine. His large chest and head, in comparison with a frail lower torso, seemed enormous. Blond curly hair billowed out from around a Nordic good-looking face, a far handsomer face than had appeared on the file photograph.

"He checked into the Clemments House under his own name," Kirkwood said as they surveilled. "He hadn't made a reservation. The Clemments House has you pay in advance. Guess how he paid? With an American Express credit card. I haven't had a debt in my life, have never been arrested and I get turned down three times for an American Express card. But they give a card to Wiggles Loftus, who has a mile-long pinch ticket . . . "

Wiggles paused at the playground, limped on across the next street and down the sidewalk, gazed into the empty lobby of the Altmont Hotel, hailed a waiting cab.

The ice-cream truck followed the cab to the Clemments House. Wiggles got out and went inside. Tailing agents, several minutes later, radioed that Wiggles had gone to his room. Agents at the Packard Arms Apartment Hotel and the Firestone Motel reported that River Rat Ragotsy and Mule Corkel could each be seen in their respective rooms . . . that neither had made any phone calls all day.

Twenty minutes later Jessup and Daughter were hurried through a back entrance at the Lafayette Inn and on into the manager's office, where they were met by a Baton Rouge Bureauman named Bass, who introduced them to A. L. Sonny Cole, a sixty-three-year-old, white-bearded, strappingly muscular man in an "Elvis Presley" cap.

"Mr. Cole is the night clerk here," Bass explained. "Has been the night clerk here since moving down from Indiana a few years back. His aunt bought this place a few years ago."

"August eleventh, 1967, is when I arrived," Cole said firmly. "Haven't missed a day's work since."

Bass displayed a reproduction of the faded sixteen-year-old photograph of Bicki Hale and explained, "Mister Cole may have seen Hale here last week."

Jessup took the picture, sat opposite the slightly stern whitebeard. "That so, Mister Cole? You think you saw this man?"

"Mighta been. Might notta been."

"You're not sure?"

"Cain't hardly tell dark from light on that camera pict're thar. But the 'scriptions fit."

"'Scriptions?"

"The description sheet we gave him," Bass said.

"Seen lots of 'em come and go," Sonny Cole volunteered. "Been clerking desks since my majority and all kinds come and go, and some, like him, make an etch. He had grips with him. Comes in the middle of the night with no reservation and five heavy grips. Leather and strapped grips with locks on the straps.

225

I carry them up two flights to three-oh-two and don't get so much as a thank-you-boy from him. Not one thin dime from him. Says he don't want no disturbing. No telephone calls and no maid coming in in the morning or any time he's in there. Only time he isn't in there is late afternoon. From four to five. Larry Doyle, the day clerk, don't ever see him 'cept from four to five. Goes out at four. Goes up the street to the right. Comes back the same way at five, sometimes with a grocery bag. One day I come to work early . . . I start at six, 'cept Saturdays, like today, when I work the early shift too . . . but last Tuesday I come at four-thirty, and when I pass the Altmont Hotel I look in and there he is, Mister Jahad, sitting in the lobby."

Cole turned to Bass. "Your friends here know about the Altmont?"

Bass told Jessup and Daughter, "The Altmont lobby reputedly is a meeting place for homosexuals."

"No maybe 'bout it," Cole said. "Been clerking all my life, and I know queer sissy boys when I see 'em. Know all about 'em. The Altmont lobby's queer sissy boy. I seen young boys go up to his room too, I didn't tell you that afore," Cole told Bass. "Three times, late at night, young boys went up to his room. I stopped the first one and asked him where he thought he was going. We're licit here. The young boy said he was picking up a delivery. I can't call Mister Jahad 'cause he don't want phones ringing. I send the boy up and sure enough he comes down soon with a package. A big package wrapped in brown paper and tied with rope. Mister Jahad comes down right after mad as mean hell. He says he don't want me interfering with his messenger boy or he'll check out. A night or two later another young boy comes in and goes up to his room. I know 'cause I snuck behind him seeing where he went. It was three-oh-two, Mister Jahad's room. He come down quick too, that boy, and carrying the same kind of big package as the first boy. The third boy, he didn't come down that fast. The third boy went up to Mister Jahad's room a couple of nights later. Went up real late and stayed long. That's the only night Mister Jahad ever made a phone call. Called the Firestone Motel and asked if somebody or other had registered. I missed the name 'cause another call came in on the board and I had to switch off a minute to take it. When I got back to listening, Mister Jahad was saying, 'You must have a reservation for him.' Somebody at the Firestone said back they absolutely didn't have a reservation or anyone registered. But no name I heard was mentioned. Later the boy comes down. He didn't have no package with him. Maybe an hour after that, just before daybreak, Mr. Jahad says he's going to check out. I bring the five bags down to his car, a station wagon. The bags are lighter now. He pays his bill in cash. He's got a fistful of twenties and fifties thick as ever I saw that he's paying with. I don't get no tip again either. Not one thin dime."

"Do you have any of that money?" Jez asked.

"All money here gets deposited the next morning," Cole said.

"And the money got deposited the next morning? In a bank?"

"It did," answered Cole.

"Was the money old or new? Old, used bills or newer bills?"

"Old and used."

"How old and used?"

"Some was in such bad shape they was torn or pasty–feeling. I remember thinking this was peculiar."

"How many days ago was it that Mister Jahad checked out?"

"Five."

"How long was he at the hotel before checking out?"

"Ten days."

"You said you couldn't recognize Mister Jahad all that well from the photograph, is that correct, Mister Cole?"

"The face shape is the same," Cole said. "And the hairline and swarthiness. The man was Arab-like 'cept the blondishness. His hair is blondish."

"Do you have his registration card?"

"It's out at the desk. I know what it reads, it reads A. G. Jahad, Beirut, Lebanon."

"Was he foreign-sounding?" asked Jessup.

"Hell, no. Spoke like he was from Kansas."

"Can you describe him physically?"

"Just like the other gent described him to me." Cole indicated

227

Bass. "Five foot eight, a hundred fifty or sixty, darkish skin, blondish, light eyes and maybe forty-five years old."

The call from Baton Rouge to Prairie Port was placed exactly at 4 P.M. Strom Sunstrom and Cub Hennessy were on the receiving end. Jessup did the Baton Rouge talking with Yates and Brewmeister listening in.

Attention centered on the interview Jez had conducted with A. L. Sonny Cole one hour and ten minutes earlier at the Lafayette Inn. If A. G. Jahad was indeed Bicki "Little Haifa" Hale, and their descriptions certainly seemed to match, then the five suitcases carried up to the room might very well have contained money stolen from the Mormon State vault. Old, worn currency like that used to pay the hotel bill. The two bulky packages carried from room 302 by the first two young men could have been shares of stolen funds being distributed to gang members waiting at different locations in Baton Rouge. Following this scenario further, they concluded the lobby of the Altmont Hotel must have been the contact point between each robber and the gang's paymaster, Little Haifa Hale . . . that on two different occasions Hale had gone and sat in the known homosexual pickup spot and rendezvoused with two different robbers, worked out times and addresses for money delivery, dispatched the young men with paper-wrapped bundles of loot . . . that a foul-up had occurred the last night of Bicki "Little Haifa's" stay when a messenger boy was waiting to make a delivery but someone hadn't contacted Bicki as planned. Someone who was supposed to have checked into the Firestone Motel. Was supposed to have been there a day before Mule Corkel actually did check into the Firestone. Mule possibly was the intended recipient of the delivery that was never made.

Jez, Strom and Cub concluded that Sam Hammond's widow, Natalie, and his mother, Ida, may both have been accurate in their differing recollections as to which weekend in Baton Rouge the distribution of funds was to be made. Somehow, Jez and Strom and Cub reasoned, a failure in communications or a misunderstanding had resulted in Bicki Little Haifa and some of the

228

gang arriving in Baton Rouge and transferring loot before the arrival of Mule Corkel, River Rat Ragotsy and Wiggles Loftus. If Jahad was Bicki, he had been gone from Baton Rouge a full half day when Mule checked into the Firestone.

Such presumptions could explain why Mule Corkel had waited in the Altmont Hotel lobby at the same time on four consecutive afternoons for a half hour: to meet with Bicki "Little Haifa" Hale and arrange for the delivery of his share of the stolen money. Wiggles Loftus and River Rat Ragotsy might be here for the same purpose.

"What do we do when Wiggles, Mule and Ragotsy find out there isn't going to be a payday?" Jessup asked Strom long distance. "When they realize Bicki Hale has left town?"

"Maybe the arrangements are for Bicki to return at a specified time if the first rendezvous is missed," Strom suggested. "Maybe he'll be back."

"Carrying five large suitcases?" Jessup wondered aloud. "That doesn't seem too smart or typical, not if Bicki is behaving as cautiously as the night clerk suggests."

"What has our star crystal-ball gazer to say?" Strom asked. "Yates, how does this look to you?"

Yates, on an extension line in the room adjoining Jessup's, thought for a moment. "We don't know if Jahad is Bicki Hale. If he isn't, Ida Hammond might be right and the payoff weekend is this weekend. Bicki and the others could be arriving any time now. There's another possibility. It could be that Bicki ran out on some of the gang without paying them. That Mule, Wiggles and Ragotsy are three of the men who didn't get paid and they've come here looking for Bicki. I have a feeling Mule isn't here in the best of humors."

Strom, always intrigued by Yates's circuitous logic, asked, "How do you reconcile both Natalie and Ida saying Baton Rouge was the payday place, and Natalie, in particular, telling you her husband was to be away from home several weeks?"

Yates answered, "Ida never said Baton Rouge was the payday location. Ida merely said she was coming here to try to find Bicki before he left. Ida never really admitted a crime came down,

229

only that the men she named were around her house before the theft."

"Yates, are you saying you don't think this gang are the thieves?" Strom spoke with concern.

"I think they're the ones, Strom," Billy Yates said. "I'm only dealing with Ida and Natalie's statements. Ida could have been coming down here to find Bicki before he left for South America. Maybe she wanted to go to South America with him. I feel it's likely that Natalie, or Sam, got the Baton Rouge end of the operation a bit muddled in their minds. Natalie said Sam told her some of the men would be going to South America. What if Baton Rouge was merely the rendezvous point for Sam going to South America? For getting tickets and passports and all that? Maybe the distribution of stolen money took place somewhere else before this? Maybe Mule and Ragotsy and Wiggles were unhappy with their share. Maybe they got completely cut out. Mule and Ragotsy and Wiggles are sort of the Prairie Port clique, the others have to be old friends of Bicki. Bicki brought the others in. Maybe Bicki and his old friends short-sheeted the Prairie Port crooks. Maybe that's why the Prairie Portians, Mule, River Rat Ragotsy and Wiggles, are here, to get even, or get their money before Bicki takes off to South America."

"How do you come up with these ideas, Yates?" Strom asked.

"You asked for the possibilities as I saw them," Yates said. "This is what I saw."

"What happens," Brewmeister asked, "if Bicki Hale doesn't show up in Baton Rouge? Shall we go on surveilling Mule, Ragotsy and Wiggles if they leave town? Or should we pick them up?"

"I'm not sure," Strom said. "We don't have that good a case against them yet. If we surveille and they lead us to the others, we'll be in a far stronger position, convictionwise. And I'd love to have some of that stolen money back."

Cub reminded everyone, "Mr. Hoover's a fanatic about recovering stolen money."

"How effective is the surveillance, if we had to go further?" Strom asked.

"Top grade, so far," Jez told him. "They have forty men on the street right now, stake-outs at three hotels, two mobile units operative and good communications. I understand they've more than enough vehicles ready if we have to go interstate, and they work well with the Louisiana troopers. Louisiana's the best there is on highway tails."

"Interstate spreads you thin," Cub observed, "particularly if they take you in three different directions."

Jessup said, "It might be a good idea to get warrants out on the guys here, just in case. If something breaks, we're in a position to pick them up without delay—"

"Yes, I'll do that," Strom agreed. "And let's try to get that Flying Hamster Squad off its butt. We need identifiable photographs of Bicki Hale. Let's make positive identification from that hotel clerk. I'll work on Corticun, you pressure Daughter."

Kirkwood came into the office, whispered into Jessup's ear.

"We got to go, Strom," Jessup said. "They're on the move. All three of them. Mule, Wiggles and Rat Ragotsy. Each one is leaving his own hotel."

Wiggles, his right leg slapping out sideways, passed the wrought-iron fence of the Old Capitol Building. Rat Ragotsy went directly to the playground and sat on a bench. Mule followed a route his surveillers had never seen him take before, turned left from his hotel onto a cyprus-shaded avenue leading down to the river. Rat Ragotsy got up and left the playground.

Yates and Brew, in a dented, unmarked 1968 panel truck following Wiggles, heard over the cab radio that Mule had gotten into a taxi . . . minutes later learned the taxi had stopped to pick up Ragotsy . . . shortly after that were told the two suspects had gotten out and entered the city zoo, a hundred-and-forty-acre tract of forest and walkways and animals where surveillance would be doubly difficult.

The driver of the panel truck told Yates and Brew it looked as if Wiggles might also be heading for the zoo. The prediction came true. Wiggles, a quarter of an hour later, limped onto a

231

narrow zoo path leading into a thick growth of trees and disappeared.

Walkie-talkie in hand, surveillers deployed along the zoo's perimeter, kept in touch with one another, dared not penetrate too deep inside the compound out of fear they'd be seen.

Yates and Brew became restive and wandered into a zoo refreshment stand. Then, munching sandwiches and sipping sodas, they meandered up a slight rise, sat down on the grass and surveyed the surrounding terrain as best they could . . . on a visible stretch of curving lagoon-side walkway saw Wiggles and Mule. Wiggles limping into view from the left, Mule emerging from the trees to the right, with neither one knowing the other was there because of dense shrubbery in the nook of the bending path. They moved closer to one another. Saw one another. Stopped as if surprised by the sight. Wiggles held out his arms, seemingly to embrace a long-lost comrade. Mule snatched a thick stick from the undergrowth and, hand on high and face lowered, charged Wiggles. Smashed into him headfirst. Knocked Wiggles down onto the path and began beating him with the stick and kicking him and shouting at him. Jumped onto Wiggles and tried to thumb his eyes out. Wiggles, thrashing his head from side to side to avert the gouging, twisted sharply and heaved and dislodged Mule and leapt back up and tried to explain something . . . and was charged again. Tumbled to the ground again with Mule on his chest shouting and pummeling. Wiggles fought back, punched and rolled with Mule. Rolled both of them into the waters of the shallow lagoon . . . found a rock and began pounding Mule in the face with it.

Rat Ragotsy came along the path from the right, saw the battle, started running to them shouting they should stop. Ragotsy reined to a halt yards short of the combat. Pointed off to the left. Cupped his hand beside his mouth shouting at them. Ran off as a moped-riding zoo ranger appeared on the arching path to the left.

Speaking into his walkie-talkie, the ranger debiked, went down to water's edge and tried to separate Mule and Wiggles. Wiggles smashed the ranger in the forehead with the rock. Mule clubbed

232

the ranger with his stick, kicked Wiggles in the chest and knocked him back into the water, ran up to the path and straddled the idling moped and rode off to the right. Wiggles scrambled up the path and directly into the woods behind. A second moped ranger came in from the left. Dismounting, he rushed to the aid of his bloody and motionless comrade, raised the walkie-talkie and spoke into it.

Yates and Brew, too far away to have either stopped the brutal fracas or chased after the fleeing suspects, ran back to the panel truck and radioed Jez at the command post what had happened. Jez phoned Strom in Prairie Port. Strom, hearing his suspects were in flight and might not bother to return to their hotels, made an immediate decision: pick up Mule, Rat and Wiggles as quickly as possible, pick them up on whatever charges possible until Prairie Port obtained federal warrants for bank robbery.

State and city police reinforced the Bureaumen and rangers in sweeping across the zoo. Desperate shouting, just before sundown, brought searchers to the base of a tree surrounded by snapping hyenas . . . a tree in which Wiggles roosted on an upper limb screaming for his life. He was taken to the city jail and incarcerated for assaulting a zoo officer. Mule and Rat Ragotsy could not be found. A three-state alarm went out for them for "assault-with-intent-to-kill."

With Mule and Rat still not in custody when federal warrants were granted at 8 P.M., Strom wasted no time in ordering an all-points federal fugitives alert for the two missing felons, citing their offense as bank robbery.

Rangers and Bureaumen, continuing their search of the Baton Rouge zoo at dawn, located the moped abandoned by Mule, followed footprints believed to be Mule's across the zoo's black bear compound and down to the edge of a moat. The towering chainlink fence beyond the moat revealed traces of ascending mud on its wire. Footprints on the other side led to a road. A police report received less than an hour later stated that at 10 P.M. the previous evening, at that very spot in the road, a car had been stopped and the driver pulled from his seat and beaten and the car stolen by a man fitting Mule's description.

Shortly before noon the assistant U.S. attorney for the southern district of Missouri petitioned the assistant U.S. magistrate of that district for the extradition of Lamar Jonathan Loftus to Prairie Port to face questioning by a special federal grand jury convened to look into the robbery of the Mormon State National Bank.

At 2:35 P.M. the Prairie Port FBI residency office accepted a collect telephone call from O. D. Don Pensler, chief sheriff of Meridan County.

"Good sirs, we jes ketched ya something fine," Pensler told Cub, who took the call for Strom. "Ketched it right outta Wallaooska Creek, trying to steal a boat . . . that Mr. Ray-goatsy y'all beena wanting. Mr. Ray-goatsy, he's a good ole fella, and we're takin' real special care of him for ya. Come fetch him when you're so obliged. Meridan County Jail House is the address. Second red light after Dunsberg on Interstate Twenty-one. And tell Mister Hoover a nice hello, hear? Tell him down here in Meridan, where men is men and the flag's a flag, he has our hearts."

Another five hours had elapsed and the sun was setting when Yates, freshly arrived at Prairie Port, crept up the ridge to where Rodney Willis and Butch Cody lay.

"That's Mule's spread down there, all of it." Butch indicated a vast tract of dusty, rolling bottom land, ringed intermittently by runs of rotting fence. The far acreage, where several thin cows stood, was what was left of grazing pastures. Closer in were corrals and stables in ugly disrepair. An ancient horse stood in one corral, four mules in another, a goat in a third. An automobile graveyard was in the immediate foreground, at the base of the rise from which the three Bureaumen watched. Between the corral and the car dump was a partially collapsed wooden house. Except for a kerosene lantern burning beyond one downstairs window, the house was dark. Ten yards from the rear porch of the house was a blazing bonfire. A few feet from the fire stood a tall, authentic Indian teepee.

"Mule's in the house right now," Butch Cody continued. "And he knows we're out here okay. He's preparing. Wait till you see

234

him, you won't believe it. He's got his squaw in the teepee, or at least a very young girl who's dressed as an Indian squaw. Whatever happens, we have to keep away from the teepee."

"Seems Mule snuck in sometime this morning," Rodney Willis said. "We thought we had this place covered pretty well, but he got in without our seeing. Could be there's a trapdoor and tunnel down there and that's how he got in."

"More than one tunnel," Butch Cody suggested. "Mule keeps showing up all the hell over the place. Popping up in the middle of a field and disappearing."

"As soon as he comes out of the house this time," Rodney told Yates, "Cub wants us to be ready to go get him. All our guys, the residency guys, will go in first. Corticun's twelfth-floor crowd follows after us."

Rodney Willis passed a shotgun and box of shells over to Yates. "Look for a flare. We go on a green flare."

. . . Marion "Mule Fucker" Corkel peeked out of the rear door of the house. A beaded Indian band engirded his brow, holding in place a solitary looming turkey feather at the back of the head. His nose was painted white. Two short, slanting white lines adorned each of his cheeks. Mule looked about, ran from the house lugging a large, tarp-covered object, zigzagged past the bonfire and ducked into the teepee. He emerged wearing a loin cloth and bullet-filled bandoleros. Stepped to the bonfire. Arched his back. Raised his chin. Crossed his arms and held them high and stared out past the fire at the setting sun. Stood motionless until final darkness arrived. When it did, Mule, with one hand fanning his war-whooping mouth and the other flapping behind him, circled the fire in a foot-stomping ritual Indian dance of some sort.

A flare gun popped, sent a tiny fireball curving up into the night sky. The ball burst into a blaze of glowing green.

Why exactly the FBI agents, charging down from the rise and in from two sides on the flat below, also let out Indian war whoops as they ran would never be fully understood. The loudest whooper of all was Les Kebbon, riding a bounding jeep driven by Happy de Camp.

Mule spun about, took stock of the assault, dove inside the teepee, moments later backed out, loin-clothed bottom first, rolling a tripod-mounted World War II light machine gun after him.

"Machine gun! Machine gun!" Bureau voices echoed in the darkness.

Mule slid in behind the gun, threw the breech, swung the muzzle around toward three nearing silhouettes. A tear-gas grenade exploded off to the side. Another detonated directly before him. Mule scurried back into the teepee, darted out of it through a rear flap carrying rifles and clusters of small round objects.

"The fields! The fields!" came shouts. "He's heading into the fields."

Mule, as he ran through darkness, also shouted, shouted the words "Vonda Lizzie!"

Hap de Camp, following the cries of "Vonda Lizzie," wheeled the jeep over the bumpy terrain, neared the zigzagging Mule, tried keeping him in his headbeams as Les Kebbon, standing on the vehicle's front seat, began to twirl a lariat over his head.

Mule, glancing back as he ran from side to side avoiding the headlights, saw the spinning rope. He grasped a small round object firmly in his hand, stopped and spun around and hurled the object at Les . . . hurled round object after round object at him and the jeep.

"Mule dung?" Sue Ann Willis questioned as her husband, Rodney, slid into bed beside her. "He threw gourds filled with mule dung at Les?"

"Les and Hap," Rodney Willis said. "Hit both of them with damn near every one he threw, which was a lot. He knocked Les right back into the jeep with a mouth full of the stuff. And Hap, I don't know if you know but Hap fought against the Japanese in World War II, made five amphibious landings and never got driven back once. But Mule Fucker sure as hell drove him back."

"Mule what?" Sue Ann asked.

"That's what they call him, Susie, Mule Fucker. It's right on his sheet. He hits Happy full in the face with dung, and Happy gets momentarily blinded and the jeep goes bumping off in one direction damn near hitting some of our guys, and Mule Fucker is running in the other direction like something wild. A real scene. Mule Fucker's dressed like an Indian with these gun belts crossing his chest and shouting out 'Vonda Lizzie,' whatever that means. He stops and knocks the jeep right out of action with mule dung and takes off again with damn near the whole office chasing him. He keeps throwing mule dung at us, and when he runs out of that he starts throwing old rifles at us. He's been carrying an armful of old rifles and he throws those too. And bullets from the bullet belts over his shoulder. Bandoleros like you see Mexican bandits in the movies wear. And he doesn't stop running, Susie. The man was amazing. Our guys are getting winded and dropping out, but this looney-toon seems to be gaining strength. He goes running across one field after another until nobody's left chasing him except Cub. Cub's chugging away right behind him like an old steam engine chugging up a steep hill. Mule can't shake Cub, so he runs right out onto the highway. This looney-toon is running in and out between highway traffic dressed like an Indian and with his nose painted white and letting out war whoops and shouting 'Vonda Lizzie' and doing everything to shake Cub. Cub finally brings him down with a flying tackle. Tackles the guy right before a tollbooth. That crazy Mule Fucker was heading right for a tollbooth.

"I can't keep a straight face when I think about that guy. I know I shouldn't be telling you this, Susie, but I've been collecting all the background stuff coming in on him, and some of what's come in today is unbelievable. You'd think I'd have been laughed out with all the laughing I already did. I haven't even gotten some of the material on him typed up yet. I just kept reading it over and over and saying, 'This just can't be, this just can't be.' "

Sue Ann snuggled into her husband, saying, "Tell me."

The following night a shocked Billy Yates, lying in bed and staring at his shorty-clad wife sitting cross-legged beside him, could barely say, "Up where?"

"You heard me plain as day, Billy Bee."

"Who told you that?"

"I'm not saying."

"Sue Ann Willis told you, didn't she?"

"Billy Bee, do you or do you not wanna know what happened to Mister Mule Fucker and—"

"Don't use that word!"

"It's his name, honey. His Christian name."

"It is not. It's an alias. An underworld nickname."

"Well, all I know is, they're deleting the whole story from the record."

"Who's deleting?"

"Mister Corticun and that snooty assistant of his who still wears pinstripes and sounds like Bobby Kennedy."

"Harlon Quinton?"

"Selfsame."

"They were deleting what? And how?"

"Sue Ann told me that Rodney had got this report in about Mister Mule Fucker and—"

"Call him Mule, can't you, Tina Beth?" he said. "Call him Marion or Corkel . . . or anything but that."

Tina Beth patted her husband's knee. "Rodney Willis had received this report about Mister Mule and the rodeo and was having it typed up when Harlon Quinton comes down and reads it over the secretary's shoulder. Harlon Quinton gets very mad and says this report doesn't belong here on the eleventh floor but upstairs on the twelfth floor, where Mister Corticun and all the men working on the out-of-town end of the investigation are. Rodney says no it doesn't. Harlon Quinton says he's in charge of the central files on the twelfth floor and therefore he says what goes where. Rodney says everything about Prairie Port people is investigated by the eleventh floor and that Mister Mule is from Prairie Port and that anything about him is staying on the eleventh floor until someone from the eleventh floor decides differently. Jez Jessup comes over and asks what the trouble is. Rodney explains. Jez Jessup sides with Rodney, and Harlon Quinton gets madder and says that a lot of what's in the report happened away from Prairie Port and therefore it belongs on the twelfth floor because it can't be verified until the flying squad checks it out.

238

He says if he doesn't get that report here and now, he's going to take it. Jez Jessup tells him he better not try.

"Harlon Quinton goes upstairs and comes back down with Mister Corticun. Mister Corticun reads the report and turns green and tries not to show it. Mister Corticun tells Jez Jessup the report definitely belongs on the twelfth floor. Jez Jessup says no it doesn't. Mister Corticun starts to take the report with him, and Jez Jessup pulls it out of his hand. Mister Sunstrom comes over and keeps Jez Jessup and Mister Corticun from hitting one another and makes a compromise. He says until everyone gets unangry and can settle things peaceable, the report stays on the eleventh floor in his office. And that's where it is, locked in his desk in the office . . . which is the same as having it deleted."

"Do you know what was in the report?"

"That's what I've been trying to tell you all along, Billy, only you got mad and started fussin' at me."

"I'm sorry, Tina Beth, for fussing."

"Are you?"

Billy Yates crossed his heart.

Tina Beth laughed her little-girl laugh, popped the pillow onto her lap, leaned forward on it. "Mister Mule is a smuggler, everyone already knows that. What they don't know is what's in Rodney's report . . . exactly how he smuggled things. And that was like I just told you, he put things up the rear end of horses and mules. Mister Mule has this horrid-looking ranch west of town where you can rent horses to ride if you want. Or you can board your animal if you're so inclined. One day a friend of Mister Mule's comes and leaves his horse there. Only this is no ordinary horse. It's a rodeo horse that has to get itself shipped on over to eastern Texas for an important rodeo. Now at this very same time Mister Mule has this business associate in Texas who is always wanting things smuggled to him. Mister Mule sees a way of killing two jaybirds with one stone, getting paid to ship the rodeo horse to Texas and smuggle something to his business associate as well. So Mister Mule puts whatever's to be smuggled in a small bag and walks up to the rodeo horse . . . and up inside the horse's rear end it goes. Well, sir, the horse arrives in Texas no worse for the

239

experience, only the business associate doesn't come by and take the bag out like he's supposed to. Instead, the man who owns the horse, a Mister Cowboy Carlson, rides the horse in the rodeo. Well, once that horse comes out into the rodeo arena with that bag up its behind and has to run, it don't act like no cowboy horse, it turns into a bucking bronco. A bucker like no one's ever seen."

Four miles across town Sissy Hennessy completed the tale of the bucking bronco Sue Ann Willis had told her and Tina Beth early in the day.

"The horse bucks from one end of the arena to the other with Cowboy Carlson holding on as best he can," she told Cub in the darkness of their bedroom. "And then the poor animal dropped dead. At the height of a buck its heart must have given out. It hit the ground and collapsed and died with Cowboy partially pinned underneath. The rodeo officials temporarily suspended Cowboy Carlson's license until an autopsy could be done on the horse, an autopsy to see if he had given it some drug. The veterinarians found a bag of stolen antique coins in the anal tract. Luckily for Cowboy, the coins weren't valuable. He pleaded guilty to a misdemeanor and served two months at a county work farm but had his rodeo license revoked for good. Poor Cowboy was barred from rodeo–riding for life."

"Poor?" Cub said.

"He was innocent, Cub," Sissy said. "Whatever his other crimes, he was innocent of smuggling. And who knows, could he have ridden in a rodeo, maybe he wouldn't have had to return to theft?"

"Who knows?"

"When Cowboy Carlson got back to Prairie Port he of course went looking for Mule Corkel. Mule Corkel was nowhere to be found. He was hiding from Cowboy. Some months later, when he thought Cowboy had calmed down, Mule Corkel surfaced. Nothing happened for a while. One night late, Cowboy Carlson was walking down the street and saw Mule Corkel sitting in Howard Johnson's having a sandwich. Cowboy Carlson ran all the way to a stable. The next thing Mule Corkel knows, he's looking up from his sandwich in the Howard Johnson's and Cowboy Carlson is trying to ride through the door on a horse. Mule Corkel ran out the back door and down the street with Cowboy Carlson riding after him on this horse, riding after him and trying to rope Mule Corkel with a lariat . . . Cub, maybe that's what Mule Corkel saw when Les Kebbon was trying to lasso him from the jeep. Maybe he saw Cowboy Carlson coming at him."

". . . Maybe."

"Cowboy Carlson chases Mule Corkel down the street. Rides behind Mule Corkel, not roping him with the noose but lashing him on the back with it. He rides and lashes and drives Mule Corkel right through a plate-glass window. Mule Corkel was three weeks in a hospital recovering from the cuts. Then he invites Cowboy Carlson to his ranch and gives him a new horse and they make up."

Sissy lit a cigarette. "Even if it was true, why would Denis Corticun hide it?"

"It is true," Cub told her. "It's been confirmed."

"But why cut it out of even interoffice reports?"

"It makes us look bad, Sissy," Cub told her. "God only knows I don't care for Corticun or Quinton or any of their headquarters crowd, but this gang of criminals is making us look the laughing-stock."

"When more comes out, you'll look just fine. The Bureau always does."

"No, it doesn't, Sissy. And it hasn't for a while. What's worse with the Mormon State robbers is, they're funny. Really funny. Chasing Mule down the highway with him dressed like an Indian with war paint on, the man was *funny*. He was yelling out the name 'Vonda Lizzie' and letting out war whoops and every now and then turning back and sticking his tongue out at me, and I almost cracked up. He had tried to cut down our guys with a machine gun minutes before, and it took all I had not to laugh while I chased him . . . but we're *not* funny, Sissy. Nothing about the FBI is humorous. We're looking bad in this. The public is amused by the crooks. It likes them. It may not like us."

Sissy turned to her husband, put her arms around him. "The

241

Bureau is fine. You're fine. You don't have to keep back reports, you just don't."

"If we want to keep them out of the press, Sissy, I think we must. Everything we do in that office of ours has a habit of ending up on the front page. Someone sees to it."

# Fourteen

It had taken the strongest agents of the residency office, E. G. Womper and Ralph Dafney and Cub Hennessy, to hold Marion "Mule" Corkel down and handcuff him. It had taken the heaviest, Happy de Camp and Hank Perch, to sit on Mule and keep him from thrashing and kicking on the auto trip into the city. One of the bravest agents, or more foolhardy, Dick Travis, had leaned over from the front seat and tried to apply a gag to the cursing, spitting, shouting white-nosed prisoner in the back. Travis was bitten three times before succeeding.

Thoughts of bringing Mule to the eleventh-floor residency office for fingerprinting and photographing, as was routine procedure, were dismissed. The media hung out on the twelfth floor, was in and around the building almost as often as the agents themselves. The media, for reasons incomprehensible to the local agents, had not learned of the raid on Mule's farm. Had either not found out about the Baton Rouge arrest of Wiggles Loftus and the "all points" alerts emanating from that city for the two other suspects or had not connected these events to the Mormon State robbery.

Mule was driven to the rear entrance of the federal building. When the coast seemed clear, was carried bodily and on the run through the door down into a steel isolation cell in the basement. Once loose in the cell and unhandcuffed, Mule, in his war paint and loin cloth, began shouting and cursing and kicking the walls and beating his head furiously against the door. Cub and Dafney and Womper and two U.S. marshals rushed in and restrained him. Shackled his wrists and ankles. Locked a metal body belt around his waist and chained the belt to a steel rung in the steel wall.

243

Legal procedure dictated the prisoner must be afforded an arraignment before the assistant U.S. magistrate as quickly as possible, must be provided with legal counsel. The assistant U.S. magistrate could not be reached, and word was left for him. Mule would not answer whom he wished to defend him, would not make a phone call . . . did nothing but twist and curse in his irons. The Bureau photographer and fingerprint equipment arrived. Four men held Mule while a fifth cleaned away his war paint. A picture was gotten. With inordinate trouble, so were prints. E. G. Womper and Ralph Dafney stayed inside the steel cell with Mule. Dick Travis waited on the other side of the door. The rest of the agents hied it back to the office.

There was excitement on the eleventh floor. And suspense. The rare sort which comes only as a great case begins to crack . . . can be expected at any moment to burst full open. Manpower lacked, that was so. Brewmeister was in Baton Rouge waiting to escort Wiggles Loftus to Prairie Port. Les Kebbon and Ted Keon were en route to Meridan County to retrive Elmo Ragotsy from Chief Sheriff O. D. Don Pensler. Three agents had been left with Mule in the basement of the federal building. But Jez Jessup had returned from Louisiana and he worked feverishly along with Strom and Cub and Yates and Rodney Willis and Hank Perch and Preston Lyle and Donnie Bracken and Hap de Camp and Butch Cody and Heck Bevins. Worked feverishly over incoming information on the eight men alleged to be the Mormon State robbers . . . and the jigsaw puzzle rapidly began falling into place. Began producing images.

River Rat Ragotsy, according to the latest informant accounts reaching the eleventh floor, had used the caves and tunnels in the area of Mormon State bank to hide contraband . . . had been doing so for years . . . had used the tunnels and caves north and south of the bank as well . . . was a scavenger in such tunnels . . . had been picked up several times, but never booked, for scavenging in the city's water and sewerage tunnels. There was no known direct connection between Ragotsy and Reverend Wallace Tecumseh "Windy Walt" Sash, but, thirty years before, both men had been listed as possible witnesses for the aborted 1941 grand jury inquiry into the disappearance of heavy machinery from the MVA hydroelectric plant inside Warbonnet Ridge. Fifty-three-year-old Wallace Sash was, in fact, a reverend of the First Church of the Holy Conversion, an Illinois-based and -accredited operation that the federal government had unsuccessfully tried to discredit as nothing more than a tax dodge. Sash had a number of arrests, but no convictions, for petty theft, petty extortion and the molesting of children. His only conviction was for a felony—extorting funds from a mentally incompetent uncle —and ended in a three-year jail sentence. An appeals court reversed the decision. Windy Walt, a native Illinoisan, was a longtime friend and alleged underworld associate of another Illinois resident, Bicki "Little Haifa" Hale. It was believed that Sash had first served as the "keep" or "holder" of stolen funds entrusted to him by Bicki Hale, that later he became a full partner in many of Hale's illegal ventures.

Bicki "Little Haifa" Hale did look Semitic, but he received his nickname in an Indiana reformatory, where he was the constant shadow of an older inmate, Clarence Highfall. Clarence had a speech impediment and pronounced his name "Cwarence Highfaw." Around the yard he became Haifa. His shadow, Bicki, became Little Haifa. Bicki Hale was a car thief and adequate lockpicker before going to reform school. He came out a journeyman safecracker. Years of subsequent practice elevated this skill, but only somewhat. According to underworld sources, Little Haifa rated as a competent box man who was far better with drills than with explosives. Where Little Haifa excelled, in the estimation of his criminal peers, was at organization. They attributed Bicki's almost nonexistent conviction record to this. To organization alone. Not to spotting the potential mark, definitely not. If Bicki picked the mark, there was every chance it was an impractical, if not preposterous, choice. Bicki was a dreamer. A Don Quixote. His eyes were far bigger than his talent. That's why he and Windy Walt Sash were a perfect pair. Both were down-home crooks who aspired to be big-time operators. With Bicki, confidential under-

245

world informants told their Romor 91 contacts, "Let the other guy spot and pick the score."

Let Bicki organize and execute and pay off and you can't go wrong, stated the question-and-answer report sent in from an FBI agent interviewing an underworld contact outside of Moline, Illinois. The full transcript went on to say:

Q: How large a score has Bicki Hale made?

A: He's in the four to five range, definitely.

Q: Four to five hundred thousand dollars?

A: That's his ballpark.

Q: Nothing bigger?

A: He could hit bigger, sure. We all could hit bigger. Luck burps, we all hit bigger. Even you.

Q: Without luck, reasonably, how much bigger a score do you feel Bicki could perpetrate?

A: I love that word, perpetrate.

Q: How big?

A: Bicki? If he gets all the luck, he could maybe bring home a million or two for the night.

Q: That's all, two million?

A: Hey, big roller, show me where I can pick it up and I don't have to talk to you no more.

Q: Is it possible he could bring off a score larger than two million?

A: Anything's possible. Only don't let him do the spotting. Let someone else find it and bring it to Little Haifa, like I said. That's how he got pinched the last time. Sent to the crapper. 'Cause he picked it too. Spotted and picked. He ain't no spotter. He's day labor.

Bicki "Little Haifa" Hale's cellmate at Statesville Penitentiary in Illinois, as revealed by data being assembled on the eleventh floor, was Willy "Cowboy" Carlson. Carlson and Hale were known to be friendly with another inmate on the tier below them, thirty-one-year-old Thomas "The Worm" Ferugli. Ferugli, a former coal miner, was associated with criminal "tunnel jobs" and petty burglaries. While pleading for a lesser sentence in court, his lawyer argued Ferugli had an aversion to guns, reasoned that if Ferguli had carried a gun when burglarizing the Alcyon Flower Shop outside of Chicago at midnight, the shop's unarmed owner probably wouldn't have attacked Ferugli with his fists . . . would have most likely stepped back and put his hands up and let Ferugli empty the cash register and escape. The judge wondered aloud what would have happened if the defendant was holding a gun and the owner still attacked. The judge sentenced Ferugli, a chronic burglar of cash registers, to three to five years at Statesville.

Lionel "Meadow Muffin" Epstein, proprietor of a modest Peoria, Illinois, wholesale hardware and plumbing supply warehouse, had no known criminal record but was suspected by state trooper intelligence of being the illicit purchasing agent for equipment needed by robbery gangs. The Q&A with the Moline informant hinted of other activities:

Q: Have you heard of Lionel Epstein?

A: I think so.

Q: Is he an associate of Bicki Hale?

A: Little Haifa? Nah, that ain't where I heard of
him from. It's Epstein's got to do with Windman.

Q: Windman?

A: Windy Walt Sash, a scam artist down southways.
Windy Walt and this Epstein run second-rate hustles.
Crooked lotto games and the like. Epstein, I think
he got this cut-rate supply house going, see what I

mean? Sells you guns and nitroglycerin and drills.
Anything for a job. Sells it cut-rate 'cause most of
it's defective. He's a real piece of shit, Epstein is.
Soft shit. They call him Meadow Muffin.

New intelligence reaching the eleventh floor on Marion "Mule Fucker" Corkel stated he was a good handyman who was particularly skilled at repairing automobiles and electrical gadgets. Mule was described as being "perhaps a borderline psychotic" who possessed an extremely quick temper and was given to sudden violent and dangerous rages.

Mule, as agents of the residency knew from earlier reports, was directly connected with Cowboy Carlson in several small smuggling activities and one horse death. Cowboy had shared an apartment with River Rat Ragotsy as well as worked on Ragotsy's boat. Lamar "Wiggles" Loftus had also worked on the Ragotsy boat, where he met Carlson, and with Carlson attempted an armed robbery which was bungled and landed Carlson in prison. Wiggles, a World War II hero, was believed to be an expert with explosives.

There was a pall, a numbing, which affected certain of the agents as the incoming information was shouted out across the room. These were not, these eight suspects, the breed of supercriminals described by the press or Denis Corticun. Not wizards or even sub wizards. Not the cream of the crime world by a longshot.

Denis Corticun, when he appeared on the eleventh floor and apologized to Jez for their argument over Mule Corkel's background report and stayed on for late-night sandwiches and an informal recapitulation of what had been learned, might have been expected to show concern over the scruffy nature of the crooks . . . over having been so inaccurate in his public assessment of their skills. He admitted being off-base, but without apparent concern. Corticun complimented Billy Yates for being right on the money in predicting what caliber of criminals had perpetrated Mormon State, reminded the other agents around the

248

table that only Yates had thought this way, or at least was brave enough to say what he thought. Corticun congratulated all the men on a job well done and called out and ordered whiskey for the room, on him, then remembering there was still much to do, Indian-gave and postponed the treat until later . . . went into the other office to join Strom, who was on the phone trying to find out where the devil the assistant U.S. magistrate was, why the devil Mule hadn't had his arraignment yet. Strom was saying that he would not tolerate a foul-up, that Mule was legally entitled to and must have his arraignment . . . must be represented by a lawyer. Strom ordered that the public defender's office be called straightaway and a lawyer brought in for Mule. Brought in without delay. He slammed the receiver down.

With Corticun gone from the dinner break, it fell to Cub Hennessy to ask the question that had plagued him, a question to which he knew the answer but hoped there was a different answer he hadn't thought of: Why, if these eight were the actual perpetrators, had none of their names appeared on any suspects list to date?

"Because they're too looney-toon, why do you think?" Pres Lyle said, surprised anyone as crime-wise as Cub would ask such a thing. "There aren't a half-dozen felony arrests among the bunch of 'em. We started with felony arrests."

It was the answer Cub feared was right, didn't want to hear.

"Felony arrests and Ph.D.s," Jez added, as others laughed. "That's where we spent half our time, shagging after Ph.D.s."

"You can't have the biggest and most spectacular robbery of the age and not have any of the perpetrators show up on a suspects list." Cub didn't know why he was pressing the issue. "It sounds dumb."

"Half those guys were over in Illinois," Donnie Bracken said. "They were small-timers in Illinois. The Illinois field offices would have gotten around to them."

"I think Ragotsy was on one of the lists here, one that I saw," Rodney Willis recalled.

"Cub's got a point," Hank Perch said. "You would have

249

thought Cowboy Carlson's name would show up here in Prairie Port. Cowboy did felony time. He's a parolee and right out of prison. He sure as hell should have been listed by us."

Cowboy had been listed, but Cub wasn't about to say he had removed Cowboy's name . . . since Cowboy had been his informant.

"Lists or no lists, I'd say we got a pretty strong case," Hap de Camp said.

"Good enough for conviction?" Jez wondered. "Don't forget, we're racing the clock. We picked up Mule. They'll be arraigning him in a few minutes and then he has to go to trial. Any smart lawyer is going to push for a fast trial."

"We're strong," Hap reiterated. "You take what we got and throw in Cowboy Carlson having Mule's initial in his record book for the night of the robbery and—"

"That page was destroyed," Cub reminded the group. "Frank Santi burned it, and I doubt if the chief of police is going to admit that in a court of law, admit destroying evidence."

"Yeah, why'd he do that?" Donnie Bracken asked. "I never understood."

Cub fibbed. "Who knows? Maybe spite."

"Even without the book we're strong," Hap persisted. "We have the tie-in to Sam Hammond and the electrical work. The fuses. Sam's mother's testimony and his wife's."

"And none of the Illinois suspects were seen at their addresses since a few days before the robbery," Butch Cody added.

"When did we find that out?" Cub wanted to know.

"It just came in," Butch said. "The last any one of them was seen in their home area was August seventeenth. That's three days before the theft came down. And all three of the suspects from Prairie Port were reported here during the score . . . Mule, Cowboy and Rat Ragotsy."

"That's still circumstantial," Cub said. "Nothing's firsthand, not even the fuse you found at Sam Hammond's garage. A smart lawyer could make us choke on that fuse."

"Cub, you saying you don't think these guys are the robbers?" Hank Perch asked.

"I don't know," Cub said. "It seems that they are, but I don't know why I won't accept it. Like I told Sissy last night, maybe I'm a little ashamed or disappointed. Maybe I started believing all that crap Corticun's been handing out about the crime of the century and supercrooks. Maybe I don't want to tell my kids I hauled in a third-rate looney-toon called Mule Fucker."

"Crooks is crooks, Cub," Pres Lyle said.

"Some are heavyweights," Cub contradicted. "Maybe that's it. Maybe I had my heart set on bringing down a heavyweight."

". . . Billy Boy," Jez said to Yates. "How do you see it? These the Mormon State gang or aren't they?"

"They did it," Yates said.

Jez turned to Cub with opened hand. "There you are, they did it. Billy knows everything. I'm proud of him like he was something pretty."

"You think what we have will hold in court, Billy?" Cub asked.

"Can't say about that, but they're the gang."

Strom, who had been watching from the doorway, asked, "Why are you so certain, Yates?"

"It plays too well," Billy said.

"What does?"

"The scenario."

"You mean the reconstruction? Your reconstruction?"

Yates nodded.

"Let's hear."

". . . Rat Ragotsy, an old-time smuggler, is wandering through the caves probably looking for new hiding places, or whatever," Yates began. "He spots dirt or rock chips falling in one of the caves. Or maybe hears noises and realizes something is being built directly overhead. He goes outside and sees the housing project going up . . . and sees the bank being built. Or he does it in reverse order, sees the bank being built and suspects there could be a cave underneath . . . checks and finds out there is. He finds the cave the bank is going up over and knows he's spotted a one-in-a-million shot. Ragotsy tells his Prairie Port roommate, Cowboy Carlson, what he's found. Probably brings Carlson over and shows him. What they need is a safecracker and organizer.

251

Carlson has just the man, his former cellmate at Statesville, Bicki "Little Haifa" Hale. Hale, the dreamer who talks a big game. Hale cases the bank and cave, is led up and down the tunnels by the man who knows them as good as anybody, Ragotsy. They go up into Warbonnet Ridge, and Ragotsy, who once tried scavenging the hydroelectrical plant there, shows them the control station for the irrigation project. I doubt if Ragotsy or Cowboy or Bicki understood how the station operated, but Bicki knew what it did . . . it let water into the tunnels. This was important because he realized then, or shortly after, that the only getaway from the robbery had to be through the tunnels . . . and that it was impossible to make that getaway walking through the tunnels carrying stolen money. The tunnels had to be flooded. Somehow he had to get those controls for the irrigation system to operate and let water into the tunnels when he needed it. So Bicki goes to his pal and partner from Illinois, Windy Walt Sash. Windy Walt had tried looting the Bonnet hydroelectric plant himself. Most every southern Missouri and Illinois and western Kentucky crook had tried that. Only Walt probably boasted he was successful at it. Walt was a bigger blowhard than Bicki. A much bigger liar. But when Windy Walt was taken down to the control room by Bicki, Cowboy and Ragotsy, he didn't have any better idea of how to get it operating than they did.

"They're stuck . . . and greedy. They smell money. Smell the biggest score any of them has ever dreamt of. And in their distorted appraisal, the easiest score they've ever come across. That's the beauty of being truly second-rate, you never realize your limitations. A bank was being built right above a cave that nobody knew about but them. They felt they had all the time in the world to dig up through the rock and cut a hole in the bottom of the vault and take what they wanted. The only catch was the getaway. They still had to flood the tunnels to get away.

"Tasting money, they went to a man they probably would have avoided under more normal situations. A crazy man who knew electricity and mechanics and thievery, Marion 'Mule Fucker' Corkel. They took Mule on the underground tour, brought him up into the control station. Mule saw that what they wanted to do about the flooding was feasible . . . and knew he didn't have the skill to bring it off. He told them so. So Bicki Little Haifa went to the one person he didn't want to approach. The person he knew all along could do what was needed, his nephew . . . his sister's son, Sam Hammond. Sam Hammond, who had trouble with the electric company's advancement test because he couldn't read all that well. Sam Hammond, who, reading or not, was a bloody genius with raw electricity and electrical machinery. Bicki always got Sam to do what he wanted in the past. He got him to do what he wanted with Mormon State. Bicki probably fought with his sister Ida over it. He probably told Ida, 'Give me this once, this one clout, and I'll make us all rich and never bother him again.' Bicki the organizer starts bringing in his specialists. One is his and Cowboy's old prison chum, Thomas 'The Worm' Ferugli. Worm is an ex-miner and tunnel man . . . has more likely than not worked robberies that required tunneling through rocks. Maybe out of friendship, maybe out of necessity, they take on another hand, a man who had wartime experience with explosives, Lamar 'Wiggles' Loftus . . . a pal of Cowboy's and a onetime employee on Ragotsy's boat.

"With an assist from Worm Ferugli, his nephew Sam and most likely Wiggles, Bicki draws up his master plan. River Rat probably helps him with the getaway aspects, with what kind of boats can best get through the tunnels. Bicki makes up his shopping list of equipment and goes to a cut-rate supplier, Windy Walt's friend and sometime partner, Lionel 'Meadow Muffin' Epstein. Epstein arranges for the purchase of certain untraceable items, tells the gang where to steal the rest. Because they will need all the manpower they can muster for the perpetration, Meadow Muffin is invited to join the robbery gang, is offered a full share of the take. He accepts. The gang is set. Sam Hammond, at this point, is no part of it. Is not supposed to participate. Sam, in fact, isn't exactly sure why he's doing what he is for Uncle Bicki.

". . . And so they begin their implausible caper. Material is gotten, and is untraceable. Sam taps into the city's main power supplies and runs cables down the tunnel to a cut-off point. Sam's not allowed to know what's beyond this point. And slow-witted

Sam, pure Sam the electrical wizard, doesn't know . . . doesn't figure it out. Mule, a seat-of-the-pants electrician, takes over from where Sam leaves off with the electrical cable. Mule strings the cable back into the cave under the bank. Lights are brought in and all the other equipment. Some is brought in painstakingly through the emergency hatch on top of Warbonnet Ridge. But there has to be a larger, closer opening we haven't found yet. One through which larger equipment was brought in. Nothing comes in through the Warbonnet Ridge hatch while Sam is there. Sam works alone, or maybe Mule comes to help from time to time.

"The scaffold goes up in the cave, and Worm Ferugli, the miner, figures exactly where, in the ceiling above, the vault is. The bank is still under construction, so the gang has another advantage. They can enter the premises with no fear of alarms going off. They do enter it, often. Can calculate from inside the bank itself what part of the cave ceiling the vault is resting on top of. Can tap the concrete vault-room floor and hear below precisely where the sound is coming from. When they're in the bank, they also check out the alarm system being installed. See that the system includes a television scanning camera and monitor screens. They trace the cable from the camera to the monitors, which is no major electrical achievement. Mule splices into the cable, which also requires minimal skill. Luck has a part. They find a fissure in the rock foundation . . . the same fissure our technicians discovered. They string the splice down the fissure and into the cave and connect it to monitor screens Meadow Muffin Epstein has purchased or stolen. They wait for the security company upstairs to activate and adjust the alarm system. This occurs the week before the robbery. Now the gang can watch, from thirty feet below, everything going on inside the bank and on the street in front.

"Sam Hammond gets the generators and motors in the irrigation–control station to operate. Also gets the pull motors at the tunnel and reservoir water gates working. Splices hot into the city's power line for his basic supply of electricity. What he pulls off isn't without a flaw or so. Activating the first generator and battery of motors attached to it causes power dips throughout the city of Prairie Port. Sam warns Bicki about this. Bicki asks what they should do to fix the situation. Sam says if he knows exactly how much water Bicki wants in the tunnel at what specific time, he can build a governing device that will automatically open a combination of gates and sewers gradually, and far enough in advance, to meet the specifications using a minimum of power. Bicki gets back to Sam and says, all right, build your device and set it for Saturday night. August twenty-first. Sam does just that, finishes the job Friday afternoon, August twentieth. Now something happens, and I'm not sure what."

Yates poured himself a cup of black coffee, sipped and thought a moment. "Remember there's a lead time involved here . . . the time it will take to flood the tunnel without using a disruptive amount of electricity. The more electricity used, the quicker the flooding. Sam's timer had arranged for a narrower gate opening, less electrical usage and slower flooding. If Bicki originally wanted the tunnel flooded with enough water to escape on by, let's say, midnight Saturday, Sam probably programmed the timer to open the gates hours before that, maybe half a day before.

"Now, on Friday, Bicki comes to nephew Sam and says the plans have changed and that the flooding has to be finished later that same night. Sam wants to know when and explains about the lead time. Bicki tells him to forget about the lead time and timing device. Bicki Hale has to do the thing he's been trying to avoid, not only tell his nephew what was happening but make him participate as well. Bicki orders Sam to operate the irrigation control by hand, do whatever it takes to get maximum water into those tunnels. In a way, it's better for Bicki and gang to have Sam regulating the water flow. That gave them more immediate control of flooding . . . they could speed it up or slow it down.

"We can be relatively certain the perpetration had to begin as quickly as possible late Friday afternoon, right after the bank's assistant manager locked up and left. But why did they change? What came up to change their plans so drastically? And to make them do the thing they had feared . . . risk causing dimouts in the city? It couldn't have been any worry about the alarm system

255

being fully activated. That wasn't to happen until Monday morning.

"There are two explanations, and I'm not happy with either one. The first is that Bicki, the impractical dreamer, had counted on the final leg of the getaway occurring on the Treachery. The gang would escape from under the bank via the flooded tunnels, come out into the Mississippi River the other end of Prairie Port and get right out midstream into the Treachery. The Treachery would take them downriver thirty or forty miles in record time. The gang might have found out, at the last moment, that the Treachery stopped flowing at about one A.M. Saturday. Stopped for over two months. So if they were going to ride the Treachery they couldn't score the vault Saturday, they had to do it the night before. Had to make the getaway and be on the river before one A.M. Saturday. That's one possibility," Yates said dourly.

"The second is that the gang somehow had learned about the federal reserve shipment of thirty-one million dollars to Mormon State. We can't assume that it was a conspiracy from the start . . . that they prepared to rob Mormon State weeks, maybe months, before with full knowledge the federal reserve shipment would be made. That would have meant a person inside the federal reserve at New Orleans sabotaged the incinerator and later made sure the truck carrying the money to Saint Louis broke down. Conspiracy couldn't have existed on the part of the armored truck company and drivers carrying the load, since they weren't hired until the last moment, had no way of knowing beforehand that they were to be hired, certainly had no way of knowing where they were to be sent or in what direction. Robbery preparations were well under way long before the truckers entered the scene.

"It's conceivable, though, that after the truck got into trouble and the federal reserve made arrangements to drop the load off at Mormon State, the gang did find out. This is a longshot. Except I see from the background report that Cowboy Carlson was still working for Wilkie Jarrel . . . that he was chauffeuring Jarrel that Friday afternoon. Chauffeured him until four-thirty that afternoon, then took off for the weekend . . . and never showed up

256

again. Jarrel's son-in-law is Emile Chandler, president of Mormon State. Once Chandler had been contacted by the federal reserve and asked to house the shipment over the weekend, it would seem plausible Jarrel was told about it. Jarrel might even have been consulted from the beginning, might have been the final arbiter on whether Mormon State should accept the shipment. Maybe some of these conversations occurred by phone . . . and maybe Carlson overheard enough to get the drift of what was about to happen.

"It's equally possible that the gang had no prior knowledge of the federal reserve shipment. That they lucked out . . . that as they were watching the monitor screens they saw the money being unloaded and couldn't believe their luck. Saw it just like they saw the early shipment from Brink's come in. That could have been why they changed plans and began the robbery a day earlier, because they were afraid the shipment might be taken away the next day . . . no, that couldn't be it . . . they had no way of knowing it was a temporary shipment, not from a monitor.

"Anyway, the decision to score the vault on Friday night was made. But Sam Hammond couldn't bring himself to go along with it. After a crying jag at home in the arms of his wife, he went to Warbonnet Ridge to see Uncle Bicki and try to get off the hook. Bicki promised him the moon, and when that didn't work, he threatened him. Maybe some of the others threatened him too. Particularly Mule. Sam ran away and hid, and terrified that Mule or the others might hurt his wife and unborn child, he jumped into the river and drowned.

"The gang has no way of knowing where Sam is, what he has done. Their concern is that Sam isn't there to control the water, to undo the automatic timing device. The device was connected and set for the next night. So Mule went up to the tunnel and into the irrigation–control station, changed wires and did everything he could to prepare for flooding. In the process he knocked the timing device out of whack, but not out of commission. Everything done in the cave under the bank works like a dream. They drill and explode right up to the bottom of the vault, then drill and explode right through. They gather the money and get into their boats. Mule pulls out every stop he can to get water into the tunnels, throws on every machine. Short-circuits half of Prairie Port into a blackout. Opens the three gates in the reservoir and sends a flood of eighteen million gallons of water into the tunnels. Knocks hell out of half the Sewerage and Water Department tunnels in the bargain and reactivates the mud volcano, but dumps the robbers and their loot out into the Mississippi . . . out into the Treachery.

"The alarm in the bank doesn't go off until Sunday morning. The flooding knocks out the main cable to the police department's communication center, and the cable didn't get fixed until early Sunday morning. By now the timing mechanism Sam had originally built and Mule had forgotten to disconnect is opening and closing, is booby-trapping the tunnels by sending more water into them. Brewmeister goes down into the cave during this time and—"

A phone call from E. G. Womper interrupted the scenario. The assistant United States magistrate had been reached and was expected soon at the federal building. A public defender was on his way to represent Mule. And the press had already arrived . . . had found out the FBI was holding a suspect in the Mormon State robbery.

John Leslie Krueger, assistant United States magistrate for the southern district of Missouri and the first black man to hold that position, met privately with Assistant U.S. Attorney Jules Shapiro and Legal Aid lawyer Andy Pantellis. Shapiro, who represented the United States government's pending action against Marion Corkel, and Pantellis, Corkel's appointed legal representative for the time being, had a joint request: that the press be barred from the arraignment about to take place. John Leslie Krueger ruled the press had a perfect right to attend. Shapiro said he could understand but pointed to mitigating circumstances, recounted the violent reaction of Corkel to being arrested and the need to shackle him in his cell. Shapiro said that it was better for all concerned if the shackles remained on when Corkel was brought into the arraignment room. Pantellis concurred with this pro-

258

posal, told of recently having visited Corkel in the holding cell only to find his new client "violent and out of control and detrimental to the well-being of those about him." Pantellis complained of not having been alerted by the FBI early enough to get to know his client's history better, accused the Bureau of technically having held Corkel incommunicado from the time of his apprehension at sundown until approximately 11:30 P.M., but felt it would serve no beneficial purpose for his client to be seen in chains by members of the press. Assistant U.S. Attorney Shapiro defended the Bureau by saying Corkel was given every opportunity to contact a legal representative of his own choosing and consistently refused to do so, that it was the FBI that did in fact contact the Legal Aid Society. Shapiro further stated the government found Corkel appearing in chains with members of the press present would be counterproductive to all parties concerned except the press. John Leslie Krueger again denied the petition, pointed out that it was, or soon would be, common knowledge the accused was a suspect in a notorious crime. Shapiro pointed out that the arraignment room was small and had a gallery of only fifteen seats and that fifty media people were already outside waiting to get in, that many more could be expected in coming minutes. Krueger suggested they move to larger quarters. Shapiro answered that might be awkward and near impossible this time of night, proposed that perhaps lots should be drawn among the media people already here to see which two would be allowed entry. Krueger said if the press agreed to a lot drawing, six should be admitted.

Nancy Applebridge and Chet Chomsky, along with correspondents from CBS, the BBC, the *Christian Science Monitor* and the San Francisco *Chronicle,* were the lottery winners . . . and the first into the small room. Shapiro, Pantellis, Strom Sunstrom, Cub Hennessy, Denis Corticun, Harlon Quinton, Jez Jessup and Billy Yates entered next, took seats in the rows in front of the media people. A clerk entered, followed by Assistant United States Magistrate Krueger.

Krueger stated that due to uncontrollable and obstructive behavior the accused would be appearing in restraints. Krueger

259

went on record voicing opposition to any man being chained, saying he had bowed to the suggestion of persons more directly concerned with the matter. Krueger motioned to Pantellis. Pantellis went to a side door, opened it, beckoned. Bureaumen E. G. Womper and Ralph Dafney entered sidewise through the narrow door, escorting between them, with shackled wrists and ankles, the shuffling Mule. Attired in his own, recently arrived, baggy clothes, Mule glanced about with abrupt head movements, casing the gathering, squinting at one observer and then another and looking on to the next. He almost docilely took his seat beside Pantellis at a small table.

Krueger explained that the federal government had sworn out a warrant against one Marion Corkel of 15 Prairieflat Road, Prairie Port, Missouri, on the charge of conspiracy-to-commit-bank-theft against the Mormon State National Bank on or about the weekend of August 20 and 21, 1971. Krueger said that the accused before him was alleged to be the same Marion Corkel cited in the warrant.

Krueger now addressed Mule directly, introduced himself as the assistant United States magistrate who must judge whether Mule was, in fact, Marion Corkel. That was all this arraignment was about, Krueger said, to determine if the right man was being charged and, if so, to establish bail. Only that. This was not a trial, just a brief arraignment as prescribed by law for the assessment of identity and bail. Mule was told he had the constitutional right to remain silent throughout the proceedings, had the right to counsel of his own choice. Krueger inquired if Mule understood all he had said.

Mule farted, resoundingly.

Krueger asked if Mule wished to change the counsel representing him, provided by the Legal Aid Society, for counsel of his own choosing.

Mule lifted a shackled leg, but no wind would pass.

Krueger announced that the proceedings would begin. The clerk asked that the representatives of the government and the accused identify themselves for the record. Andy Pantellis said he was Andrew D. Pantellis, Legal Aid Society, Assistant U.S. Attorney Jules Shapiro said: "For the Government, Jules Shapiro."

Mule stood up shouting, "I'm Shithole Ike for them what wish to dump."

The clerk urged Mule to sit down. He even said please.

"When I get ready, all right," Mule shot back. "You people make me wait this long, I'm gonna make you wait longer. I'm Shithole Ike, tenant in every bunghouse south of the Platte. Seat-licker Ike, United States Latrine Corps—"

Pantellis rose and requested of Krueger that rather than establish bail at this time he remand Mule to University Hospital for observation. That perhaps Mule had mental problems.

"Mister Corkel, and I assume you are Mister Corkel?" Krueger said.

Mule sneered and nodded.

"Do you have a psychiatric history?"

"Surest thing," Mule shouted. "I come out of a crazy pussy, and I'm gonna die in a crazy grave next to Hitler sucking Kate Smith's tits while I fuck George Washington. Because I hate you and everything you stand for, you white cocksucker."

"White!" Krueger said.

"White-livered! White-bellied! Chicken white! You take a man and beat him, what do you expect him to do? Fight back, right?"

"That's not a very effective way, fighting," Krueger told him.

"I'm gonna fight this case all the way to the Supreme Court."

"Fine," Krueger said. "Please sit down."

"I don't care if you send me to the moon in a balloon." Mule continued to stand and rant. "I'm a man and you're a man. I did what I did, which ain't what you say I did. You got the money. You got the gun. What the fuck do you want from my goddam life?"

Krueger said, "I don't want anything other than that you sit down."

"Well, God bless Missouri and all that goes with it. Send me wherever the fuck you want to send me with all the homosexuals and cocks. I'll suck your dick if you let me, goddam it. I got twenty-one cents and you got millions. Tell Nixon to kiss my ass, and Pat too—"

"Will you please sit *down.*"

Mule, to the tune of "God Bless America," began singing, "God bless Missouri, land that I love . . ."

"Shut that man up," Krueger demanded.

Mule jumped up and down singing the same "God bless Missouri" line.

"A six-twenty is ordered," Krueger called, citing the number for mental observation. Mule sang louder. Krueger shouted above him. "A six-twenty is ordered, and get him *out* of here."

E. G. Womper rushed forward. Harlon Quinton beat a fast retreat out the nearest door. What attracted Yates's attention was not the antic Mule but the reactions of his fellow FBI men. All, like Yates, were on their feet. Ralph Dafney, who was running to assist Womper, looked delighted with the challenge. Cub seemed ashamed and depressed. Strom appeared skeptical. Corticun calmly nodded to himself. Jez Jessup had no interest in anything but Yates . . . was watching Billy watch the others.

Waiting at the FBI's twelfth-floor cafeteria-lounge forty minutes later, in anticipation of a promised official statement, Chet Chomsky related for his lolling press brethren what had followed at the arraignment. "These two FBI men grab him. They're big men. Muscles. Corkel is trying to salute while he's singing. While he's being lifted up. The handcuffs make this difficult. Corkel had to bring both hands up to his face. But he does, and the FBI men, four of them by now, carry him out. Run him out. He's laying sideways and saluting and singing 'God bless Missouri' at the top of his lungs. They go on running with him along the corridor and down the steps and out on the street that way. We're running after them. They jump into a car and lose all of us except Nancy. Nancy had a cab waiting and she followed them right to University Hospital. They run Corkel in, standing up this time but still singing. Nancy, oh, our lovely Nancy, she gets right into the hospital and past the security guards in the mental wing. Borrows a nurse's outfit and tray. What does she see? The FBI is handing Corkel over to a doctor, signing a release form for him. Corkel is singing and watching. Once that form's signed, Corkel's the property of the county for twenty days. When it's signed, guess what Corkel does? He stops singing and thanks the FBI for riding him over. He's calm as can be. It was an act. The arraignment thing was an act. Corkel hustled the assistant U.S. magistrate into a twenty-day vacation on the county. Into delaying everything by twenty days. By the bye, he's one pretty funny man, this Marion Corkel. His nickname is Mule Fucker. You should hear the stories about him . . ."

Denis Corticun, at a 3 A.M. briefing, brought the press up to date on Marion Corkel, stated that Corkel was indeed a prime suspect in the Mormon State robbery and, at the suggestion of the assistant U.S. magistrate's office, had been placed under observation. Corticun said two other men believed to be members of the robbery gang would soon be in federal custody but refused to give any further information. He left the room brusquely.

Moans, arduous and painful, rose from the back seat as the car sped off the highway and into a cyprus-lined roadside rest area. Les Kebbon hurried from the driver's door, went to a pay phone, called the eleventh-floor residency office in Prairie Port collect and when the charges were accepted demanded to speak with Strom.

"You pick up Ragotsy?" Strom asked once he got on the other end.

"What's left of him," Les Kebbon answered. "That sheriff or whoever he is, that O. D. Don Pensler, is straight out of Auschwitz. He butchered Ragotsy like you don't want to see. Spent the works. Held him underwater. Hung him by the heels and used electric cattle prods on him. Everything and more. Strom, we can't let anyone see Ragotsy. He's chopped meat, and the Bureau will get blamed, I know it. We gotta get this guy to the first

263

hospital and out of sight and hope he lives. Has that fucking Corticun told the world we've picked him up?"

Strom answered, "Not by name, I don't believe. He had a press meeting a half hour ago and only said there were two more suspects beside Mule."

"So what shall I do, get him to a hospital?"

Strom had an idea, had Kebbon hold on nearly five minutes, returned to the line saying, "Can you make it to the Army base near Balmour with him?"

"Yeah, we can get that far."

"Take him to the hospital there. Maybe we'll get lucky and he'll live. Or luckier yet and nobody will know till he recovers. What the hell did he get beaten up for?"

"A confession," Kebbon told him. "The ape sheriff thought he was doing us a favor. Doing J. Edgar Hoover a favor. He beat a signed confession out of Ragotsy, not knowing that it probably won't hold up in court because he did beat it out of him. He can screw up our whole case against Ragotsy because of this. I've got the confession here, with fucking bloodstains on it, if you can believe."

"What does it say?"

The envelope containing the confession letter did bear a bloody thumbprint on the flap. The letter proper had one large and two small blood splotches on the lower right portion of the second page. The text was typewritten and began with an introductory statement attesting that this was the confession of Elmo Vorhees Ragotsy, fifty-eight years old, of 122 Wellons Street, Prairie Port, Missouri. That during the course of the confession to follow, Mr. Ragotsy had in no way been harmed, coerced or tricked. Beneath this statement were imprints of the county seal, the sheriff's office seal and the seal of the Association of Community Churches. Below these were signatures of the attending witnesses to the confession: two clergymen, the county sheriff, the deputy county sheriff, the high school athletic director, the county supervisor of road repair and the recording public stenographer.

The confession was single-spaced and read:

I am a Mormon State robber. I have been arrested before
for possessing stolen goods but I was not convicted. My
roommate, Willy Carlson, called the Cowboy, is a known
criminal and convict who is on parole. I have not seen him
in a while.

The third week of June this year (i.e. 1971) I was in
the caves and tunnels south of Warbonnet Ridge. The
tunnels was built by the WPA, I think. I often find valuable
things down in them. Sometimes I store things in them. The
third week of June I was walking in a cave and seen dust
and small stones falling out of the roof. I heard echoey
noises too, that could have been drilling. I went out
through a tunnel and up where I come in. That would be a
mile from the cave. Standing there I seen the Riverrise
Project was being built on top of where I figure the cave
was. A week later I went to Riverrise and seen that
everything is built except for the bank. They got this
shopping mall there, along the river in front of the other
buildings, and everything is complete and done. The only
construction what's going on is with the bank. The bank
is incomplete. It don't even have windows in it yet and
no name on it. But you can see it'll be a bank when it's
done. I realize this could be the noises I heard in the
cave. That the cave is right under where the bank is
going up.

I come back over the weekend with my roommate,
Cowboy. Cowboy goes and stays in the basement of the
bank. I go down into the cave. At a time we both agreed
on, Cowboy starts banging on the concrete with a crowbar.
I hear the banging real clear, and dust falls outta the
rock above me. That's how we come to know the bank is
right over the cave. Later a sign goes up in the window
and we see it's called Mormon State.

I am not a thieving man myself. If there was temptations
to do something about robbing Mormon State from the cave
I didn't give it much of a chance. There was no opening
big enough to bring equipment through for six miles. The
place I climbed down to get to the tunnel and cave wasn't
big enough to bring equipment in.  To get out of there
after the clout would mean the same thing, walking six
miles with all the money sacks and equipment you chose to
take out. I told Cowboy I did not want to rob the bank.

265

I told him if he wanted to rob it, I'd sell it to him for some of the action. Criminals have the right to sell a mark to another criminal if they find it first. I found the cave under the bank first. It was my mark.

I had gone up north of St. Louis on my boat for a freight hauling job. A two month contract job for the railroad there. Cowboy comes up to see me. This is the second week of August of this year. He tells me people of his acquaintance are going to rob the bank and need my help. Cowboy, he knows I don't have the stamina for robbing banks. He tells me I'm not going to be part of the robbing. I'm to be part of the escaping after. I'll be waiting in a tunnel near where the cave and robbing is going on. Waiting in a boat. These people plan to flood the tunnels and get out of there by boat afterwards. No one knows boats and them tunnels better than me. That's what they want me to help with, picking the right boats and getting them through the tunnels later. They're willing to pay me a full share of the take and something extra for finding the mark in the first place. I don't have to show up until the day before they go. They'll call me the night before. It's one day's work.

I say okay, sure. I tell Cowboy a list of what I want. Rubber pontoon boats with outboard motors on them. And power beams in front. I don't know how many people is taking part in this thing and I don't ask. I tell Cowboy there can't be more than two people in a boat.

I gets the call from Cowboy on Thursday night that we're going a day earlier, Friday. Right about lunch the next day I tell the crew on my own boat, my river boat, I'm going over to Emoryville and I'll be back the next morning. I drive to Prairie Port and meet the Cowboy.

We were down in the tunnel about six (i.e. 6:00 P.M., August 20). I could hear the robbery already getting started through the passageway leading up from the tunnel to the cave. I stayed on a dock in the tunnel.

There were four rubber boats. I got them ready. Put on their outboard motors and power lights. There was trouble flooding the tunnel. The water level was too low for a while. Then it was too high and fast. When the other people came running out it was almost a tidal

wave in the tunnel. The people were rushing and the
light was bad so I didn't recognize anybody except
Cowboy and a man who was naked. I don't know the naked
man's name. I think he's from near Prairie Port. Cowboy
was naked too.  The other people were all wearing
rubber sea diving suits, so you couldn't see their face
if there was good light.
   The people jumped into the boats in the nick of time.
Jumped in just before the tidal wave hit us.  I was in
the last boat. The tidal wave pushed us all the way
under Prairie Port and out into the Treachery. The
Treachery is a seasonal current in our part of the
river. The Mississippi River.

   The confession ended here. The signature and the date in the
lower right-hand corner of the page were partially obscured by
the three splotches of blood, which had resulted from Ragotsy
passing out and falling full-face onto the letter.

   Franklin Ulick, assistant manager of Mormon State National
Bank, sat at his desk studying the nine pictures Cub Hennessy and
Butch Cody had presented. The photos of Mule, Wiggles, Ragotsy,
Cowboy Carlson, Windy Walt Sash, Worm Ferugli, Meadow Muf-
fin Epstein and Sam Hammond were relatively recent. The iden-
tifying shot for Bicki Hale was still the fuzzy, sixteen-year-old
photograph the Baton Rouge Police Department had on file.
   "No, they don't look familiar, any of them," Ulick finally said.
"Only I can't see this one too well." He indicated Bicki Little
Haifa.
   "Let's think back," Cub asked. "You were around the premises
when it was under construction. Do those men look like any of
the construction workers? Painters, builders, electricians, car-
penters?"
   "I wasn't around all that much during the construction," Ulick
replied.
   "My mistake, I thought you said you were."
   "I said I was around more than Mister Julien."
   "Giles Julien, the manager?"

267

"Yes. I came here more often than he did during that time."

"Did you see any of those nine men when you did?"

"Not that I recall."

Cub produced pages of typewritten names and addresses. "This is the list you gave the Prairie Port police when they were running the show. A hundred and eighteen people who were in the premises after it was built and prior to it being robbed. Staff people and ones you were interviewing for jobs as well as others. Do any of the names bring to mind any of these photographs?"

Ulick took his time in going down the names and reevaluating the pictures. "No. I can't make any connections."

"Who might be familiar with the names you don't know?"

"No one. I know all the names. I met all the people listed. Mister Julien knows some of them because he also did job interviewing. Mister Chandler, our president, would know a few. But I know everyone on that list. With the second list it's a different story. I don't know a soul. You'd have to speak to either Mister Julien or Mister Chandler on that."

"What second list?"

"The amendments to the first list. We sent you a copy."

"No one sent us anything."

"I brought it to you myself."

". . . Tell me about this second list," Cub said.

"It was the amendment to the first list," Ulick repeated. "The changes. That first list, the master list, was compiled quickly. Within hours of our learning of the robbery. Errors were made. And omissions. I, for example, had mistakenly included two electricians on the master list who had never entered the premises, who simply had installed our outdoor sign a half mile from the bank. Mister Julien and myself, on rechecking, found several things like this, particularly with the interviews. We had listed certain interviews with job applicants who never kept their appointments. A few people who had been to the premises we overlooked mentioning. All this information was on the second list. It wasn't all that large a list of changes, I'd like to point out. We were quite accurate with our first list."

268

"You say you brought this second list, the list of changes, to the FBI yourself?" Cub asked.

"Wednesday morning, August twenty-fifth," Ulick answered. "It's noted here." He raised his red appointment book.

"Do you recall who you gave it to?"

"I was instructed to deliver it to Mister Denis Corticun. He was indisposed so I gave it to his aide, a Mister Harlon Quinton."

"You were told specifically to give it to Mister Corticun, not to Mister John Sunstrom or someone else at the local FBI office?"

"I was told to go to the twelfth floor and give it to Mister Corticun."

"Told by whom?"

"Mister Julien."

"Who gave you this list of amendments?"

"Mister Julien."

"Do you have a copy of it?"

"No."

"Who does?"

"I assume, Mister Julien."

. . . Giles Julien's suit was decades out of style. His shirt collar was starched and high. The fabric of his red bow tie was devoid of sheen. He set the folder on his desk and pushed the wire-rimmed glasses higher up on his nose. "Why did I instruct Mister Ulick to go directly to Mister Corticun with the changes?"

"That's what I asked," Cub said.

"Because those were my instructions." Julien peeked under his glasses to search the folder.

"Instructions from whom?"

"Mister Chandler."

"Emile Chandler, the bank's president?"

"That is correct." Julien held a page out to Cub. "This is what you're looking for. A list of deletions and additions for the original submission."

Looking at it together, Cub and Butch Cody saw that Ulick had been generally accurate in his description. Ten names appeared.

269

Seven were in the column to the left, which designated deletions from the original list.

The three names in the column to the right were of people who had shown up for job interviews the afternoon of August 20, the same Friday that Mormon State was robbed. All three had sought positions as night watchmen. The last man of the three was scheduled to be seen at 4:30 P.M. His name was Teddy Anglaterra.

# Fifteen

"MORMON ROBBER SEIZED!" headlined the Prairie Port *Tribune*. "LOCAL MAN ROBBER!" was the banner of the competing *Daily Portian*. Both papers reached the stands at 6 A.M. Both had completely sold out by 7:30. Second editions went just as quickly. So did a third. Elsewhere across the nation and beyond that morning, front pages carried word of Mule's arrest. Toward midafternoon more personal material began to emerge. "CROOK PLEADS POVERTY!" the Los Angeles *Herald-Examiner* declared. "21¢" took up the top half of the New York *Post*'s tabloid cover. The bottom half bore a cartoon of Mule, his pockets turned inside out, begging with a tin cup. "ROBBER SINGS . . . A SONG!" declared the Chicago *Daily News*. St. Louis's *Clarion* displayed front-page photos of Mule and Kate Smith, above which was emblazoned: PATRIOTIC ROBBER TO BOOBY HATCH! "SUSPECT ROPED, CHAINED!" protested the University of California's Berkeley *Barb*.

Rural southern newspapers, by and large, reported the incident evenhandedly. Most other publications tended, if not to favor Mule over the Bureau, then to negate FBI participation. Of two hundred and twenty-one headlines on the arrest that day and the next, only one, in the Natchez *Statesman*, mentioned the Bureau per se: FBI NABS MORMON SUSPECT.

Mule receiving media attention equivalent to what had been afforded the original robbery announcement and, later, news of the wizard, might have been anticipated. But Mule received treble this amount of press coverage and public interest. He became, overnight, America's newest pop celebrity. Had the newspapers been a trumpet obligato to Mule's apotheosis, as they certainly appeared to be, then Nancy Applebridge's article was

271

the opening movement. Somehow she was able to find a grammar school graduation photograph of Mule in a tasseled cap and suspenders, an expression of clear stupefaction on his face. Applebridge, in her press association story that appeared in nearly a thousand subscribing publications, made no mention that Mule, a chronic test-flunking truant, was five years older than his fellow eighth-graders and had racked up an even dozen juvenile arrests by the time the class of fourteen posed for the photograph before a wooden schoolhouse that had long since gone to dust—the old Samuel Clemens Elementary School not far from where Mule's horse farm was.

Applebridge's story dealt with childhood. That she managed to exhume the facts as quickly as she did was startling. The writing, admirably Dickensian, told of poverty and abandonment on the prairie . . . of Mule's drunken father and the two Indian squaws he kept, either of which, or neither of which, may have been Mule's mother. The father was a drayman of no particular aspirations who maintained a small stable. Here in the stable Mule dwelt and was thrashed. He ran away. Kept running away. Was thrashed more soundly each time he was returned by the authorities. The notion that the beatings may have caused brain damage was alluded to in Applebridge's piece. As Mule grew older, rage accompanied his recalcitrance. He beat an infant with a stick and was arrested for the first time, was officially cited as a "violent child." He became a whiskey drunk at the age of nine, complete with delirium tremens. When he was eleven he was hit full in the face by a baseball bat his father wielded. Two years later it was Mule swinging the bat full into his father's face. Mule ran and hid with an uncle, an unemployed handyman who worked as a part-time janitor at the Samuel Clemens grammar school. Arrangements were made for Mule to live in the basement of the school and attend classes. He lived there but seldom went upstairs.

Mule came of age by himself, a scavenger on the prairie. He could not relate to people. Loved animals. Spent as much time with animals as possible. There was a possibility that Mule's father had sired a daughter by one of the squaws . . . that this

272

daughter may have been the woman seen in the teepee the night Mule was arrested by the FBI. Perhaps this sister's name was Vonda Lizzie, the name Mule had shouted out as he ran for safety. Perhaps Vonda Lizzie was the name of one of the Indian squaws, the one who was Mule's mother. Applebridge posed the questions without offering answers. The final line of the article ended on Mule's eighteenth birthday . . . the day he was graduated from grammar school.

Bumper stickers reading "FREE THE MORMON STATE ONE" began appearing on cars around Prairie Port. Then across the country. When Lamar "Wiggles" Loftus was returned to the city five days after Mule's arrest and publicly cited as a Mormon State bank robber, bumper stickers were amended to: FREE THE TWO!

Unable to post the $250,000 bail imposed by Assistant United States Magistrate John Leslie Krueger, Wiggles was remanded to the county jail pending trial. His court-appointed Legal Aid attorney argued that such a high bail, with no proof of the charges yet offered, was both unheard of and unconstitutional.

Wiggles Loftus was fated not to be the darling of the media and the public that Mule was. He didn't have that certain spark, lacked star quality. Journalists, sifting through his background, chose to ignore his genuine war exploits, reported on what was routine and bland. Wiggles in jail was cooperative and bland. Particularly bland in comparison with Mule, who somehow managed, from his guarded room in the mental ward, to hold a live radio telephone interview with Chet Chomsky. Mule denied knowledge of, or complicity in, the Mormon State robbery. He did answer, when asked, that he saw nothing wrong with bestiality. Mule, in the media, was faithfully referred to as Corkel or Mr. Corkel. Everyone in Prairie Port, and probably farther, knew he was called Mule. Knew what the second part of the nickname was. Knew why.

Mule's views on bestiality spawned as lively a controversy as had his calling the black assistant U.S. magistrate "white." Some saw the "white" remark as a racial slur, others agreed with Mule. Krueger was criticized by some civil libertarians for allowing

273

Mule to appear in chains, cited the case of black activist Bobby Seale and compared Krueger to Judge Hoffman.

When Mule refused to give further interviews, the networks competed with offers of money. An agent from the William Morris theatrical talent organization sent Mule a letter suggesting they represent him. One offer Mule responded to was from a tour-bus company that bid $500 monthly for exclusive rights on bringing visitors to the ranch, as the horse farm was now being called. Mule demanded $500 a week. A settlement was reached, $1,100 per month. The girl dressed like an Indian squaw at the ranch manned a roadblock, charged all nontour bus sightseers $1.50 admission. The concessionaire within the ranch proper paid a guaranteed $100 per week against fifteen percent of gross receipts on all sales of food, beverages and souvenirs. The biggest-selling souvenir was an Indian doll of Mule. The biggest seller in Prairie Port proper was a postcard of the Mormon State National Bank with a portrait of Mule superimposed in the upper left-hand corner and one of Wiggles in the upper right-hand corner. A local rock group renamed itself "The Mule" and tried to give a concert at the ranch.

Media preoccupation with Mule had borderline advantages for the FBI, helped divert attention from the fact that four men thought to be gang members were actively being sought. So far the names Cowboy Carlson and Sam Hammond had not been revealed. Nor had the media learned who Elmo Ragotsy was or where he was being held. The less the media knew of any of this, the better for Romor 91. The FBI needed time.

Jessup sat up front. Strom Sunstrom and Assistant U.S. Attorney Jules Shapiro rode in the back. Yates drove but had not been brought along merely as chauffeur. Jez had suggested Billy help them work out a strategy. A strategy was needed desperately.

What had sent the three FBI men and the assistant U.S. attorney speeding south this midafternoon was official word that Mule Corkel would be proclaimed fit to stand trial and discharged from the hospital the day after tomorrow. He must then be immediately rearraigned before Assistant U.S. Magistrate John Leslie

274

Krueger so bail could be set, as well as a trial date. Mule's lawyer would unquestionably demand low bail. Worse than that, from the government's standpoint, he might demand specifics on the charges against his client. Might want to be told the names of other co-conspirators, in custody or being sought, as well as anything else the government possessed which might prove detrimental to his client in a court of law. The government, in the person of Assistant U.S. Attorney Jules Shapiro, who would be prosecuting the case when the trial began, would press for high bail and attempt to divulge as little as possible. Assistant Magistrate Krueger, still smarting over media criticism of his handling of the earlier arraignment for Mule . . . of chaining Mule, as the assistant U.S. attorney and the FBI had suggested . . . might side with the defense lawyer, might lower bail . . . might, and these were the two worst fears of Strom and Jez, set an early trial date and want to know if any other co-conspirators were in custody.

Trial, under present circumstance, meant action against Mule, Wiggles and Ragotsy. Jules Shapiro was content with this. He considered the three to be highly prosecutable. True, no strong corroborating witness would be presented other than Ida Hammond stating Mule, Wiggles and Ragotsy had been at her house with the other members of the gang. And Ida's reliability was a concern. She had wavered before. Had voluntarily told police Lieutenant Ned Van Ornum who the perpetrators were, then denied their complicity when talking to Cub Hennessy a few minutes later. But Van Ornum's testimony in court of what Ida had told him would account for a great deal, should she renege. So would her daughter-in-law Natalie's statements. Jules Shapiro put trust in the thesis that bank-theft prosecutions were exercises in circumstantial evidence. The evidence provided him by the FBI, circumstantial as it was, to his way of thinking would do the job. Even so, he reviewed aspects of it at the start of the auto trip with Strom and Jez and Yates.

Of paramount importance was the whereabouts of the three defendants at the time of the perpetration. Ragotsy, Mule and Wiggles all appeared to have been in Prairie Port. Ragotsy had admitted so in his coerced confession. Crew members of his boat

275

confirmed that Ragotsy left on a trip Friday noon, August 20 . . . as had been stated in the confession letter. A waitress in a Prairie Port diner frequented by Cowboy Carlson had identified a photograph of Wiggles as being the same man she had seen having breakfast with Carlson early Friday morning, August 20. Three different witnesses attested to Mule having been in Prairie Port the same morning.

No one had been developed who had seen any of the three from Friday afternoon through Sunday evening, August 22. Late Sunday night Ragotsy returned to his boat briefly, gathered up a change of clothes and left. Was gone five days. Gone until August 27. Mule wasn't seen in Prairie Port until August 28. Cowboy Carlson, following his breakfast with Wiggles on Friday, August 20, was never again seen.

The missing gang members, Bicki Hale, Windy Walt Sash, Meadow Muffin Epstein and Worm Ferugli, were all from out of state . . . had last been seen in their home areas a week before the robbery, over the weekend of August 14 and 15. The only eyewitness to their whereabouts after that was Ida Hammond, who confessed all were at her farm the week prior to the theft. Following the theft only two spottings had been made. The night clerk in Baton Rouge had thought Bicki might be the man with five suitcases. The most recent sighting came from a travel agent in Key West, Florida, who reported Meadow Muffin Epstein looked like the man who tried to charter a boat to fish the waters off Cuba.

Jules Shapiro didn't feel Ragotsy's coerced confession was as inadmissible as Strom did. Excerpts of it could always be alluded to. It might even be allowed in toto. The physical evidence found inside Warbonnet Ridge, added to everything else, made a strong case, in the estimation of the government's prosecuting attorney. Shapiro had no doubts that he could win in court. Should one of the suspects turn government witness, as Strom hoped, so much the better. If it didn't occur, no matter.

Strom Sunstrom had more than prosecution on his mind. He wanted the rest of the gang: Bicki Hale, Wallace Sash, Thomas Ferugli, Lionel Epstein. He wanted more physical evidence

276

. . . equipment with which the actual robbery had been perpetrated. Wanted to find the missing millions. Only fifty dollars in currency had been recovered. Recovering stolen monies was J. Edgar Hoover's passion.

Ragotsy, as Strom saw it, might be the solution to everyone's problems, might simultaneously enhance Shapiro's prosecution and help the FBI investigation. If Ragotsy turned government witness and merely restated what he had told County Sheriff O. D. Don Pensler under duress, little would be accomplished. Ragotsy, after all, had denied being able to identify any of the other bank thieves aside from Cowboy Carlson. However, should Ragotsy know more than he had divulged in his blood-splattered statement, as Strom and Jez and Yates suspected he did, much might be achieved. How to induce Ragotsy into such cooperation dominated conversation over most of the two-hundred-mile auto trip to the Army hospital.

Shapiro, Strom, Jez and Yates conferred with the doctors attending Ragotsy, and viewed photographs and X-rays and medical charts while being briefed. They saw as well as heard what had happened in the county jailhouse of O. D. Don Pensler . . . that Ragotsy had nearly been tortured to death . . . that whereas his face was relatively unmarked his torso and groin had sustained savage beatings and near mutilation . . . that Ragotsy was in shock for the first few days at the hospital, could or would not speak for the next few days, could or would not eat and had to be fed intravenously . . . that over the last nine days he had made astoundingly good progress . . . that yes, he was clear-minded enough to be talked to at length now . . . that no, he had had no visitors, had made and received no phone calls, had mailed no letters or gotten any . . . that all in all, he was one tough cookie to have sustained what he had and come through this well this quickly.

Shapiro never considered speaking with Ragotsy. Doing so, while not illicit or unethical, could draw criticism. He had no intention of taking such a risk. Jules waited with Yates in the hospital cafeteria. Strom and Jessup headed for the officers' wards.

277

Ragotsy, thin and tremulous and wearing blue slippers and a blue hospital robe, sat in a slant-backed wood chair on the observation deck off his private room. Lush and rolling terrain shimmered beyond in the dying reds of sunset. A hill breeze wafted. A far-off hoot owl began.

"We are sorry about the jail house business," Strom said after introducing himself and Jez. Jez went to the bench along the sidebar and sat down. Strom leaned against the railing in front of Ragotsy. "We will register a complaint with the U.S. attorney general if you like."

"A complaint?" Ragotsy watched the setting sun behind Strom.

"Against the county sheriff."

"What's that get me?"

"Revenge. Justice. Peace of mind."

"How about the letter they made me sign? Does it get me back the letter? Unsign it?"

"No."

Ragotsy's smile was slight and mocking.

"We don't believe that letter, Mister Ragotsy."

The smile lingered.

"Mister Ragotsy, you are a valuable piece of merchandise, make no mistake about it," Strom told him. "Valuable to us, the FBI. We spent most of the drive down here concocting ways to win you over. Be warned, an approach has been decided on and will be tried out here and now. We intend it to work. To win you over. Not by the means employed by County Sheriff O. D. Don Pensler, if I have my say, but by logic, Mister Ragotsy. Logic and the call of mutual interest. It makes no sense for either of us, the federal government or yourself, to remain at variance on this issue. In a word, Mister Ragotsy, we have you by the balls and intend to squeeze only gently."

"There ain't much of my balls left," Ragotsy told him.

Strom nodded sympathetically. "We arrested Mule."

"Arrest a mule? What for?"

"Wiggles is under arrest too."

Ragotsy shrugged, betrayed no sign of recognition.

278

"We have a very bright young fellow with our office, Mister Ragotsy," Strom said. "His name is Yates, and the agents joke about him knowing everything. He has an interesting theory about you. Would you like to hear it?"

Another shrug was shrugged.

"Mister Yates read your letter with great interest. Particularly the part about you not recognizing anyone else in the tunnel or cave the night of the robbery. Mister Yates, by the way, certainly believes much of what you said in the letter was so . . . that you were there and took part in it. Mister Yates believes that Sheriff Pensler might even have put in things he read in the newspaper about the robbery on his own. But there was one thing he couldn't have put in. That you had to get out into the river in time to catch the Treachery. Only someone who knew that river well would know about the Treachery. That came from you, Mister Ragotsy. Our Mister Yates says so.

". . . Getting back to the point, what Mister Yates wonders is how you could not have recognized Wiggles down there. Wiggles walks with a limp. Wiggles also worked on your boat, Mister Ragotsy. So we all think you fibbed a little bit in that instance. We think that if you fibbed once, you may have fibbed a second time. Was it just coincidence that brought you to Baton Rouge the same time as Wiggles and Mule?"

Ragotsy continued staring out at the fading sunset.

"Oh, by the way, Bicki Hale was also there in Baton Rouge."

Ragotsy, for the first time, looked directly at Strom, then quickly glanced away.

"You missed Bicki, Mister Ragotsy. He left Baton Rouge just before the three of you got there. Checked out of his hotel carrying five large suitcases with him. Have any idea what was in those suitcases?"

Ragotsy shook his head. "I don't know what the hell you're talking about. I don't know no Bicki or whatever. I don't know them other names you spoke."

"Would you like us to leave?"

"Yeah, that's what I'd like, if you don't mind, for you to leave."

"Before we say what happened to the money?"

". . . If you wanna tell me what you got on your mind, tell me. I'll listen to anything. I don't get to see many people. Only don't think I know anything about what you're saying."

Strom moved from the railing, took a seat to Ragotsy's right . . . a seat from which he could clearly see Ragotsy's profile in the young darkness.

"Our man Yates thinks, and we agree, that you went to Baton Rouge to get money owed you from the robbery," Strom said. "Your share of the money. Following the robbery Mule and Cowboy were supposed to get off the Mississippi early on, go into the Big Muddy River and land at a place where Mule's truck was waiting. They were supposed to have a third man with them, only he didn't show up. Where did you get off, Mister Ragotsy? Did you go with Mule and Cowboy when the wizard didn't show up? It was the wizard who was supposed to be with them, wasn't it? When the wizard walked out on you, all kinds of trouble started . . . like too much water being let into the tunnels?"

Ragotsy said nothing, stared rigidly ahead.

"Obviously, Mister Ragotsy, we know what went on that night in the tunnel and beyond. Obviously, someone connected with the robbery had to tell us. Don't forget, we've had Mule and Wiggles in custody for almost three weeks now."

No reaction from Ragotsy.

"I don't think Bicki Hale ever meant to give you your money, Mister Ragotsy. I believe he misinformed you about the time the money was to be divided up. The men from the Prairie Port area, yourself and Mule Corkel and Wiggles, whom you brought in, were all told to be in Baton Rouge a week later than the other gang members. The one person Bicki wouldn't cheat, his nephew, was planning on being in Baton Rouge a full weekend before any of you. Do you think Cowboy may have assisted Bicki in the holding out? Wasn't that what you suspected Wiggles of as well, being in with Cowboy on the holding out?"

Ragotsy wet his lips in the darkness.

"If you don't do something, Mister Ragotsy, Bicki Hale will get away scot-free . . . with your end of the money. He may be out of the country already."

280

Strom was on his feet, pacing. "As matters stand now, only you, Mule Corkel and Wiggles Loftus will be going on trial . . . and soon. While you do, Bicki and the other men will be spending money like water. Will be millionaires. And out of our reach. I can't say that the charges against you will be dropped or substantially reduced. But they might be if you suddenly remember seeing Mule and Wiggles down in the tunnel. Under those circumstances you would be a government witness . . . and entitled to extra considerations. We'll be making the same offer to Mule and Wiggles when we leave here. There's room for only one of you." Strom stopped directly in front of Ragotsy. "Well, what do you say? Can we count you in?"

Ragotsy lowered his head, remained silent.

"Thank you all the same for your time. For hearing us out." Strom walked from the observation deck.

Ragotsy turned and watched him go.

"Asshole," Jez Jessup said, standing up. "The man does something no FBI man I've seen does, and you ignore him. He gives you your life back and you treat him like he doesn't exist. He gives you your life and a chance to shag after some of the money with no questions asked and you sit there like Joan-of-fucking-Arc. Nah, you're dumber than an asshole. You don't even make the rank of enema. You're what they call you, a river rat."

"I don't have to take your shit," Ragotsy told him.

"You'll take anything I give you, rat ass, and love it. We own you. Mormon State's the best thing that ever happened to you. You're going to crawl on your belly begging for more of my shit . . . begging I don't give you up."

"My lawyer will think different," Ragotsy told him. "I got a right to lawyers. I wanna see him now. I want you outta here!"

"A lawyer? What kind of lawyer, homicide?"

"Homicide?"

"Like in murder."

"What the fuck you talkin'?"

"For one thing, Cowboy Carlson. Remember, he was your roommate."

"What about him?"

281

"You tell me."

"You know something about Cowboy, say so!"

"The question is, what do you know?"

"Hey, fed, can the games. You seen Cowboy?"

"In the morgue with half his head blown off," Jez said. "You musta been out of town when they fished him out of the water. He was weighted down and dumped in the Mississippi."

Ragotsy reached into his pocket for a cigarette. "Who'd wanna kill the Cowboy?"

"You tell me."

". . . This is more of your bullshit! No one would kill the Cowboy." Ragotsy lit the cigarette, puffed nervously. "And if he was killed, I didn't know nothing about it. Hey, you don't think I'd let the Cowboy get hurt, do you?"

"Somebody did."

"You wouldn't be prick enough to tag me for slamming Cowboy?"

"Not if I can help it." Jez smiled. "I still want you for Mormon State. 'Course Baton Rouge may want you worse."

"Baton what?"

Jez grinned. "Dum-dum, what kind of looney-toon are you? Mister Sunstrom just told you all about Baton Rouge. Don't pretend you never heard about it."

"Yeah, Baton Rouge. That's down south, ain't it?"

"It sure is . . . and you were seen there, asshole. Not only when you checked into the Packard Arms hotel under the name of Kenekee, but later. You were seen talking to Mule in the park. The day after that two eyewitnesses watched while Wiggles and Mule started fighting in the zoo. Then a zoo ranger comes along and tries to break it up and they attack him. Attack him just when you show up. You see them beat hell out of the ranger. You warn them another ranger is coming. That's abetting a murder, rat ass. Abetting a murder in Louisiana is the same as committing it. The ranger they hit is still in a coma. If he dies, you're up for homicide one. If he lives, you're up for attempted homicide. Either charge supersedes federal bank theft . . . Mister Ragotsy, if I may call you

282

that, you're on a one-way ticket back to Louisiana. And while you're being held for trial down there, guess what jail house they're gonna stick you in? You got it, the county lockup belonging to O. D. Don Pensler. Whatever is left of them balls of yours, you better take a photograph of . . . for memory's sake."

Jez was halfway to the door before stopping and turning back to Ragotsy on the dark observation deck. "By the way, those two eyewitnesses to the assault on the ranger were FBI agents. If it was worth their while, they might not remember seeing you there. Call me if you have a change of heart."

Hearing the particulars from Jez as they drove from the Army hospital, Strom was pleased with the sweet-and-sour gambit they worked on Ragotsy. Felt it had come off even better than calculated. Was certain Ragotsy would cave in during their next visit. Jez wondered if they hadn't underestimated the initial effectiveness of the ploy. He believed he had Ragotsy near the breaking point when he walked out on him, per plan. Jez speculated that had he stayed longer, Ragotsy might have capitulated.

Jules Shapiro thought the right procedure had been followed but did suggest a departure from the original strategy for the days ahead . . . that instead of Strom and Jez working the sweet-and-sour a second time, Jez go back by himself. Make Ragotsy feel he was all alone, trapped in a cage with the cobra.

Getting to Wiggles in the county jail and trying the ploy on him, as Strom and Jez did the next morning, proved unproductive. The gimp-legged war hero appeared indifferent, even bored, by their efforts.

An attempt to see Mule in the mental ward was embarrassingly frustrated in the downstairs lobby by the public defender, who in front of a battery of lingering news people denied Jez and Strom access to his client unless he himself was present.

Denis Corticun and Harlon Quinton arrived for the eleventh-floor meeting as requested, sat opposite Strom and Cub Hennessy at the conference table.

"What is this?" Strom held up a copy of the list of names Cub had gotten from the Mormon State bank and then shoved it at Harlon Quinton. Corticun reached for it. "I would appreciate, Denis, if you let Quinton view it first."

Quinton read, glanced up with a bland expression of ennui, said nothing.

"Look familiar?"

"Not offhand."

"It was given to you upstairs," Strom told him as Corticun examined the page.

"Many things get sent to us."

"Not us, *you.*"

"Many things get sent to me. I am, after all, in charge of the central files."

"That's what bothers me," Strom said. "Part of your responsibility is to notify us of everything that comes in. And to send copies of all data down to us. I don't remember being sent that list!"

"My God, man, we can't go traipsing after every little detail," Quinton replied. "We have nearly four hundred volumes of data up there now. Minutiae occasionally gets overlooked."

"Even when it's hand-delivered?"

"Even then."

"Hand-delivered by the assistant manager of Mormon State bank and addressed specifically to Denis Corticun and intercepted by you? You still don't remember?"

Quinton turned to Corticun. "He just doesn't understand anything . . ."

"I understand one thing." Strom talked evenly. "I'm kicking your ass off the central files. You're finished with them."

"My friend," Quinton said, "I'm headquarters. Field doesn't tell headquarters what to do."

Corticun interceded. "We can work this out, I'm sure. I remember this page quite well. I was expecting it. Chandler, the bank president, called me on it. Said he was sending it over. I may have forgotten to tell Harlon here."

"Was it investigated?" Strom asked.

284

"Investigated?" Quinton repeated.

"We got the master list the bank gave the police," Strom said. "A list of everyone who was on the bank premises prior to the robbery. We were following up on those names. The page you were given says we shouldn't bother with seven of them and that three new names should be added. Were those three new names investigated by you?"

Corticun and Quinton exchanged looks. Quinton spoke. "As a matter of fact, they were. I remember now. There were three names. We of course followed up on them. How did you know?"

"Just guessing." Storm indicated the page. "Followed up on those three names, right?"

"Yes, those three."

"What did you find out?"

"They all had alibis."

"Your memory seems to have returned," Strom said.

Quinton ignored that. "All three men, the three names, were being interviewed for night watchman positions at Mormon State, or so we thought. The first two names were men who already were watchmen for other companies. The bank had run short of applicants for the watchman jobs and turned to an employment agency which specializes in security people. An agency with offices in downtown Prairie Port that advertises in the neighboring states. All three men on that list went to the agency, where they were given a time to appear at the Mormon State bank for an interview. Two of the men went to Mormon State and had their interviews. At the time of the robbery one of them was at another job and the other was at home.

"The third man shouldn't have been on the list, that last name, Teddy Anglaterra. He showed up at the employment agency's office in Prairie Port between nine and eleven Friday morning, August twentieth. They made an appointment for him to be interviewed later that afternoon at Mormon State. He never showed up at Mormon State for that interview, wasn't on the Mormon State premises. We found out he lived in Illinois and is a drunk. He liked making appointments for job interviews but seldom kept them. That's all there was to it."

285

"And that's what you *forgot*," Cub couldn't help saying, ". . . that's what slipped your mind, all of that?"

Strom resumed pacing. "Why weren't we told about Anglaterra and the other two men?"

"Oversight," Quinton said. "Don't blow it up."

"You have no authority to investigate anything occurring in Prairie Port. That is strictly an eleventh-floor matter, particularly when the subjects may have been at the bank premises the day of the robbery. Your only obligation was to send their names downstairs to us."

"My God, we were pressed. I *believe* I mentioned that."

"You won't be pressed any more." Strom turned to Corticun. "I don't give a damn who technically has the say here, me or headquarters. Until I hear from Mister Hoover directly, I'm dumb enough to think I'm boss." His finger dropped at Quinton. "Him, I want out of here on the double, or, *my God*, I will kick his ass all the way out myself. The central files I want brought down from the twelfth floor. We operate them from here on."

After several moments, Corticun nodded his assent.

Jessup, the following afternoon, replaced one of the U.S. marshals escorting Mule from the hospital. He sat alone with Mule in the back seat talking quietly for the fifteen-minute drive to the federal building. He went upstairs and watched Mule being rearraigned before Assistant U.S. Magistrate Krueger. He witnessed Mule calmly learn his bail was set at half a million dollars . . . and meekly respond that he couldn't raise so much money, and passively allow himself to be led away to the county jail, while his Legal Aid lawyer shouted to heaven on high that the arraignment was an outrage and his client's civil rights had been denied and justice aborted. In the evening, at the county jail, Jessup again managed to be with Mule alone, to talk to him another forty minutes. The results Jez reported back to Strom were unhappy ones. Mule wanted no part of the FBI or their plan.

Jessup and Yates then returned to the Army hospital. Only Jessup went in to see Ragotsy, stayed for three hours and came

286

away empty-handed. He went back two days later, remained inside with Ragotsy less than twenty minutes. After that, Ragotsy refused to see him again. So did Wiggles and Mule.

He was as unexpected as a summer blizzard. Harry Janks, Chicago's rumpled and Wellesian and bulge-bellied "defender of the damned." Lawyer Harry, heir apparent to the red braces and stentorian spell-mongering of wondrous Clarence Darrow himself. Greedy Harry, who long ago swapped principle for profit, laid down his sword to sup at the table of the very dragons he once set out to slay. Sword or no, he cut a wide swath, Harry did. How, in his flamboyance, he managed to reach Prairie Port unnoticed, remain there unnoticed another day and a half, was nothing less than stunning. What he was doing in Prairie Port proved even more stunning . . . to the FBI.

The men had been summoned at 10:30 at night, entered the office building through the back or side entrances. All resident agents, except for Strom, were seated in the press auditorium by 11:15. So was Denis Corticun and twelfth-floor agents who had worked directly on Romor 91.

Strom, pale and shaken, entered at 11:20. The surprise, for all, was who followed him into the room. First came assistant to the FBI Director, A. R. Roland. Behind Roland strode Harry Janks.

Roland took the podium, in slow, hesitant words said that a mistake had been made which was not the fault of anyone present . . . that mistakes simply happen, occasionally, in investigations. He then thanked Harry Janks for being so considerate and going directly to Director Hoover rather than the press. Ruefully, Roland introduced Janks.

Thumbs hooked into his trouser top, he walked to the podium, confronted the audience, shook the shock of silver hair away from his eye. "I have been here before," he told his listeners. "I tried a case here in Prairie Port before most of you were born. Your Mister Grafton was the law here then. I am regretful he is not present today. He taught me a lesson with that case. My client was a young extortionist whom Mister Grafton had ar-

287

rested. A lad from a somewhat well-to-do family. The family had put me on retainer, one of the few times I ever did receive remuneration in those years of so long ago."

The hands moved up, strummed the red suspenders. "My client, the young and wealthy ne'er-do-well, afforded me a piece of evidence I felt would have won the case for me. And I would have won most assuredly . . . had my client been telling the truth. He wasn't. He was flimflamming. I lost. Mister Grafton saw I was of despair and took me to his favorite saloon. A speakeasy. Liquor was illegal in those years. We had whiskey and coffee, and Mister Grafton suggested a rule I might follow in the future: Never trust a client, even if he's telling you the truth.

"We all, of course, forget that. Yourself and myself. My clients are your adversaries, your suspects. Persons whose relationship with the truth is tenuous at best. I believe, had you invoked Mister Grafton's rule and mistrusted what several of them said, we all would have had a happier day.

"I am here in Prairie Port to represent three new clients, Mister Marion Corkel, Mister Elmo Ragotsy and Mister Lamar Loftus. I can understand your zeal and frustration concerning them, but I cannot allow, without recourse, the abuse of their constitutional liberties. My options at recourse were many, but I accepted the one at hand. A chance to talk to you directly . . . and to scold you a little.

"Sirs, you have perpetrated more heinous criminal acts in attempting to apprehend and convict my clients than they have in their misguided careers. I contend that the very warrants on which they were arrested were improper. I contend that Mister Corkel, following his illegal apprehension, was denied immediacy in contacting a lawyer, which is guaranteed by the Constitution . . . that you, the FBI, most assuredly delayed contacting the public defender until the latest possible moment. I contend that one of my clients, Mister Ragotsy, was technically placed incommunicado in a hospital after his return from the South. I know of no attempt by either you or the military authorities in charge of the hospital to contact any of Mister Ragotsy's kin.

"As to your efforts to convince Mister Ragotsy, Mister Corkel and Mister Loftus to become witnesses for the government, I must regretfully say I find them reprehensible. You were deceptive in getting to them. You were deceptive when with them. Replacing a U.S. marshal duly entrusted to guard and protect Mister Corkel so you could offer him a so-called deal is downright felonious. You may disagree, but I know the law it transgresses. And poor Mister Ragotsy, in one sentence you spew sympathy for the beating he has taken in jail, while in the next sentence you mentally abuse him even worse . . . scare and befuddle him into thinking that should he consult a lawyer you would arrange to have him accused of homicide rather than bank theft. I can assure all of you he will be accused of neither.

"Sirs, you have falsely arrested my three clients. You have trusted the worst truth of all, facts. Or should I say the misinterpretation of facts." Janks raised a sheaf of papers straight up into the air, held it there. "These here are the other facts. The true facts. They show what you either misread or did not bother to confirm . . . sirs, my three clients were not in Prairie Port at the time Mormon State National Bank was burglarized. They were in Illinois. Emoryville, Illinois. These papers contain the sworn statements of eyewitnesses who saw them in Emoryville that night and for six days thereafter . . . I will tell you something else that is not in these papers. Messrs. Corkel, Ragotsy and Loftus had gone there for the same reason they were in Baton Rouge three weeks later . . . to steal cigarettes. My clients, sirs, are truck hijackers, not bank thieves. Inept hijackers at that. They had the wrong information about what to rob in Baton Rouge and got into a fight over it. In Emoryville the shipment they were waiting for never arrived.

"Sirs, if you wish to investigate my clients for conspiracy to hijack, I suggest you alert your offices in Illinois and Louisiana. As for the homicide charges with which you threatened Mister Ragotsy repeatedly, as well as Mister Loftus and Mister Corkel, do go ahead and alert the Baton Rouge officials. Homicide is not federal purview, as we all well know. Perhaps the Baton Rouge police might wish to know why two FBI agents, who witnessed the assault, have still not told local authorities who the assailants are. Don't you think it better for all concerned if most of this is forgotten? . . . if all charges are quietly dropped and my clients agree not to sue for false arrest? I do. You and I, dear friends, will live to fight again another day at a different place, I assure you. Let us have this hour pass."

The documents were held higher. "My clients did not rob Mormon State National Bank. *They could not have.*"

Corticun's phone call ordered the flying squad into action. By morning they confirmed that every affidavit presented by Harry Janks was true . . . that eleven unimpeachable citizens of Emory-ville, Illinois, had seen Mule, Wiggles and Ragotsy in their town at the time of the robbery and for a week thereafter. Seven of the eleven were either operators or employees of the hotels where Mule, Wiggles and Ragotsy had stayed. Three different hotels . . . as had been their pattern in Baton Rouge.

# Sixteen

Edgarphobia was the word he used, said the men were in a horrid state of Edgarphobia. But that wasn't why he asked her to come fetch him.

It was raining and past 1 A.M. when Tina Beth Yates packed a thermos of hot chocolate and several sandwiches and ran out to the family station wagon and sped downtown to the FBI office and picked up Billy. Let Billy drive. Rode with him as they went nowhere in particular. Answered when he spoke to her. Listened when he thought aloud. Waited patiently while he thought in silence, which was most of the time.

They had done this before. At Ohio State University right after they had met was the first time. Tina Beth had not known Billy Yates was an undercover FBI man posing as a graduate student, only that he was vying for top academic honors in the many university courses he was taking. School had always been easy for Billy. He could achieve, without effort, grades which would rank him among the upper five percentile at any institution of learning. This was not good enough. Billy, in matters scholastic, could settle for nothing less than being unequivocally the best. He treated tests and examinations as mortal combat. Prepared for them as a general might prepare for battle. The first time Tina Beth had driven with Billy was to help him prepare for a mid-term examination in sociopathic psychology . . . a test in which he had made up his mind not to get one answer wrong. Billy had recited whole passages from lectures and textbooks as they rode, rattled off every question and answer he could conceive. They drove until it was time for Billy to go in to take the test at eight o'clock the next morning. In twenty-three pages of multiple-choice questions, only two incorrect answers were made by him.

291

They had driven again so Billy could tell Tina Beth how much he loved her and that he wished to marry her . . . that because of this he must reveal what he was really doing at the university and that if she didn't ever want to speak to him again, he understood. Billy told her he was an FBI agent. First she laughed at him. Then she got mad and got out of the car saying she never wanted to see him again, not because he was a Bureauman but because he had lied to her. Two weeks after that they were married. Never again did they use auto drives for personal matters. Affairs of soul or heart. These were discussed at home or on long walks. Autos were for professional issues such as test-taking or investigations, career decisions such as Billy considering quitting the FBI if he wasn't transferred out of undercover work.

There hadn't been, during their year-and-a-half-long marriage, all that many problems that warranted a drive and discussion. When there was, Billy's keen intelligence and deductive prowess had risen to the challenge. That was one of the things Tina Beth admired about her husband, his ability to figure out nearly everything, and to give off confidence while doing so. Now, watching Billy hurry from the Prairie Port resident office building and replace her behind the wheel of the station wagon, Tina Beth saw he was agitated and puzzled . . . sensed, for the first time, he wasn't at all confident.

Billy Yates, as he began to drive into the storming night, told Tina Beth that Mule Corkel and Wiggles Loftus and River Rat Ragotsy had been cleared of complicity in the Mormon State robbery and just set free. He said the resident office was in a state of shock and "Edgarphobia." Shock at being so wrong about the three suspects. Terrorized, or Edgarphobic, over what Director Hoover would do when he found out. Billy told her frantic efforts were under way to find new and different suspects, that to this end, everything done in the investigation to date was being reviewed.

What Billy Yates found odd was how most everyone in the office seemed to believe Harry Janks.

"Not that Harry Janks wasn't a spellbinder, because he surely was," Yates said. "He walked right into the enemy camp, into the

292

FBI office, and did his number. I'm sorry you couldn't have been there, Tina Beth. He was something to behold. Something right out of that old movie starring Spencer Tracy. Eloquent as hell. And full of hot air. Mule and Wiggles and River Rat are guilty, Tina Beth. Mark my words, they are! They have to be! Why the other agents don't see it I don't know. Maybe they don't want to see."

"They *all* think they're not guilty?" Tina Beth asked.

Yates nodded. "All but me and Brew. Could be Strom Sunstrom feels like us, but if he does he's not letting on."

"What about Jez Jessup?" she asked. "He usually thinks the way you do."

"He's the big surprise, Jez is. I would have expected Jez to say they did it too. That maybe Sam Hammond and Bicki Hale had something to do with it. But he's written them off totally. Jez thinks the Prairie Port Police Department set us up. That Captain Frank Santi and Lieutenant Ned Van Ornum nailed us good. Santi and Van Ornum were the ones that led us to Ida and Natalie Hammond. It was Ida and Natalie who named the gang for us. Mainly Ida. Jez points out that as far as we personally know, Ida has always denied her brother Bicki Hale had anything to do with Mormon State . . . that she admitted some of the other gang members were around her place with Bicki but she denied they were involved too. Jez thinks they were at Ida's farm planning a series of hijackings . . . including some in Baton Rouge, where Mule, Wiggles, Ragotsy and maybe Hale went."

"I don't understand, Billy," Tina Beth said. "Did Ida say the gang did Mormon State or didn't she?"

"She did and she didn't. She broke down and named all of them. I think she was telling the truth. Jez is saying we unwittingly fooled or scared Ida into saying the gang robbed Mormon State by showing her the fuse. It was only when Cub showed her the fuse he found in Sam's workbox that Ida let down and said okay, here're the names of the men who hung around when Bicki was at my farm. Actually it was Natalie, the daughter-in-law, who insisted they all hit Mormon State . . . Jez even has the fuse business worked out. Has it worked out two ways. The first is that

293

Sam actually built that fuse for a different group of criminals. A group Bicki Hale might have introduced him to, but which Bicki and the rest of his own gang were no part of. Jez's second explanation, which he's kept pretty quiet, is that the police planted the fuse in Sam Hammond's garage. I agree with Jez it wouldn't have been hard for the police to find out about Warbonnet Ridge before the FBI did. The geologists and God knows who else discovered the control room way before Jez and I got there. Frank Santi and Ned Van Ornum could have been down there before we were and found extra fuses, taken the fuses without anyone knowing. Then, if you want to follow Jez's scenario, they could have sat back and waited for the right situation. Or gone looking for the right situation. One way or another they might have run across Natalie Hammond, whose husband was missing. Who knows, maybe Sam Hammond was originally intended to be a member of the hijacking gang. Maybe his uncle, Bicki Hale, put him on it so he could earn some extra money. Money to buy that repair shop in Nags Head. Jez sure as hell thinks that's possible.

"Jez also thinks Bicki most likely arranged for Sam to go along with Mule, Wiggles and Ragotsy on the Illinois cigarette hijacking. And that maybe Sam did go to Illinois or maybe he committed suicide before he could go. As for Natalie Hammond, Sam's wife, insisting her husband was in on Mormon State, knowing a few things that weren't in the paper about it, Jez has a simple explanation: that Natalie herself was simple, sweet and trusting but on the dim side. Jez feels it wouldn't have been too hard for a couple of old pros like Frank Santi and Ned Van Ornum to convince Natalie her husband was actually going to Mormon State . . . to twist around everything Sam told to suit their own purposes. Jez thinks that's what happened . . . that Natalie repeated to Cub what Santi and Van Ornum had whispered in her ear, convinced her was so. That way they used her to set us up for this fall."

"But you don't think what Jez Jessup said, happened?" asked Tina Beth.

". . . I just have to believe what Ida and Natalie told the FBI was true."

"Aren't you *sure*, Billy?" There was no answer. "Why don't you and Jez go back and talk to Natalie again?"

"We would if we could find her. Natalie Hammond has disappeared. Left home three days ago and hasn't been seen or heard from. How about some hot chocolate?"

Tina Beth undid the thermos, poured a cup of chocolate. "Do you think Natalie's in trouble?"

Billy shrugged, took the cup and sipped as he drove.

"If Natalie is in some sort of trouble, then maybe Jez was right about her?" Tina Beth speculated. "Maybe the police took her away or did something to her so you wouldn't find out she was telling you lies."

Billy shook his head. "The police aren't going to go in for kidnapping to prevent it being known they made fools of the FBI. If anything, they'd take out a paid advertisement to brag about how dumb we were."

"If it doesn't matter whether Natalie is lying, why would anyone take her away?"

"To keep her from repeating the truth . . . maybe that's it. Maybe something else scared her off. Maybe she isn't missing. We don't know what conditions she left under. But we know she's pregnant. Possibly she just took a trip, but I doubt it . . ."

"What does Jez think?"

"For all we know, Jez is in on it."

"On what?"

"The conspiracy."

". . . I don't understand."

"That's why we're driving and talking, Tina Beth. I don't understand either. At times I think I do. I think I see it. See it clearly. I have this feeling our investigation, all of Romor 91, is being systematically sabotaged. Sabotaged from the inside. Sabotaged maybe by Jez. Then I start seeing Corticun as the saboteur. Or even that faceless spy that Ed Grafton was always certain had infiltrated the office. Washington's spy. I see the spy a lot . . . I stare harder, and suddenly everything falls apart. Shatters into pieces and rearranges as if I were squinting into a kaleidoscope. The conspiracy is gone, and one by one, all those inconsistencies and contradictions in the investigation start forming and collapsing. Reshaping into something else. Nothing makes sense, and everything makes sense. The more incomprehensible it becomes the more I have this feeling of déjà vu. I've been here before, Tina Beth. Whatever's going on, I've been through it before. I've got to find out what it is. What the hell is happening. Maybe if we go over it like we used to go over the tests, talk it out, hear it, I'll get some focus. Maybe just saying it and hearing it might give me some perspective. Hearing all those questions I had. Just rattling on at random. Tina Beth, you up to me rattling on?"

"Rattle away, Billy Bee."

There were immediate questions for which he had no answers, such as how exactly Harry Janks had been able to get into Prairie Port and in touch with Mule and Wiggles without the FBI knowing. How Janks was able to get to Ragotsy, who was technically incommunicado at the Army hospital. How and when he convinced each prisoner to let him represent them. How and when Janks was able to procure the eleven affidavits in Emoryville, Illinois, saying the three suspects were in that town. Had Mule, Wiggles and Rat told Janks where they were and who had seen them? Had Janks then arranged for these eyewitnesses to be interviewed at Emoryville? Or had Janks somehow managed to learn about the eyewitnesses first and gotten their affidavits and then gone to see Mule, Wiggles and Ragotsy? Janks was a very well-connected criminal lawyer, and sources in the underworld could have tipped him off about Emoryville. About who to see there. Whose affidavits to take. Was it because of these affidavits that Mule, Wiggles and Ragotsy agreed to see Janks and let him represent them? Were there intermediaries between Janks and his three new clients and if so, who were they?

Questions regarding Sam Hammond nagged. Was it conceivable Sam hadn't done the electrical work for the gang? Didn't get the generators working and the water gates open? Did not build the time-delay mechanism? Sam's work area, after all, did not contain the sort of sophisticated tools Cub thought were needed to build the mechanism. Build the fuses. If Sam hadn't built them, hadn't done the other things as well, who had? Were Corticun and Cub and most of the other agents correct in originally pre-suming an electronic engineer at the very least had been the wizard? Was it possible a different and far more sophisticated gang had perpetrated Mormon State?

No, that couldn't be, he told Tina Beth as they drove. It wasn't a different gang. It was Mule and Bicki and Wiggles and River Rat and Meadow Muffin and Windy Walt and Cowboy and Worm who scored Mormon State. If anyone had brought in a wizard other than Sam Hammond, they had. If an electronic engineer or his likes had been used, they would have had to use him. But how probable was it for Bicki and company to have access to anyone so educated and skilled? No, they had access only to someone uneducated . . . *and* skilled.

There was much about Denis Corticun that Billy Yates pon-dered, aloud and silently, while he drove with Tina Beth. Cor-ticun had originally come to Prairie Port to interview Martin Brewmeister after the robbery was discovered . . . the "first" or "small" robbery, as Yates was referring to it, of $6,500. Corticun had run afoul of Ed Grafton by going directly to the hospital room and interviewing Brew there, after being denied permis-sion to do so . . . had been humiliated first by Grafton and later by the drunken parody of him in the resident office. Through it all, Corticun had remained aloof and haughty. On the FBI's reen-try into the Mormon State investigation . . . after discovering an additional $31,000,000 had been stolen . . . Corticun seemed to have shed his skin, came back to Prairie Port an ostensibly changed man. A cooperative and caring chap who never inter-fered with Strom's dictates even though Corticun, technically, could overrule Strom . . . was in fact the ultimate authority for Romor 91. Corticun had allowed Strom to get rid of Harlon Quinton and have the central files moved to the eleventh floor. Corticun's overriding concern was public relations and press con-ferences. He hyped the crime and unknown criminals with the *joie* of a carnival barker. Corticun, more than anyone, created the illusion of the supercrime-of-the-century, extolled the un-known gang as the crème de la crème of thievery. Yet Corticun was only fleetingly perturbed on learning a stumblebum street crook like Mule had pulled off the job. Cub became, and remained, despondent over this. Other of the agents did as well. But Corticun took it in stride. Went on holding his two press conferences a day and tending to other public relations chores. When Harry Janks provided documentation of Mule, Wiggles and Ragotsy not having been in Prairie Port at the time of the robbery, Corticun was as unflappable as ever. Didn't bat an eyelash. Went back to his office and rewrote the press release he had intended for morning dissemination.

"He doesn't ring true," Billy Yates said to Tina Beth. "Nothing about Corticun rings true. He's playing games. Only I don't know what kind of games." More hot chocolate was sipped. "Jez, he could be playing games too."

"You're sounding like real paranoid, Billy Bee," Tina Beth said. "It's how I feel."

They rode on many more miles in silence. Rode with Billy squinting straight ahead through the rain-splattered windshield, biting at the corners of his mouth, swallowing dry swallows from time to time. Drove with Tina Beth watching him from the corner of her eye, sensing the turmoil.

Billy's thoughts, as they so often had, drifted back to a pair of old and troubling questions, pivotal questions that had emerged at the very onset of the investigation and lingered. Why had it taken so long to discover an additional $31,000,000 had been stolen from Mormon State National Bank? Why had J. Edgar Hoover dismissed Ed Grafton when he did?

Yates had read the flying squad's summary explanation of how the $31,000,000 came to be at Mormon State, found the reports to be, as he told Jessup at the time, as full of holes as Swiss cheese. The rush of subsequent events hadn't allowed Billy to dwell on this or Director Hoover's removal of Grafton. While he drove with Tina Beth, both questions reemerged, hovered. Billy homed in on the one for which he had tentative answers.

"If J. Edgar Hoover and Ed Grafton were such old and good pals, had fought and made up and fought again and made up again as legend held," he said aloud but not necessarily to Tina Beth, "then why would Director Hoover remove him at all?

What had Ed Grafton done that was so wrong, that would call for removal? Ed Grafton had gone on vacation. The first vacation he'd taken in five years. While he was gone, Mormon State gets robbed. Or we learn on Sunday it was robbed. Ed Grafton can't be reached, and no one knows how much money was stolen. There's no doubt the perpetration was spectacular in concept. The press starts calling it the crime of the century. Denis Corticun comes in from headquarters like a military historian rushing onto a fresh battlefield to memorialize the fight for all time. Grafton is back by then and is told by the bank and Brink's that only sixty-five hundred dollars was delivered to Mormon State just before the theft. That becomes the official loss estimate. Grafton wipes Corticun's nose in it. Corticun, of course, is Washington's man. The Brass-Balled Monkeys' man. He's a Brass Ball himself. The agents in our office get drunk and steal Corticun's pinstriped jacket and do a take-off on him . . . and he walks in on the take-off. All the agents drop their pants in front of him. Then we find out another thirty-one million was in the vault, that it's the biggest robbery in history. The press goes wild . . . but why remove Grafton? Because he believed what the bank and Brink's told him about only sixty-five hundred being in the vault? Because he rubbed Corticun's nose in it? Because the agents ridiculed Corticun? Because of the press . . . because Washington felt it needed a fall guy? Or because Washington was afraid what Grafton would say to the press when he got back from vacation?

"... Are any of these, all of these why J. Edgar Hoover would get rid of Grafton? Or are they reasons the Brass Balls in Washington would get rid of him? But I don't think the Brass Balls would dare bring one of these points up to Hoover . . . wouldn't risk his wrath if he defended Grafton against these complaints like he's defended him against everything else. Hoover, only Director Hoover, could have removed Ed Grafton. Then why did he? What would cause him to dismiss his oldest and closest friend among agents? The man he had protected and championed for so long. Could that be one explanation? That Director Hoover was protecting Grafton by removing him? Does that make any sense, Tina Beth?"

299

"Protecting him from what, Billy Bee?"

"This investigation. Being any part of Romor 91."

"Why?"

"Maybe J. Edgar Hoover felt the investigation would fail and didn't want Grafton to suffer from that?"

Tina Beth knew from Billy's tone he did not seek any comment from her, that he was merely speculating aloud, listening to how the answers sounded, how they struck him. She knew that more would be forthcoming.

". . . There are two more possibilities," Billy said after a long pause. "What if J. Edgar Hoover had come to agree with the Brass Balls who felt Prairie Port was too big a pain in the butt to deal with any more? Let's say Hoover had decided the entire resident office should be replaced. Along comes Romor 91. Hoover sees the perfect opportunity to clean house without arousing the media. Even J. Edgar Hoover might have pause at what the press would do if they found out he replaced an entire office for no good reason. We certainly have seen how Washington cottons to the media, haven't we, Tina Beth? They probably learned that from Mister Hoover himself. Yessiree, if I were J. Edgar Hoover and wanted to flush out the Prairie Port office from top to bottom, the Mormon State robbery would be manna from heaven. With Mormon State I could stand back and let Prairie Port do its own self in. Walk the plank unaided and with its eyes wide open. All that would be required was to remove the man who *was* the Prairie Port residency . . . Ed Grafton. As far as Edgar Hoover was concerned, and most of the Brass Balls for that matter, Grafton was the mind, the soul, the very blood in the veins of our office. Lop off the monster's head and the beast will die. Pluck the captain from the helm and the ship will crash onto the rocks. Let all hands perish. Then send in a brand-new crew. Answer me this, Tina Beth." He was looking intently at her now. "Why give Romor 91 to Strom Sunstrom?"

"Mind the road, Billy Bee," she told him.

He looked ahead at the highway. "Romor 91, the largest and most important Bureau investigation ever mounted . . . and they give it to Strom? Dozens of SACs and supervisors with ten times

300

the experience Strom has are bypassed for replacing Grafton. There's no precedent here. Not with a resident office. No rule saying who should take over for Grafton. It could be anyone. But Edgar picks Strom. Everything goes to Strom. Corticun, who outranks Strom, comes in and doesn't lift a finger. He lets Strom do it all. Agrees with everything Strom does, investigationwise.

"Tina Beth, you think Denis Corticun knows something we don't? You think maybe he's waiting for something to come down . . . like Strom and the rest of us? Without realizing it, you think maybe Strom's aiding and abetting Corticun? Strom's already turned over most of the residency's routine case load to Corticun and his auxiliary agents on the twelfth floor. Do you think maybe those auxiliary agents, those temporary support personnel, as they've been designated, are not so auxiliary or temporary or supportive? Do you think they're our replacements? And always have been? How much effort would it be for those thirty agents on the twelfth floor to relieve the eleventh floor of Romor 91 and have the whole kit and kaboodle to themselves? Have Romor 91 as well as Prairie Port? Think Denis Corticun was just waiting for us to stumble so he would have the excuse to take over, or . . . so J. Edgar Hoover would have the excuse to order him to take over?"

Billy's laugh was pained. "Tina Beth, looks like your old man has gone looney-toon on you. Wacko as Mata Hari Jessup claims to be about spies coming to Prairie Port to peek on Grafton. Next thing you know I'll be seeing little green Edgars under every bed . . . or on the highway in front of us. Keep your eye on the highway, Tina Beth. If you see the sign for a crazy house, let me know 'cause I haven't told you the craziest idea yet. If you see a phone booth while you're looking for a nut house sign, I can use that too."

Billy Yates finished the last of the now tepid hot chocolate. "Possibility three. Wilkie Jarrel versus Ed Grafton. Grafton and Jarrel have been going after one another for years. Headquarters and even Capitol Hill have tried to intercede, usually on Jarrel's behalf . . . tried to either check or replace Grafton. J. Edgar Hoover sticks by his old pal Grafton. No one is sure why. Maybe

301

it's not important enough for J. Edgar to do otherwise. Maybe there's nothing to be gained by not standing by Grafton. Mormon State explodes onto the land. Mormon State is important to the FBI. Wilkie Jarrel controls the conglomerate that owns Mormon State National Bank. Wilkie Jarrel's son-in-law, Emile Chandler, is the president of Mormon State National Bank. An investigation like Romor 91 needs the full cooperation of the victim bank. What with the blood feud between Wilkie Jarrel and Ed Grafton raging hot as ever, Edgar has to choose between facility and friendship. Has to sacrifice one or the other. He sacrifices Ed Grafton. After all, how accommodating would you expect Emile Chandler to be if Grafton showed up in his parlor?"

Yates glanced expectantly at Tina Beth.

"That's all?" she asked.

He nodded. "Theory number three."

She pointed ahead. "I see a phone booth."

. . . The office ordered him to go to Municipal Airport without delay.

The jet cargo plane from Chicago taxied into the National Guard hangar at Municipal Airport, swung around, stopped. The engines cut off. The nose section opened. The metal ramp behind it lowered. A large, black limousine rolled out of the fuselage hold and down the ramp and on across the hangar to where Yates and Brewmeister and a young FBI agent from Washington headquarters were standing.

"Clean it," the young man said.

"Clean what?" Yates, like Brewmeister, had been given no explanation as to why he had been summoned here.

"Clean the car. Make it glisten."

"It's glistening already," Brew said.

"There are cloths and a portable vacuum cleaner in the trunk," the young man said. "Use them. On the outside and inside."

A second young agent from headquarters, this one with an earpiece leading down to a walkie-talkie in his hand, ran forward, calling, "He's already there!"

"Where?" the first young man demanded.

"He didn't land here. He landed by helicopter somewhere else. He's already at the office and waiting."

"Jesus H. Christ." The first young man wheeled to Brew and Yates. "Let's go!"

"Where?" Brew asked.

"Your office." The first young man jumped into the rear seat of the limousine followed by the second young man.

Brew shrugged, got in behind the wheel. Yates rode beside him. They reached the downtown residency office twenty minutes later, led the two young men up to the twelfth-floor conference room/television studio.

The speaker's rostrum and Bureau crest which had been in place the night before when Harry Janks confronted the staff were gone. Standing in their place was the stage set which had not been used since the area was refurbished by Corticun . . . an exact replica of J. Edgar Hoover's Washington office. The audience comprised only men from the eleventh floor, all seventeen Prairie Port resident agents, including Strom. The two young agents from headquarters guarded the door. At exactly 8 A.M. the door opened.

J. Edgar Hoover entered. Stopped abruptly just inside the room. Stared hard at the awestruck men seated in the audience. Exuded a presence which frightened even the usually imperturbable Billy Yates.

J. Edgar Hoover strode onto the set. Seated himself behind a reproduction of his own desk. He folded his hands atop the blotter. Looked down at his hands. Remained that way.

"Here it comes," Donnie Bracken whispered to Strom and Yates, who were sitting directly in front of him. "He's exiling us to Alaska. I feel it. Nome, Alaska."

J. Edgar Hoover cleared his throat. Moved his lips silently as if he were saying something under his breath. Squinted up momentarily, then back down at his hands. Blinked. Glanced up and blinked again. Blinked down at his hands once more.

"The Bureau, like Israel, has suffered many hurts," he intoned. "Its women weep for the fallen. Its children pray for the wounded. It ill behooves one who has supped at the Bureau's

303

table to damn, with equal fervor and fine impartiality, both the Bureau and its warriors when they are locked in mortal combat. Those who must shall suffer a thousand curses. Shall be smitten by boils and blindness and plague. Their lands shall be parched and flooded. They will take to the hills like scattering sheep."

Edgar stopped talking, continued looking down at his folded hands.

"What was that about?" Brew whispered to Yates.

"Beats me," Billy answered *sotto voce*, "but the first part is a steal from a speech John L. Lewis made in the 1930s."

"How do you know that?"

"I used to know everything."

J. Edgar Hoover pinched the tip of his nose. Wet his lips. Gazed up at the resident agents seated before him. Shot his cuffs. Squared his shoulders. Leaned forward on one elbow.

"There are those who say you struck the dagger into the back of Romor 91 and that the cause is lost," he told them. "How say *you?* How care you? What is it you wish me to perceive? What is it you expect me to do?"

J. Edgar Hoover closed his eyes, lowered his head.

"He's changed his mind," Bracken whispered. "It's not Nome, it's the firing squad."

J. Edgar Hoover's head raised. The eyes opened. "Jellyfish. Punks. Mental halitosis. That's what I have to say to anybody who doesn't think you people were magnificent." He was on his feet, one hand in his jacket pocket, the other hanging loose. "You are, each of you, magnificent. You have acquitted yourselves bravely. I have come here to tell you how proud I am of you and what you have achieved with Romor 91. With God's help and your skill we will carry forward and bring to bay the true perpetrators. You shall make it so. I love you!"

J. Edgar Hoover bowed his head, reseated himself behind the desk, motioned to the two young men from Washington.

"Mister Sunstrom has brought to my attention that you fine young men have so much enjoyed reading my best-selling book, *Masters of Deceit,* you wish to have an autographed copy of my other work, *A Study of Communism.*" Strom had made no such statement. "I have therefore brought with me a copy for each of you which I will inscribe as instructed. You will receive a complimentary ten-percent discount, and the purchase price will be deducted from your salary."

Seventeen copies of *A Study of Communism* were deposited before J. Edgar Hoover by the two young men. The resident agents of Prairie Port, one by one, came forward, shook hands with the Director, said what they wished inscribed, received the autographed book, shook hands again, left the duplicate office and the studio in which it was built.

Billy Yates, on leaving, was told by one of the two young men from Washington he was to wait for J. Edgar Hoover. Was to accompany the Director on a tour of the offices and then drive him wherever he wished to go. Billy tagged along as J. Edgar was shown the rest of the twelfth floor by Corticun. J. Edgar hated what he saw, sputtered orders to Corticun for immediate redecoration . . . for restoring integrity to the space and the men who worked there . . . for making it look much more like the eleventh floor, which he had not yet visited. And did not visit.

Billy Yates escorted the Director down to the waiting limousine, drove him to the first address J. Edgar read from a typewritten list. The home of Martin and Elsie Brewmeister. J. Edgar went to the door, rang the bell, introduced himself to a startled Elsie Brewmeister. Asked if he might take tea with her inside. Chitchatted with Elsie over tea for exactly twelve minutes as Yates waited at the rear of the room. Gave her, for free, an eight-by ten-inch glossy photograph of himself. Signed the picture: To Elsie Brewmeister, a woman, mother and FBI wife . . . her obedient servant, J. Edgar Hoover. On departing told her how proud he was that she was the woman behind the man he was so proud of.

Yates drove to the home of Rodney and Sue Ann Willis. Edgar dropped in on Sue Ann as he had on Elsie Brewmeister. Stayed twelve minutes. Praised her husband and her and autographed a photograph of himself for her. Did the exact same thing with

305

Flo de Camp. Then with Sissy Hennessy. Then Tricia Dafney. Maureen Bevins. Hinky Cody. Nell Travis. . . .

"He dropped in on all eight unannounced," Billy told Tina Beth that night. "When we're leaving Nell Travis, he looks at his watch and acts surprised and says he's run out of time and won't be able to visit the other wives like he planned. He tells me to take him to the airport. I find out later that it's all crap. That he didn't have to check his watch. That he only intended to sign eight photographs. At the airport he gives me an envelope with nine more photographs of himself. Each photograph was already made out in the name of one of the nine wives he didn't visit, including the one I have here for you."

Billy handed Tina Beth a glossy photo of J. Edgar Hoover that was inscribed: To Tina Beth Yates, a woman, mother and FBI wife . . . her obedient servant, J. Edgar Hoover.

"Don't you see, it was an act, Tina Beth. He knew he was only going to visit eight wives. The eight he had not already autographed pictures for. The eight I drove him to. He'd signed the pictures for the nine other wives before he even got into the limousine with me. They were in an envelope he carried."

"What difference does it make, Billy?"

"The difference is he lied about it."

"Why?"

"You want to know why, Tina Beth? . . . because if you ask me, J. Edgar Hoover is a nut job."

"Crazy?"

"Asylum bait."

"You sure, Billy Bee?"

"Look at it yourself, Tina. J. Edgar Hoover, who never flies in helicopters, comes into Prairie Port by helicopter. J. Edgar Hoover, who travels everywhere with Clyde Tolson, arrives in Prairie Port without Tolson. Without anyone. J. Edgar Hoover, who hates riding around in strange cities in anything but one of his own limousines, has the Chicago field office airlift the limousine, store it for him in Prairie Port, only he doesn't helicopter to where the limousine is. J. Edgar Hoover, who is a tough, direct, no-nonsense speaker, gets in front of the resident office and starts babbling long, irrelevant passages from John L. Lewis and Franklin Delano Roosevelt. J. Edgar Hoover, who is nothing short of Jehovah in the wrath department when agents and offices make even minor investigatory errors, praises Prairie Port rather than burying it. Exalts all of us to high heaven for fouling up, rather than applying thumbscrews and the lash. Tells an entire office, I love you. J. Edgar Hoover then proceeds to coerce the same seventeen agents he loves into buying an autographed copy of one of his old books. J. Edgar Hoover visits the twelfth-floor offices, a space which months before he had ordered decorated in the most lavish style, and hates what he sees. He orders it totally redone. Humiliates the man he had entrusted the operation to, Corticun, by saying this in front of other agents. J. Edgar Hoover goes and visits eight of the seventeen wives and lies about not having time to see them all and sign their pictures.

"... Listen to the last thing J. Edgar Hoover does. While I'm driving him around today, we don't exchange more than one or two conversational words. He tells me what he wants me to do, and I say okay. Beyond that there's nothing said. But then at the airport . . . instead of a helicopter, he goes home by plane . . . as I'm holding the car door open and he gets out, he stops and throws his arms around me. Hugs me. Says that I am to him like the son he never had. The son he had always been looking for.

"Oh, no, Tina Beth, if J. Edgar Hoover isn't right off the wall, then I have to be. Or will be. If I don't have a nervous breakdown thinking about all of this, it won't be from lack of trying."

Strom got out of bed and hurried downstairs to the den to the ringing red phone—the direct tie-line phone to Washington that Corticun had insisted be put in.

"Yes?" Strom said into the mouthpiece.

"J. Edgar Hoover here. This is Mister Sunstrom, isn't it?"

"Yes."

"I have a favor to ask. A highly personal and confidential favor. Would you look into the adoption laws of Missouri for me?"

307

# Book Three

# Seventeen

New suspects were developed by the residency and duly announced by Denis Corticun. Mule, Wiggles and Ragotsy dematerialized into yesterday's news. And FBI-2000 rang on . . . FBI-2000, the emergency hot line telephone number used by the Prairie Port Bureau office for receiving confidential information from the public regarding Romor 91. Denis Corticun, at every opportunity, exhorted the public to phone in whatever information anyone might have, no matter how slight or unconfirmed.

The hot line number was originally connected to the eleventh-floor switchboard in the residency office. When incoming traffic grew too great, the overflow went up to the auxiliary switchboard on the twelfth floor. This system remained until J. Edgar Hoover visited Prairie Port. His orders to redecorate the twelfth floor were immediately implemented. The communications room was all but ripped out and the auxiliary switchboard installed on the eleventh floor. Following the twelfth floor's five-day alteration— the entire space had been transformed into the sterile dullness of the residency office below—it was decided to keep the auxiliary switchboard, and therefore all FBI-2000 traffic, where it was. Let it be maintained by the resident agents of the eleventh floor, who were, after all, the prime investigators of Romor 91. And it was to FBI-2000 that an unidentified woman caller suggested the Bureau look into the Elison sisters . . . that the Elisons might be the wizard.

Strom Sunstrom, in the wake of J. Edgar Hoover's departure from Prairie Port, had launched an all-out search for new suspects. Some attention was given to tracing the whereabouts of Bicki "Little Haifa" Hale, Thomas "The Worm" Ferugli, Lionel

"Meadow Muffin" Epstein and Reverend Wallace Tecumseh "Windy Walt" Sash. Routine efforts were made to find Natalie Hammond. Mule, Wiggles and Rat were ignored . . . and Brewmeister vociferously objected. He argued it was imperative that surveillance be placed on the three men, even though Rat was still convalescing at the Army hospital. He argued that more must be done to find whether Natalie Hammond was well or in trouble. His requests were rejected by Strom. Yates had consoled Brewmeister, eventually confided his suspicions that the investigation of Mormon State might be being sabotaged. Brew had had similar thoughts. They discussed Yates's questions about the J. Edgar Hoover firing of Ed Grafton as well as the curious conditions under which $31,000,000 had been shipped to the bank.

Brewmeister and Yates had decided, on their own, to look into both matters, to investigate unofficially. Brew would cover the money shipment. Yates would handle the Grafton firing . . . check out the Hoover-Wilkie Jarrel connection. They had gone as far as giving themselves first assignments. Brew was to delve into the breakdown of the armored truck bringing the millions from New Orleans to Prairie Port. Yates meant to check the phone systems used by Jarrel, try to find records to establish whom Jarrel had talked to. Brew still felt surveillance should be placed on Mule, Wiggles and Ragotsy. Yates maintained there was no time for such surveillance in light of their already heavy Romor 91 work load. As it turned out, surveillance would be the only one of their plans there was time for.

Brew received a new Romor 91 assignment from Strom, was placed with a unit of agents touring penal institutions in Missouri, southern Illinois and western Kentucky. Their quest was for an inmate, or inmates, who might divulge relevant information on Mormon State. This was part of a much larger operative channel. Nationwide, as Romor 91 headed into its third month, four thousand full-scale investigations were under way on criminals who could know about, or have participated in, the theft.

Brewmeister, during hiatuses in travel, began spot surveillances of Wiggles and Mule. When Ragotsy was released from the Army hospital and came back to Prairie Port, Brew kept an eye on him as well, or tried to . . . what with a full schedule at the residency when he wasn't on tour, Brew's time for tailing was limited. He did manage to see the three men get together for what he presumed was their first joint encounter since Baton Rouge. Brew became more interested in Mule. Spent every free evening watching Mule. Then Mule vanished. Dropped from sight. When he reappeared four days later, Brew continued where he left off, watching from afar.

Yates, during this period, was assigned to look into a subject on which he had become expert in Ohio . . . extremist organizations, particularly organizations close to the college community. The college community, Strom had always felt, was a choice place for finding and recruiting someone with the skills of a wizard. Yates was given two agents from the twelfth floor to assist him. Together they culled lists of known members of extremist groups in a five-state area. At first Billy labored without conviction or interest. His indifference soon gave way to fascination, but never zeal. He worked around the clock developing what would become the office's latest "hot lead." He hardly had time to see or speak to anyone, Tina Beth and Brew included. The reason for this began with the FBI-2000 phone call citing the Elison sisters.

The unidentified tipster said Louise and Nadine Elison, daughters of a prominent Prairie Port physician, had shared an apartment with Dwight Armstrong while they were students at the University of Wisconsin the previous year . . . that Armstrong talked Nadine, who was an engineering major, into stealing money for left-wing causes . . . that Nadine had recruited her sister Louise, a biochemistry major, to help out with the biggest theft of all—Mormon State.

The call might have been downgraded or disregarded had not the name of Dwight Armstrong been mentioned. Armstrong was well known to the Bureau. He and his brother and two other men had been indicted in connection with the August 24, 1970, bombing of Sterling Hall at the University of Wisconsin campus at Madison. The blast had left one person dead and three others injured.

The Elison sisters, Yates learned, had been on the periphery of

313

several local radical movements while attending the university but definitely had not resided with Dwight Armstrong. They had never even met the fellow. Apparently knew nothing of him other than what the media carried at the time of his indictment. But the investigation into Nadine and Louise led back to Prairie Port, where they currently shared an apartment in the bohemian part of town known as Old Port. And the apartment produced a most disturbing set of fingerprints . . . latent prints of a notorious fugitive by the name of Libby Tidwell.

Libby Tidwell had been described in New York City's Soho *News* as a "radical nihilist social butterfly." The FBI concurred. Libby, a matronly appearing woman of twenty-six, had been weaned in the old left groups such as the Trotskyist Socialist Workers Party and the Chinese Progressive Labor Party, teethed on several antiwar organizations which the Bureau deemed to be vulnerable to "subversive influences," including the Student Mobilization Committee to End the War in Vietnam (SMC), the Young Socialist Alliance (YSA) and the National Peace Action Coalition (NPAC). She had radicalized in the Weathermen, a violence-prone wing of the pre-June 1969 Students for a Democratic Society. Bolting the Weathermen, she became the political commandant of a Marxist terrorist group known as the Latin America Action Committee. LAAC was believed directly responsible for a series of bombings in Washington, D.C., New York City and Los Angeles. Just what LAAC's aims were, or exactly what its connection to Latin America was, seemed obscure. No known Latinos were involved with LAAC, and it had no connection to the Venceremos Brigade, a suspected pro-Cuban group.

Billy Yates had heard about Libby Tidwell while he was underground in Ohio. She struck him as the quintessential middle-class revolutionary of the period. A joiner more than a believer, but, with a burning stick of dynamite in her hand, extremely dangerous. Informant reports at the time stated Libby was nearby and organizing a series of clandestine conferences among LAAC, the Black Panther Party and the Weathermen. The Bureau, fearing an Apalachin of Terrorism was in the making, raided the meeting

314

site, a home in suburban Cleveland. No Libby Tidwell was to be found. No Weathermen. What was taken were several minor LAAC and Panther members and a large cache of weapons and ammunition belonging to LAAC. Libby was not heard of again. Amid rumors she had fled to Europe or Hanoi, Libby went on the FBI's ten most wanted list.

Billy Yates had feared the discovery of Libby's fingerprints in Prairie Port might trigger trigger-happy Denis Corticun into a boisterously discreet blitz of guess-who-we-have-coming-up press releases and media conferences. To Yates's relief, Corticun ignored the fact that one of the nation's ten most wanted criminals might be hiding out in Prairie Port . . . might be connected with the Mormon State bank robbery.

Louise and Nadine Elison, when asked in a three-hour interview by Billy Yates, had no recollection of the name Libby Tidwell. On being shown a picture of Libby, they identified it as Martha Salowski. They had then gone on to explain they had met Martha the year before at a rock concert outside of Madison, Wisconsin, which the sisters had attended with a group of politicized friends. The friends knew Martha. Martha and the sisters spent the night talking about nonpolitical matters. Martha, in fact, never impressed them as even slightly interested in movements, let alone as a radical. Several months later, the sisters met her at the apartment of her then boyfriend, George, whose surname they did not know. That was the last they saw of Martha/Libby while at Wisconsin.

Louise and Nadine returned to Prairie Port in early June and took an apartment. Their phone number was listed. A week later Martha called. She was in Prairie Port and needed a place to stay for a few days. The sisters let her bunk with them. Once ensconced, Martha explained she had come to Prairie Port because of her new boyfriend. He was teaching at the university over the summer and was in the process of getting a divorce, which was why they couldn't stay together. Louise and Nadine met the boyfriend. His name was David Dellafield. David Dellafield was a mathematician and nuclear physicist. Louise and Nadine had

315

no doubt he was the wizard. The more Yates learned from the sisters and subsequent sources, the more he realized David Dellafield would make a perfect wizard.

"You won't believe this Dellafield guy," Yates told Brew at the Terrace Bar. It was late Sunday afternoon. Brew, recently returned from a trip to Western Missouri Penitentiary, was talking to Billy for the first time in almost three weeks or, more correctly, was being talked to. "Dellafield is so looney-toon extreme he thinks Lenin is a closet capitalist," Yates explained. "He despises all left and radical groups. Thinks they've sold out. When you look at him, you figure he's the friendly neighborhood soda jerk. Sandy hair and baby face. Soft-spoken. Nothing in his background to show radicalization. Upper-middle-class kid, in fact. Never worked a day in his life. Smart as hell. Graduated college at sixteen. Breezed through M.I.T. Doctored in about every science there is. Never showed any political preference until he met Libby Tidwell. She rang his nihilistic chimes, okay. It was total destruction at first sight . . . David Dellafield comes over and has dinner at Louise and Nadine Elison's apartment. Sits holding Libby's hand and talking about the holocaust to come. Talks calmly and precisely. He's a revolutionary Marxist of the old school. A dialectic pragmatist preaching the 1920s and '30s gospel. The revolution must come first. Blood must flow for the sake of blood-flowing. Flowing blood is good. Subsequent to destruction comes totalitarianism. Two hundred years of mind control and subjugation. After that, true democracy will grace us all. David Dellafield scares the living shit out of the Elison sisters because he knows how he's going to finance this bloodbath of his. Robbery. And what he starts telling them is a blueprint for Mormon State . . . or any other bank, for that matter. This guy has learned banks and alarm systems and timing devices like only a scientist with a 202 I.Q. could. When we check up on him, we find he's got the fingers of a brain surgeon. He can build anything. Built it out of spit if he has to. Electronically, forget it, he's unbelievable. It's easier for him to build a TV set than walk around the corner to buy one. He knows

316

about maps too. He's been down to the city hall going through the Building Department blueprints for damn near any building in town he wants.

"The creepiest thing about him is he outlined a procedure for the Elison sisters. Dellafield wants to recruit criminals to do his work for him, only he's going about it in a reverse way. He'll let them recruit him. He's going to meet crooks and drop hints and let them try to con him into setting up a job for them. His plan is to rob them before they rob him.

"Brew, you know what this guy does on weekends and Thursday nights? He's a volunteer teacher at the county jail. We went right past him on our list because who the hell's going to think about some triple-Ph.D. professor who's a do-gooder? Know what he teaches at the county jail? Electrical repair and *lock* repair. Electrical repair was his idea. Lock repair was the idea of the Correction Department. Corrections figures the best way to rehabilitate a lock-picker is to teach him how to do his stealing better. This guy David Dellafield has access to every minor crook in Prairie Port."

"What became of Libby Tidwell?" asked Brew.

"Dellafield dumped her. Went back to his wife. That was only a few days after he had dinner with Libby over at the Elison sisters' apartment. Libby split, and the Elisons have no idea where to. Dellafield called the Elisons twice after that, suggested they come meet a small cadre of friends he was putting together. They emphasized he used the word cadre. The Elisons wanted no part of him. When the Mormon State robbery came down, they didn't immediately associate it with Dellafield. The more they heard about the wizard and what he did in the cave, the more they were sure it was Dellafield. They didn't want to contact the FBI because they don't trust us. They didn't want to contact the police on general principles. They did tell a couple of friends about it. Apparently one of those friends sold them out and called the hot line. The girls have no idea why someone would say they knew the Armstrong kid other than to try to make them look as bad as possible."

Brew asked, "What are you doing about Dellafield?"

317

"Have him under surveillance. He's popular as hell at the university. Students love him. He's nonpolitical there. Won't even comment on the Republican Party."

Brew asked, "Are you thinking Sam Hammond wasn't the wizard? Didn't go on the job? That this guy replaced him?"

"Who knows?" Yates was up and pacing the way Strom always paced. Thrust his hands into his pockets as Strom did when he couldn't figure things out. "Maybe I'm all wet. Maybe Bicki and Mule and Sam Hammond had nothing to do with it. Maybe David Dellafield did the whole bloody thing on his own."

Brew shook his head. "Mule had everything to do with it. Come on, see for yourself."

They waited until dark. Drove out to Mule Corkel's ranch west of town. Climbed the same hill from which Yates had surveilled the house and teepee on the night of Mule's apprehension three months earlier.

"I've been tailing him on and off for a while," Brew told Billy as they lay on the crest. "A week back he disappeared for four days. That gave me a chance to do some exploring, let me find out exactly where he was heading, and something else. Here's hoping he shows up tonight so you can see for yourself. It's better you see for yourself instead of me telling you."

At ten to eight Mule emerged onto the rickety back porch of the old house. Glanced about. Darted out past the darkened teepee to the standing pickup truck. Jumped in. Drove boundingly off across the fields.

Brew and Yates went down to their own car, kept a safe distance while following the pickup along a rural road. The truck's braking lights went on as it pulled over to an illuminated telephone booth at the first intersection.

"He makes three calls," Brew explained as they drove past Mule, who was walking toward the phone. "Puts in a coin, dials the number, says a word or so to whoever answers, and hangs up. On two of the nights I watched, he waited around after the last call was made. At those times someone must have rung back because he picked up the phone and started talking without depositing a coin. On the two other nights he didn't wait around after the third call. Just hung up and got in his truck and started driving." Brew pulled onto the ramp leading to the superhighway. "Mule will be taking the side roads when he's finished phoning. We can get there quicker on the highway and then cut back across town."

"Cut across to where?" asked Yates.

"Like I said earlier, it's better if you see for yourself."

The superhighway skirted the city's northeastern periphery. Coming off the exit ramp, Brew drove toward the river. Pulled to a stop inside the old railyard.

Yates followed Brew past a boarded-up roundhouse and onto the grounds of Prairie Port's first waterworks, which was now a landmark building and city park at Lookout Bluff. They went to the rear of one of the granite-block buildings, pushed through a door, descended a circular metal staircase down into a large, domelike brick structure. High arched openings rose along its curving walls. Water flowed through the arches and on into the tunnels beyond the openings. Two of the passageways seemed to be under repair . . . one on the northern side of the area, one on the west.

Brew pointed to a recently plastered and rebricked area beside the northern arch. "That's the wall I burst through when I rode the flood crest after the robbery. The wall I sprained my shoulder on. The tunnel on the other side of that wall leads due north to the Mormon State bank. Into the flood-control tunnel running between here and Mormon State. This is the shunting terminal, the one built in the 1930s to connect the flood-control network with the city sewage system. See that passageway there?"

Yates looked over to the double-width arched doorway on the western side of the structure. It had been totally reconstructed, as had much of the wall around it.

"That's what this terminal is really all about," Brew explained. "The tunnels beyond that opening lead out to the caves and underground mud deposits farther west. The idea, when all this got built, was to drain away the subterranean water farther west and dry up the mud fields and salses . . . the mud volcanoes.

"The robbery made it work in reverse. Every last drop of water let loose from the reservoir and hills came raging through here. Smashed open the tunnel leading west. This room was probably a shambles by the time I came barreling in on Sunday morning. The crest of water I was on didn't bother with the archway, it just knocked down the wall. Knocked it down in part with me. Shot me through the wall headfirst. Lucky I lived through the impact. Lucky I was swept across this room and out a southern exit to the river, instead of going inland toward the mud. Going west. Half the flood waters—how many millions of gallons was it?—went there, inland to the mud."

They entered the western tunnel Brew had indicated. Got onto the catwalk. Brew's penlight led the way through the darkness. Ten minutes later they reached a flooded cave, remained on the catwalk inside the tunnel, watching . . . waiting in the darkness. Two small red light bulbs glowed in a wall socket at the far northern side of the cave, illuminating a concrete pier. To the left on the southern wall of the cave were three tunnel mouths.

A slight, slapping echo was heard. Then one of scraping. Limping onto the pier from the darkness to the right came Wiggles Loftus. In his hand was a large portable searchbeam. He was followed by Mule Corkel, who dragged an inflated rubber boat along the concrete floor. River Rat Ragotsy emerged from the shadows carrying an outboard motor.

Not a word was spoken as the boat was dropped into the water, held tight by a tether and fitted with the motor and light. Wiggles stayed forward at the light. Mule sat amidships, shoved them off with a plastic oar. River Rat pull-roped the motor on, roared the rubber craft into the middle tunnel and out of sight. Above the roar someone could be heard shouting "Tallyho!"

Brewmeister waited until all was silent, motioned Yates to follow. He moved back along the catwalk. Stopped at a line of metal rungs leading up the wall and on into the air shaft. Climbed them. Came out in the middle of an orchard. Led Yates through the trees to an unpaved road. Indicated an emergency utility shack on the other side.

"The shack is the entranceway Mule, Wiggles and Rat just used. Their cars and the truck are probably parked in the woods beyond it."

Brew pointed at a large spread of buildings along a distant hilltop. "All this land belongs to the Benedictine Sisters. Do you remember an item in one of the papers about a nude man scaring them?"

"No," Yates said.

"Neither did I, but it was in the master file. I've been going through the files ever since we took them back from the twelfth floor. Someone on the twelfth must have clipped the article at the time, but nobody up there did any follow-up about it. I found quite a few things nobody did anything about when Quinton and the twelfth floor had the files. Such as that a few nights after the robbery was discovered a naked man pops up in the convent garage and scares the devil out of the nuns. Or at least that's the way the writer of the item put it. According to the story, the police wrote it off as a nutty prank. But I went up there earlier today and talked to the sisters. It wasn't a garage, it was the sheep-dipping shed where all this happened. The man was naked okay but covered with mud. The nuns had heard knocking from under the heavy iron sewer top in the shed. They pried it open and mud erupted. A geyser of mud shot up. In the middle of the geyser was this naked man covered in mud. He climbed out and kissed the floor and crossed himself and handed the nuns something muddy and ran off.

"The sisters did think it was a prank. There's a prep school not far from here, and the boys make life unbearable for the nuns. When the naked man came out of the sewer, they called the police and reported it as more harassment by the students. They didn't say anything about the mud, or what the man handed them. It was money. Paper money. Sixteen one-dollar bills, as they remember. They cleaned the money and donated it to charity."

321

Yates said, "And you think the mud-covered man was either Mule, Wiggles or Rat?"

"Rat?"

Yates considered. "No," he finally realized. "It couldn't have been Rat."

Brew laughed, which was unusual for him. "You have it figured then, do you?"

"Not me, you. You made it all clear."

"Let's hear."

"I don't have every last thing put together. Just the general idea," Yates said.

"Take your time. Tell me as we walk. Maybe it's me who's got it wrong."

The two men started across the field toward the eastern end of the vast convent farm.

"It begins with Ragotsy's confession, isn't that right?" Yates asked.

"How so?"

"Ragotsy, in the letter that cracker sheriff beat out of him, said the gang made their escape from Mormon State bank in four boats. They had four boats down in the tunnels and were running like hell to get in them because of the deluge of water." Yates thought for another moment. "Ragotsy said he was in the last boat. So the thing you've figured out is that Mule was in the first boat."

"Why?" Brew asked.

"For one thing, because of how surprised Mule and Wiggles were when they ran into one another in Baton Rouge. In the zoo there. Wiggles was pleased to see Mule, see that Mule was alive. He walked toward Mule with open arms. Mule was surprised to see Wiggles, and angry. Mule had thought Wiggles had run out on him and Ragotsy. Thought Wiggles had joined Bicki Hale and the other crooks in beating Mule and Ragotsy out of their share of the money. That was it, wasn't it?" he asked Brew. "Mule and Ragotsy never got any of the money. Worse than that, they couldn't find any of the other gang members, including Wiggles. Which made them believe that the out-of-town end of the gang

322

had ripped off the Prairie Port members. But Wiggles hadn't gotten any money either. He'd gone down to Baton Rouge for the same reasons as Mule and Ragotsy, to see if he could find Bicki and his money. Who Wiggles bumps into in Baton Rouge is Mule . . . and before he can say anything . . . explain anything . . . he's punched out by Mule. In the middle of this the zoo ranger shows up and gets clubbed. Mule and Wiggles light out in different directions. They don't see one another until each has been arrested for Mormon State. Whether they got to talk together before the charges were dropped and they were set free or after, when Ragotsy could join them, is immaterial. But somewhere along the line they figured out the same thing you did, didn't they? Figured it out the same way."

"What way was that?"

"Wiggles's way."

They were at the end of the convent grounds now, ducked under the wire fence and crossed the road and started for the old railroad yard.

"You were saying Mule, Ragotsy and Wiggles figured out the same thing I had," Brew reminded him. "Something having to do with Wiggles himself."

". . . Wiggles told them what tunnels he had gone through after the robbery," Yates said. "Where he had been taken with or without his rubber boat. And it wasn't the route Mule and Ragotsy had taken. It wasn't out to the Mississippi River. It was inland. Wiggles had been swept right into the shunting terminal we left earlier, but instead of being carried on into the sewerage system beyond it, like you were, he was diverted due west. Ended up trapped in the mud right under the convent. Trapped stark naked and clutching some money in his hand. Pounded on a metal hatch until it was opened by a nun. Exploded out on them in all his raw glory. And took off. Probably lit out for Kentucky and didn't talk to anybody until he went on down to Baton Rouge for his payment. Once Mule and Ragotsy learned what had happened to Wiggles, where he had gone, they knew one other thing . . . that another rubber boat had gone inland too. The boat with all the money in it. What other conclusion could there be? Ra-

323

gotsy was in the last boat, and he knew none of the money was with him. Mule was in the first boat, and there was no money there. Both Mule and Ragotsy had been washed into the Mississippi River. Wiggles was in one of the middle boats, and he was washed inland. But there was no money in his boat either. So it had to be the fourth boat that had the money. The fourth boat had to be a middle boat. That's what Mule and Wiggles and Rat must have figured once they got together, that the money was somewhere in the western tunnels or caves. Brew, that's what you deduced when you followed them back to the tunnels, saw them get in the boat like we just saw them do. From the moment they did figure it out, down into the tunnels they went." Yates paused. "I said before, it didn't make all that much difference when they made this decision. And it doesn't. But looking back, the earliest they could have been together was when Rat Ragotsy got out of the hospital, unless Mule and Wiggles went to visit him there."

"They didn't," Brew said. "I called and checked. I doubt if Rat even wanted to see them. Rat was having one sweet vacation at government expense. That Army hospital has tennis courts, a swimming pool and a golf course. Rat likes golf. He stayed on for twenty days after he was well. It was part of the deal Harry Janks worked out with America."

As they got to the car, Yates was saying, "Which means when Rat did return and meet with Mule and Wiggles, they didn't waste much time figuring it out and coming down here looking for the money. Anyway, that's how I read it."

"We're in agreement, old buddy." Brew pulled open the driver's door. "There's a bit of corroboration I omitted mentioning. The nuns say that the muddy man who jumped out of the sewer and ran off into the night . . . had a limp."

Yates got in beside Brew. "What now?"

"I say we go right on over to the office and recheck those alibis that say Mule, Rat and Wiggles were in Illinois when the crime came down."

"Where do we check on the third call?" asked Yates.

"Third call?"

"You said Mule went to the phone booth and made three calls the times you followed him away from his ranch," Yates replied. "Three calls before driving on over and going down into the tunnels. I have to assume one call was to Wiggles and one call was to Ragotsy. That Mule called each of them saying he was on his way. That they should get a move on and meet him there. Who did he make the third call to?"

It was half past midnight when Yates and Brew reached the downtown office building. Seeing mobile units from the local television station parked along the curve and reporters hurrying in through the main doors, they drove around to a side entrance, took an elevator up to the eleventh floor. The resident office, as they entered, was in full swing.

"Where the Christ have you guys been?" Cub called out. "We've been looking all over hell for you."

"It's our night off," Brew told him.

"What kind of answer is that! You're supposed to check in, right? Check in at all times." Cub was hot . . . hot at Brew. "Strom needed you. He had to go on without you. You lost us time."

"Go where?" Brew asked.

Cub stood back, glowered, then broke into a wide grin. "We *got* him. Son-of-a-gun, we got him. He's in custody and confessing. We broke Mormon State."

"Bicki Hale?" Brew asked. "You found Bicki?"

"Bicki, my ass. Bicki has nothing to do with it!"

"Then who did you pick up?" Yates wanted to know, "Ferugli? Sash? Epstein?"

"It wasn't that crowd at all . . . and thank God."

"Who the hell was it?" Brew demanded.

"The guy we should have thought of in the beginning."

"*Who?*" Yates said.

"Otto Pinkny."

Brew couldn't believe it. "Pinkny's an assassin, not a bank thief."

"He's number one on the FBI's most wanted list," Cub pointed out.

325

"What the hell does that matter if he doesn't rob banks?" Yates said.

"He robbed Mormon State, okay. I heard a little of it on the phone. If you'd been available like you should have, Brew, you could be hearing it right now. Strom's gone to get him. Strom wanted you to come along and question Pinkny more on the way back. They picked him up in South Carolina three days ago. He's been confessing for three days. Confessing things about Mormon State only the mastermind could know."

. . . And David Dellafield was quickly forgotten.

# Eighteen

He was on the short side but trim. Framed in the narrow doorway of the railroad car, he looked taller. He wore a three-piece white summer suit and a tan straw hat with a snappy blue band and white alligator shoes and chamois spats, all of which had become part of his trademark. His face was modestly pinched. His surprised eyes were wide-set and owllike. The nose, button-ish. His white, nearly albino skin made a sparse blond mustache hard to discern in the filtering light of the railroad station. His lips were fragile and bore traces of rouge. With his straw hat on and riding low, as it did most of the time, he resembled a passive marsupial. When the hat came off, doffed of course in polite acknowledgment, a radical change took place. The slightly coni-cal head with thinning blond hair was revealed, to no advantage. But so was that smile. And those white teeth. A smile so compel-ling, teeth so dazzling perfect that you wanted to shake this fellow's hand. Take him to you. Vote for him. Trust him. Hat up, smile on, teeth bared . . . and he metamorphosed, instantly, from creature into character. There was no doubt Otto Pinkny was a character. He worked at it.

Otto Pinkny smoked thin cigars and cologned with Brut and quoted Elbert Hubbard incorrectly and had authored an incom-prehensible cookbook, which wasn't all that surprising since he had quit school in the fourth grade. Writingwise, Pinkny had murdered the English language more surely than the eleven known victims of his French-made burp gun. Speaking was a different matter. Otto was as garrulous an outlaw as ever was born. "A Casey Stengel of a gunsel," *Time* had once commented. Otto had another oratorical attribute—he spoke in the third per-son.

327

"I know Otto Pinkny from a long time ago and intimately, and I can tell you he's the species of bloke who'd turn himself over to the coppers before harming one hair on a little baby in their rompers," he had proclaimed via phone to an all-night, call-in Philadelphia disc jockey show after errant bullets from his latest gun battle crashed through a window and wounded an infant girl.

When interviewed a year later in his death-row prison cell by "60 Minutes," Otto told America, "Otto Pinkny is a churchgoing bloke and don't smoke never. If chance should will it he gets himself married, he'll be faithful to his wife and won't never use no prostitutes again."

After his spectacular prison break was likened to the exploits of John Dillinger and Billy the Kid by a Baltimore newspaper, fugitive Pinkny called the paper's city editor with a veiled complaint. "Otto Pinkny is a student of history, and you better danged well believe him when he tells me to tell you that Johnny Dillinger was a stand-up bloke but Billy the Kid was a wimp who goes around shooting human beings in their backs instead of facing them face to face like Johnny Dillinger or Otto Pinkny done."

Pinkny had burst into the public consciousness in 1968 by shooting it out with a gang of Birmingham, Alabama, gunmen. Black gunmen, four of whom were killed in the fray. No one knew Otto Pinkny was responsible until he called a Birmingham paper and told them so. He chatted with a local disc jockey about it as well. Though never saying so directly, Otto implied he had killed the black men in retaliation for their having raped and murdered his fiancée. The fiancée's name was never learned, her body never discovered.

Seven months later in Pittsburgh he shot to death Joe Danker and Elroy Dobbins, notorious strong-arm men. Pinkny had explained by phone to a Pittsburgh deejay that death resulted from a dispute over money . . . that Danker and Dobbins tried to shoot him and that he was merely returning the favor. He was arrested in a phone booth the next day as he talked with yet another local disc jockey. Police assumed he must have been involved with

Danker and Dobbins in some criminal activities, but before they could question him at length Otto Pinkny broke out of jail. Four months later he went against Tough Tommy Osler on a Savannah, Georgia, street corner. Friends of Danker and Dobbins had contracted Osler to track down and execute Otto Pinkny. It was Tough Tommy who lay dead after the exchange of bullets. A great deal of publicity was given to a report that Tommy was broke . . . that his contractors refused to pay even for his funeral . . . that it was Otto Pinkny who sent the money for a classy burial. Tough Tommy's widow was outraged by this blatant lie, even allowed herself to be photographed holding up the family bank books and stock portfolio and the receipt from the funeral parlor which showed she alone had paid all expenses. The media, by and large, preferred the more romanticized version in which Otto Pinkny paid. Little play was given to the widow's proof or her complaints that Otto Pinkny himself must have been the one who spread the nasty rumor, which of course was true.

Seven victims were now dead by Otto's burp gun. Seven criminals, of varying venality, whom he had fought fair and square. Stood face to face with, was usually outnumbered by. Comparisons to Western gunfighting heroes of yore were inevitable. So too were bromides such as, after all, he's not really hurting anybody except his own kind. The funeral-payment rumor evoked Robin Hoodish images.

All these were added to in Miami, Florida. A South Miami narcotics kingpin by the name of Luis Herra had employed Otto Pinkny to help organize and protect the delivery of $2,000,000 in cash from a Miami bank to a boat captain in Jacksonville, Florida. The money was small potatoes to the billion-dollar operation run by Herra, but years of internecine war with competing dope gangs had left him irritable and overcautious. He hoped the mere inclusion of Otto Pinkny on the routine money run would discourage interference by rival marauders. Otto Pinkny insisted on transporting the money alone. Herra wouldn't hear of it and assigned his bodyguard, a killer by the name of Cortez, to go along. On the way, Cortez, who had sold out his boss to a competitor, tried to kill Otto and wound up riddled through and dead in a ditch. Otto delivered the money to the captain, went back to Miami, got his payment from Herra and, thinking Herra had assigned Cortez to kill him, told Herra to pick up a gun and defend himself . . . told Herra he was going to shoot him for betraying him. Herra managed to push a secret alarm button. Otto mowed down the pair of bodyguards who rushed to Herra's assistance. Otto forced Herra to hold a gun, let Herra raise it and take aim before blowing him away. By the time Otto had finished phoning the story to various disc jockeys he was friendly with across the country, a different account was heard, one in which Otto led a raid on an offshore-island bank controlled by Fidel Castro and stole money to help arm pro-United States guerillas within Cuba . . . and how in the transfer of this money to a guerilla ship captain in Jacksonville, Herra and his Castroite gunmen had tried to interfere.

Pinkny, for six months, eluded one of the largest manhunts ever mounted along the eastern seaboard. One in which the FBI participated for the first time, though only nominally, since the prime jurisdiction went to the narcotics division of the Treasury Department and fugitive charges were for homicide, a crime the Bureau was not authorized to investigate except in rare and specific instances. When Pinkny was finally apprehended it was in Pennsylvania, where a prior homicide warrant for him was outstanding. He was duly convicted and sentenced to die and sent to death row at the State Correctional Institution at Graterford, where he was visited by a television crew from "60 Minutes." En route to seeing himself on a guardroom television set some weeks later, Otto effected a spectacular escape, and a total disappearance.

Otto Pinkny had been, until the Mormon State robbery, the second most publicized badman in the country. The first had been Willie Sutton. Pinkny, among his peer group, was paid the rare and awesome respect of never having been dubbed with a nickname. Not Machine Gun Pinkny. Not Killer Pinkny. Just Otto Pinkny. Never Otto alone. Never Pinkny alone. Always Otto Pinkny.

Despite his notoriety Otto Pinkny seemed not to have a private

330

past. The FBI, which had entered the fugitive search for him after the Graterford prison break, found that before his Birmingham gunfight with the black gangsters no recorded data whatsoever existed on Pinkny. The underworld knew little or nothing of his pre-criminal life. The press, which did so much to popularize him, knew even less.

. . . Billy Yates, watching from the rear of the terminal platform as Otto Pinkny stood in the narrow doorway of the railroad car with one hand cuffed to a U.S. marshal and the other hand doffing his tan straw hat at the jam of media people waiting before him, wondered what the hell the flashy killer was really doing in Prairie Port. Yates didn't for a moment believe Pinkny had any connection with Mormon State. What bothered him most as Otto threw a kiss and raised his fingers in a V for Victory and started down through the throng was why his déjà vu had returned and was so strong . . . why he sensed that somehow long ago he had witnessed damn near everything that was now going on . . .

"Your name?" Strom asked.

"I don't got one," Otto Pinkny answered.

"Everyone has a name."

"Call me Everyone. I'm a friend of Otto Pinkny. That oughta be swell enough. I'm a friend of all the gents. And if I was you, I wouldn't believe nothing the law over by South Carolina said. Otto Pinkny's been thinking and he told me to tell you what he told them weren't the whole-cloth truth. Want I should tell you what Otto Pinkny told me?"

"Later," Strom said. "When were you born?"

"I can't think back that far."

"You can't tell us how old you are?"

"I don't got no age. I don't got no name, 'cepting Everyone."

"How old is Otto Pinkny?"

"Thirty-one."

"When was Otto Pinkny born? What date?"

"Like I told, even him can't think back that far."

"What was his place of birth?"

331

"I don't know. He don't know."

"He just grew up like corn?"

"Yeah, like Topsy." Otto Pinkny bared *that* smile. For the first time since arriving at the eleventh-floor residency, bared it.

"What is Otto Pinkny's current address?"

"Here."

"Before here, before being arrested, what was his home address?"

"Everywhere and nowhere like me."

"Does Otto Pinkny have a social security number?"

"Lots of 'em."

"Does he have a legitimate social security number?"

"You gotta be kidding."

"What's Otto Pinkny's mother's name?"

"He never said."

"Is his mother alive?"

Otto Pinkny shook his head.

"What was his father's name?"

"Otto Pinkny never knew his father."

". . . I was asking for his father's name."

"He never mentions it."

"Does Otto Pinkny have any brothers?"

"He would have liked to, but he don't."

"Does he have any sisters?"

"Otto Pinkny's by himself in the world. No relative at all, nowhere."

"Is Otto Pinkny married or single?"

"Single."

"Has he ever been married?"

"Someday he will be."

"Where did Otto Pinkny go to school?"

"Otto Pinkny educated himself. Read books by himself."

"But did he ever attend school?"

"Once, until the fourth grade."

"Where was that?"

"He can't think back that far."

"Has Otto Pinkny served in the armed forces?"

"No one by the name of Otto Pinkny ever put on a uniform, but he loves his country just the same. He'd die for his country. No man is worth his salt who ain't ready at all times to risk his body, to risk his well-being, to risk his life in the great cause of his country."

"That sounds like a quote, that last part."

*That* smile shone and with it those perfect white teeth. "You're pretty sharp." The tense, taut body relaxed somewhat, shifted in its wooden chair. "Yeah, President Teddy Roosevelt said it."

"You read Teddy Roosevelt?"

"I don't read nothing."

". . . Does Otto Pinkny read Teddy Roosevelt?"

"No, he only reads Elbert Hubbard. You read Elbert Hubbard?"

"We have a man here in the office who does."

Lips parted and teeth showed. "Bet the poor chump was up all last night reading Elbert Hubbard."

It was Strom's turn to smile for the first time. "As a matter of fact he was up all night with Elbert Hubbard. He read it before, but I asked him to brush up."

Strom checked his notes. Otto Pinkny, seated directly across the conference table from him, glanced around, noticed what he hadn't bothered to look at earlier: Jez and Brew sitting against the rear wall. "Hi ya, blokes," he told them. "Morning, ma'am," he said to the stenographer in the corner.

"You were arrested when?" asked Strom.

"Ain't never been arrested."

"When was Otto Pinkny arrested?"

"Want every time?"

"The last time."

"Over by a crackerville called Twin Lakes, which is in South Carolina. Dumb dog luck is all it was. Otto Pinkny forgets to stop at a red light, and who's right there shading itself under a tree and stuffing its fat face with garlic and grits, a copper. Reeks to high heaven, the fat copper does, and lucky for him Otto Pinkny only shoots his own kind. If Otto Pinkny shot fat coppers, he wouldn't be where he is today, the fat copper or Otto Pinkny.

Nah, Otto Pinkny lets the copper take him to the place, and someone at the place does the burn on Otto Pinkny, only he can't be sure. Otto Pinkny's got these fingerprints that don't print too good on account of they got fried off way back and don't hold the ink like you need for printing. And that's how they catch on finally. On the busted prints that only smudge. All them coppers is heroes now, and the fat copper's the pride of the litter. Like the man said, the whetstone may be dull but it sharpens the shiv."

"This arrest for running the red light occurred on what date?" Strom asked.

"Six days ago, whenever that was."

"Do you know the exact date?"

"Nah. A Saturday, maybe."

"Let's go back to Otto Pinkny's fingerprints. You said his fingers had been fried off? Fried so badly they didn't respond to printing?"

"All that garbage about prints not burning off is crap. Otto got his burned off."

"Intentionally?"

"Accidental."

"What kind of accident?"

"Something exploded."

"And burned the skin on his fingers off?"

"Yeah."

"What exploded?"

"Who knows?"

"Something flammable?"

"If you get burned, it's gotta be flammable."

"It could have been a nonflammable explosion. It could have been a heat explosion. A bomb? Natural gas?"

"Nah, it was flammable."

"When was the explosion?"

"Way back."

"Way back when?

"He don't remember."

"Where did it explode?"

"He never said."

"His burned-off fingerprints, do they look anything like the scars on your fingers?"

Otto Pinkny glanced down at the back of his hands. "Yeah, they do."

"So that's one thing you and Otto have in common, those burned fingers?"

"We got a lotta things in common. Mister, why you working so hard? Why you boning me while you do? I come to cooperate, didn't I? I volunteered. All you gotta do is ask and I'll answer. Anything you wanna know, I'll answer."

"Let's get back to your traffic arrest at Twin Lakes. You said it occurred eight or ten days ago."

"It ain't me what got arrested."

"Otto's arrest at Twin Lakes. Eight to ten days ago, was it?"

". . . Six days ago."

"And Otto was taken to the jail house and booked and printed, but his fingers wouldn't print and that's how they identified him?"

". . . That's right."

"How long after he was printed, or misprinted, was he identified?"

"Two days."

"He was in that jail house two days before positive identification was made?"

"Yeah."

"During those two days did he contact anyone?"

"Just sat and waited."

"For what?"

"What d'ya think, to be let out."

"You mean to be let out without being identified?"

"Yeah."

"After he's identified, then what?"

"He's gotta wait for the celebrating to end. When them coppers find out who they scooped up by mistake, they have themselves a Mardi Gras right in their station house. They're running and hugging and slapping each other on the back and kissing

335

each other on the lips and swilling beer and eating pies and cakes and chips. Them coppers is so thrilled by themselves they give Otto Pinkny some of the beer and pies, and Otto tells them when they're done good-timing, he'd appreciate making the one phone call the Constitution says he got coming to himself. The coppers give him the phone, and he calls up the FBI and says if they wanna celebrate Christmas early, they best grab some stockings and earmuffs and get right on over to see him 'cause he's gonna give them the present of their lifetimes."

Otto was comfortable now and on a roll, had slouched down somewhat in his chair with the thumb of his right hand hitched into the vest fob . . . jiggled the upraised thumb of his other hand in front of him from time to time for emphasis. "The FBI gets there lickety split, and Otto Pinkny tells them he's got this reservation problem. All kindsa places want him to come stay with them, and they've put aside rooms for him, and he don't know which one to pick. The room is on death row, and that gives Otto Pinkny pause, seeing how he's already visited the accommodations in Pennsylvania and don't really care for the view. Pennsylvania's pretty good about not frying them people it sentences to death, but dead or alive Otto Pinkny can't look forward to spending time in Graterford penitentiary. Florida's got a first-class reservation for him, too, and he don't like that one no better 'cause Florida executes more cons than any state in the country, and even if they let him off with life plus ten they'd be putting him in a prison chock full of friends of Luis Herra and all them other Latino blokes. Florida or Pennsylvania, the chances are better than not Otto Pinkny won't be taking the pipe and will become their most famous roomer. What holds for Pennsylvania holds for Florida. Otto Pinkny don't like the view from either place. State places is always run down and third class. Otto Pinkny tells the FBI he won't go third class nowhere and that a long time back he planned ahead and arranged for a first-class reservation. Why do state time when you can have a federal holiday at Lewisberg, Pennsylvania, he tells them. And then he tells them the name he made the reservation under . . . Mormon State National Bank.

"This fed who was talking to Otto Pinkny was named something or other, and his jaw fell open so far when Otto said that, it bounced on the floor and hit him back in the face. 'You telling me you got in on Mormon State just to beat state time?' the fed says when he gets his jaw put back on.

" 'The thirty-one million's got a lot to do with it,' Otto Pinkny says. And Otto Pinkny tells him he don't go *in* on nothing nowhere. Don't take orders from no man living. When Otto Pinkny does something, he's the boss. Otto Pinkny tells the fed if he wants to find out all about Mormon State, he better start asking questions before his mind gets changed. The fed goes running out of there and makes a telephone call, and brand-new feds come down and Otto Pinkny tells them all about Mormon State, and the next thing he knows, you come and talk with him and bring him here."

Strom indicated a thick folder of transcripts. "And that is the statement you made to the FBI agents in Twin Lakes?"

"*I* didn't make no statements."

"Is this the statement Otto Pinkny made in Twin Lakes?" Strom's hand was on the transcripts.

"You read it, you tell me."

"Are these the questions and his answers?"

"Yeah, it looks like what got typed up."

An upraised transcript was flapped by Strom. "I've read what this says most carefully. It was made to two FBI agents from Washington who are not as familiar with the facts as the people here. You are to be reinterviewed by six of our agents who know the most about Mormon State. If you are cooperative, and convincing, you may very well get that room with a view you prize so much. The reinterviewers will cover three specific aspects. First, the planning of the crime. Second, perpetration. Third, the getaway and aftermath. We will take a brief break and then begin."

"There are two questions Otto Pinkny won't answer," Otto Pinkny said. "He ain't saying who the other people in the score were, and he ain't saying where the thirty-one mil is. If everything goes okay and Otto gets sent to Lewisberg or someplace as

337

good, then he'll tell you. But you don't get nothing on the come. He told 'em in Twin Lakes, they don't get them two questions on the come"

"Then he may not get to Lewisberg."

"Wanna bet?"

# Nineteen

"What was your earliest knowledge of Mormon State National Bank?" Cub did the questioning. Brewmeister sat off to the side. Strom, Jez, de Camp and Yates were in the next room listening on a loudspeaker. With them were other agents assigned to check out leads as they were mentioned.

"Otto Pinkny told me," Otto Pinkny said.

"When?"

"Beginning of summer, June."

"June of this year, 1971?"

"Yeah, June."

"What exactly did Otto Pinkny say in telling you?"

"That some people was building this bank right over a cave and didn't know the cave was underneath."

"How did Otto Pinkny know the cave was underneath?"

"Eddie Argulla told him."

"Would you explain who Eddie Argulla is?"

"A bloke what helped Otto Pinkny out of his trouble in Florida with the dope people."

"Is this the same Eddie Argulla who worked for Luis Herra?"

"Yeah."

"In what way did Eddie Argulla help Otto Pinkny in Florida?"

"Luis Herra and some of his people got killed, and that's not a healthy situation for Otto Pinkny on account he's accused of doing it, and all of Luis Herra's friends is Latino and loyal and they want Otto Pinkny's ass. All of Florida was after Otto Pinkny, and only Eddie Argulla helped and smuggled him away from there and up north."

"Where is Eddie Argulla today?"

"Haven't seen him since the clout."

"What do you mean by clout?"

"Safecrack. Mormon State."

"He participated in the robbery?"

"Oh, yeah."

"I thought you weren't going to tell us who was involved and who wasn't?"

"I said there were two questions I wasn't going to answer if you asked, and that was one of them. Only you didn't ask and I felt like telling. I didn't say nothing about not telling what I felt like telling without being asked."

"Could Eddie Argulla be the same person whose body was dug up at Myrtle Beach, South Carolina, last month?"

"Eddie's dead?"

"With thirty-seven bullet holes in him."

"Who'd wanna kill Eddie Argulla?"

"Where was Otto Pinkny staying when he was in South Carolina?"

"Lotsa places."

"Name some."

"You fishing for if he ever stayed at Myrtle Beach?"

"Did he?"

"He stayed at Myrtle Beach a few nights, sure. But he never knew poor Eddie was there."

"In June of this year it was Eddie Argulla who told Otto Pinkny that Mormon State National Bank was being built over a cave, is that right?"

"Yeah."

"How did Eddie Argulla know this?"

"Cowboy Carlson told him."

"Who is Cowboy Carlson?"

"A bloke who done time with Eddie Argulla in Illinois. Cowboy Carlson comes from Prairie Port, and he tells Eddie about the bank being built."

"Was there any particular reason Cowboy Carlson would tell Eddie Argulla about Mormon State?"

"There was reasons for him telling about caves. Eddie Argulla and Otto Pinkny was doing business together and needed places on the Mississippi River to store merchandise. That's how they come to speak with Cowboy Carlson, and Cowboy told them Prairie Port was famous for the caves the bootleggers used to use there way back. Eddie Argulla asked Cowboy Carlson to show him around some of those caves, and Cowboy Carlson does, and then they come out in one cave and Cowboy Carlson pointed and laughed and said some dumb clucks was building a bank right above them and wouldn't it be funny if Eddie Argulla and Otto Pinkny was storing stuff down below which was more valuable than the money that was up above."

Cub asked, "What did Argulla and Pinkny plan to store in there?"

"Anything they could steal."

"Otto Pinkny doesn't have the reputation of a thief."

"Eddie Argulla does, and you don't know half there is to know about Otto Pinkny. Otto Pinkny is the greatest safecracker ever born, only he's so smart you never knew he was on the clout."

"You don't need something the size of a cave for the goods you take from a vault."

"They was planning some truck and barge work."

"Hijacking?"

"You wanna call it that, yeah."

"But now Argulla sees a cave over which a bank is being built?"

"Yeah."

"And after that?"

"He tells Otto Pinkny, and they talk it over and decide to take the bank."

"This was in June?"

"Yeah, first week in June."

"What part is Cowboy Carlson to play in this?"

"No part except to keep quiet and do like he's told. What Otto Pinkny wants is to wait for the bank to have their grand opening party and when they open the vault, they'll find everything is gone except a birthday cake Otto Pinkny left for them. A cake saying Otto Pinkny Was Here!"

"Did Otto Pinkny want to do this before or after he came to Prairie Port?"

341

"Who said he came to Prairie Port?"

"He didn't come?"

*That* smile showed and an eye winked. "Sure, he come. At the end of June, first. He sees the setup and decides they go after the bank."

"Then what?"

"He brings in the man with the hand."

"Who's that?"

"J. L. Squires. They call him the man with the hand on account he's so good with safes and vaults."

"Wasn't Squires in South America?"

"Yeah, Mexico. Only he come to Prairie Port. In July, and he and Otto Pinkny map it all out."

"How?"

"Busting the bank is no problem. They know they can cut right through the roof of the cave and get into the vault. They know one way or another they can kill the alarms. The trouble is scramming after the clout. The only way out is through these tunnels. There are tunnels all through the cliffs, and that's how they'll have to go out. It's almost a seven-mile walk through the tunnels to the first exit that's big enough to bring money out through. These tunnels was once used to carry water, and Otto Pinkny wondered if that was possible to do again, and he walks up a tunnel in the north with Squires and they come out in an underground center and right up on the wall of the control room are all the instructions on how to flood the tunnels. Squires reads them and says yeah, that's how it can be done. And they did it."

"Besides Cowboy Carlson, what local Prairie Port men did they use?"

"No one." Otto Pinkny's wagging thumb signaled a second thought. "Nah, there was one person they went to. To build fuses. Cowboy knew some kid who was good at building things. And J. L. Squires had him make five fuses. The machinery to flood the tunnels and generate electricity was old-fashioned. Special fuses had to be built to make everything run. Cowboy found the local kid to do it."

342

"Do you know the kid's name?"

"Sam something."

"Was Sam ever down in the control room?"

". . . How d'ya know that?"

"He was?"

"Once. For about ten minutes. The problem with J. L. Squires was he was a tequila drunk. One of the fuses got built wrong, and Squires goes wild and dragged this kid back down to the control room and pointed at what had to be done and shook the kid back and forth and threatened to kill him if he didn't get it right . . . threatened to make the kid go along with them on the job and become a hunted fugitive. Otto Pinkny damn near had J. L. Squires's hide for doing that, but it worked. J. L. Squires scared the kid into building the fuse right and into having a nervous breakdown too. Cowboy Carlson told us later the kid killed himself that night."

"Did Cowboy Carlson participate in the actual robbery?"

"He was supposed to be in on the first one but not the second one."

"What do you mean by first one and second one?"

"Otto Pinkny planned to take the bank the first day it opened, which would have been Tuesday, August twenty-fourth, because that's when he thought an opening party would be and he wanted to leave the birthday cake inside the vault for them. When he found out the bank wasn't going to have its grand opening party until a month later in September, he decided to wait and take the vault the day before the party. He still wanted to put that cake in the vault for them to find instead of the money he stole. That became the first robbery, and Cowboy was supposed to be in on it, only it created all kinds of problems because some of the people didn't want to wait around a whole month and most of the gear was ready."

Cub raised a hand. "Let's slow down and make this clear. Was the original date for the robbery Tuesday, August twenty-fourth, which was the first day the bank would be open and operating . . . or the night before, Monday, August twenty-third?"

"The night before," Otto Pinkny specified. "They was to start the clout the night before so nothing would be inside in the morning except the cake."

"And preparations to go on that date were under way," Cub continued. "Equipment was being gathered, plans being—"

"Everything was done and ready. Everything was set to go, which was what caused the hard feelings."

"Ready and set to go when?"

"Ten days before the clout."

"Which clout? The one planned for the opening of the bank, or the clout that actually occurred on Friday, August twentieth?"

"The one planned for the opening."

"But that's not the one you're calling the second robbery? The one Cowboy Carlson was not supposed to be part of?"

Otto Pinkny lowered a cocked thumb at Cub. "Let me explain it to you. We got four dates to remember. The first one is August twenty-fourth, a Tuesday, when the bank is gonna open and start doing business. Otto Pinkny plans to clout the bank the night before that, Monday. Them's the first two dates, Monday and Tuesday. Go in on Monday night so there's nothing left inside on Tuesday. Only Otto Pinkny then wants to hold off a month until the grand opening party in September. That's the third date, September. Then something comes up and makes them go on Friday, August twentieth. That's the fourth date. Cowboy Carlson wasn't no part of what happened on August twentieth. Now you got it."

". . . What made you decide to perpetrate on the day you did, Friday, August twentieth?" Cub asked.

"I didn't decide nothing."

". . . What made Otto Pinkny decide to perpetrate on that Friday?"

"Thirty-one million dollars!"

"He knew it would be in the bank over that weekend?"

"He stole it, didn't he?"

"Was that luck or did he know?"

"He was hooked into all the telephones in the bank, hooked

344

into all the alarm systems and television cameras too. He knew everything that was going on. Saw everything and heard everything. He heard the telephone call between the federal reserve people in New Orleans and the president of the bank when they set the time for the load to reach Prairie Port. That was part of the argument between J. L. Squires and the Latinos over clouting in September. J. L. Squires wanted to get it over with on the first night like was planned. That Monday night before the bank officially opened. The Latinos was unhappy about this 'cause of all the work they had done and how little they was gonna make off it."

"What Latinos?" Cub interjected.

"The ones Otto Pinkny and Eddie Argulla brought up from Miami and Colombia. They was good at working in mines and with water. Not bad at thieving, either."

"How many Latinos were there?"

"Six."

"What were their names?"

"I couldn't tell you if I was a mind to. They all got them chop suey names Latinos got. Lotsa Juans and Jesuses, but hard workers."

"And they got into a disagreement with J. L. Squires?" asked Cub.

"Wouldn't you? Look at it from where they sit. The Latinos was getting a cut of the action, and they thought J. L. Squires and Otto Pinkny was gonna wait until there's lotsa money in the vault before doing the clout. When they find out the clout's a go for opening day, they know there ain't gonna be that much money to grab. Being a bank is like being pregnant, you get fat slow. They started feeling better when Otto Pinkny finds out the bank's grand opening party ain't for a month later and he wants to wait till then. J. L. Squires is bellyaching that he ain't gonna wait around that long, and he starts in arguing for the first date or at least an early date. The Latinos wanna go as late as possible, and a tug of war happens. J. L. Squires is the only one who got paid cash in advance plus being given the second biggest per-

345

centage of the take, which is probably why he says the hell with it and walks out. Squires don't like nothing about Prairie Port and living underground and he takes a walk back to Mexico."

"When was this?"

"Three days before the real clout."

"Three days before Friday, August twentieth?"

Pinkny thought for a moment. "Yeah."

"Who is the gang made up of at this time?"

"Otto Pinkny, Eddie Argulla and the six Latinos."

"Not Cowboy Carlson?"

"I already told you nah!"

"What about Sam, the boy who made the fuses?"

"He's too scared to be any good even if they wanted to use him. One of the last things J. L. Squires done was eat that kid out for not making the fuses right."

"I thought you said all the preparations were done and ready on August fourteenth, which would have been before Squires chewed out Sam for making a defective fuse?"

"They were, and that was part of the problem. They were sitting around with nothing to do, them people. So they started redoing things and getting in extra supplies they didn't need and making spare parts like that fuse. They already had two fuses in the box and two spares, and they ordered another one and the kid couldn't get it right. J. L. Squires was chewing the kid out over a fuse they didn't need."

"When did you say Sam, the kid, committed suicide?"

"The day Squires left."

"August seventeenth . . . three days before the actual robbery on August twentieth?"

"Yeah, if you say so."

"Back in June, J. L. Squires and Otto Pinkny decided to go ahead with the robbery and then what?"

"They started deciding on people and making plans. The beginning of July they start going out and getting the equipment and bringing it down into the cave."

"What equipment?"

"All the equipment to do the clout with."

346

"Can you say what the equipment was?" Cub asked.

"Want me to tell you where it comes from too?"

"If you can."

That smile showed. "What's important working in a dark cave like under the bank is for there to be electric light to see by, and Otto Pinkny puts Eddie Argulla in charge of getting that and the other gear. Otto Pinkny's running an army down there, and all the men are his soldiers and have to obey that way or the enemy could win and you'd have to hoist your white surrender flag. The unknowing is your enemy, and the ladder of life is full of splinters, which means you don't wanna go sliding down that ladder if you can help. Otto Pinkny knows the only way up the ladder is by being organized and original, and like the man said, initiative is originality in motion, that's why Otto Pinkny's gotta run everything like an army so his people will have motion and be original and stay organized, if you get my drift."

". . . What about the electric lights?" asked Cub.

"That's why Eddie Argulla got sent to get them lights 'cause Eddie Argulla was the lieutenant in charge of that proposition from the beginning, and Eddie even hired a couple of the Latinos to be with him on this. There were six of them Latinos got hired and brung to Prairie Port, and two of them was miners who was good at working in tunnels and under the ground, and two more was sailors who could help with the boats when it got time to leave, and the last two was the sneak thieves who was always intended to help Eddie Argulla steal what goods they needed when the time come. The time had come and they needed lights, and Eddie Argulla and the Latinos who was sneak thieves take a truck and drive to Saint Louis and go to the S. and J. factory there and break in at night and take all the light bulbs and wire they need, and nobody knows 'cause S. and J. is this big manufacturer of lamps and fixtures so they ain't gonna miss the stuff."

Cub asked, "Who told them S. and J. had the equipment?"

"Any street thief knows things like that, and in this case people in Saint Louis must have told Cowboy Carlson."

"Cowboy Carlson told you about S. and J.?"

"Told Otto Pinkny and Otto Pinkny told me."

347

"Did Cowboy go along to Saint Louis?"

"Cowboy didn't go nowhere and didn't know nothing 'cause all we let him do was tell what three places had what, but only in the Midwest, and he never knew if we went to any or all of them three places he named."

"Then Cowboy had nothing at all to do with obtaining equipment other than suggesting sources of supply?"

"Cowboy got the sandbags," amended Otto Pinkny. "He was working on some barge that did construction hauling, and they bought three hundred sandbags from him for fifteen cents each, undelivered. The Latinos had to carry them from a truck down the bluff and into the hole."

"What hole?"

"The hole that was cut in the cave to bring supplies in through."

"There was a hole cut in the cave for supplies?" Cub said. "A hole from the cave under the bank leading to the outside?"

"You said that, not me. There wasn't no hole in the cave under the bank 'cause none ever got cut there. The hole got cut in a small cave to the north. There's two more caves going north from the one under the bank, and the farthest of them two was cut through. Go look and you'll see."

"After the electric wire and light bulbs were stolen from S. and J. in Saint Louis, what other equipment was gotten?" asked Cub.

"Dontcha wanna know when the bulbs got sneaked?"

"When?"

"The night of August fourth."

"What happened after that, equipmentwise?"

"Eddie Argulla and the two Latinos drove to the DPDS warehouse in Charleston, South Carolina."

"What is DPDS?"

"Navy surplus. They got this big warehouse full of all kinds of stuff. That's where Eddie Argulla and the Latinos got the rubber boats and the wet suits the people wore during the clout and the oars and the static lines and the power lights and waterproof bags and all kinds of other stuff."

348

"Did Cowboy Carlson tell them about this warehouse in South Carolina?"

"Cowboy Carlson couldn't find his way across the river without getting lost. The Latinos knew about the naval surplus at Charleston 'cause they used to steal from the naval surplus in Jacksonville and Orlando. In Florida. Why do you think Eddie Argulla hired them particular two Latinos? 'Cause they knew where certain merchandise was and they went to get it with Eddie."

"Had the Latinos stolen from Charleston before?"

"No."

"Then why didn't they go to Jacksonville or Orlando?"

"Because it was farther away and because people there coulda recognized them and 'cause if you've stepped foot in one of them big surplus warehouses, you know there ain't no trick at all to taking what you want from all the mess without nobody knowing."

"Let's get to the other items stolen."

"In Charleston or later?"

"Both."

. . . Otto Pinkny, over the next four hours, listed nearly every piece of equipment used in the actual perpetration of the robbery, and in most instances specified where it was gotten, how it was gotten and when. During his recitation, FBI men near and far rushed to cited locations. The mud coating on the walls of the second cave north of the bank was cracked away by a team of Bureau agents, who discovered the passageway Otto Pinkny had described . . . a narrow tunnel filled with hardened mud and which, once the mud was chopped through, would lead up into a field near a service road on an isolated section of riverfront palisade. Agents in St. Louis were taken through the huge S. & J. warehouse and told by company executives that yes, wire and light bulbs were found to be missing at about the time Otto Pinkny had said they were stolen, but that it was such an inconsequentially trivial shortage the company wrote it off as breakage or misplacement and never suspected theft.

Bureaumen walking into the Defense Property Disposal Service warehouse in Charleston, South Carolina, were benumbed by the array of surplus naval materiél confronting them. Literally mountains of equipment including most every item on Otto Pinkny's lists except for rubber boats, which DPDS officials assured them there were plenty of on a given day. The officials matter-of-factly let it be known there was no humanly possible way to keep track of the equipment that came in and out its warehouse other than in job-lot form . . . admitted they would have no way of knowing, and probably wouldn't have noticed, if four rubber boats and a few wet suits were missing.

Everywhere else an FBI man checked that day, he found what Otto Pinkny said was substantially so, that items were at a given location when he said. The patterns pretty much followed those established in St. Louis and Charleston. Often the equipment he cited was discovered to have been missing but never reported, as in the case of the S. & J. factory. In other instances no one at the premises was aware merchandise was gone, as with the DPDS warehouse. Some proprietors, visited by the FBI in the past regarding the Bureau's assumptions about what equipment may have been used in the perpetration, had overlooked telling inquiring special agents what had disappeared. A few proprietors had let their losses be known to Bureaumen who could never link the missing items to Mormon State.

One thing was certain as the afternoon progressed: Otto Pinkny's recitation of what material was used closely approximated the FBI's previous projections. So did Pinkny's revelations that almost every item had been stolen. Most resident Prairie Port agents, listening in on the interview from the adjoining room, were convinced that Otto was their man. Not so Brewmeister, who with Cub was now doing the questioning.

"There are no specifics!" Brew spoke sharply to Pinkny. The session was in its fifth hour. Dozens upon dozens of follow-up reports had already been phoned in on Otto's previous revelations. More were being received. "What you are giving us is too general. We need exact corroboration. There's a hundred ways you could have learned what you told us—"

"I learned only one way, Otto Pinkny told me."

"Otto Pinkny is too vague. Because equipment is missing from a given location doesn't mean Otto Pinkny or his people took it or that it was ever used at Mormon State. I want to hear about something that directly ties into Mormon State. Something stolen or bought that unmistakably links Otto Pinkny to the robbery."

"You mean something only he would know?"

"And something we can verify."

Concentration was followed by a thumb wag. "How's about the soup and sticks?"

"What do you mean?"

"Nitroglycerin and dynamite."

"What about them?"

"They was got at the Boyton Arsenal in Clarksville. There's these concrete bunkers way out in the back of the arsenal that's all fenced off. Don't seems anyone's used them very much. About the start of August, the first couple of days in August, Otto Pinkny and the Latinos slipped the lock in one of the bunkers and walked out with a pint of nitroglycerin and twenty-one cases of dynamite."

"Twenty-one cases of dynamite?" Cub could not help from calling out. Cub, like the other resident agents in Prairie Port, knew that the FBI's laboratory analysis of the crime scene had shown that nitroglycerin was the *only* explosive used in the cave. A very special brand of nitroglycerin. "You planned to use twenty-one cases of dynamite?"

"I didn't plan nothing. Otto Pinkny did, and he only planned to use nitroglycerin."

"Then why take the dynamite?" pressed Cub.

"It was there and free, wasn't it?"

"You stole all of this the first few days of August?" Brew said.

"Otto Pinkny stole it, and it was at night. August second at night."

"Then what?"

"He drove home real slow. Nitroglycerin is spooking stuff."

"He drove home to where?" Brew asked. "Where was home?"

"Prairie Port and the cave. They was all living in the cave. They brought it down into the cave."

351

Cub was on his feet and coming forward to take over the interrogation again. Having received a special briefing from the FBI lab, he was one of the few Bureaumen to know the exact nature of the explosive used in the ceiling of the cave and the bottom of the vault . . . an industrial-type nitroglycerin known as NKX-3 and manufactured exclusively by Yellow Moon Industries of Wilmington, Delaware. Due to a faulty glycerin additive, which rendered some batches of the explosive highly unstable and which left a grainy ash after detonation, all production of NKX-3 had ceased in early 1960. FBI efforts to locate existing stores of the chemical eleven years later, after Mormon State, had been unsuccessful, since NKX-3 had originally been sold in bulk and under no trade name. The most distinguishing feature was a half-liter metal canister that Yellow Moon Industries had used for shipment of the dangerous liquid. According to the FBI lab no more than two or three ounces of the NKX-3 had been used in the Mormon State vault theft . . . "Twenty-one cases of dynamite and a pint of nitroglycerin all went into the cave?"

"A little more than a pint," Otto Pinkny said.

Cub sat beside Brew. "What was used in the actual perpetration?"

"I told you, nitroglycerin."

"How much was used?"

"Maybe an ounce or two."

"Was there anything special about that nitroglycerin?"

"You mean like it coming packed in a silver drum?"

"Silver drum?"

"Small kinda silver can. Like you drink whiskey from in Prohibition."

"That how it came?"

"Yeah."

"Anything else about it?"

"It was called NKX-3."

"How do you know?"

"It was stenciled right on the silver can. Right on the packing case too."

"What happened to the nitroglycerin that wasn't used?"

Pinkny shrugged. "Probably got washed away with the dyna-mite and everything else. A box or two of dynamite floated out into the river with the men later. There was so much noise that maybe something exploded sooner without nobody hearing. Maybe the nitroglycerin exploded. Maybe it was washed out into the river too."

Bureaumen and munition experts moved in on the concrete bunkers a mile behind the main building at Kentucky's remote Boyton Arsenal. The area was restricted and ringed by electrified barbed wire which no longer carried a current. Much of what had been stored here dated back to the Korean War. The last re-corded inspection of the compound was a year and three months prior to the date Otto Pinkny claimed to have broken in and stolen munitions.

The first two bunkers, according to inventory sheets posted inside of each, had nothing missing. The third bunker did . . . twenty-one boxes of extremely unstable dynamite. Farther back in the same structure, a small wooden crate that had not been listed on the inventory lay open. Inside were five silver-blue metal canisters clearly marked NKX-3. Each container was moored snugly into a round hole in the bottom of the crate. A sixth hole was empty. Stenciling on the discarded crate lid stated that six half-liter canisters were contained within.

. . . Even Brewmeister could not fault the Coast Guard and River Patrol being immediately notified. Navigation alerts were out along the Mississippi to warn that highly explosive substances had fallen off an industrial barge and might be either floating or mudded down in the river below Prairie Port. Despite Corticun's success at getting the U.S. Army Corps of Engineers to convince a barge company to take responsibility, the media suspected the alert had to do with Mormon State, and said so.

Billy Yates got into bed beside Tina Beth and turned her to him and kissed her.

She pushed him away.

"Whatcha doing that for?" he asked.

"Your heart's not in it."

"How can you tell? I just started."

"You don't have to hear rattles to know a snake bit."

"What's that supposed to mean?"

"You're so smart, figure it out." She squinched farther away.

Billy searched for clues. "Was my heart in it last night?"

"Passably."

"The night before?"

"That was good."

"The night before that?"

"That was like the heavens that night." The girlish giggle was heard.

"But not tonight?"

"You heard me."

". . . Can I try again?"

"Won't be no help."

"Come on, let me try."

There was no answer.

He moved to her, held her, put his lips to hers.

She sat up. "Billy Yates, stop trying to change what is. I knew before you came home tonight it was gonna be no good. It's ten-thirty at night, and I knew from the first step you took in the doorway it was no good."

"I was out till eleven last night and later the nights before."

"It wasn't the hour, Billy Yates, it's you. Something's gone wrong with you."

"I'm the same as always."

"You're not and you know it, so hush!"

"How'm I different?"

"You swore you'd never lie to me again ever."

"You think I'm lying to you?"

"You tell me."

"Tina Beth, I haven't said anything to lie about."

"Where were you tonight?"

"The same place I was last night, the library."

"How come you didn't tell me?"

"There's nothing to tell."

"Billy, I know when you go down into tunnels or chase people around zoos in Baton Rouge. There's no way of shushing you up 'bout that and most everything else. But you haven't mentioned one word 'bout libraries. Why you suddenly so secretive 'bout libraries? For two days you been secretive and distant."

He lay back in the dark, after several moments put his hand over his eyes. "I *know* I've come across Mormon State before. The robbery and manhunt are familiar to me. I feel like I heard of it a long time ago, like it happened before, Tina Beth . . . anyway, part if not all of this robbery and manhunt happened before . . . I've been at the library trying to find out when and where it happened . . . which crime it was. I've come across some that are similar, some that have aspects of Mormon State, but I can't find *the one*. There's somebody who maybe could help me with this, but I don't want to go to him. At least not until I have more of it in place. Then again, maybe I'm flat out looney-toon. God only knows they warned us looney-toon was the occupational disease at Prairie Port."

She lay down beside him, looking up in the darkness. "Thank you, Billy Bee."

"For what?"

"Not cutting me out. Never cut me out of nothing in your life, Billy. No matter how small or big. I'll die if I'm not part of everything you are."

"I won't ever."

"Cross your—"

"I already did."

". . . Make love to me, Billy Bee."

And he did, like the heavens.

# Twenty

Otto Pinkny led Strom and Cub and Jez and Brewmeister and Yates and Madden de Camp and several more resident agents of the Prairie Port office on a tour which retraced various phases involved in the robbery . . . began at the small tunnel opening in the field off the service road explaining that this was where the deflated rubber boats and sections of scaffolding and explosives and all the other supplies were unloaded late at night . . . descended the narrow passageway and followed it down into a small cave and on through a slightly larger cave and along a section of irrigation tunnel and up into the very large cave directly under Mormon State National Bank, saying this was the route used for bringing in much of the equipment . . . took the party up the irrigation tunnel to the control center and power plant in the base of Warbonnet Ridge, where he explained every detail of how the generators were reactivated and electricity brought in from an outside supply line and fuses made and an automatic timing device constructed for opening the water gates which was first connected and later disconnected.

Otto Pinkny, in describing what had occurred in the control booth and throughout the irrigation system, not only confirmed everything the group of scientists had told Jez and Yates months earlier, he added new information.

"Otto Pinkny had to act awful fast when they found out thirty-one million dollars was heading this way." Pinkny was at the water gate beyond the control booth inside Warbonnet Ridge. "J. L. Squires had run out on him a couple of days before, and J.L. still had an automatic control set for the gates in that tunnel down there." Pinkny turned and pointed into the large irrigation tunnel leading from the reservoir to the bank. "Them controls

356

was set for a Monday. Now they was going three whole days before that, on a Friday, and lucky for everybody Eddie Argulla and a Latino named Jesus knows about electricity enough to come and pull out them wires from the automatic control and stick them onto the reservoir directly. Eddie Argulla's gotta be back under the bank to help with the clout and so he leaves Jesus up here and strings a telephone line from Jesus down to the cave in case the walkie-talkie radios they were using don't work for the distance. Jesus don't understand the English so good and thinks somebody said there weren't no rubber boat for him to get away in, and what everybody finds out later he done was go and savage two big spools of nitroglycerin fusing and brings lotsa fusing back up here and uses it to help build himself a raft when all he had to do was ask and they woulda gone and got him a rubber boat. This means there ain't enough fusing in the cave when Otto Pinkny needs it later, and that's okay 'cause they do something else, and lucky for everybody Jesus knows enough to get the reservoir open at the right time, only he gets it open too wide and causes this flood which almost drowns everybody."

Standing five miles downtunnel on the concrete pier leading up into the cave directly under the bank, Otto Pinkny told his listeners, "A tidal wave like you never seen comes rushing at them. From the top of the tunnel to the bottom of the tunnel it's all water. A wall of solid water, and sticking out of it and singing his fool head off is Jesus."

Pinkny indicated the pier they were standing on and the water directly below. "All four rubber boats was in the water there. Two Latinos was in the first, and one of the two of 'em specializes in boats 'cause he was a sailor back home in Colombia. Otto Pinkny was in the second boat with the money. Eddie Argulla and another Latino is in the third boat, and they got lotsa money too because thirty-one million is bigger than you think and there wasn't room for all of it in Otto Pinkny's boat. The last has got two more Latinos, and one of them is good at boats too. Then it was over. The wave hit and took everybody on down the pipe and out into the river. There's a fast tide in the middle, and they

357

got on that and sailed on down for a while before getting off and 'cause it was dark nobody saw nothing of them."

Brewmeister, who had done most of the questioning about the tunnels, asked, "They all made it onto the Mississippi? The five Colombians and Jesus? Eddie Argulla? Otto Pinkny?"

"They made it. There was some trouble when the raft Jesus was on cut into one of the rubber boats when they first got dumped into the river and that boat sank and the two Latinos on it got saved and no money was lost 'cause it was either the first boat or last what sank and you really couldn't tell which it was later, the first or last what sank, 'cause both of 'em had two Latinos in them apiece and all them Latinos look alike in the dark."

Brew asked, "What was the raft made of?"

"Made of?"

"What material? You told us Jesus used the fusing to help build the raft. Help build it out of what material? What did the fusing hold together?"

"Wood."

"Where did he find wood?"

"It was right there in the tunnel. There was this tunnel going up to the reservoir. Somebody musta tried boarding it shut with telephone poles, then gave up. There was this half a barricade of telephone poles there. Old dry poles. That's what Jesus used for his raft, them poles. He cut 'em up and tied 'em together with the fusing."

"Cut them up with what?"

"One of the electric saws. Them Latinos swiped four electric saws from four different hardware stores."

"You said no money was lost when the rubber boats went onto the river, is that right?"

"Yeah."

"When was the money divvied up?"

"A little while after."

"Where was it divided up?"

"Baton Rouge."

"How did you get from the river to Baton Rouge?"

"I didn't get off it nowhere 'cause I was never on it."

358

"Where did Pinkny and the others get off?"

"They got off just before Cape Girardeau."

"Then?"

"It was still dark out and just before the sun was coming up, and they had two of them campers parked there. Them house trucks you can live in and drive in, and they got in them and put the money in them and drove near Baton Rouge and parked in a motor park there and got sleep and then distributed the money, which took almost a day and a half 'cause there was so much of it. They already had cars parked at that motor court, and when the money was counted they each took their share and went their own way."

"Where was their own way?"

"You asking where each of them people went?"

"Yes."

"I only know where Otto Pinkny went."

"Where was that?"

"South Carolina, near Charleston."

"Did Otto know where the other men were supposed to go?"

"Nah."

"Did he have any idea where they could be reached at a later time?"

"That was it, it was over."

"He never heard about any of the others?"

"Somebody told him not so long ago that maybe Eddie Argulla got himself shot."

"Shot where?"

"South Carolina, he was told."

"The same South Carolina where Otto Pinkny happened to have gone?"

"Same one."

"How much money did Otto Pinkny receive?"

"I said I wasn't going to answer that."

"Thought you said you wouldn't say where the money was."

"I said I wasn't going to say nothing about the money at all, but since you're interested, just divide up the thirty-one among eight people."

"Otto Pinkny only got one share of the take?"

"No. It was divided into twelve shares, and he got four."

"His take was ten million dollars?"

"He earned it, didn't he?"

Cub cut in to say, "Is that all he got? Or did he grab himself a few extra shares when nobody was looking?"

"You calling Otto Pinkny a thief?"

"I'm suggesting that maybe Eddie Argulla came to South Carolina looking for something he thought was rightfully his, like a couple of million dollars of robbery loot."

"I'll tell you how dumb that is right now. Eddie Argulla and the Latinos knew Otto Pinkny didn't have no money in the United States. He let his money go down to Mexico with Jesus, so why would anyone come looking for him in South Carolina?"

Cub replied, "Okay, let's try it your way. Is the reason Otto Pinkny turned himself over to the FBI because Jesus and the other Latinos took the money and ran out on him and Eddie Argulla . . . that when Otto Pinkny found out, he blamed Argulla, who had gone to Carolina with him after the divvy . . . blamed him and killed him?"

"You one of them emotional disturbed people?"

"If anyone's disturbed, it's Otto Pinkny," Cub said. "Disturbed enough not only to kill Eddie Argulla but chop off his hands as a warning to future thieves. Did I mention, when we found poor Eddie his hands were missing?"

"It's like I told you, Otto Pinkny and the others went to Baton Rouge and stayed a day and a half. I'll give you the motor court they stayed in. People saw them. Go down and ask, you'll find out."

The fact that Mule, Rat and Wiggles had gone to New Orleans three weeks after the robbery wasn't lost on the Bureaumen any more than the fact that Sam Hammond's widow had claimed that city was to be the payoff point for the robbery.

"Could anyone else have known you were going to Baton Rouge to divide the money?" Cub asked.

"Yeah, J. L. Squires, and that nervoused some of the people but not Otto Pinkny, and like you heard, J. L. never did show up and try to take what wasn't his."

"What would have happened if he did show up?"

"He woulda gone home without a head on."

"And nobody else knew about Baton Rouge?"

"Nah."

"Not even Cowboy Carlson?"

"Cowboy Carlson was hanging around and asking questions when he shouldn't be and maybe Otto Pinkny did mention Baton Rouge, but it didn't matter. Otto Pinkny always mentioned a different date for going to Baton Rouge when Cowboy Carlson was around. A date two weeks later than they really went to Baton Rouge."

"What if I told you Cowboy Carlson was found with most of his head shot off not long after the robbery?"

*That* smile glistened. "Them's the risks."

The following morning and afternoon and early evening and morning after that, in the cave beneath the bank as well as in the eleventh-floor residency office, Otto Pinkny provided a detailed account of the perpetration, including information the FBI had never deduced or projected, such as the shortage of fusing caus-ing detonation to take place in the passageway to the south of the cave rather than in a command bunker to the north, or the nitroglycerin not detonating and the men going out into the cave and looking up at the unexploded charges in the vault bottom and someone getting mad and stamping his foot, which in turn set off the nitroglycerin and knocked all the men flat on their backs . . . or that even before this the locks uptunnel had been opened prematurely and the men had to scurry like hell to get all the money out of the vault and into the boats before the flood hit. Most every Bureauman listening believed what was said was so, had not a doubt Otto had participated as stated.

The events Pinkny had recited were, indeed, absolutely true and accurate, with one exception . . . he had replaced the real robbers with himself and his gang. Yates and Brewmeister stood nearly alone in believing this . . . were sure that the facts were real and Pinkny's alleged involvement fiction. Their frustration came in trying to prove this, or at least disprove or discredit Otto Pinkny.

Yates, in his final afternoon of cross-interrogating Pinkny on the robbery, blurted out, "I don't believe a word of this. Nothing. It's a great trick. Someone told you all about the robbery, and you're telling us. Telling us things that can't be corroborated. Cowboy Carlson, who you claim found the score, is dead. Eddie Argulla, who you say showed you the score and helped in the perpetration, is dead. The Latinos, if they ever existed, are gone to parts unknown. J. L. Squires, the legendary fugitive, is still an unlocated fugitive. There is no one to say, nothing to say, you were within a thousand miles the night of the robbery. It is all circumstantial. Everything is *circumstantial.*"

". . . You want me to prove Otto Pinkny was there, that's what you're saying."

"That's what I'm saying."

Otto Pinkny bit on his finger as he thought . . . finally raised a thumb. "The coppers could tell you."

"What coppers?"

"The ones getting their pee-pees licked."

"Pee-pees?"

"Dingles." Otto Pinkny pointed at his genitals.

"Cocks? They were getting their cocks sucked?"

Otto Pinkny stiffened, looked away, nodded.

"Where?"

"On the street in front of the bank."

"When?"

"In the middle of the robbery."

"How the hell could you know that if you were thirty feet below getting ready to blow the vault?"

"The television monitors in the command post showed it. One of the screens showed what was on the street outside. Two police cars pulled up just when the countdown to explode the vault was starting and everything in the cave had to stop. Coppers got out of each car, and one of them ain't a copper but a girl which could be seen when she lit her cigarette. One of the coppers dropped his pants, and the girl got down and licked his dingle."

"This happened during the robbery?" Yates said. "On August twentieth?"

The head nodded and the raised thumb wagged. "The picture on the monitor was so clear we could see the number on the police car . . . it was one hundred fifteen."

. . . No one noticed that Otto Pinkny, for the first time, had dealt with himself in the first person and included himself in on the robbery . . . had used the pronoun *we*.

Police Officer Herbert L. Minot marched down the carpeted second-floor corridor of the Prairie Port Police Department headquarters building and into the executive offices and presented himself to an impatient Lieutenant Ned Van Ornum. Van Ornum led the way up a short hall and through the double doors of the chief's office.

"Fellatio!" Frank Santi stood pointing a finger at Minot without bothering to introduce or identify Strom Sunstrom, Cub Hennessy and Assistant U.S. Attorney Jules Shapiro, who were seated to his right. "Fellatio!" he repeated. "Did you or did you not, on the late evening or early morning of August twenty of this year, allow fellatio to be performed on your person?"

". . . Sir?" was all Minot could answer.

"Were you or were you not on that night assigned to car one hundred fifteen along with Officer Karl Heath?"

"I was working with Karl back in August, okay, but I don't know what car we had."

"Did you or did you not, during the course of duty on August twenty, stop in front of the Mormon State bank and allow a female to perform fellatio on your person . . . as you stood up?"

"I'd never do a thing like that while I was on duty."

"I have no time to waste with you!" Frank Santi warned him. "Did what I say occur at the times specified?"

". . . I really don't remember, chief."

"Bring in Officer Karl Heath!" Santi called out.

Karl Heath entered through a side door, looked sheepishly at Minot.

"You told them?" Minot said.

Heath dropped his head.

"Aw, shit."

"I ask you one more time," Santi began, "did this event occur as described . . . when described?"

Herbert L. Minot said that it had, and thereby confirmed, in the presence of Strom Sunstrom and Cub Hennessy, that what Otto Pinkny had said was true.


Alice Maywell Sunstrom lay in bed waiting for her husband to come to sleep. When after a long while he hadn't, she tiptoed downstairs, found Strom fully dressed and standing rigid before his desk staring down at a spread of photographs and rubbing the back of his neck.

Alice moved up beside him, put a hand on his shoulder. "Problems?"

"Problems?" Strom pecked her on the cheek, moved across the room, took up the sherry bottle, poured a glass for each of them. "We have a man confessing to the Mormon State robbery. He's telling us things we never knew about the theft. We're corroborating lots of it too." He handed her a glass and they drank. "Earlier this evening he came up with something no one but a robber could know . . . he saw a cop doing something in front of the bank, and the cop verified it. It would seem our confessor was there and did the theft. And I should believe he was there and it happened. Everyone else does and I should too."

"Do Yates and Brewmeister believe it?"

"They never believe anything. It's me I'm talking about. I don't believe this man, this Otto Pinkny."

Strom walked back to the desk, placed a fist in the middle of the photographs of Mule, Bicki, Windy Walt, Ragotsy, Wiggles, Ferugli and Epstein. "These are the men who did it. What's grinding me is I can't prove it." He motioned to her to come forward. When she did, his arm reached around and pulled her

364

tight to him. "Maybe this case means too much to me. Maybe I've got to thinking I'm Ed Grafton . . . or at least wish I were Ed Grafton. I thought all I wanted was to be assigned a top-flight investigation. I know now that isn't enough. I have to do this case, this investigation, right. No tricks, no compromises. The right men have to be arrested and convicted." He dropped his fist onto the photographs. "These are the right men, Mule and Bicki and all of them here, not the hypester gunman we've been questioning. And I'm helpless. I'm going to have to help convict the hypester . . . the wrong man."

Alice pointed down at the picture of Mule. "Which one is that?"

"Corkel. The one they call Mule Fucker. How did you miss him? The press damn near ran him for President."

"You can't prove anything against him?"

"He has a nonsensical alibi we can't break. Three of them do. I think I told you about that."

"Did you? I must have forgotten," she lied. "What were those alibis?"

"That they weren't in Prairie Port at the time of the robbery. Not in Prairie Port that night and for the next week."

"What would happen if you proved one of them had been here in Prairie Port that week?"

"We could convict them, in all likelihood."

She kissed him on the cheek and started out, saying, "Come to bed soon, darling."

Alice Maywell Sunstrom had recognized the photo of Mule from the instant she glanced down at it . . . knew it was the same man whose face she had so often seen in the papers and on TV . . . knew she had witnessed him murder another man four nights after the robbery. Blow the tall Groucho Marx's head away.

Tall Groucho was Willy "Cowboy" Carlson. And Alice may have known this. Hearing conversations about the original robbery gang as well as guarded references to Cub's confrontation with police Chief Frank Santi over Willy's corpse, Alice could have come to realize she had witnessed bald Cowboy's murder at the hands of Mule. If she did, she couldn't admit it to herself,

365

just as she couldn't admit the constant fear she lived under, knowing a killer who had seen her face might be stalking her.

Alice had chosen to forget everything she had witnessed that Tuesday evening, August 24 . . . and everything she had done. There was no choice. Revealing that she had seen Mule kill another man, be it Willy Carlson or not, was tantamount to exposing her brief fling with Elaine Picket. Besides the emotional hurt that knowledge of Elaine would inflict on Strom, the professional consequences could be far graver. Homosexuality was anathema to the FBI and J. Edgar Hoover. Alice feared the slightest hint of her liaison with Elaine Picket could finish her husband's Bureau career. She knew the wrathful ways of the Bureau better than most wives, had suffered through Strom's exile with him. Strom was her life. The Bureau was his life. She could not, would not, must not jeopardize his standing in the FBI. This left frail Alice in a state of perpetual terror and anguish. Even in her dreams there was no escape. Often she had awakened from a nightmare in which Mule stood in the office across from Elaine Picket's apartment staring down at the man he had just killed . . . and then looked up and saw her . . . Alice standing in Elaine's window stark naked and staring at him.

Alice Sunstrom had gathered up all her inner strength to scour the events from memory and maintain an outward equanimity. The effort, whatever its pain, was worthwhile; she was protecting the only thing she loved—Strom. But for safety's sake she had become more reclusive than ever.

Now, walking upstairs to the bedroom, Alice decided that her silence was harming, not protecting, Strom. That somehow she must let it be known what Mule had done and *when*. Let it be known without revealing how she could have seen it. Long after Strom came to bed and fell asleep beside her, she agonized over what to do. A solution occurred. She slipped from bed and went down and picked up the phone and dialed FBI-2000.

"FBI hot line," the voice on the other end announced.

"If you wish to know where Mule Corkel was the night of August twenty-fourth, go to Twelve twenty-one Hosking Street." She spoke softly and through a linen napkin and tried to distort her voice. "He wasn't in Illinois as his lawyer said. It was four nights after the robbery, and he was here in Prairie Port killing someone in the third-floor office at Twelve twenty-one Hosking Street." As an afterthought she added, "The someone might be Cowboy Carlson."

Brewmeister said it was urgent they meet at the city morgue. Yates rushed there only to find Brew had left word to meet at the office. At the office Yates was told Brew had just gone out, saying that they should meet where originally planned. Toward midnight Yates was back at the morgue, found Brewmeister sitting in the medical examiner's office amid a sea of open records.

Stack-hunter was the phrase used at Prairie Port for an agent skilled at the examination and analysis of records and data . . . and Martin Brewmeister ranked among the residency's best. He had a nose for discrepancy and the patience to find it. Could cull through endless pages of material searching for that one fact that didn't gel, that one contradiction which could provide new insights into a problem at hand. The only drawback for the other men, once Brew locked in on such a find, was the meticulous and elongated way he explained the discovery . . . which was why, on arriving at the morgue office, Yates asked with reluctance, "Find something?"

Brew tossed a pair of manila folders across the desk. "I came down here earlier to check on an inconsistency in dates over Sam Hammond's death. Remember that Natalie, Sam's wife, had told us she thought Sam had jumped off Warbonnet Ridge and killed himself in the early evening of August twentieth. Killed himself just before the robbery began that night. But Otto Pinkny said he thought Sam had died three days before that, that he heard Sam had committed suicide after J. L. Squires reamed him out on August seventeenth. Otto Pinkny's been bothering me a lot. Who the hell could know what he knew about Mormon State without some connection to the robbery? When he told us Sam had killed himself three days earlier than Natalie said, I thought I saw a possible link . . . the chance that Bicki Hale hired Otto Pinkny to be the enforcer over the gang, over Bicki's gang. After all, what does Otto Pinkny do in life if it isn't terrorizing and executing people? I thought maybe Cowboy Carlson had given the gang some trouble and that Bicki Hale had had Pinkny blow him away. If that was possible, why couldn't Pinkny have given Sam Hammond a friendly shove off of Warbonnet Ridge? Or maybe it wasn't a shove. Maybe Pinkny killed him another way. Maybe that killing took place when Pinkny said, three days before the robbery instead of the night of the robbery."

Brew got to his feet. "I went through our office file on Sam and found out we fucked up again. No one had bothered to get a copy of his death certificate and autopsy report. All we had on his death was a burial permit and a note from the Prairie Port police saying his body had been found. So I came down here to the morgue and asked to see what they had on Sam. They didn't have a goddam thing. No file, no death certificate, no nothing. I told the assistant M.E. there must be something because Cub had seen Sam's body here a couple of weeks after the robbery. The assistant M.E. explained that could be possible because they have a public funeral parlor upstairs where bodies shipped in from other cities can be viewed before interment. If the body had been shipped in, the Prairie Port medical examiner might not have done the autopsy or even seen the autopsy report. The assistant M.E. didn't have any more time to give me and said if I wanted to go through the files on my own, be his guest. So I did. The filing system here is so disorganized it's amazing anything can be found. I finally located a report on Sam Hammond, and sure enough, the autopsy was done in Cape Girardeau, not Prairie Port. According to the data, Sam's body was pulled out of the Mississippi River near Cape Girardeau at about ten P.M. the night of the robbery, Friday night, August twentieth. The apparent cause of death was a concussion and drowning. The condition of the body, though bloated, indicated death had come within the last twenty-four hours. In other words, Billy, Natalie's version had been correct. Sam Hammond died August twentieth, not three days earlier on the seventeenth. More important for us, Otto Pinkny was wrong. Had been proved wrong and possibly caught in a lie. I knew we had cracked the ice . . . knew that if Pinkny was wrong or lying about this, we'd soon find out he was wrong or lying about a helluva lot more. That was the good news. The headache news is in one of those files you're holding."

Brew sat on the corner of the desk. "As long as I was down here I decided to search the mess and take a look at Cowboy Carlson's autopsy report too. The top folder you have is Cowboy's. It shows he was killed like we have it at our office. Shot to death four or five days after the robbery, weighted down and dumped into the Mississippi. He floated to the surface about two weeks later right off of Prairie Port's municipal pier. It's the name on the second folder I gave you that started ringing far-off bells . . . Teddy Anglaterra. I thumbed past his file a couple of times looking for the ones on Sam and Cowboy before remembering who he was. Anglaterra's autopsy report shows the Mississippi River was a pretty crowded place about the time of the robbery. Not only did Sam Hammond jump to his death from Warbonnet Ridge and float down to Cape Girardeau, not only did Cowboy Carlson get weighted and sunk, but Teddy Anglaterra's corpse drifted onto South Beach at Prairie Port on Tuesday morning, August twenty-fourth . . . was found just about the time J. Edgar Hoover was on television announcing that thirty-one million dollars was taken from Mormon State.

"The M.E.'s report says Teddy Anglaterra was the victim of a pretty brutal beating and stabbing. The actual cause of death was a stab wound in the heart. He was dumped into the river almost immediately after he died. According to the M.E. report he was killed between noon on August nineteenth and noon on August twentieth.

"You much of a statistics buff, Billy? I am. Know how many corpses, on the average, are found in the river here at Prairie Port? Three a year. Two of those bodies have died of natural or accidental causes; the third, under suspicious circumstances . . . suspicious circumstances being a catchall phrase which includes murder and suicide. But in a ten-day spread back in August of this year, from the eve of the robbery to the middle of the next week, the river coughs up one suicide, which floats on downstream, and two murders. That triples the year's quota on suspi-

369

cious deaths. There's also a fourth body found at Prairie Port during this period that I haven't mentioned. A woman. A mental patient who fell into the river pretty far upstream and drowned the day before the robbery. She alone accounts for fifty percent of the year's allotment in natural or accidental deaths. But it wasn't statistical probability that made me suspicious of Teddy."

Brew was back behind the desk again. "You're the man with the flytrap memory, Billy. Who is Teddy Anglaterra?"

"The guy who caused a to-do between the eleventh and twelfth floors, isn't he? The guy whose name was on some list?"

"That's him."

Yates recalled more. "Night watchman, wasn't it? He'd come down from Illinois to apply for a watchman's job at Mormon State, but never showed up. There was some flak about who should be investigating him, our office or the twelfth floor. The twelfth floor did it without authority . . . without telling us."

"Ever see their report on him?"

Yates shook his head.

"That's what I went back to our office to get. Here it is. Several agents traveled to his hometown, Sparta, Illinois, after the robbery. Teddy wasn't to be found. Most of his neighbors weren't concerned. Teddy had the reputation of being a drunk who went off on long toots. Teddy's nephew said the same thing." Two typewritten pages were displayed. "Here's the interview with the nephew done in Sparta on September fourth. He says his uncle came to Mormon State looking for a job and probably got drunk and kept on going. The nephew's name in the agent's report is the same as the one in the coroner report you're holding, the nephew who came to claim the body, Fred Anglaterra. When I was back at our office a few minutes ago I called the Sparta police. They confirmed there was only one Fred Anglaterra in Sparta, and that his uncle is Teddy. But the police were never aware Teddy was missing or murdered. All that their records show is that Teddy was buried in Prairie Port. That's what's so interesting. The morgue here records Teddy's body being discovered on Tuesday, August twenty-fourth. As a John Doe. His fingerprints were sent out on August twenty-fifth. His

370

next of kin, nephew Fred, was notified on August twenty-sixth, arrived and made positive identification of Teddy. The body is released to Fred, and we can presume he accompanied it back to Sparta, where on August twenty-seventh it was buried. The only thing is, eight days later an agent interviewed Fred, and Fred doesn't say Teddy is dead. He says Teddy is probably off on a drunk somewhere."

Yates took the two-page interview.

"Our reports give no indication Teddy died," Brew went on. "In fact, the file on Teddy ends with that last interview done with his nephew on September fourth. That's odd by itself, but it isn't the point. When I got back here and was waiting for you, an obvious thing finally hit me. I'd been reviewing statistical improbability of four corpses appearing in the river in a short period of time without asking the most logical question of all . . . why had one of those corpses, Sam Hammond's, been washed down to Cape Girardeau and the other corpses stayed here? Sam Hammond was the key. You listening, Billy?"

"Sorry. What was that?" Yates tried to refocus on Brew.

"I wanted to know why Sam Hammond's body hadn't washed up at Prairie Port like Cowboy Carlson's, Teddy Anglaterra's and the woman mental patient's."

"He was caught in the Treachery," Yates said. "How else could he have gotten down to Cape Girardeau that same night?"

"Exactly, he had been caught in the Treachery, while the woman who died before him hadn't and the men who died after him hadn't. We know approximately when and where the woman mental patient drifted, and we know it took her approximately one day to get from there to where the Treachery begins north of Prairie Port. By the time she reached here the Treachery had stopped running for the month. If the Treachery was running she would have been washed down to Cape Girardeau like Sam. The same would have been true of Cowboy's and Teddy Anglaterra's bodies. And that's the point, Billy. We know the Treachery was running until about one A.M. Saturday morning, August twenty-first. We know that Teddy Anglaterra was in Prairie Port, was in the security employment agency between

371

nine and eleven Friday morning, August twentieth, to make an appointment for an interview at the bank later that day, an appointment he never kept. We know from the autopsy report he was dead and thrown in the water by noon that same day. But thrown in the water where? If he had been thrown in the Mississippi River here at Prairie Port after leaving the employment agency, he would have been swept on down to Cape Girardeau by the Treachery. The Treachery was still running, ran until one the next morning. But Teddy's body didn't float into Prairie Port until Tuesday morning, August twenty-fourth. Where had he been since leaving the agency four days before? And why?"

Brew lowered his head, rubbed his temples. "Of course, this is random speculation. Maybe there's a perfectly logical explanation that—" He looked up to see Yates hurrying out the door. "What's the matter?"

Yates hardly heard. He had, at long last, found something he'd been searching so long for, the reason for the déjà vu, for the feeling he had experienced Mormon State before.

"Yates, what in Christ's name is happening?" Brew stood at the door watching Billy high-step away. "Yates?"

"Cover for me, Brew. I should be back tomorrow. Cover for me."

. . . And Billy Yates drove through the night and morning and afternoon and by early evening was in Maryland and nearing his destination.

# Twenty-one

Heeled-high and taffetaed she stood adrift looking out over a dim, distant world of demi-court and dusty pomp. A world of silent bugle, abandoned spear and waiting steed. A lost laughter and unstepped quadrille. A place of civility and form. Of familiarity. Privilege. Youth. Her chin jutted high, for she was Patricia Trask Sproul Ardmore Amory, sired by the merchant barons of Baltimore, twice wed into the British peerage, twice a countess but never a duchess. Her eyes were clear, her vision partial to a memory of parasols and esplanade. Nothing much had happened. Time was simply passing.

"Mister Yates, how nice of you to drop in without calling." She motioned away the butler who had admitted him to the somber Virginia mansion built by her great-great-grandfather. "Are you planning to stay for dinner?"

"Only to talk to your husband and leave," Yates assured her. "I'm sorry I didn't call in advance."

"Barrett is napping. Do amuse yourself until he comes down." She withdrew, saying, "I'll set another place for dinner."

Billy Yates rather liked Lady Pat, as his classmates at the FBI's training academy used to call her. He knew the feelings were not mutual, which was all right with him. After all, how chummy does a future agent want to be with J. Edgar Hoover's alleged paramour?

If the most fanciful of rumors were to be believed, Pat was the fabled Carmella Hebbelman, who long ago during Prohibition danced and drank the night away with Edgar in Zion, Illinois.

When saner heads and logic prevailed, a confirmable story told how Lady Pat and Hoover were first introduced in 1942. World War II was in full rage, and Patricia had returned to America

373

with her second titled British husband, the Earl of Ardmore. Ardmore, who was in England's secret service, had come to this country to confer with OSS chief William J. "Wild Bill" Donovan on the formation of Anglo-U.S. training programs for espionage operatives. Ardmore had created several such curriculums for Britain. Among the aides accompanying him and his wife was Patricia's cousin Orin G. Trask. Trask, a thirty-year-old scholar with a penchant for criminology, was in London researching a book on Scotland Yard when war with Germany broke out. He stayed on and joined his cousin-in-law's unit. Development of training programs for espionage whetted Trask's appetite for similar programs in crime fighting. Trask, as early as 1941, envisioned the FBI transcending Scotland Yard as the dominant postwar law-enforcement entity . . . saw a great university of criminology being established by the Bureau, a university of his design.

When the Earl of Ardmore and Pat were asked to a small dinner party that J. Edgar Hoover was to attend, Trask wangled an invitation and cornered Hoover. The FBI Director was intrigued by what the young American had to say. He was more taken by Trask's stately cousin Patricia. Patricia had been bred to believe in men. She avidly believed in cousin Orin and his work. She believed in Ardmore and his work. The same was immediately true for J. Edgar Hoover. That was the beginning.

How often and how surreptitiously Lady Pat and Edgar met during the war is problematic. It couldn't have been often. She was back in England for the duration, made only two quick junkets to America, both with her husband. J. Edgar Hoover was not known to have gone to England. But he did write, ostensibly to Orin Trask. Trask's letters back to Hoover contained sealed messages from Pat.

A year and five months after peace was declared, the earl died. Patricia, Countess of Ardmore, was devastated. Notions she had not loved Ardmore were discredited. Suspicion grew as to how much control her cousin Orin Trask wielded over her.

Since earliest childhood, independent, iron-minded Pat had always succumbed to Orin's will. Though he was a year her junior, he had always acted as his cousin's protector. She, on many occasions, acted as his. Rarely had Pat and Orin exchanged confidences. They were from private, nonconfiding stock. The idea that there had been any carnal relationship between them was farfetched. They were not a passionate or incestuous lot, the Trasks. Trask women, even before the great fortune had been amassed, married for convenience. Remained married and loyal and caring. Ruthless in defense of their own. Indefatigable in maintaining decorum. Which was why many friends doubted her relationship with Edgar ever ended in bed. A few insisted it had ... that there was no way it could be avoided, since Orin wanted it that way.

It had fallen to Orin to shake Pat free of her protracted grief and mourning. He had convinced her to abandon England and return to the family home in Virginia. To get out and be with people again. To reestablish her friendship with J. Edgar Hoover. Critics saw the steering of Pat back toward Edgar as Trask's most self-serving manipulation of his titled cousin.

J. Edgar, from their first meeting in 1942, had been ambivalent toward Orin Trask. He assessed the young Virginia plutocrat as being at once brilliant, erratic, ambitious and merciless. Opportunistically, for Edgar, there was much to be gained by an alliance with Orin. The Trask family in and of itself was respected and wealthy and politically potent on Capitol Hill and throughout the southeastern seaboard. Orin's avowed dedication to creating for the FBI a university-level training academy bearing Hoover's name was appealing. Also to be considered was Orin's cousin Pat, the Countess of Ardmore.

In the wake of Hitler's surrender, Edgar Hoover became increasingly disaffected with Orin, who was in Germany studying the structure and substance of Nazi police organizations. Trask was forever making public statements on his plans for the FBI Academy as well as shooting off unsolicited reports to Hoover. Twice he woke the Director with transatlantic phone calls, chitchat calls having no relevance. By late 1947 reports had filtered back to Hoover that Orin was not only consorting with known Nazis under the guise of research but was protecting

375

several notorious Gestapo men, as well as an SD Ausland aide to Walter Schellenberg . . . that he might even be planning to smuggle one of them into the U.S. Edgar Hoover determined to sever his relationship with Trask. Patricia returned in time to dissuade him.

Patricia came home to America and the Trask family estate, Three Oaks, in early 1948. It was there at Three Oaks where Edgar went to lunch with her. She related, as best she could, the tragic loss of her husband. But enough of me. What of you, Edgar? How goes it?

And he told her, that afternoon and most every Thursday afternoon for years to come, for Thursday was "their" day, with Associate FBI Director Clyde Tolson outside in the car parked along the great circular gravel driveway even though he could have waited inside. Edgar complained, in lugubrious detail, of each of his own troubles . . . and always ended up with detestation and fears regarding Harry Truman and an emerging intelligence organization called CIA. Unlike the military's dominant Counterintelligence Corps, the successor to OSS, which answered to the general of the Army group to which it was attached, CIA was to be a nonmilitary, unaffiliated organization answering directly to the President of the United States. Edgar had luxuriated in the fact that he alone, of all law-enforcement and intelligence-gathering heads, spoke directly to the President. But Harry Truman those days was speaking more and more to CIA boss Allen Dulles.

Future peril to the side, Harry Truman had already inflicted a blow to FBI power and prestige by stripping the Bureau of its jurisdiction to operate in Europe as well as drastically limiting its activities in Central and South America. Except for Mexico, the FBI had been reduced to a domestic service, not the international organization Edgar had come to envision. Worse yet, Allen Dulles's CIA was the new glamour service. Young men who might have applied to become FBI agents were now, in epidemic numbers, flocking to CIA.

Spying, Edgar warned Patricia, was murky business and un-American. Foreign business better done by Brits and Russkies and Swedes. America was a no-nonsense nation of right and

376

wrong, good and bad, black and white and nothing in between. No gray areas, no shading. Every American boy and his brother was either moral or immoral. Not *a*moral like the French. Espionage by definition was gray and amoral.

"With all this verbal diarrhea about cold wars and spies," he told her, "I have a mind to give that sotted billygoat what he wants and let hell thunder."

The billygoat was a junior senator from the state of Wisconsin by the name of McCarthy, who in an informal poll of Washington correspondents had been voted the worst senator in the entire Senate, which was why he was desperately rummaging for a reelection campaign issue such as communists in government, Edgar explained to Patricia. Patricia thought it might be propitious if Edgar tossed McCarthy a random communist or so to see what effect it would have on Harry Truman.

The matter of J. Edgar's faltering prestige troubled Patricia mightily. After profound consideration she came truly to believe salvation lay with cousin Orin Trask and his plans for the great training center . . . an FBI university developing unique and exciting curriculums for crime detection and prevention, nurturing generations of elite super-operatives. Edgar, however, wanted nothing as grand as a university and was wary of Trask's ideas on elitism.

"The average FBI agent today is better than his counterpart at any time in history, and this is good enough for me," Patricia's journal would record Edgar having told her.

When Orin G. Trask returned to the United States to teach at Johns Hopkins University, Edgar, at Patricia's urging, suggested he develop plans for a modest new training facility, perhaps at the very same U.S. Marine Corps base at nearby Quantico, Virginia, where the current FBI Academy stood. Edgar proposed paying a small sum from his own pocket for this service. Trask gladly accepted the assignment but insisted on personally financing whatever was required at this juncture. Edgar acceded to the funding arrangement.

Neither Edgar nor even Patricia foresaw the thoroughness, or the length of time, Trask would expend on the project. The first phase in itself, an analysis of every FBI procedure and investigation to that date, required five years of research by a hand-picked staff of think-tank experts Trask had assembled. With this knowledge in hand, a team of educators was brought in to evolve the actual curriculum for the future. Among the scholastics was the prestigious historian Barrett Amory.

Trask and Amory had both served with espionage organizations during World War II, England's SIS and America's OSS respectively. Whereas Trask had been interested in criminology and law enforcement prior to working in the secret service and returned to it after, Amory had been interested in espionage prior to, during and immediately after his stint with OSS. Amory was older than Trask, and his first love was history; his second, psychology. Trask, on recruiting Amory, suggested Amory do an extensive history of the FBI for him. Amory obliged. Several years later he expanded the history to cover crime in America.

In 1954 Barrett Amory joined the four-man steering committee entrusted with devising a curriculum for the new academy. By 1955 Amory and Trask were fast friends. During 1956 Amory moved into the great mansion, then shared by Trask and Patricia. On New Year's Eve, 1957, he married Patricia. Nothing was known of their courtship or how Edgar took the news. All that could outwardly be noticed was that Patricia's time was now divided among three men instead of two—Edgar, Trask and Barrett Amory.

Orin Trask's master plan for a new FBI training center and a curriculum was completed in 1959, ten years after work on it had begun. The achievement was remarkable, all fourteen volumes of it. What was presented, in exquisite detail, was not the "modest facility" Hoover had urged but a university more enormous and futuristic than any ever hinted at by Trask in almost two decades of conversation on the subject. J. Edgar Hoover, certain the Senate would never fund a project of such magnitude and cost, pigeonholed the leather-bound volumes without allowing anyone at the Bureau to see them, except Clyde Tolson.

Orin Trask was not all that perturbed by the rejection. Knowing the airplane would fly was for him as important as going somewhere in it. He busied himself with myriad other projects. Amory too had much to occupy his time. It was Patricia alone who was determined the university be built and, using her wile and wealth, set forth to create a power base from which to lobby Congress.

In spite of having turned down the university plans, J. Edgar Hoover was impressed by Trask's vision, was particularly taken by a teaching concept termed "cadreism," in which certain experimental courses would be taught to small, handpicked units of trainees, groups as small as four or five men who would later serve together in the field. Edgar invited Orin to try out the concept at the present FBI Academy, which boasted a student population of slightly more than thirty. Trask declined, went on declining for years. Patricia finally interceded. Orin agreed, on the condition that he could select the students he wanted in his own way. Edgar agreed to that.

Orin Trask began conducting one seminar a week in Elements of Crime Detection in the fall of 1963. It proved to be a startling, effective and popular course. And a most difficult one to get into. Trask selected only four trainees a term. Admittance became a badge of honor among the aspiring agents.

The success of the experiment prompted expansion. Trask persuaded Barrett Amory to create a seminar of his own, which he did in 1966. Psychological Profiling and Comprehensive History of Crime were the two subjects Amory's four trainees were taught.

Trask had cautioned Amory that the seminars must never become clubs or fraternities, must avoid elitism and always remain part of the overall academy, must never become competitive with one another. This was easier said than done. The tiny groups, by the very selection process which created them, were elite. Pride in their own seminar and instructor prompted student competition between the groups. Oddly enough, it was Amory's students who were the most aggressively competitive.

On the other hand, the brothers-in-law, rather than compete, grew closer. Trask, having proved his point with the seminars, was wearying of them. Longed to get away and throw himself into several long-abandoned research interests. He urged Amory to join him on one of the projects. Amory was not interested. Even so, Trask spent more and more time around the old family estate where Amory and Patricia resided. Patricia's tenacity had been partially responsible for Congress approving construction of a magnificent new FBI Academy at Quantico, but Orin showed no interest in this. While at the estate he was usually cloistered with Amory discussing some future plan or another. On occasion Trask addressed Amory's seminars. The reverse never occurred. No one, including Amory, ever set foot in Trask's seminar any more. This was starting to bother J. Edgar Hoover. Trask's students were becoming too cliquish, too competitive with Amory's students, who already were far too aggressive for the Director's liking.

J. Edgar Hoover decided to put an end to the seminar experiment, but before he could, Orin G. Trask died of a heart attack on December 20, 1969. He was sixty-seven years old. Patricia was sixty-eight. Barrett Amory was seventy-three. J. Edgar Hoover was seventy-five. Construction of a new academy had been under way for six months.

Patricia's grief was limitless. The present, like the future, eluded her. She slipped backward. Took to wearing the trappings of her bygone British past. The gowns, the parasols. Took to standing at the window and watching her garden and seeing things of yesterday that only she could see. Hearing things. Took to whispering to sweet Edmond, Earl of Ardmore. To blowing kisses to Orin.

She didn't abandon Barrett Amory. She tarried in the present long enough each day to tend to his needs. This done, she returned to the garden. To Edmond. To Trask.

Billy Yates, waiting now in the side room at Three Oaks, glanced across the grand foyer and into the main salon and saw her there, standing at the arched window in front of the garden . . . saw her in profile, her chin jutted upward, peering out through the glass. He knew all about her. Anyone who had studied with Barrett Amory did, but he knew even more. She didn't like him. Didn't like him being so bright, so independent . . . so Jewish.

Billy Yates being Jewish but not looking Semitic provided him certain advantages, or so he thought. Often, not being recognized was like possessing a secret password, allowed him to cross behind enemy lines and watch his adversaries around their campfire . . . hear what they had to say . . . what they were planning. Most of the time he didn't bother one way or the other. The whole religious issue had become tedious to him. Even so, he wasn't taking chances. As Mom said, do everything twice as good as anyone else and maybe you'll come out almost equal.

Yates, while attending the FBI Academy during 1968, was almost as equal a person as there was. And then some. Academically no one else made the marks he did. Athletically, he had only one rival in the whole institution, Vance Daughter, who ranked second to him scholastically. Daughter was a member of Trask's private seminar, the members of which had a keen dislike for anyone in Amory's seminar. Yates was the star in the tiara of Amory's seminar, a group whose feelings toward the Traskians brought new dimensions to the word loathing.

The two seminars, in the time Yates was at the academy, had both evolved into ultra-exclusive cliques, ones in which the subjects being taught were often secondary to the philosophy of the instructor. Trask's penchant for uniformity and precision resulted in his selecting young men who were brainy, aristocratic and disciplined. His students' belief and trust in him neared adoration if not fanaticism. Trask didn't discourage such fervor and obedience. Nor did he discourage clannish isolation. The Traskians ate together at the same table in the academy dining room, studied together, weekended together . . . kept together whenever else possible.

If Trask's seminar students appeared religious in their approach, then those of Barrett Amory were definitely irreligious. Amory believed in individuality, picked as his yearly four candidates brainy loners and iconoclasts. Amory, unlike Trask, kept pretty much to the two subjects his seminar was supposed to explore . . . didn't overly fraternize with his students, except for Billy Yates.

Still, whatever else, when Yates was at the academy the three Traskian seminar students were gentlemen and polite. Southern gentlemen. Regardless of their feelings, they at least treated Yates with outer politeness. Billy did not always return the favor. He good–naturedly taunted them with his Judaic origin. No one at the academy mentioned the word *Jew* out loud except Billy Yates. Yates was distinctly unreligious, quite ignorant of his people's history and ritual, but on the Jewish New Year, Daughter and each of the other Traskians had received a commemorative card from Yates in Hebrew, a language Billy didn't understand a word of. In the gymnasium, with boxing gloves on, Yates and Daughter had at one another in a war that needed no language to comprehend.

Yates, with Barrett Amory, was forever the acolyte. He respected everything about Barrett. Because of Barrett he even grew tolerant of Patricia, though she did not reciprocate. Barrett took to Yates. Was proud of him. They spent hours alone talking, very often to the displeasure of Patricia.

. . . It had been two years now since pupil and teacher had seen one another as seventy-five-year-old Barrett entered the side room.

"You look hale, young Yates, hale indeed." The old man never shook hands, only slapped people on the shoulder. He slapped Yates. "Where they have you these days?"

"Prairie Port, Missouri."

"Ed Grafton country."

"He's not there any more."

"Grafton not at Prairie Port?"

"He was replaced over the Mormon State robbery investigation, or at least that's how I see it."

". . . Yes, seem to remember hearing something about that," Amory recalled. "Probably better he's gone. He did his time. We all do our time. See the Lady Pat?"

"When I came in."

"She doesn't like you, you know."

"I know."

"Come along and eat. Whatever you have to say, you'll say over supper and wine. Come, come."

As they were crossing the marble foyer, Amory asked, "How's that religion of yours doing?"

"What a weird question!"

"You have weird habits. Joining the FBI was one of them. Still doesn't give you leave to use that religion like a cultural cap pistol when it suits you. Have us reaching for the sky one moment. Next moment you forget Jehovah ever was and ask us why our hands are up. Unbecoming trait for a fellow with your stuff. Hear you got married."

"Yes."

"Against sending announcements, are you?"

"I apologize."

"I would have liked an announcement. It was the least you could do."

The beams and wood paneling of the dining hall had come from a medieval Flemish church. The leaded windows faced out on a private lake. A banquet table ran parallel to the windows and was set with three places, two of which were taken by Yates and Amory.

"Doubtful Lady Pat will join us." Amory indicated the empty chair to his right and the setting before it. "Heard about her troubles, have you?"

"Yes, I'm sorry."

"Don't be. She's happy where she is. Gets to visit a lot of old friends, size up the territory."

A waiter appeared, placed a bowl of asparagus soup in front of Yates, then another in front of Amory.

"What's on your mind, young Yates?"

"First, tell me about you."

"Nothing to tell," Amory said. "They disbanded the seminars the year after you left the academy, which was fine with me. Had

383

enough work to do over at Johns Hopkins. Needed to get to the book I'm on too. Still keep an office at the academy and help out on curriculum problems from time to time."

"What's the book you're writing?"

"Some sort of history."

"Nothing more specific?"

"The Punic Wars. I've returned to the Punic Wars. Always wanted to. Probably discover Lady Pat poking about one of the battlefields. Now to you, Billy Yates. You've come for a reason."

Billy moved aside the soup. "Have you been following the Mormon State investigation?"

"Matters like that don't interest me now."

"But you're aware of it."

"More aware than unaware. Can't avoid the ruddy thing."

"Does Mormon State remind you of any other FBI investigation?"

"Not that I recall. Of course, the memory isn't what it once was."

"It was a case you described in this very room."

"I did?"

"One evening when I was at the academy," Yates began, "you had four of us to dinner here. Four of us from your seminar. It was just before Christmas. The Christmas tree was up, over there. We sat at this table, and your wife was with us. So were two instructors from the academy and a friend of yours from Europe. After dinner we stayed at the table and several simultaneous discussions began. I was listening to one discussion at my end of the table but overheard parts of yours. You were at the other end of the table talking about a San Francisco bank robbery that had been perpetrated in a spectacular fashion. There was confusion over how the robbers had both perpetrated the crime and made their escape. They had made their getaway by boat through tunnels nobody knew existed. Do you remember that?"

Amory concentrated. "No."

Yates said, "The aspect being emphasized by you was the spectacular method of perpetration. How spectacular it had been. Immediately after the theft there was confusion about how much

384

money had been stolen. No one could come up with a correct count. The press exploited hell out of this. Varying figures were leaked or rumored until it was finally learned that a record amount of money was taken. Once this happened the media began calling the perpetrator the cream of the crime world."

". . . Sounds like Brink's to me," Amory said. "Brink's in Boston back in the fifties. Masked bandits walked into a money room and held up the cashiers and vanished with millions—"

"Brink's was an armed robbery, a group of men marching in and taking money at gunpoint," Yates said. "San Francisco was a theft. A vault was burned through over a weekend. The perpetrators entered and escaped the premises through tunnels. Their timing in all of this had been superb."

Amory tried to recall, couldn't . . . shook his head to indicate as much.

"Perhaps I might assist you, Mister Yates?" Back arched and gown aswirl, Patricia Amory came forth from the doorway behind Billy. Barrett Amory got up and pulled out a chair. She enthroned herself. Jutted her chin in Yates's direction. "I clearly recall the evening to which you refer. And the discussion. It occurred right where I'm presently seated. Many investigations were spoken of. Tell me more of the one you overheard?"

A servant appeared with a bowl of soup. She waved him off.

"A great deal of suspense was created by the media and continued to be created over the San Francisco matter," Yates said to her. "First there was suspense because the amount of money stolen couldn't be fixed and later because each rumor of what was actually gone hinted that a new record for missing cash was about to be established. The greatest suspense was involved in tracking down the unknown perpetrators. Reward money kept escalating, and that turned the public's search for clues into something of a national treasure hunt. There was a holiday, a carnival spirit. Public sympathy seemed to be with the criminals. People were openly rooting for the criminals to evade detection and arrest. The FBI was becoming the ogre, a villain for just trying to do its job. After a time the criminals were apprehended. The evidence against them appeared overwhelming. A conviction was certain, but the media and public went on treating them like national heroes. The Bureau was receiving hate mail for having arrested them. Just before going to trial a second group of suspects was apprehended. As they confessed, it became clear that they, not the first group, had perpetrated the theft. The media and public wasted no time in forgetting the first group and embracing the second group . . . making bigger celebrities out of them than their predecessors.

"The trial for the second group got under way, and suddenly a piece of information is discovered. It's learned that the second gang had killed a bank guard during the course of the robbery. A guard nobody knew was there. A guard who had gotten his work schedule wrong and turned up for work without anyone knowing it just before the robbery. He was killed but his body wasn't found until the trial began. But I never heard why that was, why no one knew he was missing until then."

"What else, Mister Yates," Patricia began, "did you overhear?"

"That was about it. I got back into the conversation at my end of the table. I was aware the San Francisco robbery was still being talked about at the other end but I didn't hear the specifics.

"What's been driving me crazy is that I can't zero in on the robbery," Yates said. "Part of it seemed as familiar as my own name. But I can't locate it . . . in San Francisco or anywhere. I went to the library and the newspaper morgues, and there was nothing on it there, and nowhere else that I could find. So I came here."

Patricia stood facing the dark lake beyond the leaded glass. "You are quite correct, Mister Yates, nothing like it happened . . . as a whole. Only in parts. There never was such a robbery in San Francisco or elsewhere. But there was a robbery in Boston and one in New York and others in Illinois and Wisconsin from which incidents were taken. What you overheard Barrett explain that evening was a teaching device developed by my late cousin Orin Trask. I shouldn't say device. It was more an exercise meant to illustrate the pitfalls of practical investigation to aspiring law-enforcement agents. My cousin simply took pieces of actual crimes which the FBI had either failed to solve or in solving was

386

humiliated, and reassembled them into an overall scenario. Into a make-believe perfect crime. His phrase for it was, in fact, model crime. Orin theorized that if a student could solve a model crime, it would be far easier for him subsequently to solve the real thing."

She was on her feet looking down at Billy. "So good to have seen you, Mister Yates. Do come by again when you have a problem of magnitude."

Glancing toward the leaded windows that framed her past, she swept from the room.

"That answer your question?" asked Amory.

"I suppose so."

"Suppose? I don't understand you, Yates. You ask a question. You receive a comprehensive explanation. You end up supposing and glum."

"It's hard to accept the idea that a classroom exercise, a teaching aid pasted together from bits and pieces of real crimes, somehow happened three years later."

"Don't be ridiculous. You heard the woman. Accept it."

"That crime was copied," Yates said quietly. "Mormon State is that crime."

"A coincidence, Yates, and you better accept it. Perpetrations aren't shaped out of silly putty. Opportunity dictates theft, you know that. A boy of five knows that. You don't scamper out and perpetrate because a maiden aunt leaves you a set of old blueprints. Blueprints, plans, action come second. Opportunity comes first. Opportunity dictates plans and action."

Amory watched Billy staring down at the table. "Unconvinced, are you, young Yates? You'll go to your grave unconvinced you've died someday. Lady Pat could have it wrong, ever think of that? Who's to say her gray matter's functioning any better than mine? She and me, we're nearly a century and a half old between us. Never believe anyone over a hundred."

An entree of thinly sliced roast beef, mashed potatoes and peas was placed before each man. Amory dug in. Yates played with his fork.

"Did Orin Trask record any of these model crimes?"

387

"Leave it be, Yates, leave it be."

"Did he?"

"He did. Wrote down everything. Left it all to the new FBI Academy, whenever the dratted thing gets finished. Orin donated a library so his works and others could be permanently available."

"Is it available?"

"You mean are copies of the model crimes available?"

"Yes."

"I suppose they are."

"Where?"

"My office."

"Yours?"

"My office at the academy. Orin left a lot of his papers in my office. Never got around to packing it up till recently. I saw the model crimes among the material."

"And it's still there, in your office?"

"In packing crates."

"When can we go to your office?"

Amory took a sip of wine, threw his napkin on the table. "Now. If we don't you'll be stuffing potatoes in your ears trying to get rid of them fast. Can't abide the wanton wasting of food."

The drive through the United States Marine Corps base at Quantico, Virginia, ended at the solitary building which housed the entire FBI Academy, a red-brick, two-story-high former barracks. Amory led Yates along the first-floor corridor and into his small cluttered office. Two packing cases were stacked on the floor.

"It's the bottom one," Amory said. "Top one's my extra baggage. There's a hammer on that shelf."

Yates strained lifting the heavy top crate onto the floor. Stenciled on the wood slats of the crate below was the name "Trask." Billy pried off its cover. The crate was empty.

". . . Could be I got them mixed up, young Yates. Try the other crate."

Billy thought he detected a faint note of alarm in the old man's voice. He pried off the second cover. A crunch of tightly packed books and manuscripts was revealed below. Yates started sorting through. The material was Amory's. Not a page of Trask's work could be found.

"Could be they got put down in the basement." Amory didn't sound convinced. "The academy keeps the bulk of Orin's stuff downstairs."

Eight wire-fronted storage bins stood in the basement room beyond the small gymnasium. Amory walked up to the bin marked with Trask's name. A padlock hung open from a ring in the wire door. Like the crate, the bin was empty.

Amory's expression darkened.

A noise echoed. Amory beckoned they leave in silence. He stayed with his thoughts until outside and walking down a barracks-lined street.

". . . You could be right, young Yates. Right about Mormon State. Have you ever heard the name 'Gents'? I mean a group calling itself the Gents?"

Yates recalled reading a transcript in which Otto Pinkny had told Strom: "I'm a friend of gents." He said now, "No, I never heard of it as an organization."

"What about the Silent Men, that name ring a bell?"

"No."

They were at the corner now, and Amory glanced about. Across the street, beyond unshaded windows, marines were preparing for sleep. "This is between you and myself, young Yates, is that clear? This is a matter of your well-being and nothing else. And anyway, what I'm about to tell you might not be so."

Amory moved to a stone bench under a tree and sat down. Yates sat beside him.

"I'm not trying to vindicate or damn Orin Trask. He was who he was," Amory said. "The single relevant fact to remember, for our purpose, is that people like Orin are given to great passions and obsessions in their life and work. With Orin his life was his work. Whatever work happened to interest him at the time. He was changeable about that but not in the least less passionate or less obsessive. I suppose what I'm trying to say is that these passions, these obsessions, often went beyond reasonable limits

389

. . . that for a period of time Orin, in his pursuits, was possibly delusional. Knowing this, I often ignored what he was saying. I thoroughly ignored, for example, his talk about the Silent Men.

"Orin had one overriding interest in life few people were aware of: the psychology of secrecy. He would quote you whole segments from Freud's *Totem and Taboo* and from anyone else who'd written on the subject. The books didn't always have to be by scientists. He knew Aleister Crowley as well as he did Margaret Mead. I agreed with Trask that secrecy is individuality, the only means by which to protect our individual self when our privacy is challenged . . . that privacy, the greenhouse of individuality, is forever challenged and in peril.

"Orin began with that premise thirty years ago, and on and off followed it logically forward. For him secrecy in groups was conspiracy, and he studied such groups as they had never been studied before—from the Knights Templar to the Rosicrucians to the Freemasons and Tong and Black Hand and KKK and Mau Mau, no one knew secret societies better than Orin. And secret rites and rituals. He had even detailed an honorary and secret group within the Boy Scouts, for God's sake. Something called the Order of the Arrow, first and second class. It didn't have to be bad to be secret . . . take AA. But it usually was bad."

Amory paused and shook his head. "I still won't let myself get into it, will I? Keep skirting the matter. All right, here goes. There's a well-known story about Orin having been discredited for consorting with notorious ex-Nazis immediately after the war . . . that among other things he was using them as research sources in the preliminary planning of the new FBI Academy. This was true but to a lesser degree than supposed. The Nazis were high-ranking members of Heinrich Himmler's infamous Aryan Studies Department, the concocters and defenders of Germanic superiority. Most of his time with these SS men was spent researching the use of secret societies and pagan Teutonic rituals by the Nazis. One of the Germans was SS Colonel Helmut Markel, an anthropologist. Markel, at this time, was far more expert in secret societies than Orin. It was Markel who told Orin that the Gents and Silent Men had been revived. Markel claimed to have gone to see them in America during World War II, to have tried to recruit them to the German cause. Orin smuggled Markel into this country in 1950. Rumor later had it that this was done to help plan the academy. It wasn't. It was to try to track down the Gents and Silent Men. They never did. Not then.

"According to Orin, the Gents, or League of Gents, was a small, clandestine pre-Civil War group of high-born southern and eastern aristocrats, a far more refined and dangerous group than the Ku Klux Klan. Their motives were economic, to maintain their vast holdings in the South without substantial change. Their *modus operandi* was to achieve their ends through political and financial pressure, and when this failed, to have an in-house unit foment radical and violent change. The in-house unit they created for this was the Silent Men. Orin had always suspected Abraham Lincoln had been assassinated by the Silent Men . . . Orin thought the Gents had disbanded in 1870. Hearing Helmut Markel claim they had reappeared in the late 1930s and that he had made contact with them was what prompted Orin to smuggle the Nazi into America. When no trace of the Gents could be found, Markel went back to Germany and Orin returned to other subjects, not the least of which was finishing his master plan for the academy.

"The death of President Kennedy reawakened Orin's interest in the assassination aspects of secret societies. By then Orin was an expert in the subject. He had no doubt it was a conspiracy. His first thought was of the Silent Men. But it didn't prove out. At least that was the impression I got from him.

"Six months before he died, Orin had decided to abandon all his activities and write a book on the psychology of secrecy. He was still teaching his one seminar a week at the academy so he used his four students as researchers, had them scurrying about getting odds and ends for him. This, if you ask me, was the final straw for Edgar Hoover, who made known his intention to fire Orin before he could resign.

"Orin, I should point out, was in one of his manic states as the writing and final research began. More delusional than usual, which is probably why I thought so little of it when he told me

391

with great enthusiasm that he'd discovered the Gents and Silent Men. He claimed they had come to him, which made it seem all the less credible. From then on I received occasional bulletins on his dealings with them. He claimed the Silent Men were the only wing of the Gents that had survived and that whereas they took credit for shooting Abraham Lincoln, they disavowed involvement with Jack Kennedy. I ask you, Yates, what would you think of anybody who told you that?"

Amory rose and began walking. "One night Orin came to the house more elated than I'd seen him in years. And more hyperactive. If I hadn't known better I would have suspected he was on some type of amphetamine. He was at once secretive and effusive, like a cub reporter who had come up with his first scoop and was trying not to breathe a word until the story was printed. He told me the Silent Men had infiltrated the very highest echelons of government, including the FBI. He said he had known this for some time but had just that night realized what it was they were up to. And he left it at that. I asked, 'All right, Orin, what is it?' He was beside himself with joy but wouldn't answer, not that question." Amory shook his head. "When he told me the Silent Men were the only hope for America, I concluded he was indeed dippy and let it drop . . .

"Now I am worried about you, Billy Yates. I don't know what the relationship between Orin's rantings and Mormon State is, but I suspect it just might exist. You see, Orin did let it slip why the Silent Men approached him in the first place. They wanted his research on model crimes. Those two volumes. Two sets of them existed according to Orin. The original and a copy. He said when the Silent Men asked, he couldn't find either set. Later I got the impression he had found one of them. Whether he gave them to anybody, I couldn't say. After his death I came across a set on an upper bookshelf in my office. Orin was forever leaving things in my office.

"More can be drawn from this, of course. Other implications. But I don't wish to get into that. I wish to be the old man I am and comfort myself in forgetfulness. Perhaps what I've said is my inveterate paranoia catching up with Orin's talent for the absurd extreme. Let us hope there is a more rational explanation than mine for why Orin's work is missing from my office and the storage bin. After all, missing books and papers do not a conspiracy make. In any case, young Yates, I've done my duty to you. I feel there was something special between the two of us. On the off chance my suspicions are real, go carefully. Particularly you and your strutting religious ways. Gents stands not only for 'gentlemen' but also for 'gentiles.' "

"Silent Men?" Brew repeated into the telephone receiver.

"That's right," Yates's voice answered. "Barrett Amory thinks we could be right about someone meddling with Romor 91, only he's going us one better, he thinks it could be an all-out conspiracy and that—"

"Conspiracy to achieve what?"

"He doesn't know, but he implied the Silent Men are behind it."

"Silent Men? What are you talking about?"

"The guys who maybe stole the model crimes."

"Cut the clowning, Billy."

"I'm not clowning. This thing is weird enough by itself. If we want to believe Barrett Amory, it gets a helluva lot weirder. One thing is pretty clear, most everything that's happened with Mormon State so far seems to have been outlined years ago in a classroom exercise called a model crime. From here on is where it gets sticky. Amory thinks the Silent Men stole specifications for the model crimes a while back and that they put one of them into effect at Mormon State. He doesn't know why, or what's to be gained by it, but he warned me to watch out. If his information is correct the Men have infiltrated the Bureau and—"

"Who the hell are the Silent Men?"

"I was hoping you wouldn't ask that."

"What?"

"Remember Abraham Lincoln?"

"Lincoln!"

"They're the ones who knocked him over."

"Billy, for Christ's sake."

"I'm telling you what Amory told me. There was a pre-Civil War group named the League of Gents. A secret society. They formed an action wing, assassinations et cetera, called the Silent Men. The whole shebang disbanded. About the time of World War II a Nazi claimed the Silent Men had reappeared, or at least he had temporary contact with a group calling itself that. Remember Orin Trask?"

"He came to the academy after I left," Brew said.

"But you know who he was?"

"Sure."

"It was Trask who was on the trail of the Silent Men. He told Amory he found them. Now you know as much as I do. You check out those reports from Illinois yet?"

"I've got to wait till morning. Till everyone's over at the grand jury. They're running with the grand jury in the morning."

"I thought that was next week!"

"They're going now. Washington's insisting."

"Dammit."

". . . Billy, Barrett Amory really tell you all that stuff about the Silent Men?"

"Yep."

"Jesus."

Jez crossed a brick-paved, gas-lit avenue of boutiques and small restaurants and turned into Hosking Street in the bohemian, riverfront section of Prairie Port known as Steamboat Cove. The row of former stables to the left had been converted into fashionable townhouses. Across from them were several old industrial buildings. Twelve twenty-one was the number on a four-story brick warehouse that had been remodeled into offices. Jez picked open the lock with his penknife, took the steps to the third-floor landing, again picked a lock.

Three large rooms faced out onto the street. Jez kept the lights off as he wandered through the empty premises. He played his penlight beam on the wood floor. Fresh scratchings indicated the previous tenant had vacated only recently.

Near the window in the last room the beam picked up the

394

faded outline of what could have been a stain. Perhaps even a blood stain. One that had been washed and later sanded, but never varnished over.

Jez stepped to the window, looked out across the street . . . saw directly into the studio bedroom of a townhouse, could not help noticing the red-headed woman standing at an easel, painting.

He crossed the street and pushed the buzzer. A squawk box asked who was buzzing. He told her.

The door finally opened. Elaine Picket looked terrific. She made no attempt to close the front of her denim shirt. "FBI? Did you say FBI?"

"Yes, ma'am." He displayed his credentials.

"Oh, put those silly things away."

He did, somewhat at a loss.

She contemplated him, turned in such a way as to let her shirt open wider on the small, firm breasts beneath. "What can I do for you, FBI?"

"I'd like to ask you a few questions."

"Only if we fuck first." There was no doubt she meant it. "You do fuck, don't you?"

". . . When the occasion arises."

She stood aside.

He slowly entered.

# Twenty-two

Three contingents of state troopers and forty federal marshals arrived at the courthouse building at dawn, barricaded the street and sidewalks and secured the premises inside. By 6:30 A.M. media people were crammed into the narrow second-floor hall-way assigned to them. At 7 A.M. a bus with blacked-out windows entered the heavily guarded garage entrance in the rear of the building, drove down the ramp and deposited the federal grand jurors before a well-secured elevator door. The basement forces were beefed up and guns held poised when, half an hour later, siren-screaming police motorcycles convoyed a pair of cars down the ramp and up to the elevator. Strom, Cub and Jez got out of the first vehicle. Federal marshals emerged from the second, bringing with them Otto Pinkny.

The federal grand jury convened promptly at 8:30 A.M. A South Carolina police officer related how he had arrested Pinkny for running a red light. A police sergeant told of Pinkny being booked and remaining silent until being identified, then asking to talk with the FBI. A Bureau agent from South Carolina re-counted visiting Pinkny in jail and being told by the notorious killer of his participation in the Mormon State robbery. Head-quarters agent Matthew Ames told of taking Pinkny's longer confession. Strom related going to South Carolina and bringing Pinkny back with him. Jez and Cub testified as to how Pinkny voluntarily submitted to days of interrogation and how the FBI had checked on the specifics of what he told them and found most of it to be corroboratable.

Otto Pinkny went before the grand jury at approximately 9:15 A.M. . . . and for hours there would be no way of shutting him up.

\* \* \*

Brew had reckoned correctly. The eleventh-floor resident office was all but empty. The central files in the rear wing were unattended. He began his search for reports on Teddy Anglaterra and the people who had sworn Mule, Rat and Wiggles were in Emoryville, Illinois, the week of the robbery. It was no small task. Romor 91 now filled four thousand volumes, over 600,000 report pages . . . a record for any robbery investigation ever undertaken by the FBI. Nor was the material indexed as well as it might have been. He soon found himself up on the twelfth floor, which maintained its own files, copies of which were sent down to the central file on the floor below. Most of the agents here, like those of the eleventh floor, were at the grand jury inquiry.

The twelfth floor's cataloguing system was immaculate. Information was quickly located. Being in a hurry, he did what he had done on the eleventh floor and which was forbidden . . . removed a report from the file and took it with him.

Otto Pinkny was temporarily silenced and excused from the grand jury so that newly obtained evidence could be brought before the panel. An assistant FBI director was called and told the body that after secret and continuous investigation and testing by both the Bureau's Washington lab and engineers from several reputable electronics companies, an answer could now be given to one of the paramount questions regarding Romor 91: why the alarm at Mormon State National Bank had not sounded until thirty-two hours after the robbery had been perpetrated.

The assistant director went on to explain that the system operative in the bank at the time of the theft, a Thermex ultrasonic scanner, had two distinct alert capabilities. One was by ultrasonic radio to an industrial security service alarm room where Thermex leased space. The second was a direct-line cable to the communications room in police headquarters. The radio aspect was dominant. On the detection of premises penetration, the radio alerted the security service, provided specifics such as where in the bank the intrusion was and how many persons were in the premises. Should the security service not respond to the radio and confirm having received the message within thirty seconds, then the Thermex system automaticaly sent a coded message to police headquarters via the direct-line cable.

The technicians deduced that the radio-alert aspects of the system were disrupted by two power shortages at approximately 8 P.M. and 8:12 P.M. Friday, August 20. These drainages temporarily neutralized the radio transmission capabilities and also altered the wave length over which communications were to be sent. The neutralization was why no alert occurred when the base of the vault was bored into by a high-speed drill. Hours later the vault was exploded open and the radio aspect did begin emanating a message, but over the wrong channel at the wrong frequency. Instead of alerting the police via cable when no response was received from the security service in thirty seconds, the Thermex seemed to have waited fifteen to twenty minutes. By this time the cable to the police headquarters communications room had been washed away by the severe tunnel flooding. Most every cable of every security operation in the city was washed away or disrupted by that flooding. When the cable was finally restored early Sunday morning, August 22, the Thermex's coded message was received. The message was somewhat inaccurate, stating as it did that the armed robbery was still in progress.

Otto Pinkny was summoned back before the grand jury and asked the question that had previously been avoided: What, if anything, had the robbery gang done to the bank's alarm system?

"Lots was done," Otto Pinkny had been only too happy to testify. "What they did was follow the installation man home. The installation man from the Thermex company was putting in the alarms, and one of the Latinos followed him home and stole all the plans out of his truck. They made copies of the plans and put the originals back in the truck where they found them. See what I mean? The installation man never knew nothing was wrong. Otto Pinkny takes the copies to someone who knows something about it in Chicago. Otto Pinkny learns the Thermex has two ways of asking for help, radioing for it and phoning in. Radioing is what counts. So Otto Pinkny jams up the Thermex by cutting off the electricity to it. That's one of the reasons Otto Pinkny had that second generator turned on under Warbonnet Ridge when he did. It created a power shortage. Power shortages fuck up Thermexes."

"I'm looking for Mister Fred A. Anglaterra."

"Why?" The tall, scrawny young man standing at the porch doorway of the elm-shaded house in Sparta, Illinois, was hollow-cheeked and prematurely bald.

"My name's Martin Brewmeister, FBI." Brew's credentials flipped open and shut.

"That still don't answer what you want with Fred."

"I'd like to ask him some questions."

"About what?"

"You Fred?"

"Maybe."

"I want to know about your uncle, Teddy Anglaterra."

"Jesus Christ, can't you guys forget about him!"

"Then you are Fred."

"You knew that all the time. Whatcha want now?"

"Can we go inside?"

"No way."

"What about over there?" Brew indicated several neatly painted white wicker chairs down the porch.

"You wanna talk, we'll go out behind the house where no one can see. How much embarrassment you after causing a family anyway?" Fred led Brew into the backyard, sat opposite him at a wood-plank picnic table. "This gonna take long?"

"I just want to review a few points about your interview with the FBI."

"Which one?"

"There were more than one?"

"Whatcha pulling? I talked to you guys lotsa times, you know that."

Brew was well aware the index cards for the twelfth floor showed Fred Anglaterra having been talked to only once, September 4. "Let's begin with the interview of September fourth. It was conducted here at your home, if I'm not mistaken."

"They were all conducted here, all three of them. I still don't know which one September fourth was."

"The one where you were visited by special agent Vance Daughter."

"That's the last one. Daughter was here with Troxel."

"Two agents?" The filed report on the interview had only Daughter's name on it, did not mention another agent being present.

"All three times. Troxel was here all three times. Twice with some guy who didn't say a word and once with Daughter, who did the talking."

"In that last interview of September fourth, you were asked if you knew where Teddy Anglaterra was. Do you remember what you answered?"

"I don't even remember being asked that, let alone what I answered."

"Then you don't recall your answer?"

"I just told you that."

"When asked that question, you said you didn't know his whereabouts."

"If that's what I said, that's what I said."

"How could it be?"

"How could what be?"

"How could you answer that, say that you didn't know where he was, when your uncle Teddy was buried here in Sparta a few days earlier?"

"You saying I'm lying?"

"I'd just like to know why you gave that answer."

"I gave it 'cause I didn't know where the hell he was. If I'da known, I woulda said."

"You didn't know he was dead?"

"That's right."

"You didn't know he was buried right here in Sparta?"

"I told you, no! I didn't find out till a week later. Get it through your head, I don't give a shit for my uncle. He's been a disgrace to us all his life. I make a practice of *not knowing* about him. Living or dead, he's no difference to me."

"If he's no difference, why did you go to Prairie Port and claim his body on August twenty-seventh?"

"What are you talking about?"

"Did you or did you not go to Prairie Port on August twenty-seventh?"

"Prairie Port, Missouri?"

"On August twenty-seventh."

"Hell, no, not then or ever! I've not been over Prairie Port way in ten years. Mister, I think you got me confused with someone else."

". . . Tell me about your first two meetings with the FBI. With . . . who did you say the agents were?"

"Alex Troxel, that's what I wrote down," Fred said. "I never got the other one's name. Don't even remember if it was given. They came knocking on my door like you did. They told me that my uncle Teddy's got himself in some kind of trouble. I tell them Teddy is a no-nothing rummy drunk who's only brung disgrace to the family and whatever he's done ain't no business of me or mine. They say if that's the case, would I mind giving them approval to help Teddy out as best they can. I tell them, sure. They go away and when they come back a few days later they say they've taken care of Teddy's trouble and would I mind signing one or two forms for them, just to clear the legal loophole of what they did. They being the FBI, I didn't look at the papers too close. One said somethin' about Teddy's possessions, the other was giving permission to let Teddy travel somewhere. When I found out later Teddy died and had been brought back to Sparta and buried late at night with nobody knowing, I was satisfied. Only I kinda wished they could have buried him somewhere else."

"You think the FBI buried him?"

"Who the hell else knew where he was?"

"Did you learn how he had died?" Brew asked.

"Guess he was killed somehow."

"That doesn't surprise you?"

"That it didn't happen sooner is what's surprising. Teddy was always getting in terrible fights. Always supposedly going off to

401

find jobs someplace or other but really using it for an excuse to get drunk and knocked down a lot. He had a real nasty mouth when he got drunk, my uncle Teddy."

"Do you think it possible he went to look for work in Prairie Port and got into a fight and got killed?"

"Anything's possible, only Teddy never went downriver all that much. Never went into Missouri, neither, that much. East Saint Louis in Illinois is where he went mostly. Where he got into most of his trouble."

"Troxel and the other agent who came here never told you Teddy was dead, is that right?"

"That's right."

"And the two times they came to see you, Troxel did all the talking?"

"Like I said, I didn't even get the other guy's name. He stayed in the back just listening. And sweating. I remember it was hot as hell and this guy was wearing a heavy dark suit with stripes."

"On September fourth Troxel comes again, only this time he was with a special agent Daughter." Brew, of course, knew neither Troxel nor Daughter operated from Prairie Port . . . even so, Daughter's name was familiar to him. And he did know who the man in the dark suit with pinstripes was.

"That's right, Troxel came with Daughter," Fred said.

"And where Troxel did the talking the first two times you met with him, this third time only Daughter did the talking."

"That's right."

"What did he talk about?"

"He asked questions about Teddy."

"What sort of questions?"

"Where Teddy was. When I'd seen him last."

"Didn't this seem odd to you . . . I mean Troxel had said they were helping Teddy out. He and another agent had you sign certain documents?"

"What I really thought was that Teddy got arrested somewhere and this was all part of what had to be done."

"Then Daughter's questions did or did not seem odd to you?"

"Didn't seem."

"Did you tell Daughter that Teddy had gone to Prairie Port looking for a job?"

"No."

"Are you sure?"

"Yeah."

"Daughter seems to remember you saying that."

"He remembered wrong. Like I said, the only places I ever knew of Teddy looking for work was up near East Saint Louis so he could get drunk."

Alice Maywell Sunstrom examined her new coiffeur one last time in the salon's triptych mirror, carefully brought a silk Hermès scarf on up under it and around her shoulders. She couldn't decide whether to protect the hairdo with the picturesque scarf or not. She decided not and went out into the main arcade of the River Rise Shopping Mall. Alice eyed the recently opened chocolate shop next to Mormon State National Bank and thought of going in and buying Strom the champagne truffles he so liked. Once again she was undecided. The truffles would of course be bad for Strom's diet, but what with the dinner she was preparing, the *canard à l'orange*, Riesling wine and a dessert of rich Russian crème, what difference would it make? She opted to buy instead of the truffles a best-selling novel about demons called *The Exorcist*. Strom truly loved ghost and horror stories, if they were well written.

There was no particular occasion being celebrated that night by the Sunstroms. The meal was meant solely to be a diversion. Alice was concerned with Strom's disaffection over the Otto Pinkny grand jury inquiry. If indictments were handed up, as Strom was certain they would be, she knew he would be despondent. Alice hoped to surprise him with the meal. Force his mind off of this Otto Pinkny. Strom always said she was such a bad cook, and she was. But he was always delighted when she undertook what he called her "culinary adventures."

The Mall Book Shoppe had sold out *The Exorcist*. Alice bought Strom a copy of Gay Talese's *Honor Thy Father*, and for herself she got *Tracy and Hepburn* by Garson Kanin. She walked around

403

to the parking lot, got into her car and drove carefully to the lot exit. Once on the service road beyond, she felt something cold press at the base of her neck.

"That's a gun you feel, cunt sucker," a voice from the back seat told her. "Keep driving right onto the highway or I'll end it for you now."

Alice, in her horror, drove up the ramp and onto the elevated superhighway.

The gun nozzle moved around to the side of her neck and up across her jaw. "Open your mouth."

She did, and the nozzle was pushed in.

"Suck on it."

Again she obeyed, sucked on the cold metal. The person in back clambered over the seat and dropped in beside her. Glancing out the side of her eye, she saw it was Mule . . . the man she'd been terrified might find her . . . the man she'd seen kill Tall Groucho.

"Suck so you make noise," he ordered.

She did.

He ripped open her skirt, ripped away the panties beneath. "Don't stop driving. Don't slow down." He plunged his hand between her legs, spread them . . . pulled the gun from her mouth and jammed the nozzle up her vagina.

She cried out.

"We get off at Exit Twelve," he told her. He pulled a second gun from his jacket, prodded open her lips, made her take the nozzle in her mouth again. "I'm letting go of both, and if either one falls out of its hole, you're dead." He tore open her blouse and brassiere and began fondling her breasts . . . told her how he was going to rape and sodomize her. Mutilate and kill her if she put up any resistance. Mutilate and kill her just for the fun of it if it struck his fancy.

Tears streaming from her eyes, her teeth and vagina muscles straining to hold metal where it was, she drove off the ramp at Exit 12 and on along an ascending road and up the solitary lane of a vast estate . . . on up to a large, eave-roofed lodge by the side of a lake.

Mule took out the guns, dragged her from the car by the hair. Dragged her up several steps before hoisting her over his shoulder and carrying her on up through the front door and down a hallway and through a door and dumping her on the carpet and leaving.

Alice lay on the floor heaving hysterically. She realized, slowly, that she wasn't alone. Someone had been there all along. There behind her. She swiveled around. Stared up. J. Edgar Hoover sat in a straight-back chair near the window.

Edgar apologized for Mule's roughness with her but explained the matter at hand was urgent. Alice started to get off the floor. He told her to stay where she was. He chatted on idly for a bit, then wondered aloud what it would have been like if he had chosen to marry, concluded that perhaps his wife would have made him a greater man than he already was. "Just as you, Missus Sunstrom, shall have the chance of making your husband a greater man," he told Alice. "John Sunstrom is blessed, do you realize that? He carries with him the glory of the FBI. He is fated for great achievement, dear woman. The successful determination of Romor 91 will be his. Will be ours. His name shall be repeated wherever they speak of noble deeds and justice. Nothing must deny him this destiny. You above all must not deter him."

"I won't, dear God, I swear I won't."

Edgar closed his eyes. Leaned back in the straight-back chair. Interlaced his fingers over his slight paunch. "Tell me about your lesbians."

". . . My what?"

"Explain to me the sensation of embracing someone of your own sex."

"Director Hoover, I . . ."

"Come, wanton child, tell me. I know all, but I wish to hear it from you. How many times have you sodomized with someone of your own sex?"

"Only once . . ." She was hardly audible.

"Speak up."

"Once. Only once."

"Describe it."

"Please . . ." She broke into tears.

*"Describe."*

Slowly, miserably, Alice told about her times with Elaine Picket, at Hoover's quiet prodding related it in explicit detail. At his insistence, repeated certain interludes, time and time again. Once or twice, at his insistence, even attempted to demonstrate what had occurred. She became increasingly hysterical . . . nearer the breaking point . . . collapsed into uncontrollable sobbing.

When her crying had finally subsided, he asked if she felt closer to God.

She quickly assured him she did. He held out and lowered his hand, told her to take it. Asked her to swear that she would mend her ways.

She vowed that she would never again have sex with a woman.

"Sex? I speak not of sex. I speak of your subverting Romor 91. You must desist from ever again interfering with the investigation."

She told him she had never interfered.

"Good woman, did not you call the FBI office and disguise your voice and offer anonymous information regarding the perpetration of Mormon State?"

She explained that she only meant to help.

"You can most help by speaking nary a word of the evening you spent with Elaine Picket. I can assure, good woman, if you do not mention it to your husband, I never shall. Do I have your word on this?"

She nodded vigorously.

He leaned forward and shook her hand to seal the bargain, rose and announced he was placing her under the protective supervision of one of his assistants until the trial of Otto Pinkny was over. He called out. Mule entered the room and was introduced by Hoover as the man who would be supervising her.

Alice, in terror, insisted that Mule was one of the actual bank robbers . . . that she saw him kill a man.

Edgar's finger wagged, scolding at her. She was sadly mistaken. Mule, he proclaimed, was a trusted friend of the FBI and a man who had helped bring the true felon, Otto Pinkny, to justice. He warned Alice not to heed those powerful and venal friends of Pinkny, within and without the FBI, who had conspired to bear false witness against Mule Corkel and other good souls . . . revealed that these selfsame cohorts of Pinkny's were accusing Mule of other fiendish deeds such as murder . . . that, in any case, the FBI had no jurisdiction to investigate homicides.

"Heed Mister Corkel," he called out while departing the room. "For the sake of your soul, and your good husband's career."

Mule wasted no time in stripping Alice naked and hanging her upside down in a closet. He then took off his own clothes and got into the closet with her.

"Late Sunday afternoon, August twenty-second, you provided the Prairie Port Police Department with a list of names and addresses for one hundred and eighteen people who had visited these premises prior to the robbery, is that correct?" Brew had driven back from Sparta in less than an hour, was now seated in the conference room of the Mormon State National Bank.

"Yes, I provided such a list," the bank manager, Giles Julien, confirmed.

"Three days later, on Wednesday, August twenty-fifth, you presented a corrected list of names and addresses to the FBI. Is that correct?"

"It contained names, yes. Precisely how many, I can't recall."

"Ten, wasn't it? Seven names to be deleted from the master list you had compiled for the police, three names to be added?"

"That sounds right."

"And you sent this second list to the FBI?"

"Yes."

"But instead of sending the list to the Bureau's resident office on the eleventh floor, you had your assistant manager deliver it to the twelfth floor, ostensibly to Mister Corticun."

"Yes."

"Why? Why bypass the eleventh floor and send it to the twelfth?"

"Mister Chandler told me to do it that way."

"Mister Emile Chandler, president of Mormon State bank?"

"Yes."

"You helped put together this second list, didn't you?"

"Yes."

"Do you recall the name Teddy Anglaterra?"

"Yes."

"Who was he?"

"A man who was supposed to be at the bank at four o'clock and be interviewed for a job. A night watchman's job."

"Be at the bank four o'clock the afternoon of the robbery, August twentieth?"

"Yes."

"Did he show up?"

"Not for the appointment, no."

"So as far as you know he was never at the premises?"

"He was at the premises."

". . . When?"

"Sometime in the morning."

"How do you know?"

"Mister Chandler told me."

"How does Mister Chandler know?"

"He made the appointment for Teddy Anglaterra to see me at four."

"I thought an employment agency made Anglaterra's appointment."

"No. Anglaterra came from Mister Chandler."

"Did any member of the FBI ever ask you about Teddy Anglaterra before?"

"Yes, on August twenty-fifth, I believe. The day we sent the list to you. The list of changes."

Brewmeister had a copy of a Wednesday, August 25, interview with the bank manager. The name of the interviewing special agent was missing, which though a violation of procedure wasn't all that unusual with file-room duplications of reports. "A special agent asked you about Anglaterra?"

"Yes."

"What did you tell him?"

408

"That Anglaterra had come to the bank and seen Mister Chandler and that Mister Chandler made the appointment."

"You specifically told this agent that Anglaterra was on the bank premises?"

"Between nine and eleven A.M., yes."

"Was it usual for Mister Chandler to make interview appointments for job applicants?"

"No, but that last day was hectic," Julien said. "We expected to open after the weekend. What with the rush, with workmen and others around, we all tried to help out one another. We did tasks we ordinarily wouldn't have done, such as Mister Chandler making that appointment."

"Did anyone else on the premises, other than Mister Chandler, see Teddy Anglaterra?"

"I don't know."

"Can you recall the name of the agent who interviewed you on all of this, August twenty-fifth?"

"Troxel, Alexander Troxel."

"Could I speak to Mister Chandler?"

Julien flicked down the lever on the intercom, raised Chandler. "I'm in the conference room with Mister Brewmeister of the FBI, sir. He would like to talk to you about a Teddy Anglaterra. Can he—"

Emile Chandler, all six foot seven inches of him, strode in demanding of Brewmeister, "Who sent you here?"

"My office," Brew lied.

"Who at your office?"

"John Sunstrom."

"Everything I have to say on the Anglaterra matter I've said. If that doesn't satisfy Mister Sunstrom, he can speak with Mister Corticun."

"That won't be necessary," Brew assured him. "I can just check our file on what you said. Do you recall the name of the agent you said it to?"

"I do not."

"It was Alexander Troxel, sir," the manager said. "The same man who spoke to me,"

409

Brew asked, "Is that correct, Mister Chandler, was it Alexander Troxel?"

"I told you, I've nothing more to say."

"Mister Chandler, are you aware that agent Troxel is not a member of the Prairie Port FBI office, neither the regular office nor the auxiliary office?" Brew asked.

"You are trying my patience," Chandler told Brew.

"Did you 'help out' and make appointments for any other job applicants besides Teddy Anglaterra that day, Mister Chandler?"

"Good *day*, Mister Brewmeister."

Otto Pinkny finished testifying before the federal grand jury at 4:10 P.M. Twenty minutes later the panel voted to indict him as a co-conspirator in the robbery of the Mormon State National Bank. When Billy Yates arrived at the eleventh-floor resident office shortly after five, he was hardly noticed in the bittersweet atmosphere that prevailed. Most of the agents were elated over the indictment. Strom was not. Cub, of all people, seemed to have reservations. Jez was curiously dour.

Someone shouted out there was a call for Yates. Billy walked to the desk he shared with Brew, picked up the phone.

"Yates speaking."

"Keep a poker face, Billy." Brew spoke urgently. "Who's up there? Cub? Jez? Strom?"

"All three."

"Who else?"

"The whole office. Pinkny's been indicted."

"It's got to be one of them! Steer clear of Cub and Jez and Strom. Maybe even de Camp. They're connected to it. I know they are."

"Connected to what?"

"I've found them, Billy." Brew was exultant. "I *found* them. Your Silent Men . . . you were right, they do exist. At least six of them. Probably a seventh. They were sitting right in front of us all the time. Where's your car?"

"In the parking lot."

"Across from the office?"

410

"Yes."

"The keys in it?"

"Under the visor."

"I'm calling from downstairs. From the pay phone in the lobby. I may have been followed. I'll take your car. Try to get hold of another one somewhere without anyone knowing. Get to my friend Jake Hagland over at the phone company. He'll help you put a tap at Mule's place. That pay phone Mule uses up the road. That's got to be the connection between the Silent Men and Cub or Jez or Strom or maybe de Camp. Whoever's helping Mule is helping the Men. I'll explain later. And oh yeah, another surprise —Chandler, the bank president, had Teddy Anglaterra at Mormon State the morning of the robbery, or so he says. I'll fill you in on that too. I've got to get a move on."

"Where you going?"

"Emoryville . . . to put the last nail in the coffin."

Yates hung up, strolled to the window. Brew could be seen ten floors below hurrying across the street and into the parking lot. Billy watched him looking for the car. Finally Brew found it. He started to get in and as he did was machine-gunned to death by a passing van.

# Twenty-three

Martin Brewmeister's funeral was the largest ever held in Prairie Port. Corticun saw to that over the objections of Brew's widow, Elsie. Eight hundred people crammed into the First Lutheran Church, where Martin had been baptized. The press was officially barred from attending the service, but folding chairs were set up in the parking lot for them and amplifiers provided so the overflow throng of media folk could hear what was being said inside. The governor spoke, as did Brew's wife's uncle, who was attorney general for the State of Illinois. Strom made a fine tribute on behalf of the office. A. R. Roland was there to add a few words of his own. Clyde Tolson read a brief message from J. Edgar Hoover. Corticun read telegrams from other dignitaries, most of whom did not know Brew. The president of the local spelunking club provided the most touching moment by reading remarks ten-year-old Brew had written into his journal during his first weekend of formal cave exploration with the group. A U.S. senator from Missouri gave the most muddled speech. Yates and Jez were the only nonrelatives among the pallbearers.

A cortege of cars made its way up to the hilltop cemetery and the Brewmeister family plot. Military color guards were present even though Brew never been in the service. So were Marine Corps riflemen. Brew's lifelong minister was the only one to talk at graveside.

Standing beneath a tree limb on a nearby rise and staring down on the rites like some avenging deity was Ed Grafton. Cub was the first to spot him and elbowed Jez. Soon the other resident agents were aware of Graf's presence. So was Corticun, who nervously kept glancing over at the imposing figure.

412

Taps were blown and rifle salvos fired and the casket lowered into its pit. Tears were wept. Bodyguards moved in around Yates, who was perturbed by their presence. Grafton was gone from the hill. All in all, it had been a great show for Corticun.

Corticun, from the moment Brewmeister was gunned down in the parking lot, had worked quickly and diplomatically. He kept the press at bay while negotiating with the chief of police, Frank Santi. One of the few circumstances under which the FBI was allowed to investigate a homicide was when the victim was one of its own agents. Even so, Corticun felt it better to work in unison with Santi and the Prairie Port PD. Santi in turn arranged for the inquest to be held after the funeral, agreed to let Strom alone talk to Brew's fellow agents. In the one press conference Corticun held regarding the death, he acknowledged that Brew had been gunned down by unknown assailants, publicly stated his fears that the execution had more to do with the current trend of antiestablishment acts of terror than with the Mormon State robbery. Off the record he let it be known he didn't disagree with pervasive rumors of Otto Pinkny's underworld associates having gunned down Brew as a warning not to proceed with the trial. Corticun had convinced Strom that since Yates was Brew's partner these last few months, a possibility existed the unknown killer or killers might come after Yates as well. Which was why Yates was given bodyguards. Yates found this reasoning to be ridiculous. He was sure that Brew had been killed by the Silent Men. He also didn't rule out that the Silent Men had made a mistake . . . that he, Yates, was their intended target. But he couldn't tell this to anyone. Not even Tina Beth. Especially not Tina Beth. He tried to get her to go and spend time with her father and mother on the pretext of having to work day and night on Brew's murder. She would not hear of it, and in fact became overattentive. Overly inquisitive. Much of what Yates had to do now, he had to do alone . . . and he wasn't being left alone.

"Billy, this is Captain Frank Santi." Strom made the introduction in the library of his grand house, where FBI families and friends were gathering after the funeral for their own commemorative dinner. With Santi and Strom and Yates in the room was

413

Corticun. "Captain Santi will be helping us out with the homicide. I just wanted to go over a few points on the report you made out. You said that Brew called you from downstairs just before he was murdered, is that right?"

"Yes, from the phone booth in the lobby."

"Why didn't he come upstairs to talk to you?"

"He said he was in a hurry. I had that in the report."

"I know you did, Billy. And we're trying to get the whole matter in perspective for ourselves. Was it usual for Brew to use your car?"

"He was lazy about putting gas in his car." Billy was stating a partial truth. "Sometimes when he didn't want to bother gassing up his own car he'd use mine . . . whether he was in a hurry or not."

"In the phone conversation, did he say where he was going?"

"No, I told you he didn't."

"Do you have any idea where he was going?"

"No, sir, I don't."

"Do you have any idea if it was Romor 91 business?"

"Everything we did was Romor 91," Yates said.

"And after the call you went to the window to watch Brew?"

"Yes."

"For any particular reason?"

"To see if he found my car."

"But you said he had used your car before."

"He had, but there's five hundred cars in that parking lot and most of ours look the same."

"Can you describe for us what happened in the lot?"

"I didn't tell Brew where my car was parked, but he knows I usually leave it in the same place, over near the west exit. He walked in that direction and found it. He opened the door, and the van came by and opened fire."

". . . You saw him walking into the lot."

"And right on across it to my car. My car was parked on the opposite side from where he entered the lot."

"While he was walking across the lot, were you able to see much of him? See his entire body or only part of him?"

"Most of the time I could see all of him."

"Was he carrying anything, Billy?"

Yates reflected. "Not that I noticed."

"No briefcase? No papers?"

"No."

"Is it possible, when part of his body was obscured from your view, that he could have been carrying something and that he put it in another car before getting to your car?"

"I saw him cross the street before he went into the parking lot. He didn't have anything with him."

"I don't know if you're aware of this or not, Billy, but files are missing from the office. We think maybe there's a connection with that and Brew's murder."

"No, I didn't know."

Strom looked at Frank Santi. "Chief, do you have any questions?"

"Mister Yates, first I want to tell you the police will do everything we can on this. I understand you were particularly close to Mister Brewmeister, and we won't let you down."

Yates thanked him.

"You said in your report that you saw a door panel slide open in the truck and a submachine gun stick out and fire, is that right?"

"That's reverse order," Billy replied. "I saw Brew open the door of my car. He was slightly bent over from leaning down for the handle. The next thing I know he'd spun around and was standing straight up with his back against the car and his hands semi-outstretched. It took me a moment to realize he was being hit by bullets. That's when I looked over and saw the panel truck . . . saw that a machine gun was poking out through a missing panel in the truck and firing."

"You said the gun looked like a De Lisle silent carbine?"

"I don't know foreign-made weapons all that well. But from the illustrations we have in the office, the gun being fired at Brew looked like a De Lisle silent carbine."

"That's a pretty esoteric kind of weapon to make a hit with,

415

wouldn't you think? Sort of a collector's item? Last time I heard of the British Army using the De Lisle was in 1960."

"I don't know much about the British Army."

"They told me you're the man around here who knows everything."

"Up to a point," Billy said.

"Mister Yates, after the panel truck quit firing at Brewmeister, what happened?"

"Brew slid down the side of my car. Slid from view. The panel truck drove out the exit and on up the ramp to the superhighway."

"How close was your car parked to that exit?"

"Four or five cars away."

"Do you think the panel truck was waiting for you instead of Brewmeister?"

Yates shrugged.

"I mean, if Mister Brewmeister called and asked to use your car on the spur of the moment, how could the panel truck know where he was going? If the panel truck had been following him for some time and, let's say, followed him to the office building and waited for him to come out and saw him walk across the street into the parking lot, the truck could have entered the lot right there opposite the building. The truck could have shot him down anywhere along the way, instead of waiting until he was on the opposite side of the area and only five cars away from an exit. It seems more plausible that the truck was already parked inside the lot and was staking out your car . . . was waiting for someone to go to your car so they could shoot them down. Mister Yates, is there any reason you know of why someone would want to kill you?"

"No."

Frank Santi told Strom and Corticun, "I have no more questions."

"Could we have a few minutes alone with Yates?" asked Strom.

Santi complied, left the room to join the other guests.

"Billy, where were you just before Brew was killed?"

"Visiting a friend."

416

"A sick friend?"

"Not feeling too well," Yates said.

Corticun spoke for the first time. "What friend? Where?"

"You don't have to tell us if you don't want to, Billy," Strom said.

"Of course he has to tell us," Corticun insisted. "He was away without permission, he said so in his report. He'll tell us—"

"Only if he wants to." Strom was firm. "Well, Billy, what about it?"

"I drove east to see what sort of shape a friend of mine was in. He was okay, but I'd rather not say who it was."

"So be it," Strom said. "Billy, were you and Brew up to anything that needed files?"

"I didn't need files. I can't speak for Brew."

"But Brew and you still believed Mule and his crowd, not Otto Pinkny, were responsible for Mormon State?"

"Yes."

"Is it possible, without your knowing it, Brew might have taken some files to check on something?"

"If he did, I didn't know about it."

"All right, is it possible Brew took files for another reason?"

"Such as?"

"Possibly to give to someone?"

"Why?"

"For money?"

"Brew sell out? Come *on.*"

"Maybe to leak to the press," Corticun suggested. "To try to discredit Otto Pinkny."

"I've thought of doing that, but I doubt if Brew would," Yates told them.

"Billy," Strom began, "we haven't told you this before, but someone raided the twelfth-floor files. Hundreds of pages are missing. Brew was seen at those files not long before you received that call from him. I ask you again, do you have any idea what he was up to? Where he was going?"

"He didn't tell me."

"Is there anything you have to say?"

417

"There is something, but it's not what you want to hear."

"Speak up."

"I feel foolish having bodyguards. I don't need them."

Strom looked at Corticun, who frowned. "As you wish, Billy, no bodyguards. Thank you for your time."

Yates left. Chief Frank Santi came back in. Corticun went to the door and ushered in Jessup.

"I think you know Chief Santi, Jez," Strom said. "The chief is helping us with Brew's murder. We'd like to go over your statement, informally of course."

Jake Hagland was the senior supervising engineer at the telephone company. A native Prairie Portian, he had gone to high school with Brewmeister and remained a close friend. In the past Hagland had usually resisted Brew's rare requests for illegal telephone taps. On the one or two occasions he had complied, it was with the greatest reluctance. After listening to Billy Yates tell him Brew's final words, Hagland wasted little time in driving to the outdoor phone booth near Mule's ranch in a company truck. The eavesdropping system he installed was ingenious. Not only would tape recorders pick up everything said and heard in the booth, and a slowdown counter indicate just what numbers were being dialed by Mule, but Hagland also rigged it so the tap could be monitored at both his home and Yates's.

Yates's prime concern was the whereabouts of the missing files. Determining this meant tracing Brew's movements the last day of his life. Some things pointed to what these were . . . Yates knew from his long-distance phone call to Brew immediately after leaving Barrett Amory's home in Virginia that Brew was planning to check the files the next morning, when most of the agents would be away at the grand jury hearing. He was aware from the same call that after that Brew planned to go to Sparta, Illinois, and check on the interview Teddy Anglaterra's nephew Fred had given an FBI agent in September.

Yates, as a result of the phone call Brew made to him just before he was shot to death, knew that Brew believed he'd discovered the existence of the Silent Men, had stated, "You were

418

right, they do exist. At least six of them. Probably a seventh. They were sitting right in front of us all the time . . ." The very last thing Brew had said in that conversation, the very last words Brew ever spoke, for that matter, was that he was going to "Emoryville . . . to put the last nail in the coffin." Clearly, Yates decided, Brew had discovered something regarding the Silent Men in the files.

Brew, of course, never did make it to Emoryville, but Yates knew Emoryville was where eleven people had provided alibis for Mule, Rat Ragotsy and Wiggles Loftus. Billy had no doubt that Brew was certain he could discredit those witnesses. Billy was equally sure Brew had raided the files to some degree the morning of his death and then gone to see Fred Anglaterra. This was confirmed by Yates's phone call to Sparta, Illinois. A surly Fred Anglaterra said that yes, Brew had been to see him that day. That yes, he seemed to have some sort of file folder with him, or at least he knew pretty well everything Fred had told another FBI agent. Fred Anglaterra recalled that Brew had arrived at his home at about ten forty-five and had left within half an hour. Since the drive from Prairie Port to Sparta took just under forty minutes, Yates concluded that Brew had left Prairie Port to talk to Anglaterra at approximately 10 A.M. and was back in the city at least by noon. But Brew hadn't called him until shortly after 5 P.M.

Where Brew had been between noon and five gnawed at Billy, generated an endless series of scenarios. He doubted that Brew had yet discovered the existence and number of the Silent Men immediately on his return from Sparta. If he had he wouldn't have waited until five o'clock to drive to Emoryville "to put the last nail in the coffin." Other steps must have occurred . . . possibly another interview or recheck. Maybe several. And something must have been discovered at these that made Brew hurry back to the office and loot the file . . . loot it just before he phoned Billy from the lobby . . . just before he was gunned down. Strom had said that immediately before his death Brew had been seen at the twelfth-floor files. Most probably, Yates decided, Brew had visited the files twice . . . early in the morning to take out the few

419

pages relating to the interview with Teddy Anglaterra's nephew . . . then later, after a discovery he made in rechecks or interviews.

There were two questions for Yates. First, what sort of linkage had Brew established that would make him go back to the files and remove, as Strom had said, "hundreds of pages"? Second, what became of those hundreds of pages? Where could Brew have put them in the short period between being seen leaving the twelfth-floor file room and appearing on the street in front of the parking lot carrying nothing?

He was certain Strom and Corticun had searched the twelfth- and eleventh-floor offices and found nothing. Searched the lobby and whole building and Brew's car as well. Yates tried to think it out but couldn't.

Alice drove through the wide metal gate and up the dirt road. It was the third time in as many days she had returned to the site of her rape and degradation. She had no real choice. Obligation and terror had overcome her reason and pain. She had sworn to Edgar to do as he ordered. Edgar had sworn he'd protect Strom. She forgot from what.

Alice parked and entered the lodge without knocking. "You must let me go home earlier today." She was already weeping. "My husband may start asking why I'm getting home so late. He'll find out if—"

Mule slapped her.

She stifled a cry and began undressing.

Chiming persisted. Tina Beth Yates, with choice southern epithets, wrapped her wet hair in a towel, threw on a terry-cloth robe and bounded downstairs, shouting out to hold on, she was coming. Still shouting, she pulled open the door.

J. Edgar Hoover, standing in the bright morning sunshine, removed his hat and introduced himself and asked if he might come in for tea. No car could be seen in the driveway or street beyond. No aides or other persons visible.

"Tea?" Tina Beth numbly repeated.

420

"If not tea, good woman, then coffee or beer or nothing at all except fine company and crisp conversation. I am told you are crisply conversational?"

"Me?"

"Might I come in?"

Tina Beth led him into the living room, excused herself, dashed upstairs and changed into a pair of shorts and a halter, rushed down into the kitchen, searched for tea or coffee or beer, darted back to J. Edgar holding up a bottle and asking, "Apricot juice?"

"Of course," he told her.

Back in the kitchen, she found a glass. Back in the living room, she handed it to him. He sipped, smacked his lips, sipped more, sat back contentedly and folded his hands over his stomach. "The best book of the Good Book is the old book," he told her, then with his eyes flickering he began reciting passages from the Old Testament. He seemed particularly partial to Shadrach, Meshach and Abednego and Joshua at the Wall. From there he went into infertility and parenthood. He stood, requesting she repeat not a word of their tête-à-tête to a soul, including Billy. At the door he took her hand and said he would cherish having had a daughter as well as a son, and if she could only convince her husband to renounce his Judaic faith, how happy all three of them could be.

"He said *what?*" Billy Yates asked her.

"That if you gave up being Jewish, how happy the three of us could be," Tina Beth told him with a straight face.

"By 'the three,' you think he meant you, me and him?"

"No doubt about it."

"Holy shit."

"Don't swear, Billy Bee."

"After he said that what did he do?"

"He tossed a hand to the wind and walked over our front yard and down the sidewalk, jauntylike."

"No car was waiting?"

"No."

"That's all of it, everything that happened?"

Tina Beth crossed her heart.

"You must have been scared to death, hon!"

She shook her head. "I sort of liked him."

"He's mad as a screaming banshee."

She smiled. "But with a twinkle."

A week and two days after the phone-booth tap was installed, Mule's voice was heard for the first time. It was preceded by the sound of coins being deposited and a number being dialed. The answering voice said, "Ya?" Mule said, "It's on," and hung up. More coins clinked and another number was dialed. "Hi," a second voice said. "It's on," Mule repeated. Another number was dialed, but no one picked up at the other end. The phone, a moment later, rang and was answered by Mule, who said, "It's on." Whoever was on the other end hung up.

Yates was at home and listening when this exchange of calls came in. It was just after sunset. He got into his car and drove to the old waterworks complex at Lookout Bluff, descended into the underground shunting terminal Brew had introduced him to, walked along a catwalk in the dark and curving irrigation tunnel to the vantage point he had occupied with Brew. Mule appeared where he had been seen before, then Wiggles and Ragotsy. They lowered a rubber motor boat into the water and got in and sped off.

The next afternoon Yates brought his own rubber boat down to the shunting terminal and began exploring the tunnel Mule, Rat and Wiggles had gone into . . . soon found himself in a series of flooded caves and grottos.

Two evenings later Billy overheard the same exchange of calls between Mule in the outdoor phone booth and the three other persons. This time when Mule, Rat and Ragotsy started off through the flooded underground passageway, Yates was waiting for them uptunnel, watching from a shadowy alcove to see which cave they motored into. A moment later he heard another motor approaching, saw the silhouette of a second boat with only one passenger head into the same cave.

422

That same night Yates rendezvoused with Hagland, who said the first two numbers Mule dialed from the outside booth near his ranch were the home phones for Ragotsy and Wiggles, respectively. The third number called, the one on which no one answered, was a pay station in the bar around the corner from the FBI's Prairie Port office. By the following afternoon Hagland had the bar phone tapped as well.

At the office Yates was assigned to the small team of special agents aiding Assistant U.S. Attorney Jules Shapiro in preparing his prosecution of Otto Pinkny. This sharply reduced the time he could spend covering Mule and the taps as well as exploring the tunnels and caves under the western side of Prairie Port. He turned to the only ally he could trust, Tina Beth.

The outdoor pay phone near Mule's ranch rang. Mule picked up and said, "We got something hot."

"How hot?" asked a raspy voice.

"It's maybe a money sack."

"Maybe or is?"

"It maybe could be."

"Not hot enough to come out for," the raspy voice said, and hung up.

. . . Wiretap apparatus do not always make allowances for the passage of time. When they do not, one voice-activated recording follows another one on the tape even though the two calls might have been placed hours apart. Hagland's rig established the time at which each call was received or made. Because of this, Yates and Hagland and Tina Beth, who was monitoring the machinery at their home, knew that Mule had not dialed out from the phone booth near his ranch immediately prior to receiving the incoming call. No outgoing call had been recorded at that booth in over ninety minutes. The only deduction to be made from this was that the call was prearranged . . . that previous contact had been made between Mule and the unknown speaker in which it was agreed for Mule to go to the outdoor booth at a specific time and wait for the phone to ring. This further reinforced Yates's belief

423

that the fourth man seen in the tunnel and cave, the one who motored in to rendezvous with Mule, Wiggles and Rat, had his own lines of communication with the gang.

Hagland tapped into the phone lines leading to Mule's ranch, hoping this was the originating point for the prior communication. No positive results were garnered. Yates, knowing that early evening was the preferred contact time for sojourns into the tunnel, began sneaking an hour or so off from his office assignments so he could tail Mule in the late afternoons. By week's end he spotted Mule entering a pay phone near the bus terminal. Hagland wasted no time in putting on a bug. It was a busy phone. Fifty separate dialings and conversations were recorded in the next four hours alone. The hour after that began with a number being dialed and someone picking up.

"You gotta come and take another look," Mule's voice told the silent listener.

"Not now." The voice was raspy and muffled. "You take a vacation too."

"Huh?"

"Lay off. Stop going down there."

"You fuckin' crazy? We're goddam close. Any time could be the time."

"You've been saying that from the beginning."

"Now it's true. We're almost there. I can smell it."

"People are catching on. Stay away."

"No one tells me what the fuck to do—"

"I am. It's your ass if you don't listen. You stay away from there. I'll tell you when it's right to go back."

"Tell me how?"

"Call you at home and ask for Howard. You say to me I got the wrong number." The phone hung up.

The driver of a semi-truck saw her first, slowed in midhighway, waved for the vehicles behind him to stop, got out and pointed. Soon traffic had stopped in all ten lanes, the five southbound as well as the northbound lanes. All eyes looked skyward to the solitary steel trestle spanning the expressway twenty-five feet overhead. Alice Sunstrom, her dress in tatters and a coil of bright yellow nylon rope over one shoulder, crawled along the beam on all fours. Crawled shakily. Finally reached the center. Lay prone. Tied one end of the rope to the beam. Noosed the other around her neck. Rolled off the trestle and hanged herself.

# Twenty-four

Two small scars marred the striking face of John Lars Chalmers Sunstrom III, a small shrapnel wound at the corner of his left eye gotten during the Korean campaign and a dimplelike indentation along the lower right cheek resulting from a childhood confrontation with a horse's hoof. These were appropriate. Strom was to the valiant born. And equestrian. Virginia valiant and equestrian. Sunstrom's forebears were into the fray long before the Civil War . . . and long after. Save for one great-great-great-grand-uncle who was a career officer, all were volunteers. Chalmers men shed their blood at Horseshoe Bend and New Orleans and Wilson's Creek and Shiloh and Fair Oaks and Bull Run and Antietam, which family members always referred to as Sharpsburg. The Sunstroms, descended from a former Swedish diplomat who retired to Charlottesville, Virginia, in 1905, joined the Chalmers men in enlisting for World War I and World War II, with them were tabulated among the wounded or dead or missing at Château-Thierry and Belleau Wood and Omaha Beach and Anzio and Malmédy and Remagen. All but two of these citizen soldiers had been cavalrymen; in the case of World War II, mechanized cavalry. The pair of nonconformists came from both sides of the aisle. John's great-uncle, Edwin Chalmers, had been an aerial artillery spotter for the Allied Expeditionary Forces and was shot down and killed over the Hindenberg Line by a Bosch fighter pilot named Hermann Goering. John's paternal grandfather, Lars Sunstrom, an Anglican minister, was the personal padre to General "Black Jack" Pershing.

John Sunstrom, at the age of twenty-four, dropped out of the University of Virginia Law School to become a tank commander

426

in the Korean War. He was wounded three times, received a medical discharge and returned to law school with a slight numbness in his right arm and leg. Subsequent to graduation and passing the bar, he divided his time between breeding and training horses on the family's twelve-thousand-acre stud farm and working as a special counsel in the office of his cousin, Tad Chalmers, who was assistant prosecuting attorney for the State of North Carolina. The following year, 1955, twenty-nine-year-old John Lars Chalmers Sunstrom III took for his bride eighteen-year-old Priscilla Maywell. He had met Priscilla five months earlier. He had known of her much longer. Most of his post-pubescent life, in fact. She was a daughter of the Fairy Princess.

Priscilla's mother, Hope, had been a parishioner of John's paternal grandfather, Anglican minister Lars Sunstrom. The accidental death of Hope's husband left the young widow penniless, forced her and her two tiny daughters, four-year-old Priscilla and an infant sister, Alice, to leave Virginia and go to a brother's farm in Oklahoma. Reverend Lars financed the move, made sure for many years to come that the fatherless family had money enough for an adequate style of life. Hope Maywell did well running her brother's farm, eventually bought a place of her own, and prospered enormously. Bought larger places. Prospered all the more. She moved to a big house and sent her daughters to fine schools and never remarried and not only repaid every cent Reverend Lars had sent her over the years but donated the money for construction of a new chapel he had always fancied. The singular stipulation Hope attached to her gift was a wall plaque reading: "This is to attest that fairy tales come true." Reverend Lars sputtered over the allusion to "fairy tales" being posted in the house of Anglican worship. Hope was unbending, threatened to add to the inscription that he, Lars Sunstrom, not Jesus Christ on high, was the savior who elicited the miracle of her survival and success. Sputtering, Lars submitted. The chapel was built and the plaque was affixed. Hope became known, among the Sunstroms, as the Fairy Princess.

John Sunstrom, when he married Hope's elder daughter, Priscilla, called her his "fairy-tale bride," had linen and stationery inscribed PMS/FTB. And for two years they led an enchanted life. Loved one another as few newlyweds have ever loved.

Priscilla's first pregnancy miscarried. Her second pregnancy killed her. Alone with her in the Fairy Chapel, John considered getting into the coffin beside her and taking his own life, and well might have if Hope hadn't walked in on him. Staring at his tear-drenched face, Hope knew what he was contemplating and went to Priscilla and kissed her good-by and closed the coffin lid on that gentle child she had so dearly loved and motioned to John, whom she also loved, that it was best they go. He took, in silence, her out-held hand. In silence they walked from the chapel, and he knew Hope had saved his life and meant to thank her for this later. He didn't have time. Four months later Hope was dead of leukemia.

John's grief was now laid aside in his attempts to assist Priscilla's sixteen-year-old sister, Alice. Whereas Priscilla had been a pretty woman, Alice was already a full-blown beauty. And a fragile one. The double deaths of her mother and only sister sent Alice first into convulsive tremors, then into a near catatonic depression. John would not hear of her going to a hospital. He gave up his work, spent night and day with Alice. Nursed her back to life. Back to health and sanity. Back even, occasionally, to fun. She told him she loved him, and John was pleased to hear her say so but did not construe this to be a romantic love, merely a grateful one. Alice helped John partially shed his own impacted sorrows. Got him to go to movies and take trips and laugh a little again. Urged him to go back into horse-breeding and law. He confided in her he needed a change, that the law and the horse farm were too ghost pent. She coaxed him into admitting that among the new professions he'd really like to try, criminal investigation ranked near the top. Alice suggested he look into the FBI, not really knowing what the FBI entailed. The matter was passed over.

Alice and John became inseparable. Sustained one another in every conceivable way except sexually, John rejecting all notions

428

of their becoming intimate. Alice did little else but entertain such notions. On her eighteenth birthday the usually reticent Alice thanked John for the array of presents he had gotten her, then said what she wanted most, on this her majority, was to sleep with him. John, who feared such a confrontation was possible, and therefore had prepared, responded he was flattered she considered him in such terms but at the risk of sounding an old-fashioned fuddy-duddy, must decline the offer on the grounds that her virginity should be offered to her future husband only. Alice said this was the whole point . . . that she wanted, more than life itself, to marry John. That he was her life. Her salvation. Her friend and confidant. Her brother and father and child. All things and everything except two things . . . her lover and her husband. She begged him to become both. She told him she needed him. Wanted him. Must have him. Was nothing without him.

John was forthright, said he had not expected her proposal and therefore would have to think aloud in answering. He said the prospect of wedding her was appealing and that he deeply loved her, but that this love had not yet evolved into a romantic love that was necessary in a long and fulfilling marriage. He said the ghost of Priscilla was too much with him to allow for this at the time. He told Alice that if there was any chance of his love for her becoming a romantic love, as he very much hoped it would, he must somehow come to grips with the ghost, not to exorcise it but to put it into perspective. He told Alice that when he finally went to bed with her, he would like to know it was Alice he was making love to, not Priscilla.

John suggested that Alice and he put time and distance between themselves and the past. Get away from Virginia and one another for a while. Alice, after all, was to begin that fall at Beloit College in Wisconsin. Education, he told her, was important. She told him she would do what he wanted and that she would never stop loving or wanting or needing him.

John Lars Sunstrom joined the FBI, eventually dispelled the ghost of Priscilla, and married Alice. With her, he rose in Bureau prestige and then fell into disgrace and suffered exile. Without

429

her, he would have quit the FBI. Never for a minute did she stop loving him. Or he her. Their sexual love rivaled the emotional . . . until they reached Prairie Port.

Half a year after taking charge of the administrative operations for Ed Grafton, Strom stopped sleeping with Alice. Why the desire to do so left him, he didn't really know. And found it difficult to discuss. As did Alice. After a protracted period of abstinence, Alice told Strom she feared the ghost of her older sister and Strom's first wife, Priscilla, had reappeared to claim him. Strom said such a notion was poppycock, assured Alice he loved her as deeply as ever, offered no explanation for why this love was not manifesting itself in intercourse and told Alice whatever the matter was with him, it would pass. It did not pass. Alice held an exorcism at their rented home in the fashionable western hills overlooking Prairie Port. An exorcism of Priscilla. Appalled by the rite and worried about Alice's mental state, Strom, who mistrusted psychiatrists and psychologists and behaviorists, went with Alice to a marriage counselor, and in the counselor's presence was mute as to why he no longer would have sex with Alice . . . no longer could have. Alice told Strom that when he wished, she would go away. He said he never wanted her to go away. He reavowed his love for her. He swore that the trouble would work itself out. She told him the trouble was still Priscilla and never mentioned the subject again. Never brought up the abstinence. But he heard her masturbating in secret at night and, after, quietly sobbing. He knew she was reading books on how to be more attractive, more sexually alluring and provocative. Could not help noticing her more trendy makeup and hairstyling . . . her taking decorating and gardening courses at the university and trying to stay active every waking moment. This saddened him, but some inner force kept him from seeking out the root of his problem. He liquidated most of his holdings and purchased the stately old hill house he and Alice had always admired so that Alice could busy herself decorating it. Then he lost himself in the anonymity of office administration, in the selflessness of being Ed Grafton's second-in-command. He remained as passive as a minister, but not blind. He knew Alice was anguishing under the

430

rejection he had inflicted on her, winced in the dark each night listening to her muffled and ever more painful crying. Finally he told Alice what he never thought himself capable of saying, that perhaps she should take herself a man and have an affair. She was horrified by the suggestion, weepingly said that such an act would be a betrayal of her love for Strom . . . of everything they had been to one another. She said, in her pain, that she would prefer death to infidelity, but that if this was truly what Strom wanted her to do, she would do it. Strom said no, it wasn't what he wanted and expunged his suggestion from memory.

Alice ordered the painters out of the top floor of their newly purchased but still undecorated house. She herself brought in new enamel, took up a brush and painted every bedroom on the floor a jarringly bright cobalt blue. Then she cut off all her hair and went into a catatonic depression. Sat in a straight-back wood chair facing a cobalt–blue wall in the barren master bedroom. Sat that way every waking moment. Curled up and slept on the floor when it was time to sleep. Arose and sat and faced the wall again. Curled up and slept. Arose. Sat. Faced. Heard not a word Strom said to her. Was oblivious to his hand in front of her. Their doctor had offered no solution other than to send her to a psychiatric hospital. Strom, who had stayed in the room with Alice day and night, could not bear the thought of committing her to any sort of mental home . . . balked even at calling in a psychiatrist until the fourth morning. Just before the psychiatrist was to arrive, the catatonia disappeared as suddenly as it had struck. Alice got up from the floor perfectly well, cheerfully announced that she was sorry to have been away so long but she had been visiting with the ghost of Priscilla and there was much to discuss. That Priscilla was indeed upset with Alice having sex with Strom and had put a curse on Strom to keep him from making love to Alice, but that Priscilla didn't think it was a good idea for Alice to be unfaithful to Strom with another man. Then Alice went happily off to re-paint all the cobalt-blue bedrooms an eggshell white, and Strom, for the second time in his adult life, wept. A month later Alice, who now had no memory of having been with the ghost of Priscilla, was declared clinically normal. Strom noted with relief that

431

her nocturnal masturbation had all but ceased . . . that on the rare occasions she did self-manipulate, at least no crying followed.

On Tuesday, August 24, 1971, as J. Edgar Hoover was telling a Washington press conference about the robbery at Mormon State National Bank, Alice was twenty-eight and as spectacularly beautiful as ever. She was also in the third month of a lesbian affair with Elaine Picket. John "Strom" Sunstrom, who was forty-six and visibly weary of the administrative functions taken on so reluctantly two and a half years earlier, longed for a command position and action . . . saw atop a hillock the white horse rear up riderless.

That same afternoon the white horse was his. J. Edgar Hoover dismissed Ed Grafton and put Strom in charge of the office and Romor 91. That night he made love to Alice. And every night thereafter. It was like the very old days for both of them. The recent past was ignored. Alice had been as happy as Strom had ever seen her. Which was why he had such difficulty accepting her suicide, nearly fell apart. Which was why the other men of the office refused to let him see the actual autopsy report . . . why Cub and Jez and Corticun and Yates had conspired with the medical examiner to present Strom a highly edited report in which nothing was revealed other than the cause of death: suffocation due to strangulation.

What the unabridged forensic findings revealed was that she had been sexually abused in the most horrendous fashion in the days prior to her demise, abused by a male, since sperm was found in anal and vaginal tracts as well as her stomach.

The burial, like the preceding funeral service, was free of the media. Strom stood stoically at the graveside between Cub and Madden de Camp. Only once did his eyes leave the casket, and that was to glance up and look bitterly at an attractive red-headed woman on the fringes of the crowd. Yates noticed this, kept his eye on the woman and Strom throughout the rites. When the casket was being lowered, he saw the woman exchange a troubled look with Jez Jessup . . . after the ceremony watched from a distance as Jez fell in step beside the departing

432

woman. Heated words were obviously exchanged. The woman veered off in a different direction. Jez stopped in his tracks, then continued on.

Yates followed the woman home. Came up to her as she was putting her key in the lock. Stood there saying nothing.

Elaine Picket stared back at him, remained as poker-faced as he was. "Which one are you?" She spoke with contempt.

"Which one?"

"FBI agent!"

"Yates, William B."

"The bright boy?" Her scoff was half approving.

"Bright boy?"

"Alice liked you. She said Strom did too, because you're so smart. Come in."

He followed her upstairs to the bedroom atelier of the town–house.

"Coffee, booze, sex?"

"Nothing."

"Not even sex? It's all the same to me. I'm somewhat on the jaded side. Why did you follow me?"

"To find out why Strom doesn't like you. Why you had gotten mad at Jez. Why you showed up at the funeral."

She sat down in a director's chair. "I went to the funeral be-cause I loved Alice. Not in a physical way, although we did sleep together for a while. I *cared* for her. Strom knows I did. Anyway, she was a friend, and believe it or not, I am grieved. If I knew how, I'd fucking well cry."

"What about Jez?"

"You mean, why did we have words?"

"Yes."

"I think he hurt Alice. I don't know how, but I think he did."

"In what way?"

"Is he a good friend of yours? A close chum? A member of the fraternity, as it were?" She lit a cigarette. "Of course you're members, who am I kidding. Only he's no fan of yours, I can tell you that. Watch out for him."

"What did you and Jez argue about?" Billy asked.

433

"He showed up here one night, like you did. Unannounced. I believe in fucking first and talking later. We fucked." She paused, grinned briefly. "I liked him. Anyway, he explained he was checking about a robbery in the neighborhood. That's what brought him to my door. He was vague about it. Only asked if I'd seen anything in the neighborhood. He didn't press me and left. I remembered that Alice had seen something one night when she was here. I called him and told him. I didn't use Alice's name. He came back in a few hours and we made love." She paused. "Isn't that funny, I usually say fuck. I like the sound, the shock value it has. And I just said 'made love.' But that's what we did, at least I thought it was. And he got Alice's name out of me. And what had gone on. I never saw Jez again after that. Then Alice was killed, and standing at the grave, I felt sure telling him that had had something to do with her dying."

"What did Alice see that night?"

Elaine motioned to the far window. "She was standing over there. It was night. She looked across the street into the office there and saw someone get killed."

"Get killed how?"

"All she said was she saw one man pick up a gun and shoot another man . . . a small man shoot a tall man."

"Did you look?"

"Of course. But the lights were out across the street when I did. The lights were on when Alice looked."

"Did you believe Alice?"

"At the time, no. We'd had a fight. I thought she might be making it up. Looking for attention. In thinking it over, I realized it was true. Alice doesn't lie. Didn't."

"And you told this to Jez?"

"And never saw him again."

"Do you have any idea when this killing took place?"

"Right after Mormon State was robbed."

"How long after? A night, a week?"

"The Tuesday after."

\* \* \*

434

Jake Hagland had been able to determine only the first five of seven digits Mule had dialed from the phone booth in the bus station, the call to the raspy unidentified voice that told Mule to stay out of the tunnels, who had said when it was time to go back underground he would ring Mule at home and ask for "Howard." Yates had a more urgent task for Hagland, checking the phone calls made from Strom Sunstrom's home since the Tuesday after the robbery . . . since the evening Alice witnessed a murder in the building across from Elaine Picket's apartment. Strom was an early riser who routinely reached the office by 7:30 A.M. Any calls after that had to have been made by Alice. It was a slow task, but Yates began to get a picture of Alice's dependency on her husband. Strom's private number at the FBI resident office was listed on an average of three times a day in the data supplied by Hagland. Calls to the FBI's general office number averaged out at five a day. Yates presumed Alice's use of the general office number was for leaving messages for Strom. What roused his curiosity was the call made less than three weeks before, a call made late at night to FBI-2000, the Bureau's emergency hot line number for information on the Mormon State robbery.

Yates went to the eleventh-floor log in which all incoming FBI-2000 calls were recorded. Nothing was listed for the hours between 9 and 11 P.M. The call from Strom's house to FBI-2000, Hagland's data showed, had been placed at 10:48 P.M.

The office's duty roster was the next thing checked by Yates. He talked with the agent assigned to taking FBI-2000 calls that evening. As Billy expected, the man had been relieved intermittently during the evening by whoever was around the office.

At night Yates went into the empty premises opposite Elaine Picket's townhouse, searched through, found the stain on the floor. He sat down, hugged his raised knees, stared at the stain . . . began to figure things out.

Jake Hagland told Yates he had detected what went wrong with the bug he had placed on the bus station phone booth and that he had corrected the trouble and they would now be able to home in on what number Mule was dialing. Yates said this was no longer necessary, that he knew all he needed to know. He did, though, prevail on Hagland for one last favor.

At sundown Yates rang up Strom Sunstrom and then Jez Jessup and told each of them he had finally found what it was Brewmeister had discovered. He asked them to meet with him at the railroad-yard diner Ed Grafton so favored. He waited in a phone booth across the way until both men arrived, then called Mule at home and, disguising his voice, said, "Don't bother with Howard. I found it. Meet me down there as fast as you can."

Mule, as he always did when receiving such a call, hung up and called back the prearranged number for verification. Yates had anticipated this. Instead of reaching the number he dialed, Mule was shunted to Hagland's communications truck, where Yates's prerecorded voice repeated, "I found it. Get a move on."

# Twenty-five

A searchlight beam cut through the tunnel darkness ahead. The lamp itself was attached to the snub-nose prow of a rubber boat. Strom sat just behind the instrument, directing the light from time to time. Behind Strom was Jez. Yates perched on the rear gunnel steering the outboard motor.

They had embarked from the shunting terminal under the old city waterworks, with Yates saying that Brewmeister had discovered this spot by tailing Mule, that he had seen Mule and Wiggles and Rat Ragotsy get into their own boat not far from here, then travel westward through the tunnels and caves, travel into the section of Prairie Port where mud slides and mud rivers and an underground mud volcano had been arrested.

Earlier, leading the way down into the underground terminal, Yates had said Brewmeister never doubted Bicki "Little Haifa" Hale's gang were the actual perpetrators of Mormon State, and this was why, after Mule and Wiggles and Ragotsy had been cleared of implication with the crime, Brew had begun following them. When he tailed the three men into this terminal and saw them get into a boat and head west, Brew realized what Mule, Rat and Wiggles had eventually deduced: that the $31,000,000 had been swept inland the night of the robbery. It was this knowledge that kept the three felons traveling the western tunnels and caves. Brew, Yates told Strom and Jez, followed Mule, Rat and Wiggles through these tunnels many times.

Several miles westward Yates shut off the outboard motor. They were now in a series of caverns and grottos connected to one another by tunnel segments. He locked a plastic tiller to the stern, steered as Jessup and Strom paddled with plastic oars. Again, Strom, as he had earlier, wanted to know their destination.

Yates again counseled waiting until they could see for themselves, then began to relate a scenario he had come to believe.

"Long before Otto Pinkny was arrested for running a red light in South Carolina and identified as America's most wanted fugitive, Mule, Rat Ragotsy and Wiggles Loftus were propositioned by a special agent of the FBI," Yates said. "This solicitation was undertaken on express orders from someone at Washington headquarters and, needless to say, was done in the utmost secrecy. The three suspects were in custody at the time, Mule and Wiggles in federal detention in Prairie Port, Rat Ragotsy convalescing at an Army hospital as a result of the beating he took from the county sheriff.

"What they were offered by this emissary was their freedom, to be let off the robbery charges and set free, in exchange for certain considerations. The deal, obviously, stipulated that Mule, Rat and Wiggles never mention a word of the arrangement and that they follow every last detail of an alibi scheme. There were other conditions. One was that they confess in full. Provide the secret operative as detailed an accounting of the evolution, planning, perpetration of the crime as possible. And the getaway after. That had to be the hardest part, getting them to agree to this confession. But the emissary got it. Got them to record it on tape. The next step was simpler. Harry Janks, the great Chicago mouthpiece, was had for a price. Harry probably didn't know a thing about the arrangement, but he was provided with a bit of a windfall, eleven witnesses in Illinois who said Mule, Rat and Wiggles were there at the time of the robbery . . . and remained there for a week. I don't know exactly how that was worked out, but it doesn't matter. They were supplied, and Harry Janks appeared in Prairie Port with his new evidence, and then before we knew it, charges were dropped and the three actual robbers of Mormon State were let go. Of course they had to answer to Washington's secret emissary in Prairie Port. The special agent who was Washington's spy."

Yates, in the darkness, talked at Jessup. "Jez, remember how you used to joke about being Mata Hari? How all the resident agents talked about Ed Grafton suspecting Washington had sent someone to spy on him? Well, it was true. There was a spy. Not up on the twelfth floor with Corticun, but down on the eleventh. One of us, one of the resident agents, was Washington's man. It had to be. Who else had access to Mule, Rat and Wiggles? Who else knew about Wilkie Jarrel's phone setup that well? That setup was what was copied in keeping in touch with Mule, Rat and Wiggles—Jarrel's use of pay phones to avoid being overheard. Part of the original deal with Mule, Rat and Wiggles was to continually stay in touch with Washington's spy. There was a very specific reason for them staying in touch, but before this became a reality, a second use for the communication setup was found . . . a use that had to do with the tunnels we're in.

"Once they were cleared of charges and Ragotsy returned from the hospital, the three robbers were able to talk for the first time since blowing open the vault. Mule and Rat had thought the rest of the gang and all the money was swept through the tunnel and dumped out into the Mississippi River like they themselves had been immediately following the theft. Talking to Wiggles they learned he had been carried inland through the drainage tunnels, carried west. They realized this might be where some of the other gang members were taken. More important to them, that this was where the *money* might be. The three crooks had been pretty honest with Washington's spy, but they were still crooks. They told the spy they were planning to go into the tunnels and look for the money and said if he kept his mouth shut about it and helped them, they would cut him in. The spy dutifully reported this to Washington. Washington said it didn't care what the crooks did or he did, just so nobody got in trouble. The spy went along with the gang, used the intricate system of communications to be kept apprised of their progress in finding the treasure. The spy was down here himself several times to look over the situation. I saw him once myself . . ."

There was stirring in the boat. "Saw his face?" asked Strom.

"No, just his outline. He joined Mule and Rat and Wiggles in his own boat. It seems they were getting closer to the money all the time, or at least finding clues that the money was nearby, such as locating a moneybag. But that was only recently. Early

439

on when they were searching these tunnels and caves, there was an interruption . . . Otto Pinkny. Otto Pinkny gets picked up for running a red light in South Carolina, is ID'd and asks to see the FBI, or so the story goes. Most likely it was the FBI who came to see him . . . who'd been on the lookout for someone like him for quite a while. I shouldn't say the FBI was on the lookout, just a few people in Washington headquarters, including our spy's bosses. As a deal had been offered Mule and Ragotsy and Wiggles to clear them of implications with Mormon State, now a deal was made with Otto Pinkny . . . to implicate him. What had Pinkny got to lose pleading to Mormon State? Twenty years in jail? If he doesn't plead, he's going to death row. Problem is, Otto Pinkny doesn't know a damn thing about Mormon State. So they give him the taped confessions made by Mule, Rat and Wiggles. This helps, but not enough. Luckily for all, Pinkny was picked up days before the records show, maybe a week or two before, so there was plenty of time for the next step . . . bringing in someone to coach him who knew all about the robbery.

"Brew had Mule under surveillance. It was spot surveillance usually done in the early evening. For four days it couldn't be done because Mule disappeared from Prairie Port. Those four days were spent in South Carolina briefing Otto Pinkny on the crime. Washington's spy saw to Mule's secret traveling arrangements back and forth."

They were into a tunnel beyond a grotto now, a wide, curving tunnel. Strom and Jez, who had gotten tired oaring, were told their destination was near. They paddled somewhat harder.

"Everything worked out," Yates continued. "Otto Pinkny came to Prairie Port like Lindbergh returned to New York City. They gave Otto everything but a parade. He deserved one, I suppose, if for no other reason than convincing everybody he and his gang pulled off Mormon State. Most of our office was convinced, if you remember. Still are. Mule, as I said before, was fairly honest with Washington's spy. Fairly, but not totally. He forgot to mention one thing . . . he'd blown Cowboy Carlson's head off a few nights after the robbery and dumped the body in the river. Mule had said he thought one of the other gang members might have killed Cowboy. This wouldn't have mattered any more than him admitting to the murder if two things hadn't happened. One, his alibi specifically stating he was away from Prairie Port the night of the robbery as well as the week after. Two, somebody saw him kill Cowboy.

"That somebody was your wife, Strom."

The only sound to come from Strom Sunstrom's end of the boat was that of constant paddling.

"Alice had been visiting a friend that night and looked out the window and saw Mule do it," Yates said. "And Mule saw her. Saw her in a compromising situation. That's why she couldn't say anything to you. She was with who you suspected, Elaine Picket. Alice began to realize she had to say Mule was in Prairie Port. So what she did was pick up the phone and dial our hot line, dial FBI-2000. She disguised her voice and said when and where Mule had killed Cowboy. It didn't take Washington's spy and Washington long to find out and verify this. The spy even confronted Mule, and Mule owned up to the murder.

"Now the spy's boss, or bosses, in Washington had a new set of problems. Not only had they conspired with an assassin, which in and of itself could be devastating if ever revealed, but the whole charade of having Otto Pinkny replace the actual robbers was in jeopardy. If Mule's alibi could be disproved, the whole house of cards would come falling down. So they solved it very simply, they gave Alice to Mule. Whatever was done to her, whatever Mule did, she was trying all the time to protect you, Strom. When the pain, and shame, got to be too much . . . she killed herself."

Again, only the sound of paddling was heard from the bow.

Yates steered the rubber boat into a recess beyond a curve in the tunnel. "So who was this spy? This confederate of ours who brought all this down? If we think back, it isn't hard to figure out. Which one of us was ever alone with all three suspects before their release . . . alone with Mule, Ragotsy and Wiggles?"

"Are you trying to say it was me?" Jessup said.

"Had to be, Jez." Yates had his gun out and pressed to Jessup's neck. "Hands up, nice and easy. Strom, better see if he has his gun."

441

"I don't, and you're looney-toon." Jessup seemed unconcerned.

Strom searched Jez, found nothing.

"It was left to you and you only to get the final confessions from Wiggles, Mule and Ragotsy. You went to see each one of them two or three times. I chauffeured you a few of those times but never went inside. Nobody saw them except you. You told us it looked like they might confess. But all the while you were working out the deal with them. When it was finally negotiated you told us they refused to see you any more. They did refuse to see you any more, because you had told them to do it that way."

Jez turned in the darkness. "Strom, he's full of shit. He and his buddy Brewmeister brainstormed this crap and now he's trying to—"

"Strom, you know who in our office took the call the night your wife dialed FBI-2000?" Yates asked. "It was Jez. He was sitting in at the switchboard so the duty agent could go to the john. You know who went and looked at the address Alice gave, and then went over to talk to Elaine Picket? Jez. Know who got Elaine Picket to tell him what went on the night Alice was over there, say that Alice had seen someone get shot? Jez. Elaine Picket couldn't describe what the person looked like that Alice saw, but Jez had a better way of finding out. He asked Mule, or beat it out of him.

"No, from top to bottom it was you, Jez, always you," Billy told him. "And at the end, when Brew and I wouldn't buy Otto Pinkny, wouldn't let up insisting it was Mule and Rat and Wiggles who were it, only one person wouldn't bother to argue with us . . . only one person looked the other way."

"You're damning a man because he looked away?" Jez's voice was scornful.

Yates jabbed the gun hard into Jessup's chest. "Keep your voice low. As for damning, you've done that to yourself. I broke your line of communications, Jez. The same line of communications Wilkie Jarrel used, the same system of phone booths and call-backs we have listed in our reports on him. Wasn't it you and

442

Brew who did most of the investigation on those reports? It doesn't matter, I've got you on tape."

"You're crazy." Jez turned in the dark to Strom. "He's *goddam crazy*, believe me, he's—"

Strom was on him, in the refraction of the search beam had lunged forward and gotten Jez by the throat, was choking him with all his strength. Yates struggled to keep the boat even, telling Strom, "Stop and you can have them all. For God's sake, stop. Wait for the rest. They'll all be here."

Yates, in desperation, kicked his leg forward, caught Strom in the shoulder and knocked him back. Jez lay on his side, wiping blood from his mouth.

"They're coming here to meet you, Jez," Yates told him. "I know about Howard. I imitated your voice. I called Mule imitating your voice and told him not to bother with Howard and to come down here and meet you where he did last time. When he called back to verify, I was tapped in again and confirmed he should come here. Know whose phone number he called to confirm, whose number I was tapped into? Yours, Jez."

"Then you couldn't have heard anything like that because nobody would have called me." Jez spoke calmly and started to sit up. Yates pushed him back down.

Sounds were heard in the distance.

"Can you cover him without shooting him?" Yates asked Strom.

Strom said he could, took the gun Yates handed him, trained it down on Jez.

Yates unfastened a rifle from inside the prow gunnel. "Better kill the light."

Strom placed his foot on Jez's chest, reached behind his back and snapped off the search beam.

Putt-putting echoed far off. So did the voice of someone singing "We're in the Money." Light flickered in the darkness of the tunnel to their left. Putt-putting turned to the constant whirr of a motor. The lyrics grew louder.

Yates brought the rifle onto his lap.

443

The tunnel to the left filled with glaring light. The deafening roar of an outboard motor resounded. A rubber boat burst into view carrying Mule, Wiggles and Rat Ragotsy, all of whom were singing at the top of their lungs "We're in the Money."

As they passed the dark recess in which Yates, Jez and Strom were hidden, Jez, in one fast move, shoved Strom's foot backward, knocking Strom down, and jumped up and into the black water. Hitting the water, Jez grabbed hold of a guide rope on the side of Mule's boat, yelled for Mule to get the hell going. Mule threw open the throttle. The boat lurched into the darkness.

Yates hurriedly arranged a dazed Strom on the floor, started up the motor. Seeing nothing but blackness ahead, he stretched forward and snapped the search beam on, stood up to follow the turbulence in the water ahead. The tunnel opened into a small water-filled cave, then a large cave, then into a wider, curving tunnel. Speeding into another cavern, he heard gunshots ring out. Strom, now recovered, snapped off the searchlight as Yates zigzagged the boat, reduced the power, followed the sound of Mule's roaring outboard motor. In the next stretch of tunnel, the light went back on. Gunshots ricocheted back off the tunnel walls.

Yates was gaining on the boat, around another turn in the tunnel momentarily caught sight of it . . . and caught a hail of gunshots. Strom answered the fire. They sped into a narrower maze of tunnels. More shooting erupted from ahead. Again Yates and Strom had to kill their searchlight, travel at half-power.

Tunnels gave way to cavern after cavern, each wider and higher than the last. Colder too. Yates felt his fingers numb. Strom was shivering. But the caverns offered an acoustical advantage . . . Yates and Strom could now hear the motor ahead in the darkness more clearly. They briefly caught sight of Mule's boat. Yates threw open the throttle. Strom began to fire. The fire was returned. Mule's boat turned off its light. Strom turned on his search beam, sighted in on Jez kneeling down and firing back at them with an automatic weapon. Again Strom switched off the light.

444

The chase crossed more caves. Mule's boat was gaining speed, outdistancing its pursuer. Again Yates reduced power so he could follow the sound of the motor ahead of him in the middle of a grotto. The sound cut off. Yates shut down his motor as well. There was a slight current in the water. He let the boat drift. It bumped against the grotto wall, moved along the wall until an opening was found. Yates and Strom paddled through into what seemed to be a narrow corridor. Shafts of light flickered in the distance. Navigating toward it, they reached another opening and started in.

They floated out onto a vast underground lake spread across an enormous cavern. The walls had a pulsating blue sheen to them, a sheen that cast shimmering reflections onto huge mud stalactites hanging from the arching ceiling high overhead. At the far end of the lake was an island. On the island, and draped between odd-angled, truncated telephone poles, were string after string of glowing, low-wattage light bulbs. Running from the lights to a pile of industrial batteries that powered them was a frayed cable. Mule's boat was drifting just off the island. All four men in it, Mule and Jez and Ragotsy and Wiggles, were standing. Standing motionless as if frozen by what they were encountering. Drawing closer, Yates and Strom saw what that was.

Sitting cross–legged on the island, in front of the charred logs of a burnt-out fire and clutching canvas money sacks, was the decomposed corpse of Meadow Muffin Epstein. Jessup and Ragotsy noticed something else. So did Strom, who nudged Yates to look beyond the island and higher up, to look at the mud-crusted cavern wall curving up behind Meadow Muffin and the mud-covered ceiling arching down over the island. There, frozen in the mud, were the bodies of the remaining gang members . . . Bicki "Little Haifa" Hale and Reverend Wallace Tecumseh "Windy Walt" Sash and Thomas "Worm" Ferugli, each contorted in the final postures of struggling mortality. Embedded amid the corpses, like the treasure from some great Pharoah's tomb, were the artifacts of their last lost achievement, the tools of Mormon State . . . torn rubber boats and parts of a large log raft lashed together with strands of fusing cord and segments of

445

outboard motors and sections of metal scaffold and shovels and picks and hammers and walkie-talkie radios and drills and thermos bottles and dollar bills and waterproof crates of dynamite and a shattered television monitor screen and a field telephone and a first-aid kit and a bottle of whiskey and cans of beer and bits of food and faded packs of cigarettes and pulpish leftovers of magazines and comic books or whatever else was read or looked at to kill some time while preparing for the heist. Tattered rubber wet suits and hardhats with plastic visors and hip-high fisherman's boots lent an eerie animation to the gigantic frieze of robbery and death, made it appear as if a cavorting band of specters, in parts and in whole, were performing some mad and ghoulish dance.

"Don't shoot," Mule hissed out rather than shouted.

Yates looked down to see Strom standing beside him with a rifle raised at Mule and Jez. Their two boats had drifted within twenty feet of one another.

Mule waved his hands frantically and pointed to the ceiling. "There's nitroglycerin in them ceiling and walls." His tones were still hissing and low. "Dynamite too. Enough to blow us all to kingdom come."

Sunstrom, his gunsight alternating from Mule to Jessup and back to Mule, tried to control his rage, his hatred of the two men who had conspired to violate and murder his wife.

"We're in the salse," Ragotsy, who was standing beside Wiggles and Jez, whispered urgently. "The heart of the volcano. Them blue lights at the other end of this place, them's from the salse. You don't need dynamite to send this whole place up. A sneeze can do it. Don't fucking shoot no gun."

The image of Alice won out. Strom fired at his old friend, the man who had once kept him from seriously harming a SAC who had impugned his wife. Jez collapsed into the boat, his shoulder splintered. As he did, Wiggles ducked down, came up a split second later brandishing a submachine gun. Strom fired again. Wiggles dropped . . . and as he sank, his dead finger contracted on the trigger. The submachine gun fired into the air. Into the ceiling.

Something detonated. A chain reaction of explosions began, each one more powerful and shattering than the next.

Yates knocked Strom down into the boat, scrambled to the stern, jerked on the motor, sped across the lake as segments of ceiling began to fall . . . as dropping segments themselves began to explode. Mule, too, was speeding his boat through the subterranean holocaust, reached the cavern exit moments after Yates and Strom sped through. More explosions followed. Then came a rumble of terrifying proportions. A lateral quaking of untold immensity. The underground mud volcano, the salse, erupted.

The caves and tunnels through which the two rubber boats were fleeing trembled and shook, split at the seams in many places. Lightning flashed, thunder volleyed. Torrents of water, greater than any unleashed when the reservoir had been opened after the robbery, poured in. Long-dormant pockets of underground mud began to flow in avalanche enormity. A phenomenon known as "tunnel wind" occurred, sent gusts of up to sixty miles an hour whistling through the subterranean passageways.

The boats, one following the other, found themselves being swept along the rampaging waters at a dizzying speed. Yates concentrated on survival. Strom was obsessed with Mule . . . he waited and watched the lightning-streaked darkness behind him for glimpses of Mule's boat. Mule's boat, like their own, had the search beam on.

It was in a wide bend of tunnel that Strom found his chance. The other boat had been brought almost parallel with their own. Mule was at the outboard motor, holding onto a gunnel cord for dear life with one hand, trying to steer with the other.

Strom dove out across the darkness, caught Mule around the neck, dragged him down into the turbulent current, forced him under . . . tried to hold him there. Mule thrashed and twisted and broke loose long enough to get a breath. They were in the darkness and alone and being carried along at great speed. Strom was on Mule again, trying to pull him under, strangle him or drown him.

Abruptly the combatants were sucked backward and spun up-

447

side-down around a maelstrom and spat out into a side tunnel of shallow water. Mule ran off, splashing through the tunnel trying to escape. Strom caught him, punched him, again tried to strangle him. Mule somehow freed himself, trudged up onto dry concrete flooring, was hit by a small piece of tunnel roof, glanced back to see Strom coming after him, ran forward, dodging falling concrete.

Strom brought Mule down with a tackle, wrestled him over on his back, put his hands on Mule's neck and began choking. Mule had no strength left, could do nothing . . . began to die.

The chunk of falling concrete struck Strom squarely on the back of the head and instantly killed him. Mule didn't realize what had happened. Let Strom lay there motionless on top of him, thinking, hoping maybe the FBI man had changed his mind about murdering him. When Strom's fingers loosened and fell away from his neck, Mule realized something else had happened, soon determined exactly what it was.

Mule stripped Strom's pockets of money, a penlight, credit cards and an FBI shield, then went trooping up the unflooded tunnel. For a brief stretch the footing was dry. Then mud began to appear. So did the end of the tunnel and an electric light. The light was beside a metal door. Mule pulled it open, switched on a second electric light. He was in an underground supply room belonging to the water or sewerage company. He climbed onto a high concrete shelf and immediately fell asleep.

Yates's boat was rocketing through the sewerage tunnel under Prairie Port. Ragotsy, a wounded Jez Jessup and the corpse of Wiggles rode in the boat directly behind. They were traveling at breakneck speed and the water currents were growing faster. So was the water turbulence. Yates's craft was the first to capsize. The other boat overturned moments later. Yates managed to get to Jez, kept him afloat as they were carried along. He got a hand on Ragotsy too, tried to hold him up but couldn't, and in the dim lights of the sewerage tunnel watched him drown.

". . . I'm sorry . . . I'm sorry," Jez began mumbling. "I never meant for Alice to get hurt . . . for Strom to suffer . . ."

They were spat from the tunnel mouth, arched ten feet out into the air before dropping into the Mississippi River. Jessup landed badly, face first and where the currents were especially fast. By the time Yates reached him he had gone under once and was being carried downstream.

Yates attempted the rescue with a one-arm crawl. The current started pulling them backward. He told Jez to hold on to him around the neck so he could swim with both hands free.

"I don't have the strength," Jez yelled.

"Just fucking *do* it."

"So I can get hanged?" Jez clutched as instructed. Held on as best he could with blood pouring from the wound in his shoulder.

Yates battled the current. "Who are the Silent Men?"

"Never heard of them."

"Who gave you your orders?"

"The Director."

*"Hoover?"*

"Yes, he'd call and say what he wanted me to do . . . or sometimes an assistant called, but the Director always verified instructions." Jez gasped for breath. ". . . No one wanted to hurt anybody, I swear to Christ, Billy . . . I was sent here to protect Ed Grafton . . . from the beginning, the Director wanted Ed protected, and I helped Strom way back when . . ."

"Who was the assistant who gave you orders from Hoover?"

". . . Freddie . . . Freddie was the name we used . . . the voice was covered . . . could have been a woman . . . a secretary . . . who I thought it really sounded like was Sissy Hennessy . . ."

"Who did Hoover want you to protect Grafton from?"

Jez's grip loosened. ". . . Can't make it, Billy . . . can't hold on any longer . . ."

Yates felt Jez's fingers slip, grabbed back for Jez's arm . . . and missed.

Jez Jessup was sucked into the Treachery feet first and spun over . . . feet first shot on down the river, his face in the water and his arms outstretched.

* * *

449

Mule felt the coldness and opened an eye. His arm was hanging over the concrete shelf, and he could see that mud was encasing his fingers. He scrambled up on all fours and looked down. He was on a high ledge and everything below him was mud. The door across the room was already hidden beneath mud. And the mud was still rising. He crawled, swung around on the ledge, began pounding on the wall behind him, on the wall to his left. He shouted for help, kept shouting. The ceiling fractured and mud dripped through. The wall across from him cracked around the edges . . . began moving toward him.

# Book Four

# Twenty-six

From the moment he swam ashore, Yates had puzzled over what to report about Jez Jessup's complicity with Mule, Rat and Wiggles. It was almost inconceivable to Billy that J. Edgar Hoover would knowingly be party to such a conspiracy. Yet if it *was* true, if Hoover was involved, absolutely no one in the FBI would believe it . . . or anyone in the media . . . unless far more corroboration was available than Jessup's final watery statements.

Should the Hoover connection be deleted from the report, Yates still foresaw other problems. Any mention of Jessup's actual activities might reveal to the Silent Men that he knew even more about them and their plot . . . far more than when they had tried to kill him before and got Brew instead. Besides the danger to himself and Tina Beth this could incur, he was worried the Men might panic and withdraw, cover their tracks. He very much wanted the Men, and was fairly certain he had established a direct link between them and Mule, Rat and Wiggles: Freddie, the voice on the telephone. A voice that could possibly be female and belong to Sissy Hennessy. If Sissy was implicated, Cub Hennessy might be too. He doubted if Cub was a member of the Men itself, but he could be an ally. If he wrote a report eliminating Hoover but including Jessup's role, how could he avoid letting Cub see it? Cub was second-in-command of the residency. How could he avoid letting Corticun, whom he always mistrusted, see it as well? A third consideration was crucial to Billy's thinking: the raw facts themselves, without any mention of Jessup or Hoover, would be all that was needed to stop the fraudulent trial of Otto Pinkny. So he'd give up little and avoid possibly compromising himself by not telling the real story of Jez.

453

When Billy Yates began typing up his report he wasn't aware that Strom Sunstrom was dead. Nor would it have made any difference. Billy detailed what happened hours before in the tunnels and caves and what was discovered there . . . an account in which Jez Jessup's true role as abettor of the criminals and traitor to Romor 91 was changed to co-investigating agent with Strom and Yates, a man who had sacrificed his life in the line of Bureau duty.

. . . On completion of the report Billy Yates collapsed and was taken to the hospital, where he slept for three days. Jez's corpse was found downstream in the river, and Strom Sunstrom's body washed into the shunting station under Lookout Bluff and was discovered there. Cub Hennessy was made temporary senior resident agent in charge of the Prairie Port office, and Denis Corticun was placed in control of Romor 91. The two of them, with a contingent of Bureaumen, attempted to examine the underground areas described by Yates, but ongoing salse rumblings forced them to keep their distance. Media preoccupation with the eruptions made it easier for Corticun to downplay the deaths of Strom and Jez, who were officially cited as being accidentally killed in a tunnel cave-in and flooding while on a routine investigatory assignment. Their funerals were small and private. Rat Ragotsy's body was recovered from the Mississippi River a hundred and ten miles below Prairie Port, where rural authorities, dismissing him as a drowned vagrant, laid him to rest in the local potter's field. No one around Prairie Port much noticed that he was missing or that Wiggles and Mule seemed to have dropped out of sight.

When Yates, in his hospital room, later learned that the United States was proceeding with the trial of Otto Pinkny, he put on his clothes and went to Cub and Corticun and protested. He was taken by the two FBI men down into the tunnel and caves, shown that little of what he described in his report existed as he described it . . . that the entire subterranean panorama had changed or been demolished . . . that the corpses of Little Haifa

454

and Windy Walt and Worm Ferugli and Meadow Muffin were nowhere to be seen . . . that not a single item of equipment or a dollar of stolen money could be found.

Billy Yates lodged a formal letter of complaint over the impending trial of Otto Pinkny with Cub and another with Denis Corticun. Never to them nor anyone else did Yates reveal what he felt he knew about the Silent Men or Jessup's complicity with Mule. This made him appear all the more intractable, more irrational, when Cub and other members of the residency pointed out he couldn't really expect the government to call off Pinkny's trial on his uncorroboratable say-so. Billy paid them no heed, sent letters off to Washington, sharply stating the wrong man was about to be prosecuted. He was placed on extended convalescent leave, which he refused to take. The first day of the Pinkny trial he barged into the courtroom and damned the proceedings as a sham. He was forcibly restrained and placed back in a hospital under observation. While there, he had Tina Beth go out and write down the numbers of various pay phones around the city.

Ed Grafton called at 5 A.M. and told Cub Hennessy when and where he wanted to meet him. Cub arrived at the cemetery at dawn, found Grafton standing at the twin graves of Strom and Alice Sunstrom.

"They do not belong here," Grafton told Hennessy. "This is alien clay. Send them home to Virginia, where they'll be happy. Where Priscilla is. Put them with Priscilla."

Cub recalled hearing once that Strom's first wife was named Priscilla . . . that Priscilla was Alice's sister. "Yes, I'll see to it."

"Where's Jez?"

"Over in the Baptist section." He indicated a hillside tract of burial ground. "We can drive if you want."

Grafton shook his head, laid on the graves two of the three floral arrangements he had brought, bowed his head, stalked off toward the hill.

"Where have you been, Graf?"

"You weren't told?"

455

"Not a word since you left. Strom tried finding out. He always got double-talked."

Grafton's strides were long and determined. "They put me out into what's left of the wilds. The wilderness. I like that. Plenty of bear and moose and trout. No crime, less Brass Balls."

Grafton knelt at Jessup's grave and placed his flowers. "Never thought I knew you were Edgar's angel, eh, Jez man? From the day you were sent, I knew okay." He patted the soft earth. "Thanks for keeping me out of trouble."

He stood and faced Cub. "Jez was supposed to make sure I didn't get done in by the Brass Balls or Jarrel. It should have been me watching out for him. What happened?"

They started down the hillside, with Cub saying, "Jez, Strom and the new agent, Yates, went down in the tunnels and got caught in that mud volcano. The damn thing explodes with them in it. Explodes and floods the tunnels. Strom dies inside one of the tunnels. Jez and Yates make it out and Jez drowns in the river . . . in the Treachery."

"I heard," Grafton said, "that Jez had a gun wound."

"He got that inside the caves and tunnels. According to Yates they were tracking some of the early suspects in the Mormon State crime. They got into a chase and gunfight with them. Jez was wounded in the gunfight."

"You said 'according to Yates.' Does that mean you don't believe there was a chase and shooting?"

"I believe that part okay. I just don't believe those three had anything to do with Mormon State."

"I'd like to talk to Yates."

"So would we. He's escaped."

"Escaped?"

"The thing in the tunnels and caves was too much for him. He flipped out. He was ranting all kinds of blather. Rushed right into the courtroom and tried to disrupt the Pinkny trial. They put him in the hospital under guard. He climbs out a window and jumps three stories down into the back of a truck filled with mattresses . . . a truck his wife, Tina Beth, was driving. That was three days ago. He and his wife are gone."

". . . What happened to Alice Sunstrom?"

"She committed suicide."

"Why?"

"She was never all that well upstairs, you know that."

"I heard she was raped."

Cub sighed. "And her female parts badly mutilated."

"What have you done about it?"

"Nothing yet, but we will."

"Why did Yates run into the courtroom and try to disrupt the trial?"

"I told you, he was off his rocker."

"How did he disrupt the court trial?"

"He barged in shouting Pinkny hadn't robbed Mormon State."

"Did he say who had?"

"He claims it was Mule, Rat and Wiggles."

"Who are they?"

"Boy, you really *have* been in the wilderness. They're three of the early suspects in the case."

"The ones Jez, Strom and Yates were following in the tunnels? The ones who shot Jez?"

"Yes."

"But you said those three had nothing to do with the robbery."

"I'm telling you, Graf, it's Otto Pinkny. Otto Pinkny did it, not those three—"

"Then why would Strom, Jez and Yates bother following them in the tunnels and caves?"

Cub was ready with the answer. "Yates was always coming up with something or other to prove Rat, Wiggles and Mule were the real gang. But their being in the tunnels and caves meant nothing. Rat had a history of scavenging the tunnels for any kind of loot he could find. Mule and Wiggles were third-raters too. Why the hell wouldn't they forage in washed-out tunnels in the wake of big floods? It's a perfect place to find junk."

Graf considered, then began walking away.

"Where you going?" Cub asked.

"Back to the wilds . . . to my moose and bear and trout."

* * *

457

Billy Yates was placed on "leave without pay" by the Prairie Port resident office. A week after that, with his whereabouts still unknown, he was listed by Denis Corticun as a "missing person," and alerts for him went out to law-enforcement agencies across the land.

# Twenty-seven

They were driving, Yates and his Tina Beth. Had been since they left Prairie Port two weeks earlier . . . traveling north up into Minnesota, then west across South Dakota and Wyoming and Idaho, up into Canada. Tina Beth had rented the car on a credit card made out in her maiden name, so there wasn't all that much chance of their getting picked up.

Cards came into play in another way. Flash cards. White index cards on which Yates had written all the questions that bothered him about the investigation, all the thoughts and comments he could remember having along the way. Only one comment or thought or question was written on a single card. At the beginning of the trip he drove and dictated while Tina Beth took down what he said. By the time they reached Canada, three hundred cards had been filled out. Tina Beth took over the wheel and Yates pored through the stack time and time again. Reviewed with Tina Beth or himself what was said on each card. When they reentered the United States, a hundred and ten cards had been eliminated from the stack and further consideration. A long night in a Duluth motel saw another seventy-five disqualified. As they headed into Chicago, the card count was down to under fifty. As they were leaving Chicago, two days later, only nineteen relevant cards remained. Each one contained a question rather than a thought or comment.

It was at Starved Rock, Illinois, a state park on the Illinois River with high bluffs not unlike those of Prairie Port, that the final reckoning came. Starved Rock had been one of Brewmeister's favorite places, the spot where he had often gone camping with his wife and young children, a place, he had told Yates, where he could always think and figure things out.

459

Tina Beth and Yates had happened on Starved Rock by accident, had seen it announced on a highway information board and on a whim decided to stay there for the night. Since they had been camping out for most of their trip, they were well prepared for their sojourn in the state preserve, could easily cope with the early spring cold spell. Around a campfire four more cards were eliminated. Beside Starved Rock itself, the next morning, seven more were discounted. By sunset, at river's edge, Billy Yates was down to five cards . . . five questions which he was certain, if answered, would explain all there was to know about the deception-riddled Mormon State investigation and the Silent Men.

A pair of the questions were the first two he had ever asked regarding Romor 91: Why had J. Edgar Hoover chosen the exact time he had, the onset of the massive Romor 91 investigation, for replacing his old chum Ed Grafton as head of the Prairie Port office? Secondly, why had it taken two days from the time the alarm sounded before anyone realized an additional $31,000,000 had been in the vault and was missing?

A third question had once seemed trivial to Yates, then gained more importance in his thinking: Where in Prairie Port did J. Edgar Hoover land by helicopter? The morning after Harry Janks had cleared Mule, Wiggles and Ragotsy of complicity in the robbery and secured their releases, Yates was sent to the Prairie Port airport to meet an incoming J. Edgar Hoover and chauffeur him into town. Hoover never appeared at the airport. He was told, instead, that he landed by helicopter "elsewhere" and had already gone to the local office. The exact location of "elsewhere" fascinated Yates.

Question number four was, what had become of Natalie Hammond? Yates suspected the answer to this would provide a direct link to how the conspiracy to replace the actual robbers with Otto Pinkny had evolved.

The final question was not where were the hundreds of pages taken from the twelfth-floor files by Brewmeister, but rather, what had they contained that allowed Brew to discover the Silent Men?

460

For a time Yates considered adding a sixth question: How much of what Jez had said in the river before drowning was true . . . and relevant? Billy believed Jez had answered to Hoover or an intermediary called "Freddie" and that Jez's secret mission was originally to protect Ed Grafton. Yates concluded that Jessup had probably been recruited by Edgar after Sunstrom had arranged for Jez's transfer from Texas to Prairie Port. Being known as Strom's man was an ideal cover from which to keep an eye on Grafton. Jez, just before his death, had sworn he didn't know who the Silent Men were. Yates thought this was also possible, felt that the Silent Men might very well have controlled Jez by directing orders to him via "Freddie." What Tina Beth found incredible was that Sissy Hennessy could be "Freddie." Billy didn't want to belabor the point. Nor was the matter that urgent. Ultimately the sixth question was dismissed by him as being redundant. If he could answer the first five questions, Yates believed everything else would fall into place.

Tucked tight beside Tina Beth in their sleeping bag, staring up at a ginger moon, Yates spoke out his strategy. The fifth question, the matter of what in the files had allowed Brewmeister to determine the Silent Men existed, seemed the least urgent. And the one offering the most available material to examine. Billy Yates might occasionally forget what he had heard, as had been the case in part with Orin Trask's model crime being discussed at the other end of Barrett Amory's dinner table some years back, but seldom, if ever, did he forget what he had read. When it came to remembering the written word, Yates was blessed with near total recall. He had read much of what was in the eleventh-floor files regarding Romor 91 . . . and the eleventh-floor files were the master files, constituted the entire casebook for the investigation. He could recite nearly verbatim the key parts of individual reports, recall names and dates and places and other specifications, including who the inquiring special agent had been.

Lying in the silent darkness of Starved Rock, Billy told Tina Beth that a recapitulation of those files, to see how Brew had deduced from them what he had, could come later. The files

461

were always there when needed, safe in memory. No, where he would begin was with the fourth question—with what had become of Natalie Hammond.

"Know what Brew said to me from that booth?" Yates spoke softly up at the night sky. "Know the very last words I heard him speak before he was killed?"

"What?"

"He said he was going to Emoryville. Said he was going 'to put the last nail in the coffin.' Know what Emoryville is?"

She knew because he had mentioned it before, but she said, "Tell me."

"The place over in Illinois where damn near a dozen people provided alibis for Mule, Ragotsy and Wiggles. Swore under oath that the three were there in Emoryville the night of the robbery and for another week. When Brew said he was going there to put that last nail in," Yates continued, "I figured he meant he was going to discredit the alibis, disprove those testimonies. For a time I went on thinking that. After all, Brew got murdered just before he was going to do it. That's part of why Alice Sunstrom died too, knowing Mule wasn't in Emoryville when the robbery came down. But then I started to think that maybe there was something else at Emoryville, besides witnesses, that Brew was going to check out. Something to do with Natalie Hammond."

Yates rolled over, and propping his chin in his hand stared at Tina Beth. "Hon, I want you to go home."

She looked past him. "Fiddle–faddle, I'm going with you."

"Nick and Nora Charles time is over, Tina Beth."

"I don't know who those fine folk are, and I don't care. If you felt it appropriate I come this far with you, it's appropriate I accompany you still farther. Shush up, dear child, and get some sleep." She rolled her back onto him.

Yates hadn't wanted her to come this far with him but at the same time desperately needed to be with her, to know she was safe, to have her there to help him. She was, and always had been, his one ally. He functioned best with her. Reasoned and figured things out best when she was close and listening or discussing.

462

The time now had come to go on alone, and he knew he couldn't tell her that directly. He knew he couldn't say that, more than anything, he wanted her far off and out of harm's way. Where he really wished she would go was to the safety of her parents' home. He knew at best, using all his wiles, he could only get her to return to Prairie Port. He had pondered how to accomplish this. Speaking of the danger they might run into if they went on together, such as from the unknown assassins of Brewmeister, would only reinforce her determination to stay with him. Saying she would be in the way in Emoryville and after, which was true, would trigger feelings of betrayal. If worse came to worse, though, he could settle for betrayal. What he had searched for in preference to this was a plausible diversion. Something in which she could feel she was contributing as a partner but yet be willing to separate from him. The diversion he came up with made him uneasy; it might bring her much too close to the case for his liking. On the other hand, he very much wanted the information.

"I need you to go back to Prairie Port for me," he told her. "I need to know where Hoover's helicopter landed in Prairie Port."

"If I go back to that town, Billy Bee, I'll be detained and questioned about where you are. I'll have as much chance to ask after helicopters as a warthog has of being handsome."

"If you don't go back, hon, I'll have to."

Tina Beth's tears had a way of letting themselves be known in the dark. "That's unfair and unkind, Billy Bee, putting it that way. You know you can't go back to Prairie Port for being arrested."

"I need that information, I need it real bad."

The tears silenced themselves.

110 Sumpter Place was a large, white, wooden boarding house on an elm-shaded side street in Emoryville. It was also where Mule Corkel was reported to have been at the time of the robbery by three eyewitnesses, all of whom resided here . . . two permanent guests and the owner-operator of the establishment. Yates did not go in, only watched the location for a bit. Little was

to be observed other than a woman in her seventies on the front porch, moving gently back and forth on a glider, and an elderly handyman mowing the spacious rear lawn.

A four-block walk along the tree-lined, porch-fronted streets brought Yates to Hitzig Arms, the boarding house where four employees attested, in sworn affidavits, that Wiggles Loftus had been when Mormon State was robbed. This was a shabbier edifice than the one at 110 Sumpter Place, more run-down but pretty nonetheless. The few people Yates observed entering and leaving were in their sixties and seventies.

A half-mile away, at the Marchonet, a long, red-pebbled drive-way traversed the wide hillside lawn and ran up to a sprawling, turn-of-the-century wooden resort hotel, a five-story, double-tur-reted main house flanked on both sides by two-story verandaed wings. Here was where the balance of witnesses had said Rat Ragotsy had been at the time Mormon State was perpetrated. The Marchonet made no secret of its advantages, boldly listed them on a directional board near the main house—a swimming pool, miniature golf course, tennis courts, croquet lawn, tea garden, rock garden, solarium, clinic and child-care center. Yates noticed that the people wandering on the grounds were considerably younger than those seen at either Hitzig Arms or 110 Sumpter. Several of the women were pushing baby carriages.

Yates, before arriving in Emoryville, had suspected that any or all of the three locations supposedly stayed at by Mule, Rat and Wiggles could have been "safe houses" used by one governmental service or another. At the Marchonet this view was somewhat substantiated. The Marchonet, while not being the type of place the CIA or Bureau people might use for a safe residence, had a distinctly institutional ring to it.

Having lunch at a popular diner in the heart of town, Yates learned that the Marchonet was used as a vacation spot by several out-of-town industries. Checking at the local library, where copies of the city plats were available to the public, Billy saw that the Marchonet belonged to Marchall Industries of Ames, Iowa, whereas the Prairie Farmer Association held title to both Hitzig

464

Arms and 110 Sumpter Place. The Prairie Farmer Association was no stranger to Yates. It owned the tallest building in downtown Prairie Port, the one on which the electric time and temperature sign had blown out the night of the robbery. Billy had also run across Marchall Industries in his perusal of back cases in the office file. Marchall Industries was owned by the same corporation as the Prairie Farmer Association . . . the Grange Association, of which Wilkie Jarrel was board chairman and chief operating officer. The same Grange Association which, through another subsidiary, controlled Mormon State National Bank. The same Wilkie Jarrel whose son-in-law was president of Mormon State.

Yates returned to the Marchonet, stood on the grounds. Eventually, three young women came into view, chatting happily. Two were pregnant, the third was wheeling a baby carriage. He had no trouble recognizing the one with the carriage. It was Natalie Hammond.

Billy left. He had been far luckier than he had expected. He had answered not only the fourth question but the first as well . . . not only had found out what had become of Natalie but also had connected Wilkie Jarrel to the conspiracy.

Over the course of Romor 91, Billy Yates had come up with three possible explanations for why J. Edgar Hoover had chosen the moment he had for removing Ed Grafton. One was that Hoover felt the Mormon State investigation either was going to fail or would run into heavy criticism and therefore wished to spare his old pal Grafton from such an embarrassing eventuality. Second was that Hoover, for whatever his reasons, wanted Romor 91 to fail, to this end had stripped the Prairie Post office of what he considered to be its prime asset, its leader, Ed Grafton.

The third possibility dealt with the ongoing feud between Ed Grafton and Wilkie Jarrel. Imperative for the FBI, in any robbery investigation of this nature, was the maximum cooperation of the victim bank. But how much cooperation could be expected from Mormon State, which was controlled by Wilkie Jarrel, the very man Grafton had sworn to indict? Worse yet for the FBI, Jarrel's son-in-law, Emile Chandler, was the bank's president. What could the Bureau really expect should Ed Grafton walk into the bank and start asking questions? Without Grafton around, the prospects became rosier.

Yates had always postulated that once Grafton was gone J. Edgar Hoover could sit down and talk man-to-man with Wilkie Jarrel. For this to occur, Hoover himself would have to remove Grafton, since in all of the Bureau only he had the power to do so. Yates had believed J. Edgar Hoover would never sacrifice Ed Grafton except under the direst of conditions. Billy, as he drove from Emoryville, was getting some idea of just how dire those conditions were.

. . . Driving farther, he was pretty certain he had the answers to all his questions except one: the identity of the Silent Men.

She was waiting at the phone booth in Prairie Port he told her to be at, waiting at the time he said. The phone rang.

"Billy?" she asked, picking up.

"Howya, hon?"

"I miss you, Billy Bee."

"Double here. What's happening?"

"Cub came to see me," she told him. "I couldn't have been in the house more than an hour and he was there. He told me he was having the house watched, hoping you and I would be coming back. Cub said that Denis Corticun had put out an alert to have you picked up, but then Cub talked him into taking it back. Cub says he put you back on extended leave and that if you come back to town by this weekend there won't be any trouble. He says he and the other RAs understand how you feel about the killings, but he says if you don't get back right away, things could get serious. He wants me to let him know what you say."

"I'll tell you later. Anything else going on?"

"Billy, trust Cub, please trust him. And Sissy too. I know what Jez Jessup said about Sissy and maybe making phone calls to him, but I don't believe it. Cub and Sissy are the only friends we've got. And Billy, we need friends right now."

"I'll think about it, Tina Beth. What else is happening?"

". . . I found out all about that helicopter, Billy Bee. I went right

466

on down to the airport and talked to an air traffic dispatcher and he was nice as punch and took me for a coffee and told me who the pilot was. The pilot flew his helicopter up to Saint Louis and picked up Edgar. Then he flew Edgar back to Prairie Port and landed at Thurmond Hill. That's the big estate out past the highway that belongs to Wilkie Jarrel. Wilkie Jarrel has his own heliport there at Thurmond Hill."

"Know the phone out in the Shop Now supermarket parking lot?"

"Yes."

"I'll call you there at eleven tomorrow morning."

Billy Yates wasn't surprised at learning where the helicopter landed. . . . had pretty well figured that out before leaving Emoryville. What concerned him now was expediting the discovery of the Silent Men, which was why he drove hellbent for leather toward Carbondale, Illinois.

The very first summary report to come in on the newly installed twelfth-floor teletype machine the night the FBI entered the Mormon State investigation dealt with the origin of the $31,-000,000 in used currency and the shipment of this amount from the branch Federal Reserve Bank in New Orleans to Prairie Port. The shipment had been destined for St. Louis, but a series of circumstances saw the funds diverted for overnight safekeeping. Yates had found the summary to be, as he put it, "full of holes" and had always meant to get in touch with Alexander Troxel, the special agent who compiled the summary. That never occurred. Reaching Carbondale, Illinois, at two in the morning, he did the next best thing . . . he went directly to the Majestic Garage at 45 Clayton Street.

According to the Troxel summary, a U.S. Treasury official by the name of Klines had contracted with the Gulf Coast Armored Security Corporation of Corpus Christi, Texas, to pick up and transport the money. The truck crew consisted of company vice-president David C. Swoggins, company security director Allen J. Noble and Jack W. Manly, a company guard. Mechanical trouble along the way caused delays and prompted a decision to drop off the load at Mormon State National Bank in Prairie Port so the truck could be repaired. The summary showed that after reaching Mormon State and transferring the funds into the vault on Friday evening, August 20, Manly, Swoggins and Noble took the truck to Carbondale, Illinois, to the Majestic Garage at 45 Clayton Street ... that by Sunday morning, August 22, the repairs had been made and the three men started back for Prairie Port, and en route learned of the robbery.

Yates found the main door of the Majestic Garage open. The night attendant, sitting in an enclosed glass booth just inside the door, was dozing. Billy entered without being seen, followed the signs up to the office, tripped open the door with a plastic credit card, went in. The files were well kept, showed that a truck belonging to Gulf Coast Armored Security of Corpus Christi was serviced on August 21 for radiator problems. The bill came to $677.82 and was paid by check.

Billy compared the serial number on the bill with others in the file. Though it wasn't in exact chronological order, it was in the general sequence for that week.

Leaving the office, Yates wandered through the four-level premises. Parking was on the upper levels, repairs and fueling on the ground floor. He left through a rear door, wandered to the adjacent street, walked up a hill to the side of the garage and beyond and found, just below the crest, a perfect vantage point ... the deepset doorway of a factory from which he could see most everything below.

The Chevrolet sedan was black and had a powerful radio antenna attached to the rear. Its windows were dark, which made seeing into it difficult. Tina Beth hadn't noticed the Chevy following her the night before, and even though she glanced back and around, didn't spot it tailing her into the Shop Now parking lot. Noticed nothing getting out and going to the outdoor pay phone. A phone which began ringing as she neared.

"Billy?"

"You all right, Tina Beth?"

"I wish you were here, Billy."

"I am, down the walkway in front of Golb's Bakery . . . only look up slow."

She did, saw him standing fifty yards away, heard him say into the phone, "When you leave here, tell Cub I'll meet him at seven tonight out at the railyard diner Ed Grafton used to go to. Tell him I can't make any decision till I talk to him, and I'd rather he come alone and not tell anyone where he's going. What I'd also appreciate you doing, Tina Beth, is getting me some clean clothes. Put them in a suitcase. Have Cub bring them to the diner."

"What are you going to say to Cub you need a suitcase for, Billy?"

"I don't know what I'm going to say, Tina Beth."

"Try to trust him, Billy Bee. Cub's a good man. Give him a chance."

Billy Yates very much wanted to trust Cub Hennessy. Doing so might insure Tina Beth's further isolation from the danger involved with his immediate plans. Cub, if he chose to cooperate, could allow Yates much needed assistance. If Cub didn't prove out, or refused to help, Billy would be sitting on a time bomb, would have to implement his plan in a matter of hours instead of days . . . implement it alone. "I want to trust him, hon, believe me. But I have to be sure of him first . . . have to test him out."

Tina Beth moved the receiver closer. "When are we going to be alone?"

"Soon."

"Can't you come out to the house just for half an hour? Come after dark?"

"You know they're watching the house, Tina Beth. Do like I ask, please. I'll talk to you later. Nine tonight, I'll call you at the next number on your list, the pay phone in the laundromat."

Tina Beth glanced over to see him walk away, then hung up.

Cub came slowly up the diner aisle carrying the suitcase of clothes and sat opposite Yates in the last booth.

"I need some help," Billy said. "I said in my report that Jez was with us in the tunnel, with Strom and me. That was wrong. He was with Mule, Ragotsy and Wiggles. The bullet wound in Jez's shoulder came from Strom's gun. Here it all is, Jez's part. This is a report I made out but never turned in."

Cub took the pages handed him by Yates.

"Read it when I leave. Jez was Hoover's spy all along. And someone else's. Whether he knew it or not, Jez was taking orders from a group of people calling themselves the Silent Men. That was the reason Brewmeister was killed. Brew found out about the Silent Men, found out that they were manipulating the investigation. Brew was going to blow the whistle on them. Those reports he supposedly stole from the twelfth floor had something to do with that. I know all this might sound looney-toon"—Yates was leaning forward—"but it plays. I found Natalie Hammond. I traced Ed Grafton's removal from his post right into the living room of Wilkie Jarrel. J. Edgar Hoover and Wilkie Jarrel are in bed together. I believe I even know how it hooks into the Silent Men, but I need help corroborating that. Your help."

". . . These Silent Men," Cub asked, "do you know who they are?"

"Not all of them, not yet. But I'll have it tied up soon."

"What do you want of me?"

"Authorization to go in and confiscate records at a garage in Carbondale, Illinois. The garage where the armored truck was repaired, the truck that brought the money to Mormon State."

Cub shook his head. "Billy, you know I can't do that. Carbondale's out of my jurisdiction, to begin with. And I'm not in charge of Romor 91, Corticun is."

Yates got up. "Coffee's on you. Thanks for coming by."

"Hold on, Billy, we've got things to talk about."

"Later. I've got to get those records."

He was gone.

Yates drove across the Mississippi River and on toward Carbondale. He stopped at nine o'clock and called Tina Beth at the laundromat. He told her that he would be on the move now . . . that he could no longer arrange any pre-set times and places

470

for their conversations . . . that in spite of the risk of a phone tap he would have to call her at home from here on in.

Sissy Hennessy heard the familiar sound of automobile tires rolling to a stop in the gravel driveway. She set the book she was reading on the rumpus room coffee table and, straightening her wool bathrobe, went to the kitchen. She opened the refrigerator as nearby a car door slammed. Sissy paused. It wasn't like Cub to make noise this time of night . . . to be unthoughtful and risk waking the children. She listened. Footsteps crunched forward outside, Cub's footsteps. Sissy smiled and continued taking a tray off the middle shelf. Never in all their years of marriage had she not waited up for Cub. Never had she not prepared a late snack. Tonight the fare was a cold platter of sliced roast beef, smoked breast of turkey and Polish ham with ample side dishes of cole slaw, apple sauce and potato salad. The diet soda was for her. The pitcher of beer she poured was for Cub.

Backing into the rumpus room with the tray, she called out a hello. Cub wasn't there. Nor could Sissy find him in the dining room or living room. She glanced out the patio doors . . . saw him at the far end of the patio with one foot up on the low stone wall.

She moved outside, set the tray on a wrought-iron table and went to her husband. "Hi," she said, kissing him on the cheek.

"Hi." He hugged her with one arm, went on staring out at the moonlit prairie beyond their braeside home.

"Problems with Yates?"

"He's going to cause trouble, Sissy, lots of trouble. Trouble for himself, for me, for everybody." Cub spoke softly, sadly. "Billy says Jez betrayed the office. Gave me a report on it. Says Jez was directly responsible for Alice's death. Says J. Edgar Hoover was directly responsible too. That's for openers. Billy says our office was set up from the beginning, was thrown to the wolves . . ." He looked at his wife. "He wants me to help him prove it."

"You're not, are you?"

Cub turned back to the night prairie.

". . . What does he want you to do?"

471

"There's a garage in Carbondale where a truck was repaired. The truck that brought the money to Mormon State just before the robbery. Billy needs the records there. He'll steal them if I don't help him."

"He's crazy, I always told you he was crazy—"

"What if he isn't?"

Sissy moved back a step. "Cub Hennessy, you're in charge of the office. This is what I've always wanted for you. It's what you've always deserved. Strom had no right being named to replace Ed Grafton, it should have been you. Now it is, and you have to behave like it. You have to behave like you're in charge. You've protected Billy Yates far too long. If he insists on doing something criminal in Carbondale, you have to stop him."

Cub looked curiously at his wife. "Sissy, can't you understand, he may be right?"

"Right isn't the issue. Being in charge is. You are what you behave like. And don't stand there looking down at me like I'm some creature to be pitied and understood. I cared about Strom and Alice and Jez as much as anybody. I grieved at their loss and still do, probably a damn sight more than most of the others. But they're not of consequence here. You are. We are. Our future in the Bureau is. You can't protect one man against the whole organization, particularly when the one man may be . . . well, crazy."

". . . What is it you want me to do, or not do?" He spoke without looking at her.

"Protect the organization. Act responsibly through channels in letting the FBI know about Yates's intentions—"

"Tell Corticun, is that what you mean?"

"Yes."

Cub shook his head. "Maybe I lack the guts to help Billy out, but I'll be damned if I'm going to shoot him down." He walked off down the hillside.

Sissy went indoors and called Denis Corticun at home and, on behalf of her husband, informed him of Billy Yates's plans.

Carloads of FBI agents deployed around the Majestic Garage. Corticun himself, forever motioning with one hand and holding

472

up a walkie-talkie with the other, stood on a street corner directing the operation.

Yates watched it all from his vantage point on the hill, then
ambled off in the opposite direction, got into his car and drove.
A hundred miles east of Carbondale he phoned Tina Beth at
home to say they could no longer count on Cub, but not to fret
because things might still work out for the best. He told her he
would call her again at nine in the morning.

Precisely at nine he stepped up to the pay phone in Washington's Mayflower Hotel and dialed Prairie Port. Tina Beth answered.

"There's nothing much to report," he told her, "except for
saying I love you. How you doing?"

"Worrying."

"Don't. This all sounds worse than it is."

"Where are you?"

"Safe. Probably be home driving you crazy before you can say
Jack Robinson."

"Who's Jack Robinson? Why you always talking about people
I don't know?"

"Don't get mad."

"I'm not mad."

"Sure you are."

"I'm not mad. I just had something to say, and you didn't listen,
that's all."

". . . What was it you had to say?"

"Never you mind."

"Please, Tina Beth, what is it?"

". . . Well, it struck me a little while back, of all the people we
didn't mention as being a Silent Man, we didn't mention the one
with the most to gain if the investigation didn't do good."

"Who's that?"

"Ed Grafton. It would prove they couldn't do good without
him."

Billy, indeed, had never thought of Grafton. Now, as he drove

473

across Washington, D.C., considering the idea, a certain plausibility did emerge. Only it was too late. Billy Yates had committed himself to one path of action. And the detonator was ticking away.

# Twenty-eight

Yates had become aware the black Chevrolet with the high rear antenna was following him just outside of Columbus, Ohio. He knew Columbus well, had served undercover there. Even on foreign terrain, Yates was unrivaled at losing a mobile tail. He had tried, in Columbus proper, shaking the black Chevrolet. Raced up and down obscure avenues, turned and reversed course half a dozen times. Each time he seemed to be in the clear, to have succeeded in losing the surveiller, the Chevrolet reappeared.

Yates had encountered only one man who had been able to stick so closely to him under these conditions, Vance Daughter during their training days. Since Daughter already loomed large in Billy's thinking, he had relaxed, proceeded on down into Washington, D.C., at a leisurely pace, one which would make tailing him all the easier.

After talking to Tina Beth at nine in the morning, Billy went for a drive around Washington. The Chevrolet managed in capital traffic as well as it had on the open highway, was forever present in Yates's rear-view mirror. Remained present all through the drive to Quantico, Virginia. Veered off and away only when Yates drove onto the U.S. Marine Corps base.

Classes were in session, and the casual hubbub Billy counted on prevailed at the FBI's two-story training academy. He walked down the main hallway and into the basement without being stopped or questioned. The storage area for the registration office was right beside the empty bin designated for the papers of Orin G. Trask. Billy had noticed it when Barrett Amory had brought him down here months before.

Back attendance records for the time Yates had trained at the

475

academy were easily found. So were those for most every class from 1963 through 1969, the years during which Orin Trask conducted his experimental seminars.

. . . And in these records, for those years, Yates was to find everything he expected he would.

"Call Frank Santi," Billy told Tina Beth. He was in an outdoor phone booth watching the Chevrolet, which was parked down the block. "Santi's the chief of police. Tell him everything you know. Everything I've told you about the investigation and everything else." Billy checked his watch. "Tell him I'll be going to Three Oaks . . . he'll have to act fast and get hold of the local authorities. I'll be there at eight o'clock. Have the police outside by then. Do you have all of that?"

"Yes—"

"And don't worry, hon, there's nothing to worry about."

"You're walking into the lion's den, aren't you, Billy Bee?"

"I think so."

"Can't you wait until I talk to Frank Santi?"

"Nope, they're right on me." He was still watching the Chevrolet. "Better I bring the fight to them."

"What about Cub, shouldn't I call Cub?"

"Cub sold me out, Tina Beth. He set up a trap for me in Carbondale. I love you, Tina Beth . . . love you like crazy."

He drove through the afternoon, drove around greater Washington, D.C. The Chevrolet was prominent in his rear–view mirror throughout. At dusk it cut away. Nor did Yates spot it when, several hours later, he reached Three Oaks, the Virginia estate belonging to Barrett and Patricia Amory.

Barrett received him alone in the great hall beyond the dining room, didn't seem surprised by the impromptu visit, offered him whiskey and water. Billy, who didn't drink that often, accepted.

"Have you learned anything else about the Gents or Silent Men?" Yates asked.

"That's what brings you popping over, young Yates, that nonsense?" Branch water was debottled.

476

"Yes."

"I haven't had time to look into it. Haven't had time to do most anything since we spoke last." Raising the tumbler to eye level, he added bourbon to the branch.

"I've had a good deal of time to look in." Yates walked over and took the ready drink from the old man. "It's all I've done."

"Sounds a worthless endeavor." Whiskey poured into Amory's own tumbler.

"If you call seven lives worthless, then I guess it is."

"Seven lives?" Amory set the decanter on the sideboard.

"Seven people have died because of the Silent Men."

"Tchin-tchin." They clinked glasses and drank.

"Now for your saga, young Yates, what do you wish to impart?"

"It will be of as much interest to Missus Amory as to you."

"Lady Pat is indisposed."

"I know what went on, Barrett. All of it. About the Silent Men. Patricia should hear."

"She is indisposed." Amory was curt, which was not his style.

"Allow Mister Yates his say, Barrett." Patricia, statuesque and stunning, dominated the doorway. "He has gone to great bother, no doubt."

She flowed forth into the chamber, swirled and dipped into a chaise that was form-fitted to receive her elegance. A wall of leaded windows stretched behind her. Through the windows was a shimmering waterscape of lake and cloudy spring night. "Do begin, Mister Yates."

"Thank you, Missus Amory." Billy had begun to pace much as Strom used to pace. "What I'm about to provide is a reconstruction of the events leading to, and ending with, the corruption of Romor 91. In the worst sense of the word it is a conspiracy. A conspiracy of spirit as well as intent. If some of my early assumptions are slightly off, it makes no difference. The essence exists. A germination of deceit.

"We'll have to go back a bit to get a clearer perspective, go back a year or two before the Mormon State robbery. The FBI and J. Edgar Hoover himself were in deep trouble with the public and on Capitol Hill. Time and the media were catching up to

Mister Hoover. Catching on, as well. Deglossing the Bureau's rose. Besmirching the Director's person. Bright young prospects were shunning the FBI and hurrying instead to get into the CIA or State Department or other 'hot' organizations. The very bedrock of the Bureau, its funding support in the Senate and the House of Representatives, was eroding. The media, correctly or not, perpetuated the notion that the President would at any moment be curtailing FBI authority and jurisdiction. J. Edgar Hoover, who in the past could have handled each and every one of these problems with ease, seemed to be at a loss, seemed not even to be aware the peril existed, didn't seem to realize that he and his beloved FBI had become, to many, an embarrassment.

"But there were Bureau partisans. And many of them searched for a solution to the dilemma. Most agreed that what was needed was affirmation of the FBI. A return to the glory days of old. One particular group decided it knew exactly how to do this . . . and possibly take over control of the FBI in the bargain. This group worked from the logical and simple premise that the easiest way to recapture the glory of the old days was by having the Bureau do what it had always done best in the past: solve and exploit a great crime . . . another crime of the century. Which came first, the exploiting or the solving, was immaterial . . . as it so often had been in the past.

"So this group started looking for just such a perpetration. Since some of them were strategically placed within the Bureau itself, they could monitor most anything that came into Washington headquarters and act on it. And they had another advantage . . . the specifications of exactly what was desired had been spelled out by Orin G. Trask in his so-called model crimes. In retrospect, it isn't all that hard to figure out what those specifications were." Yates held up six fingers. "There were a half dozen of them. Number one, the crime they were looking for must be spectacular in its perpetration. Number two, it should be a crime against property rather than persons, preferably a robbery of cash or gems or other valuables from a large institution. No one sympathizes with a large institution . . . with impersonal wealth. Number three, the perpetrators must make a clean getaway and for a time not be found. Number four, the public and the media must show an immediate interest in the perpetration and escaping felons. The public perceiving the unknown criminals are heroes and rooting for them not to be caught would be advantageous. Number five, the crime must appear to be nonviolent at the outset. Information that innocent bystanders or company employees were harmed by the criminals must be temporarily suppressed. This fifth requisite, the nonviolent aspect, is pivotal to the whole plan. It alone must provide the desired response at the most propitious time. It's the ultimate opinion-shaper. And this fifth aspect is what went haywire in the Mormon State conspiracy. What brought everything tumbling down . . .Teddy Anglaterra.

"The sixth requirement is that the perpetration be record-setting in the worth of the valuables stolen. America is addicted to old records being shattered."

Yates went to the sideboard, indicated his empty glass. "May I?" he asked Amory.

Amory did not reply.

Billy poured himself another whiskey. "So there they were, these do-gooder supporters of J. Edgar Hoover and the Bureau, waiting for the right crime to come down the pike. A Trask-like model crime. They did Trask one better. They devised their own contingency measures in case a perpetration came along that was somewhat under specifications, one that might possess many but not all of the desired requisites. Don't get me wrong. Trask was in no way denigrated by our schemers. The opposite was true. Trask, or the memory of Trask, was held in near-messianic esteem. They even named themselves after one of his favorite secret societies, the Silent Men."

Yates was back to pacing. "How long the Silent Men watched and waited for a Trask-like crime to take place, I can't say. Anyway, on Sunday, August twenty-second, the Prairie Port police responded to an alarm and found the vault had been looted at Mormon State National Bank. We, the resident office, sent our first reports back to Washington. The Silent Men read them and, sensing what they were looking for was at hand, dispatched one of their own members to Prairie Port for a closer look. Now they saw first-hand that Mormon State filled their bill, or at least met most of Orin Trask's specifications.

"Then a seventh requirement, one which Trask had never anticipated, was encountered . . . bank cooperation. Wilkie Jarrel controlled Mormon State. The time had finally arrived when Bureau needs were more important than J. Edgar Hoover's loyalty to Ed Grafton. J. Edgar himself probably made the first phone call to Jarrel. Whether the dumping of Grafton came up then or later doesn't matter. Grafton was to go. J. Edgar left the details for this and other matters to his private spy in Prairie Port, the same agent he had recruited to watch and protect Ed Grafton, Jez Jessup. Jessup wasn't a Silent Man. He never knew they existed. But the Silent Men knew all about him. Knew he was Hoover's spy. The Men figured out a way to transmit direct orders to Jessup . . . orders which Jessup, to the last, believed had come from Edgar.

"There was a forty-eight hour delay between the discovery of the robbery on Sunday, August twenty-second, and J. Edgar Hoover's announcement the FBI had entered the case on Tuesday, August twenty-fourth. Part of this time, these two days, was spent in negotiating with Wilkie Jarrel . . . getting him to go along with their plan. Other issues had to be tended to as well during this period, some of which included Jarrel, some of which didn't.

"With Jarrel's cooperation in hand, the FBI publicly launched Romor 91, launched it with Hoover's Tuesday announcement. A planeload of equipment landed in Prairie Port. Support agents flooded into the city. And it all worked. Worked better than ever imagined. Worked so well the Silent Men had nothing to do now but sit back and watch. The Mormon State robbery and investigation, in and of itself, was seen as truly a crime of the century. The public ate it up. There wasn't enough the media could say about it. And an occasional well-placed false item, such as letting it slip that millions of stolen dollars may have fallen into the river, thereby turning the lower half of the Mississippi into a gigantic treasure hunt, didn't hurt the Silent Men's cause either.

"Then something happened that wasn't in the script . . . Mule

480

and the gang. I believe the Silent Men would have preferred that no major suspect be found this early." Yates turned to Amory. "After all, wasn't the name of the game maximum exposure?"

Barrett Amory again did not respond.

"Whatever the Men's preference," Yates continued, "the body of Sam Hammond and the statements of his wife and mother forced the issue. We swooped down on Baton Rouge, followed three of the gang members hoping they would lead us to more, then when they got into a fight and took off, we began picking them up. If it had been Bicki Hale or some of the other thieves the media focused on, that might have been all right. But the problem was compounded. Unfortunately for the Silent Men, the press and public fell in love with Mule Corkel . . . Mule, the deviant sideshow attraction. No modern criminal had been given the kind of attention he was getting. And this was serious business for the conspirators. Beyond not being the image they preferred for a supercrook, Mule was a dark, unwitting clown. The public laughed *with* Mule but laughed *at* the FBI.

"The Silent Men decided they had to get rid of Mule and his two pals. To do this they reverted to an auxiliary measure prepared for just such an eventuality. First off, they needed witnesses who could provide new alibis for Mule, Wiggles and Ragotsy. This could have been done through several safe houses other government organizations ran. But since Wilkie Jarrel was already part of the conspiracy, they prevailed on him to let them use facilities he controlled in Emoryville as fronts. The Silent Men now had 'Freddie' send orders to Jez Jessup in the name of J. Edgar Hoover. Jez, thinking he was carrying out Hoover's wishes, went to Mule and Wiggles and Ragotsy offering them freedom in return for cooperation. They agreed, as anyone in his right mind would have. It doesn't really matter who brought in criminal lawyer Harry Janks—Jez or the Silent Men. The point is, Janks arrived and did his job, and the FBI's case against Mule, Rat and Wiggles fell apart."

Yates thought he noticed the dark silhouette of a man standing outside one of the lakeside windows. He turned back to Amory and Patricia. "The Silent Men were at their best now, were think-

481

ing trigger-fast and with frightening precision. Realizing that the resident agents of Prairie Port were confused and depressed by the turn of events and could become even more demoralized, the Men decided to bring in J. Edgar Hoover to bolster spirits. Scheduled his arrival into Prairie Port's metropolitan airport. At the last moment a snag occurred in the person of Wilkie Jarrel. Jarrel, directly or indirectly, was now a full partner in the plot. Not only was his bank cooperating and subsidiary operations producing false alibis, but he was responsible for the sheltering of Natalie Hammond and her baby at the maternity clinic of the resort where Ragotsy allegedly had stayed at the time of the robbery. Natalie Hammond was originally interviewed by Cub Hennessy. After deciding that Mule, Ragotsy and Wiggles were to be removed as suspects in the robbery, the Silent Men felt it wise to transport Natalie Hammond out of the range of inquisitive agents who might discredit their plan. Natalie had always told the truth and wouldn't change her story. The Silent Men didn't even bring up the matter. They simply enticed her away with promises of free medical and infant care for herself and her unborn baby. The facilities and services were excellent. It was no problem convincing Natalie to stay on after the birth.

"Wilkie Jarrel learned about J. Edgar Hoover's impending arrival in Prairie Port at the last moment and demanded an immediate meeting with the Director. Knowing that no liaison between the two could be kept from the press after Hoover's arrival, the Silent Men diverted the incoming aircraft to a nearby airport, probably Saint Louis, then had him helicoptered to Jarrel's estate west of the city. It wasn't enough for Jarrel that he had forced Hoover to replace Grafton as head of the Prairie Port office, he wanted the whole loaf. Once Jarrel had Hoover alone, he pressed for the expulsion of Ed Grafton from the FBI. Hoover said no. Grafton might have been better off if he'd agreed. Grafton's probably in exile at the North Pole right now. Anyway, after leaving Jarrel, Hoover drove into the city and met with the discouraged resident agents. Even though their case had fallen apart, he praised them for their work.

"I'm not sure but I doubt that Director Hoover knew about the

Silent Men . . . or that he could have comprehended the whole plan even if he did know. From what I've seen, Director Hoover's mental faculties aren't what they used to be . . . maybe this made it easier for the Silent Men to get him to replace Grafton at Prairie Port . . . get him to do all those other things he did for the conspiracy, some of them pretty ugly things.

"The Silent Men learned something else about Mule, Ragotsy and Wiggles . . . that they were going into the irrigation tunnels running under the western section of Prairie Port looking for the stolen money. Jez thought he was reporting this directly to Hoover, but the communication was actually with a Silent Man . . . with 'Freddie.' Jez even let Freddie know the three crooks had offered him a share of the take if he left them alone to look. The Silent Man told Jez he could do whatever he wanted so long as he kept an eye on the three actual robbers. Jez, I'm sorry to say, accepted Mule's offer of a share, set up a secured system of communications with the thief and on occasion went down into the tunnels and caves to check on progress.

"When Otto Pinkny was arrested in South Carolina and identified, he didn't demand to see the FBI any more than he was held in jail only three or four days. He was probably in jail some two weeks negotiating with the Silent Men. It figures he was first identified by FBI handprints and talked to by local Bureau agents. But when the Silent Men in Washington found out, they sent down their own people to make a deal with Pinkny. Terms were finally worked out, and Pinkny listened to confession tapes Mule, Ragotsy and Wiggles had made as part of their freedom deal. When more details were needed, 'Freddie' called Jez and Jez arranged for Mule to go to South Carolina and brief Pinkny directly. Then Pinkny arrived in Prairie Port and stood up under the toughest interrogation our office could manage. Everyone but Brewmeister and Strom and myself was convinced Pinkny and his gang had done Mormon State. What's more, the world had taken to Pinkny as it would to a matinee idol. Took to him exactly as planned. It was the Silent Men's supreme moment. Pinkny fit their image as a supercrook. The final ploy, the master-stroke, was as good as assured. The price to pay had been a pittance, not more than a fib or two. But the price was about to go up."

Yates spotted two men standing outside the window, paid them no attention. "As brilliant as the plan had been," he said, "as well as it had worked, now the opposite began to happen. Alice Sunstrom called the FBI hot line and told them, anonymously, that she saw Mule kill a man in Prairie Port at a time he was supposed to be in Illinois. Jez Jessup was the person who took her call and soon verified what she said. The Silent Men suddenly realized that they were conspiring with a known murderer. Like it or not, there wasn't much they could do about it. They were tied to Mule. If Mule's alibi was disproved, as Alice could make happen, their whole conspiracy could come tumbling down. But there was another threat to the conspiracy—Brewmeister and me. What we'd discovered was the biggest blunder the Men had made to date . . . dumping the corpse of Teddy Anglaterra into the Mississippi River. Anglaterra was a drunk who had nothing to do with the Mormon State robbery. He'd been killed in a drunken brawl a hundred miles away, and the Men found him there and brought his corpse down to Prairie Port and dumped it into the river. Then, with the connivance of the bank president, they added Teddy's name to the list of people who had been at the bank the day of the robbery. What they intended to do, at the right time, was prove that Teddy was actually employed at the bank at the time of the robbery and was killed in the line of duty defending the premises. This was to fulfill Orin Trask's fifth requirement . . . that the crime must appear to be nonviolent at the outset. Outset was the operative word here. Trask and the Silent Men knew that once violence was established, the public would turn against the perpetrators. Teddy Anglaterra was to be used in this fashion. The announcement that he was killed by the robbers, the Silent Men were certain, would make any suspect into a public ogre . . . and thereby elevate the image of the FBI.

"As things turned out, there was no need to use Anglaterra. The reason was two unexpected deaths. If the Men needed to trump up a dead victim of the crime they could always say Cow-

484

boy Carlson or Sam Hammond had been killed by the robbers. So the Silent Men tried to ignore Anglaterra, but Brew and I discovered him, or at least his records. And Brew tripped up the bank president on whether Teddy had been at Mormon State the day of the robbery. It was Teddy Anglaterra who made me re-member hearing about the model crime that the Mormon State conspiracy was based on. You, Barrett, tried to warn me off by telling me about the Silent Men. Brew verified the Men's exis-tence and figured out how they operated. And figured out how many there were. Seven was the outside number he came up with, seven Silent Men.

"Either my visit here or Brewmeister's discovery forced the Silent Men to make their worst blunder . . . a blunder that in-stantly transformed them from ill-advised crusaders into assassins . . . the murder of my friend Martin Brewmeister."

Three men were now standing outside the window, revealed in silhouette. Yates sensed a fourth might be behind him, but he didn't turn to confirm this. "Right after Brew's death came the suicide of Alice Sunstrom, which was really another murder. The Silent Men had two scalps to their credit. Homicide had become a *modus operandi* for them.

"I was left to figure out the riddle Brew had already solved, who the seven Men were and how they operated. The prime clue had come from Brew, who said in his final phone call to me that the evidence had been sitting in front of us all the time. When I learned Brew had stolen Romor 91 files from the twelfth floor, the answer should have been evident, but I was a little bit dense. After all, the twelfth-floor files contained only out-of-town case reports. That's what slowly dawned on me. The Silent Men had controlled Romor 91 by controlling the out-of-town investiga-tions and reports. The plan was so brilliantly conceived that it really took only four men, all of them special agents of the FBI, to complete the operation, to control and alter the critical aspects of it.

"I said before, I was a little slow in realizing all this. And I did it in reverse order. What I figured out first was what Brewmeister had done with the missing files, where all the Romor 91 case

485

reports he had stolen were. The answer, when it came, was as simple as pie . . . and it more clearly indicated who the Men were."

"What was that answer?" the voice behind him asked.

Yates knew it was Denis Corticun before turning and seeing Corticun standing with a gun in his hand . . . a gun pointed at no one in particular.

"The answer, Denis, was that the files had not been stolen, at least not by Brew. They'd been removed by the Silent Men working on the twelfth floor and then returned. The files right now are where they've always been, with certain deletions." Glancing off, Yates saw that the three silhouettes beyond the window were gone.

"What deletions?" Corticun said.

"Four names."

"What four?"

"The four Silent Men who controlled four critical aspects in altering the investigation. When it was learned Brewmeister had been at the twelfth-floor files just before his death, the Silent Men had a pretty good idea what he had found. When he was killed, by them, they pulled reports they wanted and claimed Brew had stolen them. Once they'd altered the four names, changed them to those of friendly agents who would cover for them, they put the reports back into the files. I'd say this was among their worst moves. By now the Silent Men were falling apart—"

"Do you know what four names were deleted?" Corticun asked.

"Yes."

"Who are they?"

"Headquarters agents. And former students of Orin G. Trask. That was the common bond among the conspirators. All of them had been in Trask's seminars. Were Trask disciples. Acolytes. Worshippers."

"Name them."

"Most are gentlemen I've never met—"

"*Name* them."

". . . Let's begin with Matthew Ames, a Trask seminar student,

486

circa 1968. Would you like to know what part he played in the conspiracy?"

"If you know," Corticun said.

"Ames was the headquarters agent who went to talk to Otto Pinkny in South Carolina, the one who offered Pinkny the deal."

"Who else?"

"There was my old classmate from the academy, Vance Daughter. That was Daughter standing outside the window a moment ago. I recognize his bowlegs. Vance was probably tailing me."

"And what part did Daughter have?"

"He was jack-of-all-trades. He helped with Anglaterra, arranged for false receipts to be in the Carbondale garage files about the truck repairs, and most likely talked Natalie Hammond into having her baby in Emoryville. Next comes Alexander Troxel, Trask student, class of '68. Troxel not only worked the Anglaterra ploy with Daughter, he controlled the reports dealing with the arrival of thirty-one million dollars at Mormon State. Troxel may also have assisted some with the alibis, but that was mostly the work of William Esper. Esper secured and wrote up the eleven alibi reports out of Emoryville for Mule, Ragotsy and Wiggles. Esper was in Trask's final seminar in 1969. Those were the four field men, the workhorses of the conspiracy—"

"You said *seven* Silent Men," Corticun pressed.

"There were seven."

"What of the last three?"

"One was at your elbow all the way through," Yates told Corticun. "Harlon Quinton. Quinton was in the very first seminar Trask gave in 1963. His job was to keep the investigation under review, which was no trouble when control of the files was on the twelfth floor. After Strom Sunstrom demanded the main files go down to the eleventh floor, it made Quinton's job a little more difficult but not all that much. When the main files were directly under Quinton's scrutiny on the twelfth floor, no one could get to them long enough to detect that certain agents' names, Silent Men names, reappeared consistently on critical out-of-town re-

487

ports. When the files were moved downstairs, it was decided by the Men that there was now so much material amassed, so many report pages to go through, that no one would be able to pinpoint their actions. Then the Men learned Brewmeister may indeed have gone through the files. That's not what prompted Brewmeister's death. I think Brewmeister was killed by mistake. Not that they wouldn't have killed him later. I was the intended victim that day, not Brew."

Yates turned to Barrett Amory. "At the time of my visit here to you the Silent Men had no way of knowing what Brew had discovered. It was me they were after. You may have warned me about the Silent Men, but at the same time you signed my death warrant. The Silent Men panicked when they learned I'd been told of their existence and tried to kill me for no other reason than that. The only way they could have found out you told me, Barrett, was from you. And you're still alive and well. You're one of them, Barrett. You may damn well be their leader."

"Preposterous—"

"That accounts for six," Corticun said. "What about the seventh?"

"You, Denis. Trask seminar student, class of 1966. Prime architect of the scheme along with Amory. Chief operating officer of the plot. You called the shots all along. And you had a ringside seat to do it from."

"And what did you say our motivation for this so-called conspiracy was?" Corticun asked.

"I gave you my assessment, Corticun . . . why don't you tell me yours?"

Patricia Amory began applauding. "Bravo, Mister Yates. Bravo indeed. You have bagged the scruffy lot at last." Her handkerchief fluttered. "Mister Corticun, do make the introductions."

Yates turned to see Vance Daughter, Harlon Quinton and two neatly dressed young men he didn't know standing in a row along the wall to his rear. Corticun introduced the shorter one as Alexander Troxel, the taller as William Esper.

Patricia resettled herself on the chaise and posed in quarter-profile, her chin high. "There is, Mister Yates, one particular

488

blemish in your otherwise brilliant and accurate reconstruction of the event and characters. Shall we say a fifty-percent error? There was indeed an Amory involved, but not dearest Barrett. Like most male-oriented associations, the Silent Men have also succumbed to the emerging feminist reality of our day. There are not, in fact, seven Silent Men . . . there are six, and one rather garrulous woman. Myself. You were quite astute in believing an Amory was the boss. I am. But of course you suspected that too, didn't you, Mister Yates? Otherwise you wouldn't have insisted I be present tonight."

"I suspected you could be Freddie, yes."

"The maker of phone calls to your Mister Jessup? I was indeed. He received his orders from me. All the gentlemen did.

"Where do we go from here, Mister Yates? You know about us, we know about you. We must assume you are intent on destroying us . . . we know your wife was instructed to contact police Chief Frank Santi. The reason you don't see Matthew Ames here now is that he is in Prairie Port attending to our security needs. We have your wife, Mister Yates, but I assure you no harm will come to her if reasonable heads prevail."

Billy winced and said nothing.

"Reason is your only salvation . . . and ours," she told him. "Should reason fail you in this instance, should you in a fit of sublime duty decide to sacrifice your dearest Tina Beth, there is still nowhere for you to go. The only place you are safe is here with us. Or didn't you know . . . as of late this afternoon you are being sought as a suspect in the murder of Martin Brewmeister. New evidence has been found at your home by none other than Frank Santi, the murder weapon and ammunition. It seems that Mister Brewmeister had discovered you were in league with Mister Marion Corkel in seeking missing robbery funds and was about to report you. You steered him to your car, set him up, as it were. More evidence will come to light as needed. Your wife has been advised of this, which is why she did not contact Captain Santi as you had asked. We told Tina Beth we would help you if she cooperated . . . told her we doubted if you would ever be convicted of Mister Brewmeister's murder, but then again, who can know for certain?" Patricia lowered a regal finger. "Come sit down, Billy Yates. Let us chat as we used to."

Yates stood where he was. "We never talked much."

"That was because I disliked you. I still do. But we must try to get on together. There has been too much killing. Matters have gone amok. I wish no harm to you. Whatever our differences, we must reach an accord. Even the bitterest of enemies negotiate, the most barbaric. That is the only civilized way. If we become deadlocked, only barbarity gains. Hear me out, Billy Yates. Do hear me out."

Yates came forward, sat down opposite her.

"Edgar Hoover is a great man gone atrophied, Billy," she said, still keeping her profile to him. "You must have seen that atrophy for yourself when you were driving him. You know about it from your wife, whom he visited. Nonetheless, I love him very much. Had I no personal stake in him, decency alone would have told me he must not be abased, belittled. He has a right to the glory which was his. It is not so much a matter of saving the FBI as it is of restoring the honor of the man who *is* the FBI. This prompted our actions, Billy, as you suspected. Bestowing upon him, in the relative dimness of his sensibilities, a little bygone glory. If doing this meant helping the Bureau as well, so much the better. And we have helped, Billy, you see that. Mormon State will go down as one of the FBI's crowning achievements."

"At what price? Seven dead people, four of them Bureaumen and family."

"Wars are fought for less noble causes. And it isn't the lie or the truth that ever prevails, it is the idea. J. Edgar Hoover is a noble idea. He is the image of justice incarnate. And he had done grand work, great work. He is the hope of decency surmounting evil. He *cannot* be lost, what he represents *must not* be lost."

She had swung around full-face to talk to him. "What difference does it really make whether Otto Pinkny or Mule Corkel is charged with the robbery? They are guilty of crimes against decency, let alone law. Mule Corkel and his cohorts have paid a far greater price for their venality than any court would have levied. Otto Pinkny is a convicted assassin who will never be executed. Is it so indecent for him to go to prison for a crime he didn't commit if a greater good is served? If America benefits?"

"Can't you understand, *three FBI men and one FBI wife died because of this—*"

"That wasn't intentional."

"How unintentional was gunning down Brewmeister?"

"I agree that matter got out of hand, but what would be gained by our confessing what had happened?"

"Justice, for starters."

"What price justice? Would the public good best be served by Otto Pinkny being cleared of charges and a scandal within the FBI exposed? And a scandal of monumental proportions would result, Billy Yates. The overwhelming number of your good Bureau people would be as severely damaged as the few bad. Bad by your lights. Political enemies of J. Edgar Hoover would band together and try to wrest from him whatever power he has left. I assure you these enemies could control the Bureau for decades to come. That would not be wise for either law enforcement or the public good. J. Edgar Hoover may have engaged in politics more than he should have, but he also kept politicians out of Bureau affairs. Each of you has profited from that.

"Edgar is unaware of any of this, as you pointed out. He has never heard of the Silent Men. They were, after all, my invention. At least the modern ones were. The few times he participated on our behalf, he was tricked into doing so."

"Tricked how?"

"Edgar depends on me, relies on me. He comes every Thursday afternoon to sit and chat with me. I am his one and only confidante. I do things on his behalf. Often official things. Make official phone calls and afterward tell him what was said. He values my opinions . . . and my advice. I induced him to go to Prairie Port and console all of you and your wives after the real thieves were provided alibis. I convinced him Mister Marion Corkel was in fact an ally of the FBI . . . was being maligned by enemies of the Bureau. Everything that Edgar did or thought regarding Romor 91 was me!"

491

She rose slowly and with majestic aplomb. "So what will it be, Mister Yates, your pound of flesh or the FBI?"

"Someone must pay for Brew and Strom and Alice and Jez," he told her.

"As I suggested, why not Otto Pinkny?"

He shook his head.

"Mister Yates, you are asking us to atone for these tragic deaths at the very moment the Bureau needs us most. Don't you comprehend? J. Edgar Hoover is aged and ailing. He could die at any moment. With him gone, there is no one to save the Bureau but us. Reconsider, please reconsider."

"And if I don't, will I be shot down on the spot and the police later told that I was a wanted murderer trying to escape arrest? That would make it all legal and tidy, wouldn't it?"

"Join us now," she urged. "We need you. Be with us for the great victory. I swear to you once the Bureau is secure, the Silent Men, and their single distaff member, will disband."

"Even if I did agree, would you believe me?"

"Yes."

"And dissolve the Men?"

"Of course."

"You can't dissolve them," he told her. "You never intended to, not after Wilkie Jarrel had joined the cause."

It was Patricia who did not answer.

"You and your Men have the Bureau, Lady Pat, why give it back? I doubt if Wilkie Jarrel would let you give it back."

Corticun spoke up. "You've said enough, Yates. For once in your life be quiet and smart."

"I was always loud and dumb, Denis. Why change now?"

"I'd like to hear about Wilkie Jarrel," Patricia said.

"Of course, Lady Pat," Yates said. "Jarrel consolidated your conspiracy, made it real and to the death. A high-rolling powerbroker like Wilkie Jarrel didn't come along with your plan merely to get rid of Grafton. Didn't force his son-in-law to commit perjury, didn't tolerate homicide just for that. No, there were bigger stakes for Jarrel, there had to be. Lady Pat, you promised him the Bureau . . . he promised once you were in charge of the

Bureau he would use his wealth and political clout to make sure you hung onto it.

"Hoover's helicopter landed at Jarrel's estate in Prairie Port and Jarrel did try talking him into drumming Grafton out of the FBI. But there was another reason for the meeting. You, Lady Pat, talked Hoover into seeing Jarrel so Jarrel could judge for himself that J. Edgar was senile . . . that you and the Men were in control of him as you had claimed. Controlling J. Edgar Hoover was synonymous with controlling the Bureau. And taking over the Bureau, if this was true, might be easier than anyone thought. You could have Hoover name his own successor. A successor whom you picked and who was a Silent Man, like Denis here. You could even make Hoover clean house at headquarters, get rid of most all the brass you didn't want and replace them with more of the Men. The Director then, at your prompting, could step down and retire. Your Capitol Hill allies, along with Wilkie Jarrel's, could make sure Congress kept the Men in charge.

"And Wilkie Jarrel met with Hoover and saw that what you said about him was so. Jarrel threw in with you. From there on in, the game was for real. Now you can't get out of bed from one another. You've murdered together, deceived together, are bound together.

"So what possibly started as a ploy to bolster J. Edgar Hoover's image and prestige blossoms into a full-fledged conspiracy . . . a murderous power grab. Who knows, you may still pull it off, may go on from there."

"You still won't join us?" Patricia asked.

"You'd never trust me," he replied.

She smiled at that. "Perhaps not . . . well, good-by, Billy Yates." With a sigh and a toss, she glided off.

Corticun and Quinton moved in beside Yates, stripped him of his gun and started leading him away. Billy stopped at Amory. "Will you be hurt because of this? Because you tried to warn me?"

Amory looked down at the floor. "I'm afraid not."

# Twenty-nine

Yates was taken to the gatehouse of Three Oaks and locked in a room. He heard a car drive off and someone start typing down the hall from him. The typing ended. Not long after, a nearby phone rang. Quinton and Esper entered and cuffed his hands behind his back.

He was led out to a car and put in the back seat. Quinton got in beside him and refused to talk during the journey. Esper, who was driving, was as quiet as Quinton, which caused Billy to accuse them of taking their Silent Men routine too seriously. The car ahead of them carried only Alexander Troxel. Vance Daughter drove alone in the car to their rear.

The convoy wended its way southeast down through Virginia. A scare was had outside of Newport News when Vance Daughter thought he was being followed. A revised, more desolate route was taken. No tailers could be seen behind in the darkness.

They drove out along a lone beach section of Kitty Hawk in North Carolina and turned into a thick stand of trees. Waiting in a field beyond was Yates's car, the one he had driven east in. Beside the car stood Denis Corticun. Resting in the high grass, not far off, was a chair.

Yates was brought to Corticun, who presented him with a typed page to sign.

"What is it?" Billy, of course, knew.

"A suicide note."

"Was I despondent after my work-induced near mental breakdown, or did the guilt of murdering Brewmeister weigh too heavy on my troubled soul?"

"It's just depression. The Brewmeister allegations will be publicly discounted by us in the morning."

494

"If I don't sign?"

"Your name will be forged."

"And attested to by one of your experts as being authentic?"

"Yes."

"And the suicide happens out in that chair?" Yates nodded at the chair in the field.

"Only if I have to kill you. If you do it, you can pick anywhere you like."

A rustling was heard. The Silent Men brought out their guns, deployed, looked about. Saw nothing.

"What will it be, Yates?" Corticun asked. "Do I do it, or will you?"

Yates thought for a moment. "You do it, Denis."

Corticun took the gun Quinton handed him and marched Yates into the field.

"That my gun?" Billy asked.

"You know it is."

Squinting ahead as they neared the chair, Yates asked, "Why the chair? That Silent Men ritual or something?"

"It is."

"What's the origin?"

"Simply that a gentleman dies sitting down, with his legs crossed, and smoking."

"I'm a gentleman?"

"In this instance."

"I get a cigarette?"

"If you like."

They were at the chair. Corticun put on chamois gloves, eased Yates onto the seat.

"You're not undoing the handcuffs?"

"No." He lit a cigarette, placed it in Yates's mouth.

Billy inhaled, blew the smoke out slowly. "I can't stand filters."

"Shall I throw it away?"

Yates shook his head, took another drag of the extended Marlboro, exhaled slowly. "This is a pretty shitty way to die, I want you to know."

"I suppose it is."

495

"I mean you're fucking up my week."

Corticun held the cigarette closer. "Last puff."

Yates took it.

Corticun ground the cigarette into the soft earth, withdrew the gun from his pocket, stared at it momentarily . . . cleared his throat.

Yates, who was perspiring, noticed the hesitation. "Ever assassinate anyone like this before, Denis?"

Corticun didn't reply.

"No last question either?" Billy pressed. "No little wonderment about how goddam brilliant I was at figuring it all out?"

". . . There was one question," Corticun said. "How did you know there were seven people involved?"

"I didn't. Brew did."

"There was no way he could have known from the reports that there were seven of us."

"I know. He took a lucky guess. Probably figured there were five agents, including Quinton, mixed up with the reports. Knew none of it could have happened if you weren't involved. That's six. If you ask me, Brew pegged the seventh man wrong. I think he thought it was A. R. Roland."

"But you knew it was an Amory, didn't you? Knew it was Patricia, not Barrett."

"I'm a real smart fuck." Yates's nervous laugh ended abruptly. "Isn't that something," he realized aloud, "I never fucking swear, I never use the word F-U, and now that I'm about to die, that's all I'm doing. I'm F-ing all over the place. Which gives me license to tell you what a fucking asshole you are, Denis, what a loathsome, two-timing scumbag fuck you are." He strained forward hoping Corticun would come closer, close enough to be tripped or kicked.

Corticun, instead, moved around beside the chair, raised the revolver barrel toward Billy's temple.

Shouting came from two directions. Then gunshots. Corticun was grazed in the side, dove for cover. Yates jumped from the chair, dove into taller grass.

"No pinstriped enemas kill my people and don't get their asses blown off in return," thundered the stentorian voice of Ed Grafton. He had materialized from nowhere and was charging down on the startled Men. "Let the wife of one of my people get raped and murdered, will you! I'll whip ass for this, whip your puny asses into cheap raw leather and hang it out to dry!"

Vance Daughter tried to fire at Grafton but was shot in the knee by Cub Hennessy, who was coming at them from the opposite side. Corticun took off into the woods. Troxel, Quinton and Esper just stood there.

"Who gunned Brewmeister?" Grafton demanded, his hand at Daughter's throat. *"Who!"*

". . . We drew lots."

"Who *won?"*

"Corticun . . . Denis shot him."

Corticun was past the road and halfway down a steep oceanfront dune when Grafton caught up, tumbled with him onto the beach. Corticun broke away, ran to the water's edge, sprinted along the crashing surf. Grafton brought him down with a flying tackle and spun him over and swatted him back and forth across the face in what seemed one quick and uninterrupted movement.

Yates, still in handcuffs, reached the top of the dune to see Grafton sitting on Corticun's chest, forcing the barrel of the gun into Corticun's mouth, shouting and cursing Corticun as he did.

Before Yates could yell out for him to stop, Grafton had pulled the trigger.

Free of his handcuffs, Yates joined Cub in restraining a raging Grafton from executing the prisoners. When a tenuous calm was achieved, Grafton demanded Yates recapitulate what had happened. Yates, fearing a new outburst of temper, was reluctant. Grafton insisted. Yates detailed certain aspects of the conspiracy, summarized the rest. Grafton grew pensive.

"I was fifty-eight years old last week," Grafton told Cub and Yates. "I have served with the FBI since I was twenty-two. I have put in my mandatory two decades as an active investigator and can retire from the Bureau, in honor, at any time I want. I have

497

carried a letter of resignation with me for many weeks now. I am going to present it to Edgar myself. This is my last investigation. This will be Edgar's last investigation too, I pledge you that. This very night I am going to kill him . . . kill him with this." Grafton displayed a revolver. "With Denis Corticun's gun."

Cub and Yates argued with him, grew more persistent. Grafton trained Corticun's revolver on them, relieved them of their own guns.

"Edgar executed my men," Grafton said. "Out of his mind or not out of his mind, he has to answer for it. Answer right now. If one of you wants to come along, fine. The remaining man can cuff and hogtie these enemas and take them to headquarters."

"Not the police?" Yates asked.

"We are the FBI," Grafton pronounced. "We will settle our own affairs our own way."

Cub, Grafton decided, would arrange for the captured Silent Men and Corticun's body to go to Washington while Yates would accompany him to Hoover's home. Billy and Cub could only hope that during the trip Yates might be able to dissuade Grafton. Grafton would not discuss the matter or anything else as they drove back through Newport News and Richmond and Fredericksburg and Arlington.

The house stood at Thirtieth Place near Rock Creek Park in northwest Washington, was three stories high and built of red brick. An Astro Turf lawn spread before it. An unattended limousine waited. Grafton and Yates pulled in across the street. The time was 7:58 A.M., Tuesday, May 2, 1972.

"Stay in the car," Grafton ordered. "Later you will tell the authorities you drove me here for a meeting with Edgar, that to the best of your knowledge I had phoned Edgar about the Corticun death and he had asked me to come right over . . . that I was behaving peculiarly . . . that when you heard shots you immediately came after me."

"Did I catch you . . . or did you get away?"

"I haven't decided yet." Grafton checked his watch. "It's about time for him to come down to breakfast. You can say I knew his

498

routine pretty well. That I had been here many times before."

"Had you?"

"In better days. Edgar breakfasts in the dining room. Comes down and eats in suspenders and shirt and tie. There's a house-woman and houseman on the premises. The woman is Annie Fields. The houseman goes by the name of Crawford. Both keep out of the main part of the house at this hour. The driver of the limousine keeps out of the main part as well. It will be simple as punch. Say I said so." Grafton started to get out of the car.

"The Director was *used* by the Men," Yates insisted. "It wasn't his fault."

Grafton hesitated, then said, "Don't believe Edgar was senile. It was an act he began to play years ago. I saw him do it many times. Nothing ever happens in the FBI without Edgar knowing. Nothing. He found out what the Silent Men were up to, and when he did he turned a deaf ear because it suited *his* purpose. He could have stopped it and he didn't. He's responsible. He allowed it to happen."

. . . Grafton went to the front door. Picked it open with ease. A photograph of Edgar and President Richard Nixon was promi-nent on the entrance hall wall. Pictures of Edgar with other Presidents and politicians and celebrities festooned the front rooms. Rooms in which antiques abounded. And bric-a-brac. Grafton moved silently past an eight-sided basket made of old popsicle sticks. Then a wooden stork from New York City's de-funct Stork Club. Then a salt-shaker with a nude woman de-picted on the side. Made his way to the dining room. No one was there. He sat down at the round, highly polished table. A teacup and glistening silver waited in front of Edgar's place. The morn-ing papers rested beside the setting. It was 8:07. Edgar was run-ning late. At 8:12 he still hadn't shown. Grafton grew edgy, and knew he mustn't. The hell with it, he told himself, no more waiting. Let it be done and over.

Grafton went to the staircase and started up. Hushed voices could be heard somewhere above. He stopped, pressed back against the wall, drew the gun . . . Corticun's gun. The voices

499

moved out of earshot. Grafton continued up. Faint rapping came from afar. Again he stopped. The rapping repeated. A door opened. Urgent tones trailed rapidly off into the distance. He eased up and onto the landing, wondering if he'd been discovered. The hallway was empty. He started along it. A phone was being dialed. Sweat was running down his face and he knew why. He'd never executed a man in cold blood, let alone a comrade he'd long admired. He paused, tried to erase the slate, clear his mind. He told himself to concentrate only on what he had to do and how he'd go about it. He realized that time was working against him, that he mustn't hesitate. Mustn't allow Edgar so much as one word, one glance.

He regripped the revolver, decided he would walk through the door firing. He moved down the hall. Quickened his pace. Raised the gun. Turned abruptly into the bedroom . . . and saw that he was too late. J. Edgar Hoover lay naked on the floor, dead from a heart attack.

# Thirty

The body of J. Edgar Hoover rested in state in the rotunda of the Capitol. Yates and Hennessy and Grafton were among the first of 50,000 persons to walk past the catafalque. Billy and Cub did not mourn.

Grafton did.

"He was a great man," Grafton said as they descended the hill and hailed a cab. "Only he stayed in the game an inning too long."

On the plane back to Prairie Port with Cub and Yates he repeated the sentiment, then fell asleep.

In flight Cub told Yates that after Sissy, for decent if misguided reasons, contacted Corticun to say Billy was en route to the Carbondale garage, he had tried getting in touch with Grafton.

"I figured you needed some help," Cub said. "I didn't believe what you were saying any more than before, but I wasn't going to let you be out there alone. I had no way of knowing Graf was already on your case . . . that's why I couldn't locate him. Graf told me later he was always suspicious over why he'd been removed from Prairie Port. Brew's murder got him thinking hard. The deaths of Strom, Alice and Jez pushed him over the edge. He took a leave of absence and came down to Prairie Port. Kept out of sight and poked around. He began putting two and two together. Began looking for you while I was trying to find him. Well, he got hold of me, all right, and I filled him on the parts he didn't know. Then he knew it was time to ride the big white horse again. That's what Graf calls a hot investigation, 'riding the big white horse into battle.' I apologize, Billy. I should have listened to you a long time back, only I was too pigheaded."

Yates assured him, "You did just fine."

"No. I didn't. You spotted what was really going down and Graf smelled it. I should have too."

"I just kept on the trail out of my inveterate sense of skepticism," Yates said. "Graf followed up out of his ego, on account of being replaced as senior resident agent. You approached the facts like a normal, sane person should, objectively."

"Which is just what the Silent Men wanted, wasn't it?"

". . . After you and Graf got together, what happened?"

"We started looking for you," Cub said. "Graf had been tailing Tina Beth, and she led him to you. Then he followed you while I covered Tina Beth. When Matthew Ames turned up at your doorstep trying to scare Tina Beth into cooperating with the Silent Men, we were there and waiting."

"We?"

"Happy de Camp and myself. Happy stayed behind with Tina Beth, and I lit out and joined Graf in D.C. Graf and I tailed you to Barrett Amory's and on down to the shore. We thought of rushing them while you were still at Amory's, only Graf was afraid they hadn't done anything to incriminate themselves. Nothing we heard or saw, at least. We were listening in as best we could. Good thing we didn't lose them when they drove you to the beach, huh?"

"Good thing."

Cub pushed back a notch in the reclining seat. "I can't get over Mormon State being dreamed up by Trask . . . being a looney-toon classroom exercise. It's wild."

"I didn't get a chance to tell you and Graf the last step," Yates said. "Maybe that's the wildest of all. It was the sixth requisite Orin Trask had for his model crime, the matter of the *amount* of money stolen. Trask realized that nothing intrigues the public quite as consistently as riches. Often, stolen riches. Pirate treasure. The perfect robbery, according to the model crime scenario, would have to rival the fabled wealth of yore, or at least beat the modern record-holder for cash stolen in a nonviolent theft. And it was this that took the Silent Men more than forty-eight hours to work out . . . two days from the time the robbery was discovered Sunday morning to the time Director Hoover made the announcement on Tuesday morning of how much was missing and that the FBI had joined the investigation. I'd always wondered why over two days had gone by before anyone realized how much money was gone. The answer is that the Silent Men had to implement the auxiliary plan for the sixth category.

"The first phase of that plan was removing Grafton and getting the cooperation of Wilkie Jarrel. Jarrel could see to it that the shipment of money would be duly recorded by his son-in-law, Emile Chandler, the bank's president.

"Alexander Troxel was in charge of this operation, and he did quite a job. Of course a good deal of groundwork had been laid before, like the recruitment of a high-placed Treasury Department official who could dispatch necessary funds to whatever location was needed . . . could also, if need be, contract a carrier for those funds. And he contracted and arranged for the shipment of thirty-one million dollars to Mormon State. More money than had ever been stolen before. A fabulous amount. Also a fictitious one. *Not one cent of it existed.* It was all done on paper, Cub. The Silent Men, through false documentation provided by the Treasury Department contact and the cartage company, had created a nonexistent transfer of funds. A record–breaking, but imaginary, shipment that the head of Mormon State National Bank, Emile Chandler, verified had arrived and was later stolen . . . verified on the express orders of his father-in-law and boss, Wilkie Jarrel.

"All that was in the vault at the time it was robbed was sixty-five hundred dollars. The same sixty-five hundred dollars Grafton had first reported as being stolen . . . the same sixty-five hundred dollars that caused Cowboy Carlson's death when Mule thought he and the rest of the gang were holding out on him, not cutting him in on the additional millions. Of course the media wouldn't have been all that interested in only sixty-five hundred dollars being gone, would it? The media and the public? A measly sixty-five hundred wouldn't have brought the glory . . ."

They drove through the wide metal gates and up the forest-choked drive and past the lodge in which Mule had raped and sodomized Alice Sunstrom, drove on to the great mansion on top of the hill. Grafton got out first, then Yates and Cub and Happy de Camp, led the way over to where Assistant U.S. Attorney Jules Shapiro waited beside a car.

"Here they are, Graf." Jules handed him the warrants.

Grafton studied the documents, turned them over in his hand like a rare objet d'art. For him it was as prized a possession as could exist, one he'd been trying to obtain for many years . . . one that, in a way, had precipitated the tragedy known as Romor 91. Grafton looked up at Yates, held out the warrants. "You do the honors."

"No, sir," Billy told him, "it's yours, all yours."

Grafton replied, "I'm no longer with the Bureau. Better take this too, or I may use it." He gave his service revolver to Happy de Camp. "Shag ass, Billy Yates."

Yates walked across the pebble driveway and up to the great manor house. Rang the bell. The double doors opened. Wilkie Jarrel himself came out. Behind him stood his lawyers.

"Mister Wilkie Jarrel?" Yates said.

The gnarled old man said, "Yes!"

"I'm William B. Yates, special agent of the Federal Bureau of Investigation. I have here warrants for your arrest for the crimes of conspiracy to murder a federal officer, conspiracy to commit bank theft, conspiracy to commit fraud against the government, bribery and eighteen other federal violations. Will you please come with me."

The promenade ran eight and one-tenth miles on top of the riverfront palisade from just below Mormon State National Bank on down to Lookout Bluff and around to Steamboat Cove . . . ran through thickets and stands of trees and across parks and playgrounds and gardens and campsites and an athletic field and past the new sports stadium . . . ended at the not yet completed two-block replica of the main street of Hannibal, Missouri, being built on the near side of the cove.

The promenade's official name was Clemens Lane, and at least one recently published history of the area, bolstering the beliefs

504

of numerous oral historians, maintained that Mark Twain once walked the entire distance while apprenticing as a riverboat pilot, may even have conceived the ideas and plots for his later stories here. Certain authoritative accounts held that the walk was an old buffalo path which later became an Indian trail, even though buffalo and Indians were seldom known to have traveled over solid rock for so long a distance. The CCC labor gang that actually laid down the walkway and did the landscaping back in 1933 hadn't noticed any trails and paths, old or recent, in the area. Nevertheless, it was a lovely place to stroll. Had become Tina Beth's most favorite place for early evening walks with her Billy.

Tonight the stroll was longer than usual, had begun at Steamboat Cove and gone upriver many miles and come back down again, with Billy recounting in relentless detail the conspiracy of the Silent Men . . . and their fate.

"Wilkie Jarrel doesn't as much as bat an eyelash when I read off the counts and arrest him," Yates told Tina Beth. "The guy looks a hundred years old and has trouble standing up straight and walking, but he's built of cold steel. I arrest him and he says, 'Take me where we have to go and don't waste time.' I take him on out to my car. When he passes Grafton, cold steel meets cold steel. Those two guys have a hate-on for one another like you've never seen. But Jarrel doesn't stop when he passes Graf. He just gives a fast look. And Grafton gives it back. I thank God that Grafton didn't get in the car with us. For a minute I thought he was going to, but then he walked off with the assistant U.S. attorney. So I take Jarrel in and turn him over to the U.S. marshals. He was arraigned and got out on one million dollars' bail. But he's finished, Tina Beth. They got him good. He's going to do some time."

Tina Beth asked, "What about Mr. Grafton?"

"He went back to the office and cleaned out all his stuff. I never realized it before, that he had never come back to Prairie Port after getting relieved of command. What Strom had done was seal Grafton's desk as it was and move it into the storage room. He sealed Graf's locker too. So Graf went through all his stuff.

505

Donnie Bracken and Pres Lyle gave him a hand. He threw out damn near everything. By this time I was back in the office and we had a conference call with A. R. Roland over what happened to Corticun and the other Men. Roland was pretty teed off we all left Washington without permission. We told him the truth, that Grafton told us he had cleared it with headquarters. What we didn't know was that Grafton had quit the Bureau before we got back to Prairie Port. That letter he was carrying, he sent it in to Clyde Tolson. Tolson is the acting head of the FBI now. Grafton told me to tell Roland exactly what I saw him do to Corticun, and I tried to, but Roland wouldn't listen. He just said they'd handle it their own way. Cub and Happy think that means Grafton is off the hook, that no charges will be brought against him.

"Anyway, Grafton waited around the office until he heard what was happening to the Silent Men and Barrett and Patricia Amory, then said good-by to all of us. Shook every hand and then hugged each one of us. It was real touching, Tina Beth. He cared about each one of us. I got tears in my eyes while he was saying good-by. The last thing he told me was he was putting the great white horse out to pasture, then he left. Donnie Bracken drove him out to the cemeteries. Grafton put flowers on all the graves, Strom's, Alice's, Brew's, Jez's. Then he went to the airport and got on a plane to Montana. At the airport he didn't say what his plans were, just turned and walked away."

Billy and Tina Beth were at Lookout Bluff now. Had stopped at the railing. The Mississippi River lay beneath them, whirling past a delta island. Beyond the island bubbled the midstream current called the Treachery.

"What happened to Patricia and Barrett Amory?" asked Tina Beth.

"They've been arrested. The arraignment's in the morning. Their lawyers and friends will put up one hell of a battle for them. And do some fancy bargaining. They might even get off with suspended sentences. At the worst, Amory will plead so Patricia can go free. It's the Men who are in the soup . . . Quinton, Ames, Troxel, Esper, Daughter. They've been turned over to the Justice

Department. Hoover's gone. There's no way to protect them. They're going to pay the price for everyone."

"You don't sound too happy about that."

"They're FBI men, Tina Beth."

"Guess that answers my next question."

"What question?"

"Your intentions 'bout staying with the FBI or not."

"I haven't made up my mind."

"Sure you have, Billy Bee, only you don't know it yet." With a giggle she turned and leaned back into the railing. Rearranged her skirt. "Billy Bee, when Patricia said I was being held a prisoner and would be killed if you didn't do what she wanted, what was it you did again?"

It was a question he had hoped would not be asked. "Want me to be honest?"

"Cross your heart?"

"I tried not to think about you, Tina Beth. I tried to . . . ," his voice cracked, "tried to forget you . . . and what I was doing to you. And I couldn't, Tina Beth. All I thought about was you after that. All I could see was you. I was screaming inside. Even when Corticun had me out in the chair, even when he was getting ready to fire, all I saw was you. And know what, Tina Beth?" He crossed his heart again. "I think I was just about to tell him, 'Okay, don't shoot. I'll do anything you want if you let Tina Beth off. Let her off and I'll be your puppy and you can kill me later or I'll kill myself.' Only we don't really know if that's what would have happened, do we? Grafton showed up first."

"I know." She kissed him and started sashaying down the gas-lit promenade. "See that bench right over there, Billy Bee?"

Yates, as he began to follow her, looked over at the wooden bench under a shade tree. "What about it?"

"Nothing, 'cepting that's where Mark Twain sat and wrote *The Man That Corrupted Hadleyburg.*"

"Who told you that?"

"Sue Ann Willis."

"How would Sue Ann know? She can't read."

507

"Sue Ann is third vice-chairperson of the Samuel Clemens Restoration Society. She knows all about those things. He wrote it in 1889 sitting right there. Or do you want to defy known truth?"

It wasn't the truth, he knew, but his eyes were on revealed truth . . . her swinging hips, and below. "Whatever you say, Tina Beth."

"I feel sorry for Patricia."

"Sorry?"

"She lost Edgar."

"My God, Tina Beth, she was a Lucretia Borgia!"

"I think she was sweet. And Edgar too. I told you that about him way back."

"He was a lunatic."

"No, he wasn't, Billy Bee, no, he wasn't. Like you told me Ed Grafton told you, Edgar liked pretending he was crazy so he could get away with more. Edgar was as sane as you and me, Billy Bee. And just as much in love. Don't you see, Edgar loved Patricia. He was her love-slave. He had to obey her. He let her believe she was helping him because he loved her so much. He didn't want to disappoint her and hurt her feelings by telling her to stop helping him the way she was."

"Are you serious?"

" 'Course I am."

"That's the next thing to saying Hoover condoned the actions of a monster like Mule—"

"Maybe when you looked at Mister Mule Corkel, or I looked at Mister Mule Corkel, we saw a monster, but not Edgar. He saw who Patricia told him to see. She like cast a spell over Edgar, gave him a secret potion. Dear child, Edgar would have fallen in love with Mister Mule Corkel if Patricia had so wished, just like in William Shakespeare."

"This isn't a play, Tina Beth. It's real life."

"And *love*, Billy Bee. Oh yes, love. Why can't you understand that? Edgar did it all for love. Isn't that romantic? A man of his age being so amorously inclined?"

She had stopped under a path lamp and was smiling at him. He was, for the moment, bewildered.

"How amorously inclined is a man of your age, Billy Bee?"

She turned before he could answer, began walking down the path, walking and sashaying . . . discarding clothes as she went.

. . . The call went out on the park patrol's radio band at 9:07 P.M. as 122 and 188 offenses, a disturbance of the peace as well as a violation of the city's decency code. A follow-up alert revealed that all cars should proceed to the sports stadium, where, reportedly, a stark-naked man was observed scrambling across the infield in pursuit of a fleeing stark-naked woman. The witness, who declined to be identified, said he had never . . .